Cassandra

PRINCESS OF TROY

HILARY BAILEY was born in 1936. She is the author of eight novels, including the bestseller, *All the Days of My Life*. She lives in London.

HILARY BAILEY

Cassandra

PRINCESS OF TROY

PAN BOOKS

First published 1993 by Jonathan Cape Limited

This edition published 1995 by Pan Books Limited
an imprint of Macmillan General Books
Cavaye Place London SW10 9PG
and Basingstoke
Associated companies throughout the world

ISBN 0 330 32128 5

1 3 5 7 9 8 6 4 2

A CIP catalogue record for this book is available from the British
Library.

Phototypeset by Intype, London
Printed and bound in Great Britain by Cox & Wyman Ltd,
Reading, Berkshire

For my son, Max, and The Eagles (1989)

Part One

ONE

Thessaly

I SIT HERE at the stone table outside my house with my writing materials and the wind is already lightly rattling the leaves of the lemon tree beside me. Most of the herbs in the herb-bed I have been watering throughout the summer heat will not live much longer now autumn is here; the cistern in the corner of the walled yard is nearly empty, the wells nearly dry. We wait now for rain, after such a long, hot summer, when the plague was fierce at Pinios, our port, some ten miles off. It even reached its tentacles out here into the quiet farms of the Thessalian coast, beyond Mount Olympus, on the borders of savage Thrace. Soon the leaves will begin to fall from the olive trees on the slopes behind our fields. The barley and what corn we can grow here is reaped, the vines are stripped, the year's hard work is over. In a month, or less, the winds will grow harsher, there may be snow on the mountains, even, perhaps, down here. The seas will grow rough; there will be storms. From now on we shall be living on the barley stored in the barn, on our olives, our onions, the meat we have salted down and what we can hunt and fish.

As ever at this time of year I pray our stores will last until spring, that the tax collector will be fair, that there will be no raids and no sickness in the family. I pray of course that there will be no war, the prayer I have prayed for nearly thirty years now, since I was ten years old. I begin to believe there will be an invasion and war here in Greece soon. It chills me, even though these people are my enemies. Nothing is worse than war. I feel I have known it all my life.

My own children have never heard the brutal music of swords and shields clashing, never seen what happens when the sword comes down on an unshielded body, the sudden gape of flesh and the bright blood springing out – they have not heard the terrible sobbing sighs and grunts of men fighting for their lives, the screams and groans of the wounded. They have not seen men's lives put out like candles, not heard women scream as infants are tugged from their arms, seen them on their knees in the dirt, sobbing over their dead children. They have never smelt a city burning, that odour so different from the cooking fire, or the logs in the hearth, or bonfires of chaff and old leaves. Only the burning of old, soiled clothes or of rank meat can sometimes revive that dreadful memory. My children have had none of this.

This is why I am writing.

My servants look at me curiously as they go to and fro, fetching water for the house from the cistern, carrying clothes back from the grove where we dry them, carrying the last baskets of olives through the entrance at the end of the yard up to the stone shed where we keep the press.

My maid Naomi's little son stands in front of me wearing only a small shirt and little goatskin boots. He stares with his thumb in his mouth at the spectacle of his mistress making black marks on yellow-brown

4

sheets. He is curious, being only three. The others may be waiting for some positive result from this peculiar activity – barely any of these Greeks can write, high or low. Their princes employ clerks from other nations to do their accounts and necessary correspondence. So the servants may well be expecting some practical result from my activity – that my pages will suddenly produce a bolt of cloth, a lamb or a calf. I have been mistress of this farm for twenty years, first a young wife, now a widow with the last of my five children married. How could they imagine this woman, thirty-seven years old, in the middle of life, to be doing anything but filling corn jars, weaving cloth, doctoring sick animals, binding up wounds? At all events, whatever they think I am doing they must believe it is connected with my land, my crops, my livestock, my family – connected somehow with a predictable future. But, sitting here in my blue gown in the fading sunshine, my concern is only with the past. I can write and I write easily. I shall enjoy telling my tale. Iphitus, my husband, died last year. He is not here to fear, or disapprove. My daughter Iris was married a few months ago to crafty Telemon, who now owns a few acres of wooded hillside, but will own a great deal more in future. So there are no matches to be broken now because the wife of Iphitus of Tolos is mad or eccentric and sits during the day scratching bird's footmarks on sheets of pressed reeds, which cost her, if the truth were known, the profits from a whole year's harvest, and the price of two fat ewes as well. There's no one here to ponder, wonder and begin to ask dangerous questions. Now I can reclaim my skill from where it was buried, and tell

5

my story in memory of my family and my people and for the sake of justice.

Naomi, my slave, my old friend, guesses, I think, what I am doing. A little while ago she emerged from the house and stood in front of me, spindle in one hand, wool in the other, the embodiment of a good serving woman, and asked me some unnecessary questions about the household – were the twenty fish hanging in the smoke-house ready to come down; what had become of the two linen sheets for the biggest bed? She was trying to call me back to the life I have created for both of us. She was trying to pull me back to safety in time. She thinks if she can catch me now, like a piece of cloth on the loom when the web has begun to waver, she can unpick the faulty part and go back and get it right. But I don't think she can, not now. I am at the right tension: not too tight so I'll break, not too loose so my fabric will be thin and gaping. Now I need only to weave my story.

Soon the wind will grow stronger and the trees begin to rattle. Snow will spit down the chimney into the fire and I shall set up my table in front of the fireplace and go on to the end. The house is empty now. There is no husband to whom I owe silence, no children to whom I cannot tell my tale. When I've finished I shall wrap all my pages into a strong linen cloth and give them to Iris. She'll keep them; Telemon will keep her and their children safe during the bad times to come. He will betray his country for profit. His barren acres command the coast down from here, to the east, a perfect spot for secret landings. His disloyalty may help to bring down the Greek states. I have no love for these states and have seen too much death and bloodshed in the name of patriotism to

6

condemn my son-in-law. He will ally himself with the victors, Iris and my grandchildren will be preserved. They may never sing heroic ballads about Telemon, but he and his family will live, and that is what matters.

Poor Naomi came back a moment ago, still carrying the spindle. 'What are you doing?' she said. (She guesses, anyway.) 'The neighbours will see – the servants will talk.'

'Don't worry,' I said. 'Trust me.'

She looked at me doubtfully and went inside again. She'll return to the attack though, soon, no doubt of it. I shall have to tell her we are in greater peril than we have ever been, that what I am doing is the least of our worries. Nearly every night I dream of danger from the sea. The outline is misty now, as it always is, always has been, but each night the details become clearer and sooner or later the future will reveal itself to me, as it always has. I shall know who is coming and why. But when I tell Naomi, will she believe me?

She was given to me in Troy when I was fifteen years old. She was anything between ten and fourteen; she did not know her age. She was lying in the stable courtyard, flea-infested and half-starved, wearing a torn tunic of filthy flax. She was beside a chained group of captives but they hadn't bothered to chain her, just roped her hands together to prevent her from stealing. My mother, Queen Hecuba, picked her out because she noticed that Naomi, though half-way to death, as she must have been nearly all her life, underneath her fearful air looked fierce and intelligent, like a sick dog which still retains the capacity to decide, as you approach it, whether you have a stick or a piece of meat in your hand. My

7

brother and his party had got her from hillmen in bearskins far to the north, but before that she must have changed hands many times already, during a fight, for a few pounds of salt, or for a young ram (she would not have been worth a ewe). She said she had originally been taken from her tribe in a desert far beyond the Taurus mountains by some Amorites, or Ammonites or Edomites, she could never remember which. She wss probably four or five years old. Later she had only memories like a stray dog, of being cold, hungry and kicked. She had probably only survived because she was a skilled thief, thus the binding of her little hands.

All she remembers of her childhood seems to be walking through deserts with her tribe. She was carrying a baby. Then, one day, there was shouting and fighting, screams and the bleating of goats. Then her mother fell, and after that she was caught up and dragged away. She remembers dropping the baby. Before that, only a mother giving her food and water, sitting under a tree with her brother; being carried sometimes on her father's back. Also that she had to throw herself on the ground when their priests carried past a big coffer with two handles at each end. This, she says, contained the laws of her people which had been given to their king by a god at the top of a mountain. She often says if she knew what those laws were, she would obey them. There, Naomi's respect for writing, and laws, comes to a finish. She can write a little, though, but chooses not to.

My writings frighten her, but I shall go on, as the leaves fall, as the storms begin, as the winter closes down. I will not be silenced now. I will be heard. I am known as Iphianissa of Tolos but I am King Priam's

daughter, Cassandra. I am supposed to be dead. I will be heard.

TWO

Troy

OOR TROY, poor city, once my home. They
describe it now as rich and stately, these singers in Orestes' hall at Mycenae and all the
other Greek lords' halls, as the wine goes round. Rich,
noble, proud and stately, they say (those who were at
Troy, or now say they were), as they rehearse their
old boastful tales when the singer ends his song. Rich,
stately and noble are their plunderers' words. It was
my home before they burned it.

The city lies some quarter of a mile from the sea,
the beautiful Aegean. It had high walls, then, and
great gates to the east and west. From the walls, the
port, to the east, was easily visible.

I remember that every spring our nurse used to
carry us, my twin brother Helenus and me, to the
ramparts to look down over the plain below the city,
down to the sea. As we grew older we could take our
short legs up the many steps which ran up to the great
towers which stood at either end of the ramparts.
Later we sprang up them nimbly, beating our nurse
to the top, and there we all stood, celebrating the start
of spring. There the sheep grazed in pasture to their
knees, the lambs suddenly skipping up out of the green
like clusters of white blossom, then sinking down

again so that only the tops of their little white heads showed. There, too, were our few cattle and the many horses we loved and prized, foals running, mares and stallions grazing. Suddenly it was the time for the flowers to grow high in the grass, for the sunshine, for the freshly-rigged ships we could see at a distance, in the bay, to start out on long voyages. The city lay between two rivers – on the big one, Scamander, ships sometimes sailed, seeming to be sailing through fields.

The year I remember, Helenus and I were eleven years old, twins born on the shortest night of the year. We were standing on the ramparts, gazing over nearly a mile of flowers, yellow and blue, down to the great expanse of the sea where we could see our ships' white sails. There was a cool wind blowing. But a normal child's delight in the sunshine and in the new colours of spring was spoiled that day. We both had prophetic gifts, a torment and a blessing. As we pestered our nurse to take us down to the meadows, the harbour, the sea, there came to me (and to my brother, too, I found out later) that familiar stilling, where there seems to be no sound, where everything has frozen. I was alone, seeing what I should not see, hearing what I should never have heard. I saw that sea of flowers in the meadow as a sea of armed men, saw bright sunshine glinting on helmets and shields, saw tents pitched, the smoke rising from stray camp-fires, saw tethered horses, heard their neighing and whinnying, smelt smoke and the smell of roasting meat, the odours of men, the smell from the piles of horse dung on the outskirts of the camp. It was not spring; it was a hot day in summer. This vision came in spasms, coming and going like the creaks and bangs you hear alone in a house at night, which you first attend to, then forget, then hear again. As I say, I think I had seen these things before, when we were both younger, always at the start of spring, on the day when all the flowers seem to have come into bloom at once. But this year they were clearer and more frightening.

When Helenus and I compared notes at last, and found we had both seen the same things, my brother told me he always thought he must have been seeing ghosts. Indeed, he said he had hoped so, for if it was a vision of the future, it was a dreadful one. We were only beginning to understand the gift we had been given, or inherited. We were learning to control and interpret its messages. But this was beyond our understanding. All we experienced was the weariness and ferocity of the men below. We understood the soldiers were not our own people, though some wore our armour, carried our shields. And we felt fear.

Scene on scene, in shattered fragments, crowded into my head on that spring day in my twelfth year. I could at one moment feel the cold wind, see the grassy plain, Helenus leaning over the rampart and Adosha, our nurse – then, again, the terrible sights and sounds of war. I did not know Helenus, too, was hearing the cries, the shrieks of men and the screaming of horses. Looking back, I am sorry for those two thin children (we were always hungry in winter, and sometimes in summer, too) in their woollen tunics, whose joy in spring was being marred by their terrible and unwanted gift.

That time, I saw Adosha's mouth open and knew she was speaking to me, then I began to shiver. I fell and she half-carried me back down the stairs.

'Why did you say "the white horse is breaking

loose" before you fell down?' Helenus whispered to me that night in the great hall. We had eaten, the room was growing dark. Our parents had gone off to make up the day's reckonings in the room where the accounts were kept. On the long table in the middle of the room some of our brothers were playing dice. Our sisters, some of the ladies and my father's other wives were at their looms as usual, producing the cloth which was part of our city's trade. We were crouching at one end of the long fireplace. In front of it were several men, some on a bench, some on the floor with their arms round their knees, talking and swapping stories.

'And then the barren mare,' declared one, 'produced twin foals next year, and then year after year, foal after foal.'

'I thought I saw a battle,' I said to Helenus in a low voice, 'a lot of men, in armour. They were camped outside the walls. There was a chariot with two white horses, the driver was struck by an arrow and fell out. One of the horses panicked and started to break loose. It was very dim – it was a frightening dream although I was still awake.'

'I tell you,' said the man at the fireplace, 'she would not produce a foal by the black stallion. I told Advenor. Would he believe me? No – so much the worse for him. I bought the mare.'

'I've seen that battlefield,' came Helenus' voice in my ear. He sounded very sad. 'On the sea side of the city. I've seen it in the spring but not much. Now it's getting worse.'

'You've seen it?' I said. 'What have you seen?'

'Campfires, shapes of men fighting, all grey, like shadows,' muttered Helenus. 'I saw two men fighting.

13

One brought his sword down on the other's helmet. It split and the blood leaped up through the top, like water leaping up when you throw a big stone in it. I've heard yells, too, and horses screaming – clanging, like swords on shields, and I can smell it all, too.' He was shivering. 'Bards sing songs about battles, and tell stories. It's not like that. It's more like the slaughterhouse.'

There was a burst of laughter from the fire, one of the women got her lute and began to sing, there was a fracas in the doorway as five of our big fighting dogs tried to burst in and were kicked back. There were cries for the dog-trainer. I could see, even in the near-darkness – there were now more cries, for torches to be brought – that Helenus' pupils were dilated and his pale face paler than usual. I knew he couldn't be allowed to stay as he was, any more than I could, when I was like this. When we had been younger the next stage was normally a screaming fit, or an attack of meaningless babble, where we said any words or sentences which came into our heads, or we simply stared into space for minutes at a time, unconscious of anything said or done around us. All these manifestations caused awe, or terror in the witnesses. We prize our oracles and priestesses. We know they often tell us the truth and advise us wisely. But we, Helenus and I, were very young, and very strange.

Our mother – who had borne six strong sons and four skilful daughters since she was fifteen years old and was also extremely busy with many other tasks – put us in the care of Adosha with instructions to keep us as calm as possible and out of the way for much of the time. Her instincts were probably as good as usual. She knew the result might be madness or prophecy – there is not always such a gulf between the two – and she made the best choice of nurse when she found Adosha. At that time Adosha was only twelve. Her father was a relation of our father's. She was the oldest girl in a large family and instantly accepted the burden of the king and queen's two mad children, which was probably rather lighter than the burdens borne by the oldest girl of a big family on a poor farm. She took us for granted and doled out a mixture of indifference, concern and slappings which turned us, especially as we grew older and more in command of what was happening to us, from children generally seen as mad and going madder, to children accepted as sane. For my mother, I think, we were the night side of the bright day she wanted to live in. She had allied herself to the sun and given birth to the moon. Helenus and I, with our quick glances at nothing and our sudden, long, awestruck starings into empty space, were not what she wanted, even if the glances and stares were part of something holy. Our births seemed to indicate a strange, even malign, fate coming upon the family, although now it seems to me that we were a prophecy in ourselves, a hint of coming darkness.

Meanwhile, as they brought in the torches, I knew I must break Helenus' mood. We would both suffer if any more of the visions came in on us. I said, 'Let's go and make sure the horse has enough to eat.'

By this season the barns were emptying and the slaves who fed the horses were inclined to be economical with straw and fodder. Okarno was an old, rough pony, one of the local breed, not one of the fast horses we bred from southern stock. We had him only because his foot had cracked and mended badly and he commanded little attention in the stables. But we looked after him, groomed him, tended his bad foot because we loved him and because the ownership of any horse, even if it was only Okarno, gave us prestige. The palace stables were part of the palace itself, opposite the great hall, a four-sided block, built round a small courtyard. You could also reach the stable by leaving the palace and walking along the road which led up from the town below.

Behind us lay the warmth of the fire, on which they were piling more logs; the dice were rattling, wine going round and the women beginning to bandy words with the men.

We took the long way, walking the path round the palace walls, looking down at the lights winking from the houses on the levels below. At the bottom, torches were being carried into the temple beside the great gates of Troy. The whole of the lower area of the city – temple, granaries and tanneries, metal-working shops and potteries, stables, shops, storehouses and smithy – covered less than an acre. Inside the city a cobbled road rose, with houses, gardens and workshops, to the palace, armoury and stables at the top.

Helenus and I, clutching our arms around our thin chests, hurried in the wind, scurrying along the wide, paved path, broad enough for a chariot with a pair of horses, round the palace wall and through the stable gates.

Advenor, the man who looked after the horses, was a slave captured somewhere in the wild mountains and as broad as he was high. In spite of his youth and savage appearance he was respected by everyone – was he not in charge of our fortune, the horses? He was out of his hut beside the gates in a

16

flash, torch on high, peering through the dark, calling, 'Ah – it's you, my prince, come to see your charger.' We had only managed to secure stabling for Okarno in the royal stables because we were the king and queen's children. Advenor had the power not only to evict Okarno from the stables but to send him to the pit outside the city where the dead horses were thrown. We looked at Advenor nervously as he stood there with his torch. No point in arguing with him, he was too powerful. He could, as they said, bring a dead horse to life. He knew at a glance what a horse was like, body and mind, and it was by our horses and our wool and cloth that we lived. The farm produce kept us alive, but without our trade we would have had a thin time of it.

'We've come to see to Okarno,' I said. 'I brought him an apple – and you also.' I took the apples out and gave them to him – they were rare at this time of year – and he said, 'All right,' and didn't prevent Helenus from fetching more straw for Okarno, who had gone short in the distribution of litter.

We sat down behind him, with our backs against the stable wall. It was warm and soothing there, with the straw bunched round us and Okarno snorting and breathing in front. 'Were they camped all across the plain when you saw them in your vision?' I asked Helenus.

'Tents, huts, fires,' he said. 'Rows of horses, pickets on the outskirts. They looked settled in. Many ships were anchored in the harbour and along the beach beside the harbour. I could hear the horses and the scraping of armour being cleaned, and talking and singing. Not in our tongue.'

'Is it true?' I asked.

'You know it is,' he said calmly. 'It's worse for me – I shall be a man soon and expected to fight. What good shall I be when someone runs at me, blade raised?'

Mercifully for us at that time, although we saw the visions we could not interpret what the real consequences would be, if they were true. We could not imagine the future for the land, the city, the people, and our own family.

Here, perhaps, I should speak briefly of my land and family, not as the Greek ballads do, but as they truly were. My father, King Priam, ruled the city of Troy, its prosperous harbour and the surrounding area, the Troiad, or, as our Hittite neighbours call this, the Seha River lands. This is a fertile area some hundred miles square bounded to the west by the Aegean Sea and to the north by the Sea of Marmark. Further down the Aegean coast lay our friendly neighbours, the Mycians, Lycians, Carians and the rest. To the east were enemy tribes, such as the ferocious Black Sea Gasga. Beyond them, from where the mountains begin, lie the territories of our ally, the great and powerful Hittite kings.

My father, King Priam, had married twice, divorcing his first wife, with whom he could not agree, in favour of a happier and more practical alliance with my mother Hecuba, daughter of the King of Phrygia, from the mountainous country to the east of the lands of the Troiad. They had many children. Oh, my brothers and sisters, now dead! As I write, all those sharp memories, deliberately put aside in order to continue my life, assist my husband, rear my own children, return. I weep for them now, and for Priam and Hecuba, my parents.

I weep for my brothers and sisters, for brave Troilus, stalwart Hector, Paris, the beautiful, and for merry, cynical Deiphobus. And for Polites and young Pammon, my half-brothers who both died so early on in the fighting. For Polydorus – little brother – whom we thought saved. I remember my sisters, Creusa, Aeneas' wife, and Laodice, and Polyxena, the youngest.

My poor mother's sister was queen of neighbouring Lycia, through our grandmother. In Lycia women rule, make the laws and own almost everything. The Lycian men are famous warriors. I think now my mother had always been afraid of her powerful mother and even felt at a disadvantage with her sister for she was not a queen as Borea was, just queen to a king. Here my tall mother was less influential than she might have been, for although in Troy women could inherit property and leave it as they wished, and had much independence, they did not rule as they did in Lycia.

Some thirty years separate me from the child sitting in straw in a stable with her brother. My mother and father have been dead for twenty years. She must still be sad, Hecuba, even in Paradise with the Great Mother. The Greeks call her bitch and Dog Queen. The winners give such titles to the defeated. Virtually none of her fine children lived out their lives to a natural end, as people should. Probably only Helenus and I, her strangest fruit, are still living. It's a terrible thing for a woman to carry children, then bear and rear them, then have them thrust, too young, into the insatiable mouth of death.

*

In the stable Helenus said, 'Shall we tell? What we've seen? Who are they?'

'I believe it's the Greeks,' I told him. 'I believe I saw Agamemnon. I think I saw his blue eyes staring from under a gilded helmet.'

I call these men 'Greeks' for reasons of convenience. They would not have found the word friendly. Agamemnon was King of Mycenae, his brother King of Sparta. When the nations eventually coalesced they saw themselves as an alliance of separate states – from Mycenae, from Sparta, from Boetia. King Nestor came from Pylos, the Thessalians were led by Achilles, there were men of Crete and Rhodes; the Ithacans were led by the intelligent Ulysses. Any of these warriors would have scorned to have been called by one name – Greek.

I knew Agamemnon for he had come on a visit with some lords less than a year ago. Even then he had claimed he was leader of all the kings of Greece. My father doubted this; my mother said he would be leader so long as he could band together with the stronger lords to kill the weaker ones and take their lands and property. If he were the Greek leader – and she doubted it – it was only as the biggest and most powerful wolf in a pack is leader until a stronger wolf comes along and kills him. Agamemnon, a great, fair man in a red robe hung about with necklaces and bracelets, shining with gold, had frightened me. Suddenly, there in the stable, I saw what Helenus' vision had shown him – the great warrior in full armour, his gold armbands pushed up his thick arms and glinting in sunshine, and his huge sword raised over the head of Helenus as he was now, just a boy.

'You wouldn't have to fight him,' I said. Suddenly

everything seemed vague, hopeless, incredible. Were we saying this? What were we saying? Were we, Helenus and I, really here or dreaming?

'Perhaps it's just bad dreams, waking dreams,' I said to Helenus and added, 'I can hear Advenor coming. He wants to lock the gates.'

So we got to our feet. 'Come on,' said Advenor from the doorway. 'It's dark and I want to lock up – thieves could sneak in. Are you talking to the horse? Nothing you two do could surprise me.'

He walked behind us as we went out of the high wooden gates.

'What shall we do?' Helenus muttered to me.

'I'll tell you – you won't like it,' I said.

Advenor drew the bolts of the gates behind us. 'This way,' I told Helenus. He followed me across the paved road to the high city wall which overlooked the plain on one side and the sea on the other. In a corner between the wall and the high tower, from which we could hear only the wind and the faint sounds of celebration from the palace, I said to my brother, 'We must go to the oracle.'

'Oh,' groaned Helenus, who, I think, had known in advance what I was going to say, but did not wish to hear the words. 'No – I can't go. I don't want to. You go. Take Adosha.'

'They won't let her inside the cave,' I told him despondently. I knew the priestess would only let the two of us in. Even our mother, who had first taken us there when we were four years old, had been obliged on that occasion to wait at the cave mouth while we went in alone. At that time the oracle had frightened both of us, but not nearly as much as the journey to the cave, or the inside of it. She, it was easy to see, in spite of the robes and chalky face, was only a woman.

'You'll have to come,' I told Helenus. 'You said we had to tell. She's the person we must tell.'

'You don't tell her things,' Helenus said. 'She tells you.'

It was a weak argument and he knew it. In the end he agreed to go, as he had to. 'We'd better go back,' he said. 'It's freezing.'

At the corner he looked down at the winking lights of Troy and said, 'It's Helen.'

'Helen?' I asked. 'Who's that?'

He just said again, 'Helen.' I didn't ask again what he meant. I felt as if my head was in a thick fog and I couldn't see. A huge noise filled my head, as if I were standing close to a waterfall. All I wanted to do was sleep, but Helenus and I had been concentrating on fear and disruption for hours now, trying to piece together images of war. I dreaded to sleep, being afraid of dreaming and waking my sisters and the other women in the room where I was supposed to sleep. It had happened often before and they were annoyed when I disturbed them with my cries.

'Let's ask Adosha if she'll let us sleep on the rug by the brazier, under the sheepskins, like we used to,' said Helenus. One of the prices paid for increasing age and sanity was that we had been separated six months before, Helenus to go to the men's room, I to the women's. Our brother Hector was undertaking the job of training Helenus to use arms as a man ought – he was nimble and competent but a little cowardly, said Hector – and so night after night he had to go to the big room, containing thirty men. He hated it, complaining that the men were noisy and often drunk, quarrelled and talked about women half the night and threw smelly sandals and clothing all over the room. If he had a bad dream, they swore or laughed at him. I was not much happier among the women, who also quarrelled, talked about prospective husbands half the night and made the room smell of stale scents and old incense. They complained when I used their combs and pins. Still, I was lucky not to be in the room where my father's other wives, their babies and small children all slept.

Nevertheless, because it was tacitly admitted that Helenus and I were quite young to be in the big rooms with the others, we were often able to persuade Adosha to take us into the little stone room we had once shared. So that night we rolled up like puppies under our sheepskins by the brazier and managed, without saying anything to each other, to will ourselves to sleep without thoughts of an army between our city and the sea.

Half-way through the night I heard scratching and whispering at the door. I heard Adosha get up from her palette bed and say, terrifyingly, 'Die – go away and die! Stay unburied until your bones show on the earth!' But I fell asleep again, partly because I was used to Adosha's ungentle tongue, partly because I knew the midnight visitor was my brother Hector, who was beginning to pursue Adosha, who did not very much like him.

Next day we woke up frowsy in our rugs to Adosha's excitable shrieks. An embassy from Mycenae had docked in the harbour at dawn. The palace expected a royal visit. We managed to evade her – a swig of goat's milk and we were off, bits of bread in our hands, wrapped in sheepskin cloaks against the early chill and the mist from the sea. We ran out through the main gate with the others, and took the road down to the harbour.

Half the city had urgent business down at the port that day; half the nearby countryside had got its cart on the road, with bread, casks of wine, what was left of the apples, dried figs and raisins, tubs of olives and sausages. Others were rushing across the meadows with a cheese, a couple of hens tied together, wings flapping. A small man with bandy legs carried a whole slaughtered sheep on his shoulders, with some of the blood still dripping down his neck; three boys were trying to keep a herd of goats together. The Greeks might only have been at sea for three or four days, but people reasoned they would still be needing supplies.

Half a mile out of the town, jumping aside for carts, pushed and shoved by women with baskets and men with loads of planks, we felt the sun on our heads and saw the mist disappearing from the fields. There were cries behind us, and rattling, and, looking round, we saw Paris, our brother, standing up in his chariot behind two matched black horses, charging up at a fantastic pace, with people dropping away from the road on to the fields, as fast as they could, to keep out of his way. No one minded; everyone smiled; I think he could have knocked a child or an old woman flying and still received everyone's blessing.

Paris, now twenty-five but still unmarried, was as handsome as a god, very dark, curly-headed but with huge, dark blue eyes, which shone out from his dark skin like pieces of lapis luzuli. And Paris was brave, kind as a mother and calm as a meadow. He was

Dionysos at the festival at the solstice, when Dionysos made love to the priestess to bring back the sun and rekindle the earth. Children were not supposed to be present at the festival but, as children do, we spied and I don't think very great efforts were made to stop us. I once sat in a tree beside the sacred grove and watched as the great surge of men and women, some masked, some not, raced over hills and fields to the sound of pipes and drums, torches flaring, people shouting and crying out. Was the priestess my mother on those occasions? I could not tell if it was my mother under the bird mask she wore, although I knew Paris was the lover because he wore no mask. I don't think that to this day I have seen a man as beautiful or as good as my brother. Of course, it was that beauty and generosity which helped us to our doom. Had it not been for Paris my family might have lived. I might have been a happy woman. He destroyed us but no doubt was fated to do so. In any case, with his strong arms holding the reins, his hair flying back in the wind of his chariot as it sped and his brilliant, open smile, he was a joyful sight on that spring morning. Spotting us, he pulled up short, the horses snorting. 'I'll let you ride,' he said, 'but before we arrive you'll have to drop off and disappear into the crowd. You're too young and too unwashed to meet the guests. You'd bring shame on us.'

'How many ships?' I asked.

'Two,' he answered, as we jumped in. He urged the horses on through the crowds. 'No warning,' he said, partly to himself. 'They should have sent a messenger by an earlier ship. Perhaps they came on impulse – but why?'

Our relationship with our violent neighbours

across the sea was never happy. We were a major port on that coast. Suppiluliumas, the Hittite king, from his capital Hattusas, six hundred miles away, relied on us to protect the coast, part of his sphere of influence, from pirates – chief among whom were the Greeks. Consequently, our ships were forever in battle with theirs – while our own ships raided their coasts when possible. I think we took it that these Mycenaeans were mad. Their ancestry was short, but the records said that ever since their arrival in Greece they had been leaving their poor land to ravage their neighbours, looting, burning and enslaving. Mighty Crete had fallen to them, and Rhodes and many other places. Now they had gold, weapons and land. They lived in well-defended fortresses, for when they were not conspiring to attack foreigners they would be turning on each other. They seemed always violently angry, as unpredictable as poorly-trained dogs and as furiously deprived as week-old babies left to cry in the dark. Happily for us we had the support of Suppiluliumas, but even so the sudden arrival of our deadly neighbours made us uneasy.

Paris had eventually been despatched to make a hasty welcome, while Advenor would have been unhappily selecting some horses as a gift, the palace being made ready, waggons sent out to the farms for supplies, and my parents preparing themselves to greet the unwelcome guests. Behind Paris would follow a couple of chariots, harnessed up in haste, to convey the Greeks to Troy.

Helenus and I were silent. The prospect of seeing the disembarkation had been exciting, but now that we found ourselves near the harbour, we both dreaded seeing the figures from our nightmares, and the thought was sobering.

'How long will they stay?' I asked.

'Weeks, I suppose,' said Paris. 'We don't know the reason for the visit. They will want something – they usually do.'

A woman with a basket on her back turned when one of the horses brushed the basket, toppling out some dried figs. When she saw Paris, she smiled. The woman she was with, her sister perhaps, also smiled and bent to pick up the figs and put them back in the basket. The child she had by the hand grinned at my brother. All down the route people told each other, 'The prince's chariot is coming.' Carts and laden men and women moved off the narrow road to let us through. Graceful, smiling, the sunshine seeming to make his face gleam, Paris could do no wrong. Finally, with the ships in sight, we had a clear pathway to the harbour. Paris raised his whip, planning to arrive with our fine horses galloping and panting, to make a show. He said, 'Jump out!' and as we both tumbled off the side into the crowd he brought down the whip and dashed off, stones flying up from under the black horses' hooves.

I didn't see what happened after that. I lost Helenus immediately and, wedged between a big woman with strings of onions all over her and three large men from the mountains, with two small children immediately in front of me and a crowd behind, I had a job to keep my feet as the travellers all hastened forward to try and get a glimpse of the arrival of Paris and the descent of the Greeks from their ships. Later there were many accounts of the event, but none from Paris. I don't think he remembered much.

It seems he reached the harbour at a gallop, turned the chariot sharply at the entrance, sped the horses over the paving of the dock and pulled up short, opposite the gangplank of the largest ship, which had a big golden bird at its prow. The horses shuddered, then stopped tidily on their polished hooves, making a fine sight. They were unused to such brusque treatment, but Paris, obviously dragged from his bed to produce a respectable display at short notice, while the king and queen prepared an official welcome, was doing his best. He stood upright in his chariot, waiting.

The Greek leaders, appearing on deck as if from nowhere, began to come down the gangplank. The crowd stood silent as two tall men, both in red, one with bright red hair, the other blond, both heads circled with gold, walked slowly down to the dock. Behind them, with two women servants, came a tall woman with golden hair, elaborately dressed in plaits and curls, wearing a white tunic of some fine wool which reached to her knees. She wore golden sandals, a gold circlet, lost in the colour of her hair, and a small necklace of dark, blue stones. 'The exact colour of her eyes,' Adosha told me afterwards. (Adosha had somehow arrived before us, and was to the front of the crowd.) 'And of Paris' eyes,' I said.

The Carians were, legend has it, the original people of Troy. They are a small, dark people, fine-boned, with brown eyes. But Troy is a port, and we have in us the blood of the Phoenicians, Hittites and even the Greeks themselves. Thus it was that in my own family men like Hector could be so mighty, Paris have eyes of clearest blue, while Helenus and I, as if representing the original Trojans, when the city was a fishing hamlet and the port just a beach with a few boats drawn up, were brown-skinned, brown-eyed and showed signs we would always be smaller in stature than the others.

As the two kings touched land Paris leaped from the chariot and advanced quickly, arms outstretched. It must have been at this point that he properly noticed the woman as she followed the two men down. He and she looked at each other. By this stage Adosha, panting in her best clothes, had got nearly to the front of the crowd, telling everyone loudly she was looking for the king and queen's children, which she was not. As she elbowed the last person aside she caught sight of the woman on the gangplank just as she, seemingly, noticed Paris for the first time. Adosha said that suddenly hers was the face of a girl looking at her first lover just after they had made love in some wood or grove. Impossible, said Adosha, to describe the softness of her face, or the hunger, or the look of that very red, gently parted mouth. She looked at Paris, said Adosha, as if she and he had been in bed all night and she never wanted to get up. She said she couldn't see Paris as his back was to her, but what she noticed was that he had stopped a few paces from the two Greek kings, with his arms still outstretched, as if he'd been turned to stone. It looked as if the taller of the two, the fair-haired one, Agamemnon, had been forced to step forward and grasp his outstretched arms just to get his attention. The red-headed king, behind, looked grim behind his smile. To them it must have seemed as if Paris were trying to play the great king, waiting to be approached, rather than approaching. The touch of the man, said Adosha, seemed to bring Paris to himself.

There was an exchange of remarks, unheard by

the crowd, there were smiles, clasping of arms and larger-than-life gestures as is customary on such public occasions. The woman had by then come down on to the dock with her servants and had her expression more under control, which, as Adosha said, was a blessing, since there can have been few in the crowd who hadn't read her countenance and seen what it was saying. By that time anyway, most people were looking at the two heroes and taking in the details of their entourage, now disembarking. There were five nobles among them. White-haired and leaning on a staff was their priest and adviser, Calchas. There were about forty soldiers in full kit, with bright helmets, breastplates and swords. They had even brought ten large horses. This, of course, was why there were two ships, but it was an over-large, over-military display for a simple diplomatic visit between allies.

Agamemnon and Paris stood at the front of the chariot, Paris holding the reins. Behind stood Agamemnon's brother Menelaus, King of Sparta – and Helen. The woman Adosha had pushed aside muttered, 'She's married to the red-headed brother, it seems – but you can see which man she wants.' Adosha told her, 'And he's no Greek.' There was a laugh from those around them, Adosha said. Our Trojan women, of course, lived more freely than the Greeks. Here among the Greeks, as I have learned in Thessaly, the rule is that anything un-Greek which doesn't move is seized or burned, anything edible is eaten and anything human, which is un-Greek, is killed or enslaved. This rule applies to all women, Greek or not. For my own safety I have had to live as a Greek woman. It is like living in chains.

Meanwhile Paris, affected as he probably was by the woman standing behind him, whipped up the horses. They left the harbour and drove up the long road to the city. Two additional chariots for the other Greeks had by then arrived. Paris passed me, standing in the chariot with the reins in his hands, looking handsome as the young god himself. But there was something on his face which reminded me of Hecate's priests when they have drunk sacred wine and can dance all night, or slash themselves with knives to feed their blood to the fields and never seem to feel fatigue or pain. He was entranced. And there were the two fierce kings, both, though young, with identical lines carved from nose to chin and across their brows, and there Helen, Menelaus' wife, the most beautiful woman I have ever seen, perhaps the most beautiful woman anyone has ever seen. She silenced the crowd. Those who saw her pass could do nothing but look. Moments after the chariot had gone by, people started talking. 'It isn't human,' said a man. 'I'd murder to have her – I know I would. It isn't human.' Most of the men seeing Helen must have thought when they saw her, only of having her – then, of how they never would. Women, I think, were beyond envy for that woman seemed of a different kind. No one in our world looked like that. No one ever could. She was like a creature from the sun.

When they had gone, half the light seemed to have gone with them. I felt cold and tired, as a child will who has sprung out of bed early and run a mile or so, on an almost empty stomach. While those with something to sell remained, I joined the others who had just come for the spectacle and began to walk back to the city, behind the contingent of Greek

31

soldiers marching fast in a double column. Naughty children mimicked their heavy, armour-laden tread. Helenus ran up after me, offering me half a smoked fish and a piece of bread he had come by.

'Helen,' he said. 'That's the queen's name.'

'You told me that name,' said I.

'Did I?'

'Last night.'

'I think I remember.'

Had he heard the name somewhere once and then forgotten it? It wouldn't be very surprising, for her beauty was a legend and so was her history. Everyone, everywhere, even then, spoke of Helen. This kind of foreseeing is often not pure magic, just memory and intelligence working too fast for the thinking brain, which goes plodding on, step by painful step, to follow.

'The other king's married to Helen's sister,' he reported. 'She's beautiful, but not as beautiful as Helen.'

Adosha caught up with us now. 'Oh,' she said, 'such beautiful kings – did you see the sun glinting on their gold circlets and that beautiful woman's hair, brighter than gold itself? A goddess, she must be. We'll never see a sight like that again.'

'No,' Helenus and I found ourselves saying together. Helenus then said, 'Will you take us to the oracle today, Adosha?'

She was astonished. 'The oracle? Today? You both want to see the oracle? And today, of all days?'

'We must,' I told her.

She looked at me angrily. 'You fear the oracle. Don't you want to stay in the palace today and see the kings and hear their discussions? What about the banquet? If you must see the oracle, wait till the kings have gone.'

'Today,' I said firmly. I knew Adosha herself wanted to stay in Troy and see what was going on and hear all the gossip. She would have to be made to go.

'They'll expect you to be there,' she told me.

This seemed hardly true. In the bustle of the kings' unexpected arrival and the attempt to understand why they had come, no one would notice our absence.

'We've got to visit the oracle, though we don't want to,' I said, 'and you have to come with us.'

She began to see we were serious and her face changed. She shivered. 'If we must,' she said.

We had stopped on the road, where it curved round to meet the city gate. People walked round us. Helenus was very pale and I expect I was, too. In the great hall my mother would be in her blue robe, her hair plaited on her head beneath the great gold headdress she had brought with her at her marriage. My father would wear his huge embroidered coat. His grey-black hair and beard would be curled. All the famous and dignified men and women of Troy would be greeting the guests, waggons would be drawn up outside the doors and carcasses of sheep and goats and heaps of loaves from the baker would be unloading. The servants would be hauling great jars of wine towards the hall. There would be music. But Helenus and I had to go up the frightening hill, past the black altar, to see the oracle.

THREE

Thessaly

IT IS full autumn here now. The last leaves are
fluttering about the yard as I sit, wrapped in my
cloak, writing. The cistern and the well have to
be cleared of leaves daily. All the crops are in. Olives
are standing in big jars in the storehouse, apples,
apricots and plums are drying on their racks, the wine
is pressed and I can hear the olive press thudding
down on the last of the crop. Next week we begin
slaughtering the beasts we will not be able to feed
during the winter. The smokehouse fire is already lit
and the barrels are filled with salt. I shall be driven
indoors at last both by the cold and by the bellowing
of cows, rams and ewes in the yard as they are slaughtered. Years ago, when there were many to feed and
not enough servants to do all the work, I used to help
with this myself, holding the animals as the big knife
was pulled across their throats, but always, as I
helped to hold down the struggling beasts, I had to
push away the thought of the knives thudding through
cloth to strike flesh, always heard, in the crying and
bleating, human cries, calling 'Treachery! Revenge!
Blood for blood!' Nevertheless, I held the animals as
they died – twenty people had to get through the
winter with full stomachs. Having seen so much

death, I wanted all the more to preserve life. Those who saw what I saw – there are some of us left – will never be able to forget. Our minds are stained with memory nothing could wash away. We will never be able to say, 'There it is, fresh and good as new. You'd never suspect it had ever had a mark on it.'

But the children are grown and healthy and my patient husband beyond harm or help now. (Where is he? Stalking gloomily among the shades of the Greeks or sitting with the Mother in her pleasant pastures?) And now the venerable Greek mother and widow can rise early, despatch the day's business and sit down at the bench to tell her story. Naomi makes faces when she sees me dragging the old Arabian cushion from the house to lay on the stone bench, in preparation for hours of sitting. That long cushion, with the strange birds woven into it in red and green, used to lie in front of our fire in winter. All the children wanted it. 'I want to sit on the bird.' 'No – I do,' they'd cry in their high voices. My husband would always say the three boys, Diomed, the oldest, Dryas and Phaon, should have it and the girls should go on carding their wool, and winding it on to spindles; then, as they grew older, should take their places at the loom. It galled me to see Penelope and Iris, grand-daughters of Priam and Hecuba of Troy, working at the loom in the chill while their brothers sat playing at knucklebones and fondling the dog in front of the fire. But I could hardly protest and boast about my children's birth, unless I wanted to die, see my oldest son killed and make sure my daughters would never marry.

What would the claim mean, anyway, where all Trojans are slaves? Only my brother Helenus is free, many miles away across the mountains, the Epirus, a wild place where the Greeks, rulers of this land, have little sway. That place is still under the moral protection of the great Achilles, who would not allow Helenus or his wife to be troubled. I have seen others of my countrymen often enough over the years, on the few occasions when I have left my home. They are pulling ploughs and hauling water, they are being beaten and used until they die. They are often easy to recognise, being smaller-boned than Greeks with small, high noses, high cheekbones and big, slightly slanting eyes. Only three years ago I bought some sheep from Vanno, Adosha's brother, at the annual fair. I knew him by the burn on his cheek he got when she pushed him on to a brazier when he was two years old. Vanno was well dressed and healthy for a slave, but his eyes were dull and turned to the ground when he spoke to me and I had no doubt his back was scarred with beatings. It takes many floggings and tyings up to take the light from the captive's eyes like that. He didn't recognise me. Why should he have? His eyes never met mine anyway, and I doubt if he could have recognised in the slackened body of a prosperous Greek landowner's wife the Trojan princess he last saw twenty years before. And if he had looked me straight in the face he would have seen eyes as dull, almost, as his own, blanked by time and the effort to put on a suitable face for this public appearance. Not hard to keep your eyes down and timid when you are afraid, as I was, in the market-crush of confident Greeks.

Vanno and I had last met at the gates of Troy when he was fourteen, I sixteen. He stood in a great group of men and boys, wearing armour which was too big for him. The first battle of the war was about to begin. Adosha was clinging to him, trying to wrestle him away, saying he was too young and inexperienced to fight; why didn't he steal away home? She, his older sister, ought to have had some influence with him, but he wouldn't listen. So Vanno went. Later she saw Vanno fall, hit by an arrow, and then disappear under chariot wheels in the mêlée of fighting men and rearing horses. He must have survived and been taken back to a Greek ship.

I couldn't tell him who I was. He might have been happy to know I was alive, but twenty years of bullyings and beatings can turn a man into a traitor, for gain or to get off a punishment, or even, the greatest trap of all, can make a man who believes his enslaver is his superior. He could have betrayed me to get a pat from his master.

Soon, none of this will matter. Each day I see more clearly what will happen. The crisis will come soon and the Greek nations will not survive.

Naomi has been telling me off. 'The servants are talking about what you're doing. They'll tell others. They may think you're making spells against them. We can't afford curious people. We've hidden successfully for twenty years. Why not let us go peacefully into old age?'

'It doesn't matter,' I said.

'Why? Do you think you're going to die? You look healthy to me. Don't try to foresee your own death – it may be beyond your powers. Anyway, even if you die, I may not. Think of that.'

'It's not our deaths – our deaths will come when they come. It's Greek deaths I see.'

'Don't promise me they'll die, the bastards,' she

said. 'They'll never die. Cut off one of their heads and another ten spring up from somewhere else.'

'They'll die,' I told her.

'I'll pray for it,' she said.

'To which gods?' I asked. 'Ours, theirs or your own?'

'To all of them,' she said. 'Tell me when it's coming and I'll take knives to them myself.'

Naomi had been married (she called it) to a fish merchant before we left Troy but never saw her husband again. She had been given to the Greek soldiers even before we landed. She had strangled at birth the child she bore to the platoon in the shed where they kept the Trojan women. They beat her for this, too, weak as she was. The marks where she had cut her wrists with a piece of flint were still there. Not long after I had come to the farm, I found her in the slave huts at the port and, pretending that I needed her help, persuaded my kind husband to buy her. Otherwise I suppose she might have tried to kill herself again, and that time succeeded.

'So what are you writing?' she said, standing in the chilly wind, without a cloak, shivering.

'The whole story,' I said. 'The story of those days we have hardly dared remember, in case they showed on our faces.'

'So when their doom comes on them, they will know why,' she said.

'That's a fierce god you had there as a child,' I told her. 'I can still see his traces on you. He believed in justice and revenge, and bad men being punished and good ones rewarded. And men in deserts pointing bony fingers at the bad, denouncing them. After all you've seen, do you still believe your enemies will be

38

punished, or that they'll be abashed by words, made ashamed because someone recites their misdeeds?'

Some years ago one of her countrymen, an Israelite, had come off a boat forced to put in because of a storm. We found him in the olive groves with some other stranded sailors, eating our olives. Naomi found out his race and dragged him back to the house. She spent a day and a whole night talking to him until they had patched the ship and could put out to sea again. All they had in common was a mangled Hittite tongue, fragments of which she remembered from those years in Troy, when it had been useful to know our chief ally's language, and which he knew from trading at Hattusas, the Hittite capital. This mariner told her about her people, who had stopped their desert wanderings, had fought the established inhabitants for their cities, overcome them and settled themselves in more fertile territories. He spoke of their religion, which still relied on those tablets she remembered (simple rules normally observed by all, such as honouring your father and mother and not committing murder). Sadly enough, he knew nothing of her parents and had not heard of her. He thought she must come from a different tribe. Nevertheless, he drew a fierce picture of this god worshipped by these former nomads. Amazingly enough, they had a single deity, one jealous god, who forbade any images of himself, as he was something like the wind, everywhere and nowhere.

Before he departed, this Israelite offered to marry Naomi – she's a good-looking woman and has quite a lot of silver hidden in her room. She refused, saying she had no desire to find herself on a trading journey through the desert pulling a reluctant camel to its feet, while the man's other wives lay about squabbling and eating figs in a tent. She told him she was already married, which was not true, but now she has a man, a servant on another estate and her small boy, aged three, is his son.

I think she must love this man, or why would she walk three miles over the mountains to visit him so often? I envy her. She is less lonely than I am, now my husband is dead and my children are away. No one will ask questions about her, a slave, but I must live without company most of the time, to keep my secret. Formerly I presented myself as a very shy woman, devoted to her husband and children, never leaving my own home, which gave me a good reputation among the Greeks, where women are trained to cling to their thresholds and make sure their daughters never stray out of sight of the house. This retired life meant I never had to account for myself. Now, all these years later, I don't think anyone would ask who I once was, where I came from or who my parents were. I have grown into the landscape like a tree.

I turned back to writing, but before I did so I said to Naomi, 'The victors compose the ballads about their wars, saying how great and brave they were.'

She bent towards me and said, 'You must tell me more about what you expect to happen. We shall have plans to make. And how soon?'

'What can happen before the spring?' I said. In my dreams I had seen men coming up the beach from ships.

What I had not foreseen was an immediate visit. Yet, as I spoke, a man ran into the courtyard and shouted, 'There's waggons coming along the road, about a mile off – rich waggons. Someone important's coming!'

I jumped to my feet in alarm.

FOUR

Troy

ADOSHA, HELENUS and I scrambled up the narrow track on the wooded hill to the oracle's cave. It lay almost a mile inland from the sea, behind the city and up the steep path which at that time of year was blocked with bushes, and with stones which had come down with the winter rain. It was a hard climb. We did not have to go right to the top for the cave of the oracle was two-thirds of the way up the hill. The mouth of the cave ran into the hillside. In front of it was a glade. All around were trees hung with the animal masks used in our ceremonies and bells with muted clappers, which made a sound between banging and ringing. Also dangling from the trees were strips of stained cloth, the skeletons of birds and small animals and clay bowls, hung on strings, containing offertory objects.

Before you arrived at the oracle's cave you had to pass, at the centre of the grove near the steeply mounting cliff, the black slab of the altar. In front of the altar lay the pit we called the blood-pit, its sides hard with dried blood. In wet weather the pool in the pit was red. At the bottom lay bones and scraps of half-burned flesh. The smell, especially in summer, was terrifying in itself. Thoughts of those sacrifices, at night, when the adults were not the people we knew in daylight, thoughts of the beast struggling and crying out as the white-faced priests and priestesses cut its throat, the idea, the possibility, never discussed, that sometimes the sacrifice on that black altar had been human, not animal, and might one day be so again – all that awed adults and frightened children. No child, however brave, ever played on that hill, even on the sunniest day.

Adosha, thin, only eighteen years old, was wearing her best dress, long and red, secured at the shoulder with a large, bronze brooch (she was dressed to impress the Greeks). Once we had scrambled up the hill she took our hands in hers and, after a pause to pluck up courage, advanced across the grass. We must have been a strange sight – Adosha in her long gown, Helenus and I, undersized for our age, pale and gazing fiercely through our almond eyes at the altar some ten yards away – we were not frightened – no, not we! After a few more paces we stopped again, hearing only the sigh of the wind in the trees, the muted sounds of the bells' clappers, the song of birds. We all three stared at the black altar, mounted on four blocks of greenish stone and then slid our eyes to the cave-mouth. Bushes grew in front of it. Out of sight from where we stood was the pit into which they rolled the animals after the sacrifice. Hanging from the trees all round us were the animal masks – the bird-mask, with its beaked nose and feathers, a plume at the top – the hollowed-out skull of a big dog, the mask painted black and red – the goat-mask, with its horns – the flat-headed snake, painted yellow and black in whorls, with tiny horns at the top – the mask of a lion, painted with black rings round its eyes.

Adosha, afraid of the place, afraid of what we would do in it, or what would happen to us, said brusquely, 'Come on,' and pulled us both in the direction of the altar. Meanwhile for me, and for Helenus too, I guessed, the light dimmed. I felt a trance coming on me. The animal masks seemed to grow bigger and loom down. Helenus said later he saw the snake-mask's mouth open and heard a hissing. None of us wanted to look at the altar, with its grimly-stained surface, or down into the pit. Nevertheless, as we got closer I saw from the corner of my eye a goat lying half-burned at the bottom, its horns in earth and its head thrown back as if pleading for mercy. There were flies buzzing round and a rat leaped from the pit as we got closer still. But the real horror of the pit was the fear of seeing the remains of a human being lying there – a woman's face peering up through the ashes or a half-burned baby or the stretched-out figure of a young man with his throat slit, the priestess's son-lover who used to be sacrificed there each year in the old days.

The light was dimming and then came that time I – we both – dreaded, always half-forgotten until it happened again. It was the time when time stopped. Nothing moved. There was no sound. Then, into that void the visions would come crowding.

I was only half-conscious of the big eunuch-priest in his dark robe coming stooping from the mouth of the cave. I saw his mouth move and I knew he was speaking to me but I could not hear him. Already I saw men sitting round campfires, their helmets and weapons stacked on the ground nearby. I saw them cutting pieces of meat from a sheep on a spit, heard voices, and laughter. At the same time I was aware

44

the priest had me by the hand and was leading me into the cave, and I felt sympathy coming from him. I knew Helenus was there as well. Then my mother was crying out from one of the towers of the city as, from below, came the sound of swords hitting shields, the neighing of horses, the swish of a flight of arrows, a sudden yell of pain, sounds of a storm rising.

Then I was staring, scarcely seeing it, into the chalk-white face of the priestess, an old woman with long white hair, a great necklace of jagged lumps of blue stone round her old neck, a scarlet dress, heavy with gold embroidery hanging from her thin shoulders. Her face was painted. Her lips were very red, there were black lines around her eyes. She sat in the depths of the cave on a stool, in front of a brazier giving out aromatic smoke. The thin red slit of the woman's mouth opened and a voice, neither a man's nor a woman's, said, 'So you have come to tell me what you know. Tell me quickly. Neither of you can stay long. You are too young for this.' Then I found myself speaking, although sometimes the voice seemed to be Helenus' as well. And my father was saying, 'How many more sons shall I see killed?' There was a terrible chorus of voices, men's and women's, crying, 'Send the woman back. Send the woman back.' There were children crying.

'Send the Greek queen back to her husband,' came Helenus' voice, but it was not exactly his voice.

'It's the port they want and not the woman,' came my mother's voice, speaking reasonably. 'Send her, send our daughters, too. It will make no difference.'

A chariot went round and round the walls, something dragged at the back of it. Men dug a deep trench by the sea. A band of weary men came through the city gates, the wounded leaning on the fit – the live carrying the dead over their shoulders. The heavy gates were closed behind them. Children cried, a man's voice called, 'Water!' 'Send the woman back,' someone said. There were screams.

'Five years and then we burn,' came Helenus' voice.

'No stone shall be left standing on another,' I murmured.

'Children wrenched from their mothers' arms, their heads shattered against stones.'

'The swords will come down and down, the stones will run with blood.'

'Treachery.'

'Death.'

The oracle's white face loomed over us and, 'Enough,' she said. Her priest was pulling both of us to our feet. She said, 'I have also seen what you have seen. That is what you came to find out. Is there anything else you want to know?'

But I knew the woman had finished with us. She wanted no questions. I felt myself being pulled away. The priest was half carrying me through the dark and cold of the cave, on and on, into daylight. Then I was lying on the grass and heard another body drop down beside mine. It was Helenus. Gradually the sound of the birds grew louder. I could hear the wind in the trees again and the muffled clang of the bells in the trees.

I asked, 'Are you there, Helenus?' I saw Adosha's feet beside me and heard her shocked voice, 'He just threw you on the ground and went back into the cave. No ceremony there.'

'I don't think we brought good news,' Helenus told her.

Even as we helped each other up I could still see dim figures at the altar, like ghosts. A tall woman was raising a knife before bringing it down towards the black slab where a boy lay, bound and screaming. I glanced at Helenus, hoping he had seen it too but he was standing weakly there on the grass, head bowed, like someone grateful to have emerged from high fever. The terrible thing was that my vision showed me that the woman killing the boy was my mother, Hecuba.

As we returned Adosha said little but she was kind. She helped us down the steep places on the track, even carrying Helenus down the sharpest and rock-iest part of the path when his legs were slipping under him, while I sat at the top, waiting my turn. She knew that after these attacks we were always very weak. So we went slowly downhill to the plain behind the city, through the pasture surrounded by the ewes and their lambs and back to the palace. We must have been a terrible sight, Helenus and I, pale and exhaus-ted, with our hair all tangled from the climb and our arms and legs streaked with mud.

Unfit to be seen by our distinguished, unwanted guests we entered the palace by the courtyard near the stables, where sweating slaves were basting three whole sheep on spits across a huge fire. A cauldron hung over a smaller fire and in a corner heaps of fish were being gutted and piles of onions chopped.

'Your brother was looking for you both,' one

47

woman said over her shoulder. 'He said you ought to be in the great hall.'

We went to wash and change our clothes. 'Just sit there quietly,' Adosha instructed. 'Don't look at anybody and don't say anything.'

Helenus had on a heavily embroidered tunic and I had a long skirt with stiff pleats. Adosha had fetched these things from the chest in the storehouse where the ceremonial clothes were kept.

Seventy people could dine and two hundred stand comfortably in the great hall. On that day it was full to capacity. There were landowners from within a radius of twenty miles, citizens of Troy – bakers, blacksmiths, wealthy traders, merchants, fishermen, potters and warriors. There were Egyptians and Phoenicians and two tall Africans, head and shoulders above the rest.

There was a continual murmur of conversation, comment and translation as the words of the main protagonists seated before the fireplace passed back and forth.

On one side sat the two Greek kings, legs apart, hands along the arms of their carved wooden chairs. Opposite them were King Priam and Queen Hecuba, also sitting formally and motionlessly. All four were posed to be seen, by those attending the council, like the characters on a wall painting. Blind Calchas, with his long white hair and staff, stood behind his king, Agamemnon. Next to Calchas, beautiful Helen stood behind her husband. My parents had at their backs Anchises, their adviser, and my brothers Hector, Deiphobus and Troilus. Next to them were two insignificant-looking Hittite men of business, recognisable as what they were by their robes, and by their pointed hats and the scrolls they held. They could not have reached the city from their capital Hattusas, many weeks' journey away. They must have been summoned from somewhere nearby.

Beside the chairs of Agamemnon and King Priam stood the translators to clarify and supplement what they were saying. They could also slow things down when one side needed time to think. Seated cross-legged on the floor were my younger sister and brother, Polyxena and Polydorus. Around them, on stools or standing, were Trojan dignitaries and the rest of the Greek party. Behind the throng in the room, Greek soldiers, in armour, leaned against the walls. They had come in after the conference started and should not have been there.

Though the four seated figures by the fireplace sat still as statues and spoke unemphatically, the faces of the tough, scarred Greeks and the large concourse of hardy Trojan dignitaries betrayed the fact that this assembly had turned into a show of strength on either side – Greeks and Trojans were displaying equally affability, cordiality and willingness to defend themselves. An important aspect of the display was the family of Priam and Hecuba, particularly their sons. But, I wondered, where was Paris on this important occasion?

Helenus and I had slipped through the crowd and dropped on to the floor beside Polyxena and Polydorus. I felt, rather than saw, the chilly blue gaze of Agamemnon on me. I sat quite still, looking at the floor, hoping, I suppose, like an animal, that if I did not move he would forget about me. From the corner of my eye I saw the kings' big, muscular legs ending in gilded sandals. The reddish hairs on Menelaus' legs seemed unnatural. For reassurance I glanced at my father. He was a grave, hieratic figure, his beard and shoulder-length hair both crimped, a long robe in severe folds round his feet, a high gold crown on his head. He was different, but still my gentle father, the man of the port accounts, rent tallies and archives, who would spend all night in the stables with Advenor, holding up a lantern for a foaling mare. I looked at my mother, again for reassurance. Her face was grave and still but I sensed that underneath her calm she was displeased by what was happening. I looked for reassurance, but found too little. I was losing control; my panic was mounting.

The discussion in progress concerned the old vexed question of harbour tariffs. The Greeks were suggesting they should pay no tax for docking and harbour facilities. My parents were refusing politely.

As the talk went on I felt myself drifting helplessly. Helenus took my hand. He glanced round at the room. It would have been impossible to leave without a fuss. The room was packed. There were men and women's legs right up against our backs and all eyes were in our direction. Behind me a woman turned to her companion and muttered, 'In the next breath they'll ask us to send shiploads of free food to Pylos.'

'The blind man's whispering in the Greek king's ear again,' said the man. Then an 'Oh!' and a shout went up at some unpopular statement by Menelaus.

Then I felt I was far away, smelling the reek of fish, a lamb-fat tallow candle, sweat and sex. I guessed my mind had taken me down to the docks where, I knew, in some corner my brother Paris was with a girl, helping to pay her dowry. Why was he there?

Then I was returned to the great hall. I saw the

blond hairs, like tiny gold threads, on the huge muscular legs of Agamemnon. I caught the odour of the Greek queen's musky scent. She stood behind her lord, clad in white linen. Her skirt was long. Only one tiny foot in a blue sandal trimmed with silver emerged from the folds. Blue beads were wound into the gold of her elaborately dressed hair. Her face was white marble and very still. Her red lips were slightly parted and her blue eyes moved with polite blankness from the face of my father to that of my mother. I was reminded of the faces of the women at our ceremonies, their minds wiped by drugs and chanting, of the beautiful madman who sat in a corner of the temple and thought he was an eagle. I felt sorry for her and did not know why. I saw Hector, standing behind my father's chair, looking at her and knew that loyal husband as he was, at that moment he desired only Helen. And that would be why Paris was trying to find forgetfulness in a corner of a warehouse with a woman from the port. He dared not see Helen. She was irresistible.

The sun became hotter. Slanting beams came through the windows striking the barely moving figures in their chairs. The voices of the leaders and their interpreters went on and on, droning the same points over and over. The close-packed crowd shifted and muttered. The smell of roasting meat came into the packed room.

The afternoon seemed eternal. They told me my shrieks broke into the mumble of voices, shocking everyone. I imagined my own small figure in the elaborate, too-heavy costume, standing, head thrown back, pointing at my brother in the doorway. I cried out, 'Take him away! Make him go! He'll be our ruin!'

The entire room, they say, fell silent. The Greek kings, though angered by the interruption, did not move. My mother's head turned to me but she did not move either. My father half-rose from his chair. Adosha pushed through from somewhere, grasped me under the armpits and started to haul me through the crowd. Helenus was beside her, whispering to me, 'Quiet, Cassandra. Quiet.' And I was screaming, 'Ruin! Ruin!' while they pulled me through the room and past Paris in the doorway. But even as they dragged me through he was not looking at me. He was staring, transfixed, at the Greek queen, Helen. And she was looking back at him, that familiar half-smile on her face.

My father resumed his seat once I had been removed. He covered the situation by saying that alas, I was suffering from a fever, and King Agamemnon nodded coldly and delivered conventional phrases of sympathy.

Polyxena told me later, 'It was horrible. The eyes of that blind priest of theirs found Paris where he stood by the door and even when the discussions started again he went on looking at him, just as if he could see.'

Adosha, having dragged me up a flight of stairs and smacked my face hard on both sides to discourage any further visions, now leaned exhaustedly against the wall while I lay, sobbing with pain and fright, on the stone floor of the landing. Helenus had run after us. She turned on him. 'Helenus,' she said furi-

52

ously. 'How dare you run out of the room after your sister! Go back into the conference as if nothing had happened. Sit down in the same place quietly.' He went off downstairs.

I struggled to my feet and went to the arched window looking over the plain to the harbour, where the Greek ships bobbed lightly on the blue waves under a blue sky. 'Don't you see?' I said to Adosha. 'Don't you see the land full of fighting men, my brothers dead, the city – '

'Shut up!' Adosha cried. 'Shut up, you crazy little bitch!' Her voice was cracking. 'The queen will have me beaten for this. You, too, and not a moment too soon. I'll laugh to see it. You should have been whipped from the moment of your birth, from when you could stand up. That would have cured you – why your mother didn't order it I shall never know. She had too many duties; she was worn out when she had you. So – she handed both of you to me, let me try to rear you – I'd rather have had two apes given me, two Numidian tiger cubs to control than two mad infants with their eyes rolled up, twitching and starting, ranting from the moment you could speak, telling me things I never wanted to hear – ' She was sobbing now. 'That my uncle would die in such pain, my sister would have three children at one time, three ugly boys – ' She wiped her eyes with her arm and raved on: ' – both of you, forever cursing. Now this – I could throw myself from that window, smash myself on the rampart wall – what will she do to me, Hecuba, Hecate, the Goddess? What place have you here? You should be in the blood-pit,' Adosha went on, unforgivably. 'I wish I'd pushed you in – if the gods want you, let them have you, I say . . .'

53

I leaned my head against the stone wall by the window. Adosha had never said such terrible things to me before. Now she told me what I knew, though only a child – that there was no real place, anywhere, for an individual like me, who was, in some ways, less than human – I was the same as the man who thought he was an eagle, as deformed as the boy in the fishmarket whose legs had never grown, who ran about bearing baskets of fish above his normal head on little stumps of legs. I said to the wall, bitterly, 'You're going to make up a bundle, Adosha, and run away and leave us before my mother catches you and beats you.' (That much anyone could tell, without prophecy.) 'Because of what I did, Helenus and I will lose you.'

There was a silence. Then she said, 'What else do you expect me to do, Cassandra? It's your own fault – '

'Go,' I told her. 'I'll be alone then. They won't let me be with Helenus much longer. They'll take him.'

I could feel already how lonely I would be. I turned then and added angrily, 'Still, let me tell you – you're carrying Hector's child.'

I think she had already guessed, but she denied it furiously.

'Bring up Hector's child,' I ordered. 'Go now and leave us. Perhaps the child will live. Perhaps.'

I'd frightened her. She took off up the stairs at speed, calling behind her furiously, 'What makes you think I'd let it live?' She stopped on the next landing, calling down, 'Why would I let it live? I could be unlucky. It could be like you. Who would want to give birth to anything like you or your brother!'

I stood shivering on the landing, alone and frightened. I looked at the Greek ships in the harbour. A few minutes later Adosha passed me, running lightly downstairs with a bundle tied up in a good linen sheet and wearing my sheepskin coat. Passing, she said, 'Come and see me when the fuss has died down.' Then she ran on. She'd taken off her sandals for the sake of speed and silence. I went upstairs, lay down on the rug by the dying brazier in the scattered room and fell asleep.

In the event there was no beating for anybody. My mother sent a messenger after Adosha when it was discovered she'd gone. The messenger, mounted on horseback, caught up with her walking the rutted road back to her parents' farm. He presented her with a new dress from the queen and an assurance she could return safely. Adosha, nearly home by then, sent the man packing, rescued the bundle from where she had hidden it, with my coat, under a roadside hedge, and trudged on. My mother then sent her five silver coins, for her dowry, and a message of loyalty and gratitude – a sincerely meant gesture, no doubt, but Hecuba also knew that Adosha had three strong brothers whom it would be pointless to alienate when Troy might have need of them. She recognised, too, that there might be some basis for my hysterics about the Greeks – she was a priestess herself. Also, there are punishments for those who punish an oracle, or anyone connected with him or her, if the oracle speaks truly. She did not want to attract bad luck. So the queen dealt kindly with me and Adosha, and told the Greeks we had been beaten sorely, when we hadn't. But she declared that hereafter Helenus must stay with the men, and I with the women. She hoped, no doubt, if we were split up firmly and forever, the prophetic gift we both had would dwindle.

Adosha did not return, though, but married a cousin who was pleased by the silver and just as pleased, I expect, by the birth of a strong son. Without my brother or Adosha I was lonely. No one noticed. Nor did they notice I was neglected and neglecting myself, becoming thinner and dirtier. The Greek kings and their retinue stayed for a month, as if determined to eat us out of house and home, and the work and expense took everyone's attention, to the exclusion of anything else. They cost us a whole ox or five sheep a night, the kitchen was in turmoil, carts arrived daily with the remainder of the year's wheat, oil and figs coming from further and further away because the farmers close at hand had already sold the last they had to the palace.

'The old trick,' my father muttered after three weeks. 'The early spring visit, after your own planting's over, when your own stock of cattle and wheat is running low. Then you go on a visit and live on your host's exhausted stocks.'

Since the women didn't particularly want me among them, and an eleven-year-old girl can be almost invisible, I roamed about continually, like a ghost, in and out of kitchen and stable, taking long walks in the countryside, slipping unobserved in and out of rooms. One day I slipped unseen into the room where my parents and their advisers were sitting, and sat on the floor against a wall, my hands round my knees. Major conferences took place in the great hall, generally after a feast. Nobles, landowners, merchants came, and even the humblest people had some access to the deliberations. Next to the great hall was a smaller room, where the immediate household would gather. This was where my parents now were, with Anchises, my father's old friend. His son, Aeneas, was married to my sister, Creusa.

'We'll visit them next year,' promised Anchises.

'We'll visit without warning,' said my mother.

'And with soldiers, and without cordiality,' my father said. 'Just as they've visited us. Let's pray Deiphobus returns soon from his trading journey. With any luck he'll have some slaves, and swords and vessels we can present to our guests when they depart. Otherwise I'll be unhappy when I open the treasure-house door to search for suitable gifts. And all the time,' he said, with his hand on his temple, 'I ask myself the reason for this unannounced visit.'

'Low stocks at home, as you said,' Anchises said.

'They're roaming the countryside,' said my mother. 'That's why they brought horses. Why are they doing that? They're spying out the land.'

'They want their harbour dues halved,' said my father, 'on the grounds that the volume of trade they wish to do will justify the reduction. They offer us a similar concession at Tyrins and other ports they command, but they know, as we do, that the reduction gives them access to all our surrounding territories and turns them into competitors, whereas our trade with them has always been limited.'

'They prefer war to trade in any case. It's easier to take what you want, paying only with wounds,' said my brother Hector, coming suddenly into the room, greeting my father and mother on one knee as was customary. His voice was bitter.

'I dread them,' said my mother. 'Anywhere you bite that apple you find a maggot.'

'Pray only Menelaus or his brother don't discover what Paris and Menelaus' wife are doing,' said Hector. 'If that happens, there'll be bloodshed.' There was a silence. 'We must acknowledge what's happening,' Hector said bluntly. 'For if they find out lives might be lost, when the fighting starts.'

'How can they not know?' exclaimed my mother. Our customs were less ferocious, perhaps because each year Trojan men accepted into their families children conceived by wives at the January festival. Hecuba sensed a resistance among the Greeks to this practice. Their customs, originally much like ours, were changing. A Greek husband might kill his wife and her lover and be seen as normal by his friends. 'Hector is right,' she said. 'If they find out, the consequences will be dreadful, worse than we could ever imagine in such a case.'

'On the other hand,' my father said, 'they may never suspect. Greek women have little influence, even Helen. So they are rarely looked at. As for Helen, while present she's almost like the image of a goddess. Her beauty is so startling you scarcely notice the woman underneath. Who she really is, none of us knows. I think even Paris doesn't know.'

I knew Paris treated the Greek queen somewhat like a child, from whom he expected no equal response, but also as if she were magical. I suppose she was. At any rate, she had made Paris, the man, disappear. Now he barely existed, blind to anyone but Helen, only alive when in her presence, a shadow when out of it. He thought of no one and nothing else. I had always loved Paris more than Hector for the reason that Hector usually ignored me. Now I felt reassured by his solid presence. He might have lusted after Helen, but I doubted if he would have lost himself to her as Paris had. I doubted even if he would have risked everything for her, as Paris was now doing.

I had been asleep in the stable next to Okarno one night when Paris and Helen came into the yard. I was so miserable in my bed in the women's room, I had taken to escaping to the stables, just to sleep in the hay to the sound of the pony's noisy breathings and shiftings. There was a small hole at the bottom of Okarno's stable wall where the mortar had gone and I could take away some of the stones from outside and scramble in. That time I heard Paris and Helen's voices, then their entry into the empty stall next door. Paris must have been giving generous presents to Advenor to let them go past him so silently. Hearing noises, I woke and looked through a crack in the wooden partition. I watched Paris light a torch he had with him and put it into a metal ring on the wall. They were very bold to use a light, especially on a wooden stable wall, where lights were forbidden by Advenor, except at times when a horse was sick or foaling at night and someone would be there to prevent fire. Paris really must have paid Advenor well.

As soon as the torch was lit the two figures came together in an embrace so close they seemed to be struggling to bond their flesh together, and as that happened, their arms moved gently and the clothes seemed to fall from their bodies, until they were naked. Paris was then really in Helen's body, as they still stood, eyes fixed on each other, their hips moving rhythmically. They sank into the straw, and the two bodies, Paris' dark one, Helen's whiter than the body

59

of any woman I had ever seen, were lost to me. I stopped watching. After that came the gasping breaths, the murmured words, sighs, Helen's scream, beginning loudly, then muffled, Paris' long groan, and the act of love was finished.

All the while I was removing the two big stones from the back of the stable as quietly as possible, realising they were unlikely to hear me, and timing my exit through the hole in the wall for their moment of climax. After that, again as quickly as I could, I replaced the stones, knowing that this time they would hear me, but perhaps be too absorbed in each other to notice, or to care. At any rate, neither could afford to raise a hue and cry at that time, and to the best of my knowledge they didn't bother about it, for they went on using the stables as a meeting place. You could, if you looked, see the faint glimmer of their torch from some of the palace windows on some nights. Anyone seeing the light would of course think someone was up at night with a horse.

That night altered my feelings about my brother. It diminished him in my eyes. Some might say that was because I had been a little in love with him before – as most people were – and that seeing him with Helen made me turn against him out of jealousy. That might be true, but truer still was that, knowing he was creating such danger for himself, his family and for all of us, I could feel only bewilderment and, finally, a certain contempt. In retrospect I conclude Paris had every virtue but good judgement. For this lack of sense we all paid – although perhaps only a man of stone could have resisted Helen once she offered herself to him. As for Helen, she believed herself to be a goddess; her beauty and high birth combined to make people treat her as such. I don't think she could conceive of anything bad ever happening to her. She was twenty-eight years old and for half her life she had been able, through men, to move the world. My parents and their advisers, my brothers and sisters might wince at the sight of Paris and Helen in the room together, dread some moment when Menelaus became suspicious, and within seconds the Greeks got their swords out and began to hack and chop our flesh, but the happy pair, drugged by love and strangers to misfortune, believed they were safe forever.

It must have been only a few mornings later in the great hall that my father stood up, kicked the fire – it was a cold, late spring that year – knocked the heel of his hand against his brow and said, as if to himself, 'Will they never go?' It was one of those hasty conferences, occurring by accident, when people arrive arbitrarily and serious discussion begins.

There was no way of asking honoured guests to leave. There was no way a host, without loss of reputation, could hint to a guest even the possibility of a departure. Now ten people in the room debated urgently what to do.

'Pile up rich gifts in their ships,' Hecuba said. 'If they stay on, pile up even richer gifts in their ships. Their greed will triumph in the end.'

My father was a frugal man but he sighed and nodded, adding, 'But just a few more days, whilst we wait for Deiphobus and some gain.'

Hector said, hiding fury, 'Mother. Bribery will only work for a short while. Then they will return.'

'This cannot wait,' Hecuba said. 'Paris is being reckless. Menelaus and his brother are not stupid men. There could be bloodshed at any moment. Even as we speak a servant may be betraying them – one of Helen's maids, Paris' men. Tomorrow I shall order the treasury doors to be opened and start making noisy arrangements for the presentation of jewellery, a bronze cauldron for cooking, ornamented buckles – Advenor will have to find me ten good horses to be loaded, and a dozen bales of woollen cloth,' she said. 'And the two Cimmerian women slaves from the slave houses.' She was resolute, seeing the death of Paris and her other sons who would go to his defence, foreseeing the Greeks might burn the palace. 'They're looking for a reason to attack us,' she said. 'We have to get rid of them before they find it.'

'We should then attack Mycenae,' Hector said. 'Strike them first. The others in Greece, King Nestor, the Prince Achilles, many others, will curse us in public but they may support us in private. They fear the Mycenaean brothers as much as we do. Better to attack them on their ground than continue to dread them at home.'

Beside him the grey-bearded merchant Archos said loudly, 'I would kill them now.'

'While they're under our roof?' my father said, appalled.

'Do you think if we visited them they wouldn't do the same, or arrange an ambush as we left?' Archos demanded.

There was a silence, as there so often is when the practical, but unthinkable, is said.

Anchises moved towards Archos. 'Say no more, Archos. That is enough.'

Archos was unrepentant. He even glanced at me, as if to say to the others, Do you all, really, still believe Cassandra mad?

'I dislike being threatened by these Greeks,' mused Anchises.

'All men and women are threatened by something,' Hecuba said steadily. 'Plague, bad harvests, famine, childbirth, an overlord's whim – ' She looked sternly round the room catching each councillor's eye. 'We may have to load them until the ships are groaning. We may have to ask all to contribute flocks, produce, silver pieces. But we must get rid of them.'

And this was agreed.

Later, in private, Hector said bitterly to my father, 'I still dream of falling on these Greeks suddenly and killing them all.'

'And have all their Greek kin mount an expedition against us as soon as they can get a fleet together?' Priam said. 'You'd do better to speak to your brother. He's our danger.'

'I've tried. He avoids me. When I do manage to speak to him he can't hear me. He's a man in a dream.'

'I asked him to leave the city. He refused. If only we had sent him to Hattusas with the trading party, not Deiphobus,' said my father.

The two men gazed at each other.

I thought I would have drugged Paris' wine and carried him off on a horse. Then my mother saw me and shivered. 'Cassandra,' she said, 'you've heard nothing. Say nothing. These Greeks – they question children.'

I nodded. I went out and ran upstairs. I found Helen, sitting idly in a small room with the two Greek

63

women who had accompanied her. A brazier burned in the middle of the floor which was decorated with bright rugs she must have brought with her, though the style was not Greek but Cretan. Through the archway I saw a great bed which she must also have brought and had erected in her own quarters. The room smelled sweetly of some herb her women must have flung on to the fire. Though she was Queen of Sparta, she had the seductive customs of an Egyptian or a Babylonian. She sat in a ray of sunshine from the window and I was awed by her. I fell on my knees and said in a low voice in my broken Greek, so the women could not hear, 'Lady, I am Priam and Hecuba's daughter. I plead with you to persuade your husband to take you home. Say you are sick, say you are expecting a child, say anything, but please go, or you will bring a horrible fate upon us.'

She smiled that meaningless smile, which filled her face with light, but no sense, and looked at me, saying, 'What horrible fate do you expect, child?'

'Death,' I said. The women both heard the word, and went to their mistress. 'Please,' I said, 'please – please go. Paris will not listen. You must.' The women were looking at me suspiciously. One had already pulled the big brooch from her shoulder, with its long pin like a narrow dagger. They expected treachery, even in the form of a child. And Helen put back her head and said with pride, 'I love him.'

'If your husband finds out – ' I said, and she looked even prouder, said something to the women and they hustled me out of the room. 'You'll kill us all,' I screamed in the doorway, and the women shoved me forward so violently I fell on my knees.

How could I expect her to believe me? Her beauty

had made her fate – she had been abducted when she was fourteen years old, then stolen from her captor by Menelaus who made her Queen of Sparta. At twenty, all she knew was being taken by violence, then seducing her captor. From my scraped knees I screamed, 'Hecate's dogs will get you, bitch.'

The sound of my child's voice cursing in my own language brought one of the women, laughing, back to the doorway. But now I was on my feet and her smile faded. 'Tell her she'll make the world scream, and she'll be screaming loudest,' I proclaimed. Helen and her women stared from the doorway. Blood may have been dripping from my knee, but my gaze was fierce, arms wide above my head, fists clenched – in the old gesture of power, I held the priestess's ancient stance. Helen was frightened. 'What is your name?' she asked.

'Cassandra,' I said, 'and I always tell the truth.' I did not add the rest, that I was never believed.

She gave me a blind stare. Her woman, horrified, pulled herself together and led her back into the room. Satisfied that I had frightened them, I left. But how long would Helen's fear last, I wondered?

Menelaus passed me, not noticing a skinny child. He lurched towards his wife's room, with burning eyes. Paris, Menelaus and Helen were now all strange to me, as if they had dropped from the moon to the plains of Troy. Being a child accustomed to mad people beating their breasts in the street, or rushing about foaming at the mouth, with a crowd after them trying to catch them, I now assumed they were in the same state and not much more predictable. In any case, 'All Greeks are mad,' was now the watchword of the palace, for underneath the manners of the two

65

kings and their henchmen we observed their slyness, their mistrust – they believed they were continually being lied to; they had the air of fierce dogs kept barely under control by some invisible master. They behaved as if they were among enemies. They slept with guards across their doors. They sometimes unaccountably refused food at the banquet until they saw Trojans eat it, so that we came to believe they thought we might poison them. This was why we considered them mad. But Hector, who thought more like a Greek himself, told my parents, 'They only suspect us of doing to them what they would gladly do to us.' Even so, the madness of Helen, Menelaus and my brother was of a different order. They had been cursed with passion, I thought. None of the three could help themselves.

I retreated to where the servants were lighting fires and sweeping up for yet another banquet in the great hall. At dusk the Trojan nobles, and the Greeks back from their foraying in the countryside, or conferences in the palace, or from tending their ships, sat down. At the head of the table were my parents, the two Greek kings and Helen; others sat on stools or benches near the fire. I found a place near the end of the table with my little sister Polyxena. Half an ox, huge platters of bread and salads, huge bowls of spiced lentils were brought in. Silver, gold and pottery jugs of wine were at first carried round, then placed on the table for the guests to help themselvs. They mixed it with water from large pottery jugs. The two flute players played airs and dances as we ate. In spite of the hospitable atmosphere, hosts and guests did not appear happy and the men became drunk quickly. I went to as few of these meals as possible, but if

I didn't, I was reduced to hanging about the kitchen taking what food they would give me, which, as they were so busy, was not much. I was driven to these uneasy feasts by hunger.

That evening Menelaus was barely watering his wine. As the torches on the walls were lit I saw his brother warn him about it. Helen, lovely and straight-backed in her chair, seemed to be elsewhere. While the flutes wailed, the party at the top of the table was largely silent and the meat and bread turned to lead in the stomachs of all. Paris, happily, was not there. He had at least the discretion not to join in the convivialities of the table with the man he was cuckolding, or stare at his lover in the torchlight, imagining no one could interpret his look. I suspected Hector had warned him to stay away and ordered him on to picket duty – at the edge of the two farms behind the city belonging to the palace, a small force usually guarded against raiders or thieves. He was either there or on harbour duty or patrolling the coastal areas against pirates, a fairly nominal duty at present, since the prime coastal pirates were at our table eating heartily.

Meanwhile, an air of sourness and mistrust pervaded the atmosphere, in spite of my mother's desperate attempts to stint nothing, show the guests nothing but courtesy, pay flautists, harpists and singers generously to give of their best. The blind old man, Calchas, moved his head about, following the sounds of the room. All too often his face, when I raised my eyes, was turned in my direction. He knew me for what I was. Perhaps he also knew Menelaus was being betrayed by my brother, I thought, but he would say nothing, fearing Menelaus' sword. My father's manner was strained. He was now resigned to my mother's opening of the treasury to our guests, who were becoming discontented. The ostensible reason for their visit was to negotiate that they should pay no harbour fees. My father had refused. The harbour fees constituted half the money the city could expect annually in cash and the Greek offer of a reciprocal arrangement at their own port was hardly more than a trick. The gain to us would be nominal and they knew it. My parents had offered to halve the normal fee, and that offer had not so far been refused or accepted. (Hecuba was right: the only way now was to pay them to go.) Meanwhile they stayed on, lowering suspiciously, especially Menelaus, with his notion that something, he didn't know what, was wrong. We Trojans affected ease and dignity, while feeling afraid, like hens when they sense a fox is on the prowl.

Polyxena, my sister, her head in her hand, said, 'I think they find our piper tedious. I think they do. Do you remember the visit of King Tudhaliyas?'

This great king of the Hittites, now dead, had arrived last spring from his city in the mountains to confirm our allegiance to him, with a glittering train made up of his servants, two of his wives, and four of his concubines, the women all dressed in vivid scarlets and blues with headdresses jingling with gold. He brought gifts of gold and spices, and five musicians. There were two harpists, two flautists and a drummer, all eunuchs of the great priestesses of his kingdom. To add to the excitement, his guards were a contingent of twenty tall women soldiers. The palace had filled with scents, and the sound of women's laughter and jingling ornaments.

At the evening meal each night during the Hittite

king's visit, the air had been full of music. As his retinue had been small, his women soldiers – there were two hundred at his own palace – sat among us. These troops were much dreaded by other armies for their ferocity. They came from high mountain villages and, when they became too old and began to tire of fighting, they returned to the mountains where, using their pay as dowries, they bought land and married the men they chose (except for the ones who loved each other, who went back and lived together as they had while serving as soldiers). On campaign the Amazons bivouacked together, away from the men, who were forbidden to go past their pickets.

The Hittite king was a dark brown man with a clear black stare, a crimped black beard and crimped hair to his shoulders. His right arm and both his legs were heavily scarred. He had a ready, hearty laugh. I told Adosha I would marry him when I was older. Adosha said if I wanted to be his ninety-ninth wife, and live in a palace, however magnificent, with ninety-eight other wives and countless concubines and children, then she felt sorry for me; she would rather be the only wife of a poor farmer – at least she'd see her husband more than twice a year. She told my mother of my childish ambition.

'Why do you want to marry the Great King?' she asked. She would not have been blind to the political advantages of a marriage between him and her daughter.

'He laughs,' I said. 'And as for all the other wives – I could make sure he loved me best.'

My mother, who I now believe had decided I would be better off as a priestess of Hecate, looked at me doubtfully.

'I could tell him who to fight and who to trust,' I said persuasively. 'What better dowry could anyone bring, better than a thousand silver cups and a thousand herds of cattle, sheep and goats?'

They did not know what was to befall us or they would have made the match for me then and there and exported me to the Hittite court, where I might have become in time an influential queen, mother of an emperor, though not by Tudhaliyas, for he was dead.

But the gaiety of the Hittite visit was gone. Now we sat, some forty of us, my father's friends, nobles, older children, landowners and their wives, at meat with our gloomy hostile guests. As the meal continued the atmosphere grew, uncheckably, worse. The guests got drunker. Half-arguments arose. Many sat silent. Unfortunately, the flautist gave way to two singers, young sisters from the mountains, who sang of love, and Menelaus sat plunged in gloom next to his brother, while Helen sat opposite, erect in her chair like a dancer, a half-smile on her face, waiting. For what? For Paris? I think he was only a shadow of what she really wanted and needed. They called her the child of god and a human woman, and her sister, too. They might have been. Neither could endure plain human life. Both wanted more, tried for it, and ruined lives. In the semi-darkness the faces of the Greeks seemed more deeply lined, their aspect more violent. The two sisters sang a lament, wailing filled the air, increasing the gloom. Calchas' lined face moved about blindly. You could almost see the thoughts, impressions and calculations moving in that tortoise head.

The big wooden doors were flung open. Five servants entered, bearing gifts obviously marked down earlier for the Greeks. There were two golden bowls, bronze buckles, gold pins, a necklace and earrings made of gold and lapis lazuli, a vast ivory drinking cup, carved with elephants. All this treasure was set, item by item, in front of the Greek chieftains. The guests exclaimed, the Greeks got up and crowded behind the chairs of their leaders to examine the spoil, much of which glinted a little in the light. It would be redistributed by their leaders to the loyal and faithful later. My father bent forward, obviously making a dignified speech, saying the gifts were unworthy of the Greeks, but he hoped they would none the less accept them. I could hear little of his words from my end of the table. In turn came Agamemnon's bass voice thanking the king for his generosity. He tried not to stare too calculatingly at the costly gifts. During the excitement I slipped out, went to my cold room and sat waiting for Helenus, for I had felt he would come to me. He arrived not long after and shivered as he sat down on the rug in front of the empty brazier. He heaped another sheepskin round our shoulders and said, 'I don't care what happens. I'm so miserable. You can't imagine how smelly and noisy it is living among the men. They're drunk every night now the Greeks are here. If you step out at night to relieve yourself you come across some oaf fucking a servant against a wall. All I want to do is marry a nice woman with a farm and live there in peace. I'd rather marry you, but you haven't got a farm.'

'You can't marry your sister.'

He went on, 'There's one friendly boy from Lycia, but I've frightened him with my nightmares. I think he's going to die, anyway. I've seen it. I'm so tired –

tired of seeing the future, tired of waiting for a catas-trophe no one else is expecting, I'm like a dog or a cat shivering before an earthquake. Let's go and sleep with Okarno tonight. No one will notice. The atmos-phere's getting worse. Those gifts will make every-thing more complicated. They'll only want more.'

'I think they'll go soon,' I said. 'They've fattened themselves and their horses enough – they have their growing crops to tend now. Time to return before their slaves grow lazy, wives out of order, neighbours greedy. And they know now what they came to find out – the lie of the land, how many farms, the size and nature of the people.'

There was a fight that night between the soldiers and the palace guards. We heard it from the stable, where we were burrowed under the hay. Next day, they said, twenty or thirty Greeks and Trojans had clashed swords on the walled road beside the palace, overlooking the sea. There were drunken shouts, clat-tering of swords and shields, and a scream; then Hector, it sounded like, and one of the Greek captains, were bellowing in their own tongues at their men. Then came sounds of sulky withdrawal as order was restored.

In the morning, when I entered the hall, many men were asleep on their arms over the table, as the serv-ing women crept about, clearing up. Plates and goblets lay on the floor, the dogs had dragged the remains of the meat from the table, even now a bitch and her four puppies were at work on a cow's thigh bone in a corner. There was a smell of vomit and piss. It had been a night of disgrace for all.

My mother arrived in a white robe, her hair loose, her face grey with fatigue. She thrust brooms into our hands and said, 'Sweep out every corner.' My sister, dark Clemone, daughter of my father by an Egyptian woman, looked sideways at me, but we took our brooms, and swept.

When we had finished, and rinsed our foul brooms in a bucket, we went to the ramparts and stood by the tower, watching the sun rise over the sea to the left and the greening land below us on the right. The clashing of pots and the scraping of tables being moved inside the hall went on. Weary men passed us, going to the hall. There was now the faint smell of bread baking from the kitchens. Clemone said, 'They took my brother for the men's hall last night.'

'He's seven years old,' I said.

'And several others, no bigger. What do you think it means?'

'You know what it means,' I told her.

The Greeks breakfasted in the cleaned hall, on fresh food. Hosts and guests were silent. Heads ached, no doubt, and the clash of soldiers the night before had been embarrassing for all. Clemone and I returned to wait on the guests as well-brought-up young women are trained to. I approached the massive form of Agamemnon with my eyes downcast, offering him a cup of well-watered wine. His great hand took the goblet, not round the stem, but round the bowl. His hand, large, well-shaped and well-manicured, touched mine. Darkness swept over me. Then I saw what I should not have seen, never wished to see – and I fainted. Clemone said my mother leaped forward from nowhere, like a cat leaping from a corner, and bent over me, took me in her own arms and carried me at a run from the hall. Meanwhile, said Clemone, King Agamemnon re-seated himself

73

and drank, smiling, from the cup I'd given him. The spectacle of my proud, clever mother running and crying out amused him, it seems.

All I remember is regaining consciousness on the floor, my mother leaning over me in the small council chamber. 'What did you see, Cassandra?' she was asking urgently. 'What did you see?'

'Nothing.'

She did not believe me. 'Tell me.'

But how could I? She would not have believed me anyway. She looked at me in despair as I rolled my eyes at the carvings on the ceiling, pretending to be in a state far worse than I was. And then a servant ran in without ceremony, hissing at her, 'They're leaving – shouting for waggons. They've sent a messenger to the harbour, telling the captains of their ships to make ready.'

My mother sprang up, forgetting me. As the wind filled the Greeks' sails later that day it was as if we all, my mother, my father, old Anchises, Hector, all gathered on the quay, were blowing them full with our sighs of relief. My parents gave their still and dignified salutes, one arm raised at the elbow, the crowd cheered. I grasped Helenus' hand, half afraid the wind would change, a storm come up, the ships turn before they went out of sight and sail back into the harbour. But they didn't. On my other side I knew my brother Paris stood, tears on his face as Helen, with her husband Menelaus, went over the sea to her home.

FIVE

Between Troy and Mycenae

THE BROTHERS Agamemnon and Menelaus, and their priest-adviser, Calchas, sat on stools in the prow of their longship as it bounded over the waves. The sails were filled and there was no need for rowing. The fifty warrior-oarsmen sat on deck, talking and playing dice. The two younger men wore white woven cloaks, the blind man wore an elaborate woven cloak in reds, greens and blues, two winters' work by a patient daughter. All looked in the direction of the coast of Greece, more than a hundred miles away. They discussed their visit to Priam in voices which could not be heard by the others.

Agamemnon said drily to his brother, 'They honoured us well, our Trojan friends.'

'They fear us,' responded Menelaus.

'We should take Troy in the autumn,' declared Agamemnon.

Menelaus turned his eyes towards his brother's bold, enthusiastic face. Calchas' blind eyes still looked towards Greece. Agamemnon went on, 'Imagine the wealth. Imagine controlling that harbour they make us pay to use. Consider the trade.'

Calchas broke in. 'You tell us nothing. But you're mad. Over-excited. You haven't eaten or drunk since we left Troy this morning. To attack Troy with the men and arms we have would be absurd.' He counted the points off on his fingers as he spoke. 'The walls are thick. The neighbours of the Trojans would rally to help them because they hate us. The Hittite king would send reinforcements – he, too, hates us. Since we took Miletus on the coast, he's come to fear we'll establish ourselves on the mainland and begin to challenge his influence with his puppet-kings.'

'I know these things,' Agamemnon told him. There was threat in his tone. He was in no mood to be challenged.

'I'm merely repeating what we all know,' Calchas said, 'to soothe your agitated feelings.'

Agamemnon's anger, which was fearful, was not far off. He told Calchas, 'Your value to us, and great it is, is as a soothsayer, not a planner, still less a warrior. I would not attack Troy in the conventional way. How could you believe I would? But if we could land by night, get an advance party of men quietly up to the walls of Troy to wait, then send out a larger force, in chariots, shouting and making a noise, to attract attention, we might get into the city quickly. As the Trojans woke, our first party could get the gates open. By the time our second force arrived several hundred men could sweep into the city. With the advantage of surprise, we could take the city.'

Menelaus did not seem to be paying great attention. He looked out to sea. Calchas said, 'Priam has many friends and many sons.' Perhaps, he thought, Menelaus was uninterested because he knew his brother was talking for effect. Perhaps he had other thoughts.

Calchas pondered about what those other thoughts might be, horrified by his own conclusions. He said, 'Priam has many sons within the gates. Surprised or not, they might overcome us. That done, our warriors would be finished for good. I think the risk too great.'

Menelaus' attention had been caught, though. He turned his eyes towards Calchas. The priest had touched a sore point. Agamemnon and Menelaus, younger than Priam, had been faced during their stay with an older man constantly surrounded by tough-looking henchmen, a great many of whom were his grown-up sons. How many were there? But Menelaus had only one child, a daughter, Hermione. Agamemnon had three children, but two were only daughters and the boy, now twelve, had often been ill in childhood, hard to rear, and even now, unlike many twelve-year-olds he still had the appearance of a child. Agamemnon was returning to a household consisting of women and girls, weaving, and an all-too-often enfevered boy. The brothers did not look weaklings, Calchas thought, and their wives were both acknowledged to be the most beautiful women in Greece, Helen, of course, being irresistible. But for all the women's beauty and the men's strength, both couples lacked sons. Neither wife had borne a child for seven years. The brothers, admittedly, were often away, in battles on the mainland or raiding the islands of the Aegean. Nevertheless, other women of often-absent husbands conceived son after lusty son. These women did not. Calchas, a seer, was privy to many of those parts of the world women kept secret. Was this infertility the result of a curse, or was it some magic art they practised, he wondered?

As Menelaus stared at Calchas with some

unspoken question in his eyes – a question Calchas never wished to hear him ask – Agamemnon prevented any further comment by taking something from the pocket inside his cloak. 'Look,' he said, the same fierce stare in his eyes. The object was a spearhead, black and pitted. The broken shaft of the spear, a jagged-edged piece of wood only three or four inches long, was splintered at the end. He slipped from his stool, knelt on the deck, raised the spearhead and brought it down onto the deck, driving it into the plank with all his strength. It lodged about two inches deep, splitting the plank slightly.

Menelaus jumped, then peered down at the exposed part of the weapon. His face cleared as he understood. 'Where did you get it?' he demanded.

'From Deiphobus,' his brother told him. 'Yesterday I intercepted that caravan from the mountains they were expecting. It was twenty miles out of Troy. They were making a secret of it, but I found out from one of the servants that they were waiting for his return from Anatolia. So, I thought, I'll ride out on the sly and see what's happening, what he's got. True enough, the caravan had come from King Suppululiumas' city and was loaded down with good things – tin, rare fabrics such as you've never seen, and many bales and chests I could not decently ask to see. Suffice it to say I became friendly with Deiphobus, a strong and personable young man, quite intelligent, on one of the stops. He knew nothing of our visit and sold me this – he could hardly refuse. And now do you see why we must take Troy? They have access to mountains of iron. Suppululiumas is shy about trading it. He has hills full of it and slaves at work digging for the ore. He has smelting sheds in all the villages close to his stronghold – but he won't trade. Deiphobus says he's even written to Pharaoh, claiming he can't send any. Deiphobus accepts Suppiluliumas' explanation that the Great Mother wishes iron to be used solely for objects connected with her worship (he told Pharaoh a different tale, that he had not sufficient refined ore, but that's not true either).

'No,' Agamemnon said indignantly, 'the Hittite king knows if he alone has it his ploughs will plough deeper, his scythes reap more quickly, his billhooks prune faster – and with his weapons he'll be able more easily to keep what he has – and get more, with his indestructible spears, his strong swords – this is what we face: Suppiluliumas, that greedy king – and his claims about the goddess's wishes – convenient claims.' He began, the great muscles of his arms bulging, to work the spear-head out of the plank in which it was stuck.

Calchas spat to one side. He respected and worshipped the new gods of Mycenae, painted pottery figures with angry faces, which now stood in the sanctums. But he held more strongly to the ancient Triple Goddess, worshipped for generations throughout the countryside. These new, fiercer gods were city-gods, but had they the power of the maiden, the woman, the crone? He wondered. It was to them he sacrificed, when he could. In any case, what soothsayer would speak ill of the Great Mother of all Asia? Who would take the risk?

Agamemnon watched him spit. He said broodingly, still working at the spear-head, 'Swords, ploughshare tips, scythes—' The arrow came out suddenly from the plank. He stood up, stared at it lying in his big palm. His hand closed round it. '*This* is what we want!' he asserted, almost shouting.

Menelaus said irritably, 'The Trojans have no iron. I watched Aeneas, son of the king's adviser, ploughing one of his father's fields near the palace with a bone plough.'

'They are closer to the iron than we are in Greece,' Agamemnon said grimly.

'Troy is only part of your plan,' said Calchas. 'You dream of attacking the great Hittite king.' He felt Agamemnon's fury but went on, 'That is a vast, dangerous ambition.'

'Smoke!' cried a voice. 'Smoke on the horizon off the Trojan coast.' All three men stood. To starboard, behind them, thick columns of smoke rose into the clear blue, dispersing higher up, waving into the sun. All the men were standing, staring at the smoke and talking.

'From Tenedos,' Agamemnon said. 'But who?'

'Achilles,' muttered Calchas.

'Achilles,' Agamemnon said in a low voice. 'Just so. Now tell me we shouldn't try to capture Troy – while he and his men are everywhere, on the islands, on the mainland, taking what they want and growing stronger.'

Calchas sighed. Agamemnon was angry and impatient, but that anger, impatience, and his fierce ambition had served him well in the past. And it was true that though he and Menelaus as a pair made the most powerful kings on the mainland, as long as the other Greek kings and princes were harrying and looting ships, attacking cities all over the Aegean, there was no guarantee they could hold their position. One man, or several working together, grown stronger, could overturn them – as their grandfather had overturned and driven out his predecessor. But he, their grandfather, Tyndareus, had sons. His son had had sons – these very men, Agamemnon and Menelaus. Between them they had only one son, too young to fight, perhaps never strong enough to rule.

Agamemnon's jaw was set. He brought his foot down on the deck in an angry stamp. 'And us with only two ships. If we had five, perhaps only four, we could change course and go there – take from Achilles what he has got.'

But the ship bounded on for Tyrins and home with a good sweet wind in its sail and sun shining in the sky. Menelaus stood discontentedly in the prow looking back at the pillars of smoke on the horizon, while Agamemnon brooded, with the spear-head still in his hand. Unhappy men. Calchas looked inward. He saw war, contention and folly. He thought of the delights of victory if it ever came, the clash of weapons, screams of the captives as they were led away, the heaps and handfuls of booty hurled down into the streets.

Below, in her cabin, Menelaus' wife, the beautiful Helen, sat and thought only of Priam's son, her lover, Paris.

SIX

Thessaly

AS MY servant shouted 'Rich waggons – someone important's coming!' Naomi instantly began to sweep up my papers and bundled them, written and unwritten sheets alike, into a basket on which she shut the lid. She asked, 'Who would come here, at this time of year? This bodes no good. Will you take to your bed and pretend to be ill?'

I nodded, picked up the basket and went to my room. I hid the basket behind the wall hanging, a piece of weaving I and my daughters had done many years ago. It was all vivid greens and reds and showed our daily lives, the sowing, the digging round the olive roots, the lambing in spring, the summer crops; our sparse barley fields depicted as vast acres of yellow corn. It pictured the harvest, the autumn slaughter, the pruning. All these matters were presided over by the rural gods of these parts, a girl, a grown woman and a crone, with their familiars, an owl on the girl's shoulder, the woman leading a cow, the crone with her black dog. They were close enough to the goddess of my youth, this girl, this pregnant woman, this old crone. They were shown as homely figures – the girl wore a short skirt, the woman in a longer dress was pregnant and holding a child in her arms, the crone, in a dark woollen cloak, stood by a bare tree with her dog.

Who was this visitor, coming unannounced up the rough track to the house? I was not anxious, felt no threat. In any case, my children were safe now, even Diomed, safest of all, under the protection of the Pharaoh of Egypt.

I sat down on my bed to wait, dreaming. We were at our looms for five winters making that hanging. Each of the families to whom Iphitus had given our daughters had hinted the tapestries should be part of the dowry, but I had pretended not to know what they were asking. As I now did when they eyed my farm and wondered, aloud sometimes, why I was still there, alone, running the farm by myself, instead of handing it over to one of my sons, or sons-in-law. They would certainly put more pressure on me to go, as time wore on, but I knew, though they did not, how little time there was for any of us now.

It was this thought which brought me out of my room. Formerly, when strangers had come – and they were few – I had hidden, pretending to be ill. Now the time for hiding was over. As I went into the hall, Naomi looked up startled, from the fire, where she was hanging up a pot of lentils to cook, since we would have to entertain these visitors, whoever they were. Two plucked birds and a hare lay beside her, ready to go on the spit over the fire. I went outside to the courtyard and stood in the bright late afternoon sunshine, preparing to give a proper welcome. Through the gates in the high wall two men were carrying a litter, the handles ornately carved, the whole structure shrouded in bright tapestries. Behind, two other men led a waggon laden with bales and

drawn by two white mules. Behind them were three
mounted, armed male servants. Inside the litter was
a person of great importance, evidently. It must be a
woman, or an old man – an active man would have
ridden. Standing in my old gown, short, as is the
custom in these parts, with a cloak of undyed wool
round me, because of the cold, I felt hardly fit to greet
this entourage. I had seen nothing like this for twenty
years.

I advanced into the courtyard, bowed, spreading
my arms wide to express the honour I felt, and though
I was gazing down at the stones of the courtyard, I
could just see the litter put down, the curtains parting
and the feet of two men assisting the woman inside
to get out. I saw a blue cloak, misshapen feet in sandals, the big toe joint on one white foot was swollen
and so was the ankle-bone on the other. Yet they were
feet I knew, still so white, but distorted now, no longer
as lovely as they had been. As I raised my head, I
knew who I would see. She was heavily painted in
the Egyptian manner, with black lines round her blue
eyes, her face very white, lips very red. She was a
painted version of herself when young, damaged, still
beautiful. There in front of me stood Helen, Queen
of Sparta, Troy's doom. I was horrified, though I'd
always known I would see her again one day. And,
though I was believed to be dead, I'd known, too, one
day someone would find me. It seemed horribly right
that my discoverer should be Helen. So I raised my
eyes and greeted her.

The woman was lined under the paint. Egyptian
beauty-doctors, skilled slaves from everywhere, many
magicians must have done their best to save her
beauty, but time had been stronger than they. She

pushed back the hood of her cloak, gazing at me, almost apologetic, as women are when you meet them years later and their beauty is lost. They'd said the two sisters, Helen and Clytemnestra, were daughters of a goddess, but it seemed they were all too mortal. Clytemnestra was dead, murdered by her own son, Helen alive, but appearing older than her years. She was not well. I felt only anger. Sick or well, she was alive, had survived twenty years longer than the men who'd been killed in the war she'd caused. She had lived as a queen. I, another of her victims, had lived in hiding and exile.

As I greeted her, formally, without any warmth, I wondered, Why had she come? How did she know I was here? The exchange of greetings took place outside in front of the servants. I noticed she used the courteous language she'd have used to a princess, not a farmer's wife. I wasn't pleased by this and hoped none of the servants, hers or mine, would observe this. However Naomi, behind me now, noticed, and I felt her stiffen.

Then we walked in. I poured her wine, warmed by Naomi because Helen shivered and pulled her blue cloak about her. I gave her a chair close to the fire, where the pot was bubbling. 'We live simply,' I explained.

'I rejoice to see you,' was her response.

'And I you,' I replied, though this was far from true. I still wondered why she had come and feared for my own safety. 'I live alone,' I pointed out. 'My husband died last year. My children are married.'

She nodded. Obviously she already knew this. She was too polite to ask directly why I had not gone to one of the families of my children, nor offered one of them a home on my farm. She sat stiffly in the chair, her back very straight in her fine, pale woollen dress, the distorted feet in their golden sandals placed straight, a little apart, on the rug before the fire. Her golden hair was pinned up with gold combs, studded with small turquoises. I still stood, to honour her. Naomi was impassive by the thick door. It seemed to me that this thickset servant of mine, with her gnarled feet, legs like sturdy little treetrunks and workworn hands had, at that moment, as much dignity and power as either of us. From outside came the sounds of Helen's servants unloading the mules and unharnessing the animals. Like me, Naomi would be wondering how long the queen and her seven servants planned to stay.

I was still awe-stricken. This was Helen, who had betrayed her husband for my handsome brother Paris and become, if not the only cause, at least one of the causes of his and all our deaths. Then she had been taken back, how or why none could tell, by her abused husband. Trying to conceal my feelings, I said, 'Will you allow me to speak to my servant for a moment, to give instructions?' I moved over to Naomi and told her to prepare beds in the big building beside the farm, where my sons had slept when the house became too small for them, to light the fire in the yard, get bread baked, fetch a fresh jar of the summer wine.

In an undertone, as if asking about all this, Naomi hissed, 'We are in danger now. Shall I prepare for a journey?'

'No – or not yet,' I told her.

Then Naomi left. 'Gifts for you,' Helen said and her men came in bearing bundles. I sat down as they opened them, undoing the coverings to reveal a rug made of the skin of a brown and shaggy animal I had never seen before. Wrapped inside were a pair of painted vases. There was a woollen cloak in red, blue and green stripes, the dyes more vivid than anything I had seen for many a year, a bronze urn, finely worked with a picture of warriors on it, a bale of finely-woven wool, light as feathers. This booty lay, bright and sumptuous, on my wooden floor, the gleaming pot on the great skin rug, the cloak nearby. They were royal presents. There would be no way to return such gifts – they represented a life-time's farmwork, dawn to dusk in summer heat and winter cold.

I said, 'You are truly generous.' I poured her more wine, taking some myself. From the yard I heard the sounds of wood being hauled in, the clatter of grids and pots being set in place. Naomi set up the spit in the fireplace, speared the birds and hare on it. Their blood spattered into the fire. She glanced sideways at me, asking silently if I knew the reason for this visit. I signalled I did not know why the woman had come, without warning, at the beginning of winter. She wanted something, of course.

'I hope your journey wasn't hard,' I said, 'or dangerous.'

'I wouldn't have cared to venture much further east into these mountains,' she replied.

'With such costly and beautiful gifts, it might be dangerous,' I agreed and then, because I had to ask, 'I trust your husband is well.'

'He grows older, as we all do,' she said.

I had an immediate image of a vast red-headed man, fattening, discontented, uneasy, surrounded by men who might have been glad to seize the throne. Together, he and his brother had decided to be great kings, commanding a mighty empire. Now Agamemnon was dead, his weak son reigning in Mycenae. Menelaus, with no son to follow him, was ageing. His wife now sat in my remote farmhouse, face painted, thinking – what? I didn't know, except that it was nothing good. At all events, it was a miserable story. Of Menelaus' and Helen's only child Hermione I did not enquire.

The gifts still lay on the floor. It was growing dark in the room. Perhaps Helen had been told by an oracle where I was, even urged to visit me. It came to me suddenly that she wanted her fortune told. It was incredible that this woman, who had done me and mine nothing but harm, would come to me like a village woman in a market-place finding a fortune-teller – but she had. I was sure of it. My mouth tasted of iron.

I tried to keep wonderment from my eyes, as we sat opposite each other. Politeness demanded that we should eat before raising the issues between us. But her presence was unbearable to me. It threatened me. I did not want her there.

'Time and fate have played tricks with both of us,' she said finally. 'You told me true when you came to me as a girl, screaming that I should go away. If I'd done as you ordered—'

I interrupted her. 'As you well know, that could not have happened. I was fated to be disbelieved.'

'I wanted to know – is it still true?'

'That I'm disbelieved?' I asked her. 'Is that why you tracked me down?'

'I wished to see you,' she replied. Royal dignity is like an invisible shield, hard to penetrate. For a moment I accepted her courteous remark, then the old farmer's wife, accustomed to bargains, children's and servants' evasions, took over and I broke with politeness. I asked her, 'Why? Did you want your fortune told?'

My bluntness shook her, though she tried to conceal it. She reproved me, 'Your circumstances have made you uncivilised.'

'That's so,' I said. 'Therefore I should like to know why you've made this hard journey to visit me. And how you found me. Let me be honest – I don't seek out my memories. There's much I prefer to forget. It may be said that by forgetting I fail in my duty to my family, I allow my parents to go unremembered, my brothers and sisters unrecalled, but remember, I'm believed to be dead, or was, so let it be as if I were.'

'You've failed in your rites towards your kin, certainly,' she told me.

'My kin were mostly buried in the ruins of Troy,' I pointed out. 'I had no means of finding them – and, remember, our beliefs were not yours. I'm confident they wait to greet us all in the fields and groves of Hecate.'

She flinched, imagining, I expect, her meeting with my dead kinfolk as a series of oaths and reproaches, my mother cursing her, my father's terrible gaze, my dead brothers and sisters clustering round, squeaking and gibbering. Our beliefs were different and mine were the more merciful. The violent and greedy have their violent greedy gods – those who try to conquer and enslave others can only conceive of an afterlife on those terms. No wonder Helen feared the vengeance of the dead.

But she hadn't answered my question. She was

still a royal personage, accustomed to the formulas, but I no longer was. I was a farmer and only used to farmers' ways now. I asked her again bluntly, 'Why are you here? How?'

'I have visited Helenus,' she said. 'He told me you were alive and where you were.'

'Helenus,' I said. How sad I felt. She had been free to see him. She was fortunate. I did not dare see my brother though he lived only two days' journey away. 'How did you find him? And his wife?' I asked. 'Did they welcome you?' I could not imagine how they would have greeted her.

'They treated me well,' she said.

'How could they have?' I demanded.

'I think they pitied me,' she said simply. 'Especially Helenus' wife.'

'I wonder why – you seem – fortunate,' I said, gesturing at her, at the gifts on the floor. 'She's very kind if she imagines your lot to have been worse than hers, a blameless girl who saw her first husband killed, then her own child, and nearly all her kin, then was passed from hand to hand like an old cloak. Why should she pity you? Am I to pity you then? Are we all? Why should that be?'

'She pitied me as a woman,' Helen said. 'At least your brother and Andromache are safe, protected by Achilles' kin.'

I heard the screaming of a boar as it broke from the hands of huntsmen, ran round and round a glade spurting blood in all directions, bellowing, squealing. I saw Helen's nephew, now Mycenae's king, running through my yard half-naked, in darkness, screaming, mad with fear – and I laughed. I might have thought Helen, by revealing where I was, could destroy me

90

and what I held dear, but I knew in my heart that whatever she did, or did not know, she could never harm me now. And if I thought she could, or would harm me, I think I'd still have laughed.

She was startled and tried to speak. I interrupted. I taunted her, 'What do you want, lady? I know what you want. You want forgiveness, but are too proud to ask for it. But more, like any servant on market day, you want your fortune told. You'll get neither here – and as for the fortune-telling, my gift has flown. Was that why you visited Helenus? Your own oracles did not convince you? You needed a man whose visions had been right in the past. He told you as a boy you'd bring ruin on all of us – as you did. You know now he was right. You were Troy's ruin. You know him now for a true oracle. He called you a destroyer and you were. So, you must have thought, let him again foretell my future. Perhaps, you thought, it might be better this time. Perhaps he will be kinder. This is what you thought. Well – did he give you the prediction you desired? Perhaps. He was always kind. And his wife forgave you – she was kind, too, always. But you weren't satisfied. Perhaps you came here for confirmation of his prophecies. Or perhaps he would not help you. You came to find me.'

'You are very bitter,' she said.

'Like a snake, I lead my quiet life, harming no one until I'm disturbed. You tread on me and I bite you. I tell you, my gifts are gone.'

I had been rude enough to make anyone other than a slave declare they would leave the house. But the Queen of Sparta did not move or show any rage. She said, 'Surely not.'

'I tell you, my gifts are gone.'

After a pause she said, 'Helenus told me otherwise.'

I stood up. I said, 'Lady. I have not seen my brother for many years. I cannot visit him as you can. He cannot visit me for fear of betraying me to others. Now you dare to come here. You tell me what he says of me. He does not know. Expect no kindness here.'

There was a silence. The logs spat. There was a shout from the kitchen. Naomi came in to turn the spit. She saw my face and did not speak to me, did what she had to, shot a glance at Helen and left.

Helen leaned forward: 'What do you see – what?'

'Nothing,' I told her. 'If he spoke, he was mistaken. We're both older. My gift has gone. So, perhaps, has his own.'

She leaned forward angrily. 'I don't believe you. Remember, I can betray you. I can have you captured and taken away.'

'Being captured by King Menelaus is an old story – if he will do what you ask,' I said unkindly. Instinct told me half her trouble – her roaming in search of forgiveness, oracles, the rest, however queenly she was, came down to the old story of an ageing woman whose husband may be asking her to leave his home. Or worse. As I thought, I saw in a half-vision that dreadful king in a great hall, lit by flares, heard the wild music of flute and drum players, saw naked men and women and boys, mad on wine, or the concoctions of herbs and mushrooms made by women to drive men into battle, or love. I saw mad and terrible deeds. The face of that evil man, Menelaus, came close to me, his eyes clouded with insanity, and I shut my own eyes, to blot him out. But I could still hear the drums and pipes. Naomi came in with bread and put it on the table. She ladled lentils into a wooden bowl. She returned to the fire to turn the spit. I gestured towards the table, saying, country-style, 'Will we eat?' I did not apologise for the plain food. She rose and sat down.

I and this painted queen ate, though neither of us can have had any appetite. We were chained together by a terrible past. As we sat opposite each other, even Helen, a woman without guilt, must have remembered something, and I remembered too much.

SEVEN

Troy

AFTER THE Greeks sailed away from Troy that spring with our gifts on their decks, and the last of our winter corn in their bellies, our own lives resumed their normal course. Those last years of peace were good – the rain was plentiful in spring, the summer was hot and there were no storms. Harvests were abundant. There were no diseases other than the usual among men and beasts and the harbour was busy with many ships. It was almost as if our visitors had never been. Even so, every autumn when the declining sun lay over the rooftops of the palace at the top of the hill which was Troy, gilding the walls and our two great towers, my mother would order some work to be carried out – the walls to be repaired and thickened at their weak points, more storage jars placed in the storehouses beneath the palace. These things indicated she did not believe the Greeks would be quiet forever.

Helenus, now in the men's house, was often not available. The men and boys there, in addition to their normal duties running the harbour, tending horses and other beasts, fishing and hunting at the right seasons, were working harder at their arms practice. After the Greeks left that spring my brother Deiphobus rode the six hundred miles north to Hattusas with messages of loyalty, which were returned, unequivocally, in letters they brought back before winter, along with many gifts of furs, and silver cups. I knew Suppiluliumas would ask for me to be a wife and that my mother would say I was too young. This also happened, and meanwhile we hoped for peace and prepared for war, as people do.

Now I was nearing fifteen. I could have married; it might have profited Troy to have had me at the Great King's court, as it turned out, but I knew my parents would refuse the offer. My mother was afraid of offending him by sending him a girl who was better suited to be a priestess, who might have a seizure at the wrong moment, give out accursed prophecies, become his enemy and suffer the fate of anyone who upsets a great king.

The harvest in, normal autumn ceremonies took place on a bright day. Before dawn the traders around the city gates were up and frying fish, baking bread, waggons of food were coming in, shouts and cries reached the palace. Before midday there were thick crowds down below, people in country clothes wandering, staring, up and down the road from the bottom of the town to the top. My mother was absent, fasting, preparing herself for her priestly function, which gave the palace a holiday air – corners were not swept; the cooks in the kitchen fought, as cooks always will, but without interference.

Helenus found me, as he often did, hiding in the stables. Old Okarno had been spared for another year, and it was only in the stable, with Advenor and a strong assistant at the gates with clubs, to hold off trespassers and thieves, that there was any peace. He slid down in the straw beside me and said, 'They'll find you here, in the end. But I know where we can both hide. Inside the temple, inside the shrine, where the black stone is, there's what's left of a tunnel. It's by the back wall, caved in, but it once led out of the city, I believe. I don't suppose people will remember it.'

'How do you know?'

'An old man showed me. It's very dark,' he warned me. 'I only went in a little way.'

My fear was that my mother would be guided to find me and take me with her to the ceremonies that night as a priestess. If this happened, while I was still so young, it would be tantamount to declaring I was the new oracle, who would then take over when the old one died, or lost her powers. I would have to stay in that cave on the hill with my visions for as long as I lived. So I ran, with Helenus, and got some rugs and some bread, and we went to the tunnel.

I was at fault, of course. If my mother was guided to take me to the ceremonies, I had no right to refuse. If the goddess wanted me for herself and the people of Troy, I could not deny her. But being young I was prepared to try to deny my fate. I wished to marry, see other people, other places, be a queen at the court of a great king. Sometimes even an animal will not act according to what we think of as its nature. Such as a mare who will only mate with one horse, or a lamb which attaches itself to a person, not its fellow sheep. I thought I might be defying the wishes of the goddess; I knew I was defying the strength of my own, and Helenus' visions. But I was young – young enough to believe, a little, I could alter my own fate.

We went to the temple which lay just inside the

city gates and crept unobtrusively past the priestess at the main shrine, where the great white statue of the goddess carved in marble loomed over the big court. Beyond it lay the sanctum. Inside, there was a smaller altar than the one in the main temple, and at the back a row of statues, very old, and a huge black stone on a pedestal, some ancient god, deeply sacred, almost forgotten. Helenus squeezed behind this pedestal. On the floor, masked by pedestal and sacred stone, was an entrance about four feet high, leading into nothingness. He slipped into it. I followed down five broken steps. We huddled down there; the tunnel, which was stone-clad, was large enough for a loaded donkey to pass through. We had a little rush lamp with us and saw that for a length of about two hundred yards the tunnel was intact, but at some point, roughly where it met the city wall, there had been a cave-in. A vast pile of earth and slabs of stone blocked it almost completely.

It was cold, and there was nothing to do but sit on a rug on the stone floor with other rugs wrapped round us, reciting the old poems to each other. And later, when the light went out, we had no idea of what time it was. We ate some bread and fell into a doze. I said to Helenus, 'You don't need to stay.'

'You couldn't remain on your own,' he told me. 'You know that.'

'But we don't know how long to stay down here,' I said. 'It could be night by now. Or dawn next day.'

He shook his head. It was good of him to keep me company. It was I they would put on the white horse, lead out of town in front of the huge procession and across the fields to the hill. I, not he, would have to stand by the altar for the sacrifice, face white with clay, mouth reddened, and bring the knife down into the struggling beast on the altar. Worse, if they'd decided it must be human. The drum would beat, pipes wail as the sacrifice gave its last thrust of life. As it died, the world would give a great shiver, readying itself for darkness and winter, then revival. Afterwards they'd roast the beast, drink wine, or eat the little cakes containing herbs which produced visions and transports. There would be hundreds of people there from castle and countryside, in masks of horses, animals, snakes. There would be wild music, feasting, dancing – and from me they would expect prophecy. I might never return home, be taken by the oracle into the cave for good, live permanently in that world which would suddenly go black, white and grey, freeze. I would be seized by cold myself, as in the very coldest of weather, when ice grips everything. And then would come visions, more and more, usually terrible and never believed. And that would be my life.

'I can't do it,' I said. I was ashamed. 'I believe it might kill me one day. No one can understand – only you, and the oracle, and she's given over to it. She doesn't resist. There's nothing human and ordinary left of her.'

'It's unholy to resist,' Helenus said, taking the other side. 'There are punishments.'

To be driven mad, to be torn to pieces by dogs, to hurl yourself from a cliff or stab yourself. I knew. I said, 'Perhaps next year.'

'Next year,' Helenus brooded. We both wondered about next year – and so the day wore on, in silence and darkness. We slept a good deal of the time, but my dreams were frightening – a severed horse's head, the sacrifice of a girl, but I knew it was not taking place here. There was an exhausted man on some stairs burnishing his armour, facing his death.

Later, Helenus said, as though continuing the conversation, 'Next year – it may begin next year. It gets closer all the time.'

'This tunnel could be dug out,' I said. I felt as I spoke that above the tunnel, on the hill past the open fields, the sacrifice's blood had just now been scattered. The world had been celebrated, the libation of blood given. Now the earth would rest. Later the grass would grow back, beasts give birth, trees grow leaves again. Now men and women would make love all over the fields and hills, each thrust, each groan, reviving the world. Then they would lead the priestess home. She might sit, all night, staring into nothing. No one would dare approach her. The next day, the day after, she would be my mother again, mistress of the household, Queen of Troy.

We decided it was safe to go, and crept up, round the black stone's pedestal, almost tripping over a woman with brown hair, a streak of mud down her face, lying fast asleep, face up. She woke, stared at us for a moment, then muttered a prayer and fell asleep again. We entered the temple proper.

It was dawn and the floor was covered with sleeping people, some drunk, some exhausted. A naked man slept, apparently, with his eyes wide open. Two men lay embraced, a man and two women, the air smelt strange.

The watchman at the great gate was asleep, too, stretched out on the paving beside his chair. We prodded him awake, though this morning ships would lie quietly at anchor in the bay, no carts would come in and out. Nothing and no one would stir, for the world itself was resting. Only Advenor in the stables would be awake. The watchman fetched a man and a boy from the hut beside the gate and, together, hardly knowing what they were doing, they lifted the big wooden bar from its sockets on either side and pulled it to one side. Helenus and I pushed open the gates, went out and leaned against the eastern wall, watching the sun come over the horizon. The birds were singing, horses lifted their heads and to the south, a great flight of gulls came over the sea. The cool air smelt of brine.

EIGHT

Troy

S O THAT winter passed. One morning in early
spring I rose and set out to warn my old companion, Adosha, for I had had a fearful dream
that night, seeing her farm in flames and her father
at the door of a stone barn, fighting off armed
attackers. I said nothing to anyone, for I had exhausted everyone's patience by then. Young girls can be
tiresome and nervous, with their bad dreams and
stormy behaviour. I had lost my footing in childhood
and was stumbling on new ground. My tormenting
gift of prophecy was never so bad as in that time of
immaturity. I sat trembling and telling my tales, while
the women swept and counted loaves and carded wool
and tiredly hoped, if they were going to be told anything, for a good tale, not a bad one.

So that morning in March, well wrapped against
the wind, I set out on the five-mile walk to Adosha's
farm, going through quiet fields of grazing sheep, past
farmers spreading seeds for wheat, greeting the few
people I met civilly, until I reached the farm in the
hamlet of Cassawa, where I found Adosha's mother
collecting eggs. She gave me a little milk and directed
me further on to the home of Adosha and her new
husband, and there I found her, alas, in the very barn

I had seen in my dream, sitting by a hearth, feeding a big three-year-old child I recognised, even by his hands and feet, to be the child of my brother, Hector. The sun had come up, and we went outside with the boy and sat on barrels in the yard, with hens clucking round us. There was a stream a little beyond. With the dowry-money my mother gave her she had bought this little farm. Her husband, a cousin, was, she said, on the other side of the hill, digging blood into the vine roots.

'I'm glad to see you,' she said. 'It's been a long winter in this place, with never a soul in view. I miss the palace. There was life there, and company.'

'Sometimes more than you wanted,' I said, looking at the baby.

'Ah well,' she said, quoting an old saying, ' "a child's his mother's until we learn who the father is, in the fields of the goddess". But still I miss the palace – the silence here is so noisy I wish I were back among the old sounds, quarrels in the men's room, pots crashing, loads coming in from the harbour, a caravan arriving, a horse loose, a bit of singing here and there. I even miss your screams, Cassandra. I must be mad myself. And this, I suppose, is what brings you here. Too much to hope you would come without a reason. More dreams and nightmares, a warning...?'

'Yes.'

'Mind the child. I must go to the stream,' she said and fetched two buckets, went down to the stream and filled them. She brought them back, went inside, filled a cauldron, and put it on the fire. 'Good water here,' she said. 'Good land. A good husband – a decent-natured man who works hard. Well,' she went on cheerfully, 'now here you are, walking through the cold dawn, to tell me – what? What is it, fire, flood or famine?' Those are the warnings the sensible Adosha might have taken seriously – would have stored food against famine, kept buckets filled at night in case of fire. I suspected she might not listen to my story of the coming attack on her farm.

'The Greeks,' I said. 'The Greeks –'

She smiled, the strong woman with her big baby. 'Always the Greeks,' she said.

'I've seen them attacking this barn – your house.'

She smiled again, but her eyes drifted uphill. Half of it was cultivated with olives, planted far apart, but at the top the old woods were still growing, thick, tangled and green, and beyond that hill was a taller one, cultivated low down, but heavily wooded higher up. I followed her eyes.

'Let your family fight for the last knife and beaker,' I told her. 'You take your brooches and the baby and run uphill. Hide food up there.'

'What have you seen?' She was as sceptical as she had always been.

'Your brothers fighting here, with armed men.'

She shook her head. 'Who would come here?' But her eyes were now on a horse in a field. There was only one. He must be the plough-horse, the carthorse, the horse they threw a blanket on and rode when they needed to make speed in an emergency if a child was sick, if fire broke out and they needed men to help.

I anticipated her next question. 'I don't know when. Soon.'

'Cassandra – who would attack us? We're only farmers.' She paused. 'I hoped – when you were older

103

– well – that this evil gift would vanish. You're tall now. A woman –' she sighed.

I said, 'Show me the farm.'

We took eggs, onions and bread up the hill and found her husband, a small, tough young man with a humorous gaze. We sat down among the lines of the vines, under a small tree growing on a hummock, and started to eat and talk. He was a good man, Tacho. Plainly he had no objection to the child, even if he was Hector's. He was a son after all, who would help on the farm when he was bigger. The boy was proof, too, that his wife could bear more children. Not only that, he seemed to love him. A goat with a bell on its neck wandered up and tried to join the feast. Tacho pushed it off but the child got up, ran after it, fell, cried out and it was Adosha's husband who ran to pick him up. He laughed with the child.

He told me his mother and father had sixteen children. As a half-starved boy, he had gone off to seek his fortune, drifting over hundreds of miles. He ended up working on the palace buildings of King Suppiluliumas' fortress – or his father's, he was not sure which. But the strange tongue they spoke and a winter colder than he had ever experienced – a winter he didn't believe, snow on the ground for months and, if you were outside for too long, the danger of death from cold – drove him back home again. 'Where I found almost the whole village dead,' he said. A band of raiders from the coast had come the previous year and taken everything. Then had come famine, then disease. In the end, of his family only his mother, two sisters and a brother were left to work the land, so he had stayed to help. He spoke of the mountains he had passed through, drawn by the stories of gold and plunder in the upland kingdoms of the Hittite Great Kings. 'And then, they say, over the mountains in the east was the land of two great rivers, the Tigris and the Euphrates, a golden land of palms and fruit trees. I desired to go there, but by then I was tired. I never made the journey. That winter frightened me. I believed in my own death then, as I never had before. I turned home, expecting to find safety.'

'And found trouble,' I said.

'The trouble had been and gone.' He looked at me politely, but there was a question of some kind in his eyes. Adosha had told him about me. He wondered if I had come to deliver a prophecy. Knowing Tacho now to be a man who had an understanding of the world, I told him, 'I came with a warning – in a dream I saw your farm under attack from raiders.' But all he said was, 'Who knows, ever, what is going to happen?'

Later, Adosha and I went back to the farm again, and I helped her dig over a plot for vegetables, then carry some heavy stones, which would be used to build another room on the barn, when the planting and lambing were over and there was time for the work. I embraced her and the boy and went back to Troy.

NINE

Troy

FORTY GREEKS ran silently uphill at a crouch, holding their shields away from their bodies so they would not clash on their body armour, their helmets under their arms so that no point of light would strike them when dawn came. The night was dark, there was no moon. During the frantic, silent rush, the great walls and towers of Troy on their left a hundred yards away were, to their dark-accustomed eyes, a blur. Their boats landed, they'd paused at the estuary of the river, muddying their faces, hands and bare legs on the banks so that they would not show up in the darkness. They had followed the river upstream for five minutes, then, to achieve the position they required, just below the ridge and near the massive gates of Troy, they had had to break cover and race uphill, doubled up and breathless.

They sank down in the chilly grass, quietly – only one man's sword clanged against some other part of his equipment – gasping for breath.

Menelaus' young cousin Idas (born of a savage captive of his father's, the result of a border raid on Thrace) looked from his streaked face at his brother, only sixteen, and, he thought, afraid. But his brother looked back at him and grinned. His slanting Thracian eyes gleamed with excitement and aggression taken in with their mother's milk. Perhaps, thought the boy, this raid, which some had called wolfish because it conformed with none of the rules of proper warfare – which ought to involve only the encounters of strong men in daylight – was suitable for the two of them, came nearer, for them, to the stories their mother had told of mountain raids and ambushes. Idas was relieved his brother felt no fear, though he himself did.

Menelaus, the expedition's leader, crawled through long, damp grass to talk to his sergeant, Diocles, a tough Cretan, willowy, strong, no more than twenty years old. He pointed to the fig tree growing against the city's great walls. He whispered, 'That one – when the noise comes from the main army – get the tree down.' Diocles nodded. Menelaus was relieved the trees he had remembered growing at irregular intervals along the wall during their spring visit were still there. Otherwise, the fifty men would have lacked a battering-ram for the heavy gates. His own party would cut down the trees while Agamemnon's created a diversion.

Agamemnon, brooded his brother, could fight and inspire men to fight, but he left the detailed planning to others, who trailed behind him, anxious, sleepless, hesitant. Had it not been for Achilles having seized the entire island of Tenedos, only twelve miles off the Trojan coast, they would not now be here. Achilles had not only looted and taken slaves but had left behind him what amounted to an army of occupation, small but terrifying to the inhabitants. By July, there had been Achilles, a hero of ballads sung from lords' hall to lords' hall, all concerning his victory in Tenedos, the firing of a city, the seizing of two beautiful women, daughters of a nobleman (what did it matter if the stronghold was a fortified farmhouse, the daughters less than beautiful?), and appearing to the other Greek kings more and more like a leader. With secure anchorage for his ships, a supply base on Tenedos, he was in a position to launch a raid on Troy.

Whether Achilles planned this was unknown. It would have been like him to have no plan at all. At any rate, the sight of the capture of Tenedos had first made Agamemnon brood; then he mounted six armed men and went at speed to Sparta, where he arrived late at his brother's palace after the fifty-mile ride, hardly stopping, with three of the men still behind him. The others had dropped out, they or their horses having proved unequal to the ride. He had gone furiously in to the great hall where the household was eating its final meal of the day. The men around the table were drinking their wine, talking, telling jokes and stories, when Agamemnon strode in, red in the face, already shouting. Could Menelaus and his friends sit idly eating and drinking while Achilles, that unpredictable barbarian from Thessaly, did exactly as he pleased all over the Aegean? Now he'd claimed Tenedos, leaving behind an army of occupation, taken his treasure home and was quietly helping his father with the harvest, getting their small sour grapes from their vines on the mountainside, seeming to all appearances just a farmer and devoted son, but – cried Agamemnon – with a treasure-house full of loot, fresh slaves for the farm and an heroic reputation. Hadn't he, shouted Agamemnon, said they should attack Tenedos forthwith? Take it back from Achilles before he gained a firm foothold? Hadn't Menelaus stood there with a stupid look on his face, not even considering the plan? Hadn't Calchas discouraged him too? But already, at Miletus, in Tenedos, Achilles had taken the initiative. Now, unless they were careful, Achilles would capture the prize, Troy.

Agamemnon had silenced the hall, filling it with his energy and rage, his cries and lamentations. A conference had been called. The noblemen of Mycenae and Sparta had rallied – two ships had been launched at night in secret, from the port of Tyrins, then, hugging the Greek coast, sailed all night and arrived late the next day at Aulis. They'd tied up in the small harbour there, then, next day, with a good wind behind them, sailed to Troy in a single day, creeping in cautiously while it was dark, anchoring in the bay and coming in by rowing boat, very quietly.

Now here they were, seventy nobles and fighting men of Mycenae and Sparta – Agamemnon's thirty men, hiding on the beach below, Menelaus and his Spartans crouching uphill, chilly with the cold of dawn. There was silence, very long for the men thinking variously of their fear, their hopes of victory, their families, the boats at anchor in the bay which, at a word from their commanders, would bear them home again.

There was no sound from Agamemnon, who would soon call for a noisy raid uphill to the city, and no sound from the city itself, where the watchmen must still be pacing the ramparts, telling each other, 'Quiet night. Yes, quiet night,' while their dogs slept on beside the fire. Troy slept in peace while the invaders all faced their moment of desolation before a battle, fearing lack of courage, and death, fearing for their families, for their parents dying without them, their children growing up fatherless.

Diocles came crawling up to Menelaus. 'The men are by the tree with axes. What are they doing down there?' He nodded towards the beach. Menelaus shook his head. Then the noise began. From the shore came the rattle of chariots, the sound of horses' hooves and jingling of harnesses. The warriors drummed their swords on their shields as they came uphill, shouted and cat-called at the city walls. They yelled out portions of a song-tale about soldiers attacking a cowardly army. Through all this could be heard Agamemnon's shouting voice. Menelaus nodded at Diocles, who stood and signalled to the soldiers with axes to begin cutting down the tree. At a distance Agamemnon yelled, 'Come out to me, Trojans. Come out to me, sons of Priam. It is your lover, Agamemnon who calls, I want to kiss you with my sword.'

Meanwhile cries started up inside the city. Dim, moving figures appeared behind the ramparts – the bowmen arriving. Below, the warriors would be putting on their armour in a rush. Menelaus' eyes peered through lifting darkness at the tree being felled. He heard it thud down on the turf beneath the city walls. As this happened Agamemnon's tall figure, others around him, came over the rise. He turned at the top and waved his men forward. Chariots jingled up. Arrows began to come down from the ramparts of the city, but it was still quite dark and the Greeks were almost out of range. A horse whinnied, hit, perhaps. Agamemnon ordered his own men to start shooting back at the ramparts, a futile exercise, with the enemy so far off, but it distracted attention from the activities under the very walls, as two more broke cover to join the men with the tree-trunk and helped them run it along under the walls to the Scaean Gate.

Once the small unit was in place, sheltered in the darkness against the gate itself, Menelaus stood up and signalled to the rest of the troops to move towards it. They started running. A voice aloft called, 'Men running to the Scaean Gate.' There were shouts, the sound of feet, a few arrows came down as they raced along. Menelaus' young cousin, Idas, saw a spear thud into the ground beside him as he ran. An arrow caught someone, who cried out. Idas reached the twenty-foot gates, gasping, and looked round for his brother. With relief he saw him sitting against the wall, not far away.

Menelaus had ordered eight strong men to carry the tree, four on either side, and as they took their first run at the massive gates, a warrior, behind the main party for some reason, fell ten yards from the gates, with a spear in his stomach. He lay, screaming and writhing on the ground. Menelaus and his sergeant Diocles unhesitatingly ran to him, in a hail of arrows, and dragged him to safety. Idas, standing against the wall, heard the injured man, screaming. To his left the eight men ran towards the gate with their battering-ram, thudded it against the wood, stood jarred for a moment, then retreating again, readied themselves for another attack.

Agamemnon had moved his men back, well out of range, now that the diversion had succeeded. A silence fell, broken by the groans of the wounded man, the regular thud of the battering-ram against the gates, the pause as the men steadied themselves after the shock, then the next assault. Idas looked away from them across to the horizon. A line of red lay across the darkness, the sea was silvering. Suddenly his brother was beside him, looking in the direction of the dawn. On an ordinary day, Idas thought, they would be bundling out of bed, going to the big table in their hall to find bread, to the well for water. Within minutes they would be off about their morning tasks – milking the goats, finding eggs, perhaps plucking ripe apples from their four ancient trees. And instead here they were against the walls of Troy, chilled by sea wind, with the dawn coming up and nothing, not even the sound of a bird, but the jingle of horses' harnesses, the shouts of the men of Troy aloft in the palace, the steady bang of the battering-ram against the gate – again, and again, and again.

An apathy crept over Idas, as though nothing had ever happened, or ever would: he would stand like a ghost against this wall forever. He felt the sergeant's hand on his shoulder. 'You two have done well so far,' he said. 'Keep your eyes peeled – watch the other gate. That's where they'll come from, if they come out of the city to attack us.' He nodded down the length of the wall towards the Dardanian Gate. He passed on, saying, 'I knew your father. He would be proud.' The words put some strength into Idas. Their father had been killed two years before in a sea battle with a Phoenician ship, attacked in the hope of booty.

The injured man screamed as they pulled the spear from his guts. Voices trying to sound reassuring said, 'There – we'll bind it now. Hold on – stay calm. You'll be all right now.' The man said, 'Water . . .' They told him, 'Yes – in a minute –' There came a noise, like choking, then silence. Then a voice, muttering a blessing.

Idas gazed out to sea. The light was coming. He

knew as the men became more visible their position was more dangerous. A voice from above called, in fractured Greek, 'You won't knock that gate down. It's stood for a thousand years. You can stay here all week. That gate will hold.'

Menelaus called back, 'What will you be doing? Weaving at your looms? Giving suck? Baking bread?' There was a laugh at this. Agamemnon called, 'Come out and fight like men.' A hail of arrows came down. None hit him. He shook his spear angrily, 'Come down and fight,' he bellowed. It was partly panic. If the gates did not yield to the battering-ram early on, then the Greek soldiers would be stuck there all morning, into the heat of midday, into the afternoon, into the next day, perhaps, while the Trojans stayed inside their walls and laughed. The expedition would fail.

Menelaus ordered eight fresh men to relieve the others. 'The men have no water,' said Menelaus' sergeant. His face was expressionless. The gate was not yielding. It was tougher than they had thought. The danger was that at any moment the Trojans might come flooding out of the Dardanian Gate to attack them. Worse if they waited until midday, when the troops had been at the city walls since before dawn; worse still if the sun was hot and the men thirsty. Why were there no men at the other gate to take the first brunt of the attack? He called to Agamemnon, 'Set men at the Dardanian Gate.' Haughtily, Agamemnon did nothing. What was he supposed to do, Menelaus wondered? Send a messenger running to him through arrows to whisper a message in his ear? He ordered his own men to sit down. No point in standing, listening to that incessant thud of wood striking the obstinate gates. They might as well rest. He prayed for the gates to yield. Or even for the Trojans to come pelting out in fury and at least turn the affair into a battle. With luck and skill, they might then carry the day. But why should the Trojans, safe inside their strong city, do anything? He could smell the smoke of the fires they were lighting, hear voices, hens clucking.

So the morning wore on. The men on the walls called down insults, succeeded by the women, which was worse. From inside the city came the normal sounds of the day – the blows of the blacksmith at his anvil, a baby crying, people talking. Smells of baking fish, meat and bread came to them. The Greeks sent up taunts, sang and chanted, partly to cover, for their own sakes, the sounds of that futile battering at the gates.

Idas sat dozing next to his brother against the wall. 'Wake up, boy, and fetch water,' came the voice of the Cretan sergeant. Idas stared up, startled, into his smooth face. The Cretan had found a bucket at the washing troughs near the river where the women went to do their laundry. Idas could hardly believe he was being asked to run to the river through the spears and arrows from the walls. The trip back with a full bucket would be worse. But he was not being asked to do this. The order was for his brother. 'I'll go,' he said.

'He goes,' said the sergeant. Teucris stood, took the bucket, measured the distance from where he stood to the river, three hundred yards away. The journey out involved running downhill so that most of the way he would be covered by the hill and invisible from the city ramparts. The uphill journey back, with a full bucket, would be extremely dangerous.

'Better than later – now the sun's in their eyes,' Diocles said impassively. He did not like giving the order. He did not like the position they were in, that Idas guessed, as he stared at him pleadingly, wanting to beg him to send someone else, and knowing he could not. Meanwhile Teucris said farewell to him and they embraced, briefly. It was hardly any different from any other day, when Teucris went to get water at their well at home. Teucris went off like the wind, running down over the turf with his bucket swinging. Soon he was out of sight. Nothing hit him. Idas watched the spot where he had disappeared. His chest felt like lead. He felt tears in his eyes. 'And all for a bucket of water,' he heard a voice inside him saying. 'And all for a bucket of water.' Then he saw his brother come back over the ridge. The Trojans, yelling, shot arrows and threw stones. Idas' brother set off at a slow run, trying not to let the bucket swing. Idas stood still and sent him a silent message urging him to drop the bucket and run, downhill, if necessary, to join Agamemnon's troops; but he knew he would think it a dishonour. Fifty yards away, an arrow caught him. He fell, the bucket beside him. He twitched and was still. A howl of triumph came from the Trojans on the walls, a low moan from the Greeks. Arms went round Idas, who sobbed, 'He may be alive. I'll go out and fetch him.'

'And die yourself – that would please your mother,' said Diocles. And Menelaus called to the men with the battering-ram, 'Get to work again.' Idas heard the thuds start up again and stood, tears running silently down his cheeks, gazing at his brother's body only a hundred yards off.

An hour later Agamemnon called off the attack.

Idas heard the cry, men moving around him, but it was not until a hand shook him by the shoulder that he came to his senses. 'We're going,' said Menelaus, no expression in his voice. 'You run like a goat to the ships, my boy, or your mother may lose another son.'

Idas burst out, 'Why did you send him?'

'Never mind that now,' said Menelaus roughly. 'This is a war. This is what war is like. Now, move! Do you want me to carry you?' And Idas, behind the others, began to run, stumbling, downhill. The two parties, chariots ahead, carrying too many men, horses fiercely whipped, united in a mass and began to run helter-skelter down the hillside.

Behind them ran the Trojans, who, seeing the retreat begin, had raced out of both gates whooping, shouting and yelling. Though the chariots and half the Greek force were almost at the beach, the rest, Idas among them, were cut off by a scissor movement of the two Trojan parties. 'Fight!' yelled a Greek voice. Idas was gazing into foreign eyes, under a huge foreign helmet, coils of bronze ending in a point. He sensed rather than saw the man's spear poised to strike into his chest. All around him there was the clash of swords, hisses of effort. The Trojan's shield was to one side as he prepared for the spearthrust. Idas dragged his sword from his belt and threw it, his own weight behind it, at the other man's chest, armoured only in a light coating of bronze. The sword went in. The Trojan, struck, staggered and fell, taking Idas with him. Someone helped him up, pulled the sword from the fallen Trojan, pushed it back into his hand. All round spears came down on shields raised against them, sword struck sword as the Greek force, no more than forty, fought shoulder to shoulder slowly down the hill. Idas, whose spear had now gone, hurled with insufficient force at a tall man in a plumed helmet, who had dodged it easily, bashed aside the painted shield of a young man little older than himself and stuck his sword in the other's throat. Blood spurted everywhere. The young man's brown eyes were astonished, and he fell. Idas was blinded by his blood, tripped and was caught by Agamemnon's one strong hand as the other took a slice from a Trojan's arm. Agamemnon dragged him towards the boats. Then Idas' feet struck water. The Greeks turned and raced, splashing and stumbling, through the waves, swam the last feet effortfully and were hauled aboard their ships – all but those caught, at the last moment, by the pursuing Trojans. Idas, lying on the deck, breathing heavily, saw Agamemnon leap from the deck, run through the water, haul a Greek warrior from the very arms of a captor, carry him back to the ship, throw him aboard.

When the different accounts had been given and the numbers taken, they had lost thirty men, dead, or left behind wounded in the retreat. Idas sat on deck unwashed, refusing food, mourning his brother. Agamemnon came to weep with him and said, 'The young man you killed was a son of Priam's – your brother is avenged.'

The wind dropped and the exhausted men had to row for what remained of the day. That night they slept over their oars, or stretched out on deck, armour beside them, as the ship moved slightly, at anchor in the dark Aegean waters. Below, the brothers, Menelaus and Agamemnon shouted at each other about the disaster, the plan, the execution, the muddle of the retreat. Idas, son of Paimonides, lay, bloodstained, on deck in a chilly, uncomfortable sleep, waking briefly from time to time to remember he had lost a brother.

TEN

Troy

WE BURIED Pammon, my half-brother, with much mourning after the Greek attempt to take our city. As we wept for the seventeen-year-old boy, half our grief was for our own futures and the future of the city. Five others died in the pursuit of the retreating Greeks, including old Themon, who was forty-five and should not have been in the attack force. We had been forced to act quickly and had not picked and chosen among the warriors. Later, another man had to have his leg taken off by the doctor-women, because a wound had mortified. He survived the operation.

My half-brother was the first of Priam's sons to be killed by the Greeks. He was the son of a Lydian woman. She herself had died when the boy was nine and for that reason they had taken him early into the men's room where because of his youth, his joking and his lovely flute-playing, he became something of a mascot to the men. We wept bitterly as we buried this innocent boy, who had never harmed anyone. As we wept, his dog howled and barked. This dog sat on the burial mound for three days and nights. As we mourned, unwashed and not eating, so did he. Later, none of us had time to mourn, seeing our dead decently into the lovely meadows of Paradise. Later still, of course, there was no mourning. We died and lay there like offal thrown in the streets. But at that time we could. And when the time was over, I crept out and rescued the dog which they called Smiler, because, though a long, lean, ugly animal, he had the trick of standing in odd places staring into space, wagging his tail and seeming to smile at nothing at all. So I enticed him back into the city with food and thereafter he became my dog. The men had given him to Pammon when he had entered their room, still weeping for his mother – well, the dog outlived his master and many of the rest of us.

Along with the mourning, as I say, was sadness, somehow, for a world that had passed. We were growing accustomed to our battles with the Greeks, especially the warlike men of Mycenae. They had raided the coastal towns for years. They attacked our ships; we attacked theirs. We had, indeed, carried out raids at Pylos, and once burned their harbour. Sometimes a man died, or several men, always cause for sadness, but we were accustomed to the raids and battles as, after many years, you are used to a bad neighbour. But this seemed very different. Achilles was on Tenedos. The surprise raid on our very city by the ferocious brothers was bolder. They had no mines, no products, their lands were infertile; they were away from all the mainland trade routes. However, they had all the wealth they had taken from others, a passion to take what they wanted and now, we knew, we were their target.

They said the people on Tenedos were terrified of Achilles and his retainers and neighbours, Myrmidons from the bare Thessalian hills, stocky men, quick and ruthless under their tall and unpredictable leader. They were considered strange and barbaric by the other Greeks. I did not know then I would finish finding asylum in Achilles' remote hills. Then we called Achilles 'The Madman', because his speed, strength and wilfulness made him seem like one of those lunatics who, when the fit is on them, show a cunning, understanding and strength beyond the normal. We did not know him then, apart from the accounts of others on our coast who had experienced his raids. We heard of looting, burning, men dead, families weeping for ravished or captured daughters. After these raids the councils would repair what they could, strengthen their walls, train more men and matters would resume their normal course. Then Achilles took Miletus and held it. Looking back I see that our desire to continue trading and living contentedly, as if nothing was happening, was weak. If we had joined together and raised an army then, the worst might not have occurred. After Miletus, Achilles took the island of Tenedos. We did not know what his intentions were. He made few statements of his intentions, we later learned. He was a law unto himself.

With Achilles on Tenedos, as we thought (being his father's only child he had in fact returned to Thessaly to keep him company), and with a surprise attack on Troy barely beaten off, we knew our position was worsening. 'If they'd sent more men,' my father remarked bitterly, 'they might have taken the city. They're like wolves in a hard winter now. They're sneaking up in darkness, hoping to catch us as we sleep. And they call themselves warriors.'

Many bad looks came my way. I had predicted all

this and it was as if I'd somehow caused the disaster. I was used to this from early childhood, as was Helenus. We'd taken many blows from Adosha, as she knew that some kind of visionary fit of ours concerning, say, a fire, or a dead bird, often preceded an event such as a brazier overturning or disease striking all our hens. In the heat of the moment she would take our confused dreams and visions not as predictions, but as successful, childish curses. I was accustomed to being unable to refrain from the truth, and for being blamed when predictions turned out to have been true.

After the battle and the mourning for Pammon the council assembled. I, the unattended girl, crept in and sat under a long table against a wall. They discussed attacking Tenedos and taking it back from Achilles, and decided the prospect of losing ships and men was not worth it. This, in view of what happened later, was a mistake. We resolved instead to do the obvious – to further strengthen the fortifications, double the watch on the city and patrol the bay by night. There were recriminations – what had the watch been doing to allow a contingent of Greeks even to land unobserved, still less to creep uphill to the city? There were suspicions – had the guards been bribed, the dogs drugged? No one cared to blame my mother for giving the Greeks rich gifts to persuade them to leave, and apparently only whetting their appetites for more. Though this may have been a mistake, it was only one of the many we made.

In the end it was decided to send two separate groups, one to Agamemnon in Mycenae and the other to his brother in Sparta, in an effort to make permanent peace. My father suggested that it might be wise to hint at a possible alliance between ourselves and the Greek brothers to evict Achilles from Miletus and Tenedos. As he said, quite rightly, it was doubtful who the various Greek rulers hated more – their enemies or each other. If we had to ally with one of our possible attackers, to attack another, then, so be it.

The plan should have worked – but for Paris. He was away in a trading ship carrying wool and some ponies into Sidon. Most unfortunately, as he was loading for the return trip, another Trojan ship docked at Sidon. He heard about the envoy to Sparta. This began the disaster. Paris should have come slowly back along the coast home. He did not. He claimed later, truly or untruly, that he had spotted three Greek pirate ships off Rhodes. Believing they would attack his vessel he headed into open sea in the direction of Crete. Their pursuit and unfavourable winds, he said, had driven him off course and he'd been forced to land at Pylos. Whatever the truth, the upshot was that long after he was expected back in Troy he had, without anyone knowing, met the ship carrying the Trojan envoys to Greece in the harbour at Pylos. How fortunate, he declared. He would join the diplomatic embassy to Menelaus' court. Anchises, leader of the party, did all he could to prevent Paris from going to Menelaus – and Helen – but he had no authority over him. Paris was determined.

It was a full week before Paris' ship returned without him. Even on arrival, the captain, not understanding the importance of what had happened, did not hurry to inform us. When he had eaten, bathed and dressed in good clothes, he came up to the palace with his report. I heard the news first. I had been hanging

123

about waiting for Paris and when the captain came through the Scaean Gate I asked where he was. I was dumbstruck when he told me he was at Menelaus' court. I could see this meant no good. I told him to hurry and tell my parents. Then I went to the smithy and listened to the smith grumbling about overwork and offered to fetch him some fried fish and bread, an offer he accepted. I must have been crouching in the back of the smithy, watching the big man beating our horse-shoes like a madman, and enjoying the sparks, the warmth and my portion of fish, when the storm broke.

One of my sisters, sent to fetch wine for the captain, told me my father had sat still in his chair while my mother, arms raised, stood and uttered a cry of despair. 'Menelaus will discover that he and Helen are lovers,' she declared. 'He will kill him, if he hasn't already.' They decided to send a messenger to Sparta to recall Paris, threatening that if he did not return immediately he would not be allowed back in the city at all. But a week had already gone by. The damage might be done; the message come too late.

The messenger had already sailed when next day, late at night, a ship came into the harbour. It carried Paris, the Trojan ambassadors and Menelaus' wife, Helen, with what looked like the entire contents of Menelaus' treasure-house.

The other contingent, those who had been sent to Agamemnon's court, arrived only two days later, very angry. They had barely escaped with their lives once the sweat-stained messenger from Menelaus had got to Mycenae to tell what had happened. Had it not been for Advenor, the horse-master, whom they'd taken with them in case some horse-trading might be involved in the negotiations, they might, they said, have been dead. He had fortunately been eating his supper out in the courtyard with the stablemen from Agamemnon's court, when he spotted the messenger coming through the gates in a lather. He'd seen something on the messenger's face he didn't like and managed to approach him, bribe him and find out in advance what he was going to report – that Paris of Troy had seduced away Menelaus' wife and taken half the treasury with her. He warned the Trojan party just in time for them to make a hasty getaway with nothing but the clothes they stood up in. All dignity forgotten, they'd galloped off on any beasts they could find and been forced to fight their way to their ship in a hail of arrows and spears. One man, swimming to the ship, was hit by a spear, and they'd had to leave him behind.

Yet, for everyone else in Troy, Paris' feat seemed like a triumph. We had been continually harassed by the Greeks for years. They had stayed on too long in hostility at the palace. We had sent them off with rich gifts. They had responded by mounting a shock attack against the city at night, in which Trojans had died. We, having chased them off, had then sent a peace mission. So far, all the courtesy had been on our side, all the aggression on theirs. Our position was beginning to look to citizens and nobles alike more like humiliation than restraint. Now here came Paris, who had cuckolded the Greek king and brought away his beautiful wife and many objects of beauty and value as well. The moment the word was out, and it did not take long, a procession of excited people hurried down to the quay to cheer and get the details from the sailors.

Next day Paris was greeted in the streets with cheers, applause and laughter. Women held up their boys for him to kiss, hoping for some transfer of his powers over women, no doubt. Tales circulated about the wealth with which he had returned. In short, everyone felt cheered at having struck a counter-blow at the Greeks. Even my father, though he should have known better, and in fact did, could not help being pleased. He showed many marks of love and favour to Paris and gave him a house near the palace and costly linens and woven rugs and blankets. These things Paris hardly needed, since he had returned with Menelaus' wealth. Priam had bought the house from the parents of one of the warriors killed in the battle with the retreating Greeks less than a month before – they had decided to retire to their farm now their marriageable boy was dead. My mother said this was an unfortunate move, and could bring bad luck.

Paris, in the meanwhile, swept through the streets in his chariot, smiling his radiant and charming smile, rich on Menelaus' gold and happy in the love of a beautiful bride, the man who had made the Greek kings a laughing stock.

My brother Hector was less enthusiastic about him. I think he was indignant that my father had rewarded Paris for an act of passion, and probably folly. He also feared the consequences. I was sitting quietly at my loom, making a poor job of a piece of weaving under my mother's eye as she spoke with Anchises about some official correspondence, when Hector came in, raging. He paced round the room. 'In Greece the other rulers are all laughing at the brothers. Menelaus and Agamemnon will come after us like a swarm of wasps now. Who will have to deal with them? I shall.'

My mother, looking up from her letter, said only, 'Paris, my son, alas is a fool.' And, 'One fool married to another,' Anchises said. My mother did not reprove him for the insult to her son and unlooked-for daughter-in-law.

Paris and Helen created something like a second kingdom within Troy – a kingdom of love and pleasure. Inside the magnificent house given them by my father there was no sense of any ill fate. The money seized from Menelaus' treasury – Helen claimed it was her dowry, which she was reclaiming; Menelaus said otherwise – made the couple rich. They had brought with them beautiful vases in gold and silver, worked with all the skill of Cretan craftsmen, dishes of silver, an inlaid table made of many costly woods and much rich clothing. Now mules weighed down with other rich items constantly took the narrow streets up to their house. Helen had twelve women, whose only duty was weaving the fabrics they wore, the hangings for the walls and lovely rugs. She even sent an intelligent slave out to intercept the most recent caravan from the mountainous region of Hattusas, to get first pick of its load.

I, still the neglected mad daughter most of the time, was forever creeping into the house of Paris and Helen – with Pammon's dog. I would sit in the hall, listening to the musicians, watching the dancing, gazing at Paris and Helen holding court, leaning together in a large chair, holding their beautifully-chased goblets of wine, speaking affably and affection-ately to all those who constituted their unofficial court. These were the young warriors of Troy, gallant men. Paris' particular friend was Aeneas, who came often, though without his wife, who was my sister, the patient Creusa. He was a handsome man, but I did not trust him. Those of us, and there are few, who have been from the cradle onwards given to visions, learn early about their fellow men and women. We live in the ordinary, the mundane world and the world of visions from infancy on and living like that, one is not a heedless child for long. The effort of finding reality in the midst of dream teaches much and quickly. Thus I mistrusted Aeneas' smiles, his amiability, his compliments to my brother and his wife. I noticed, too, that Hector and his wife, though welcome, seldom came to Paris and Helen's house. Hector still disapproved of the union, fearing the consequences. His wife was a quiet and loving woman, mother of a son and not fond of late nights and dancing.

I loved Paris' house, though. From the moment you entered their gates at night there was light. Torches flared on all the walls of the courtyard and even from the gates the sound of flutes, drums and cymbals could be heard. Then, as you went through the doors to the main hall, there was more light, the music was louder. There was the smell of meat cooking – how they feasted! – and the odour of women's scents. A long table contained a seemingly endless banquet. Roast meats were brought up throughout the evening. There were spiced stews of lamb. There were salads and bread. There were sweetmeats – platters of toffee, cakes of figs, saffron, honey and nuts. I ate and ate, as a child from a large, frugal household will. There was dancing. Often the men and women were drunk. At the end of the evening, as the music grew faster and the laughter louder, Paris would push me gently from his door. 'Go home, little sister,' he would say. 'It's late for you now. You must sleep.'

Paris loved me and noticed my neglected condition, I'm sure, though he did nothing about it. Helen feared me. She could not directly object to my presence but she never made me welcome. She remembered too clearly, I knew, my outburst in her room. I must have been a frightful sight for that beautiful and loved woman, every particle of her body groomed and cared for, as I'd stood there in my rough gown, eyes staring, shouting abuse like a skinny rat standing on its hind legs, shrilling and squealing, ready to bite. But I had my evenings at Paris' house and would stay and stay, until finally I was forced to slip off into the darkness always with Pammon's long hound beside me, he with his stomach swollen with food and usually still holding a bone in his mouth. Then we'd go back to the little stone-floored room I'd once shared with my twin and Adosha, and I would fall asleep on the floor, wrapped in my sheepskin, the dog beside me, crunching noisily on his bone. It sounds desolate, but I was strangely happy.

Finally, my mother noticed what was happening and realised it was most unfitting for the growing daughter of a king and queen to be skulking round in unclean clothing, hair uncombed and often barefoot, with no attendant and no supervision. She got a slave to give me some lessons in accounts and writing. She began once again to correct my manners – and she got me an attendant – Naomi.

Naomi came in on Deiphobus' caravan from Hattusas – the one Helen had intercepted. At first she seemed like a bad joke on a mad princess (and was taken as such by many). She looked like a child of ten, though she must have been older. She was small for her age, and not merely thin, but positively skeletal because of her previous privations. Initially she was dirty with the grime of never having been washed and her hair was so lousy that it would have taken months of attention to get clean, so they tackled the problem in the most radical manner, by shaving her head completely. So there we were – I the under-sized and fearsome-eyed child princess attended by a tiny, bald slave who had no language, virtually of any kind, and certainly none of our own.

She had no idea how to serve others or manage for herself. After the capture in the desert I've referred to, under the leader and law-giver (later named for her by the Israelite I've mentioned as a certain Moses) she'd been enslaved and brutalised for years. She had been too young when captured to have learned much civilised behaviour and later she had no chance. She ate badly, at first taking her food rapidly into corners as if someone was going to steal it from her, eating furtively and too quickly. She had no conception of pouring water or wine in the proper manner, taking care of clothing or hair or the body. Obviously, she had no domestic skills. But my mother had summed her up correctly, guessing that a child of that age who had even survived the life she'd led must have some form of intelligence, and noting, I'm sure, that the best side of her nature had not been quite destroyed by brutality. How it could have survived, any more than she did, I don't know.

She'd been obtained by Deiphobus when he met with a tin-trader from the Black Sea. He'd been head-ing towards the Hittite capital, a long, troublesome and dangerous journey of about six hundred miles (as the crow flies, more like eight by the easy route). For over a year and a half, when traders came into the port of Troy they had little or no tin with them. They fobbed us off with stories about shortages. Advance messages, appeals, bore no fruit – they still turned up with everything but tin aboard and we were becoming increasingly desperate for the metal. We could not patch our cooking pots, mend or replace knives. The season had come for the repair of ploughs and pruning hooks and scythes. We had lost arrow heads and broken spear tips after the Greek attack, and our store of metal would soon be exhausted. The constituents of bronze are nine parts copper to one of tin, so that, although tin makes up a small part of the metal, it is vitally important. It is also scarce, coming from areas far from civilisation. The Phoenician traders go everywhere to get it, risking voyages even to the lands of the far north, where the seas are always stormy and the sun scarcely sets in winter. We suspected, rightly, as it turned out, that the Greeks had made a contract with the Assyrians to sell them all their stock at high prices – of course they were rich with plunder and could afford this. Since the only other source of tin was Hattusas, Deiphobus, an intelligent and ambitious young man, suggested he would go there and try to make an arrangement for tin with the Great King, Suppiluliumas. This journey ought to have taken a month or more, but in fact he was back within a week, for he had met a caravan from Hattusas, led by a wild and wily Cimmerian and his savage wife. Deiphobus said she had filed teeth and a talent for fortune-telling. The trader, fortunately, was carrying ingots of tin with him.

131

There was no danger to Deiphobus as he sat round the campfire with the twenty men and women who constituted the caravan. Traders prefer peace; murder and brigandage convey only short-term advantages. The Cimmerian could make no firm arrangement for supplies of tin – the caravan was somewhat off its usual route, but he was glad to relieve himself of twenty ingots and the waggon and mules carrying them. He made it plain, though, that it would help if Deiphobus took certain other items off his hands at the same time – a dirty wooden box of bits and pieces, lucky items he called them, and a broken waggon of broken-down slaves. Deiphobus agreed, to please the trader and get the tin. The slaves were plainly those who get sold on and on and on because they are too useless or too troublesome. There was a man so old and sick that he died on the way to Troy. There was a tall, mute boy of thirteen (apprenticed to the smith in Troy, he soon grew into a giant and became very useful). There were also two wild men, possibly brothers, whose eyes were so fierce and backs so scarred with beatings that when the waggon broke down yet again, Deiphobus just let them escape. They would have been more trouble than they were worth. And there was Naomi. It is impossible to piece together her career after her capture in Palestine, but she had probably been sold on to Assyrian slave traders. She had been put on some farm in Anatolia where it snowed a lot and the slaves lived in a shed and fought for food from a trough; then she was conveyed elsewhere, to a market-place, put in a fenced compound and resold, with a woman she'd become friendly with, made a long journey to somewhere sounding like a seaport brothel, lost her friend and then went to some other farm where she herded swine with a filthy man who had tried to rape her. Travels, hunger, uncertainty, filthy work and beatings – that had been her life.

My young sister, kind Polyxena, took her on and taught her what she ought to know. She proved clever and nimble-fingered. She was put to sleep across my doorway and I would watch her wake in the mornings – first she would stir, then, as she woke, she would sit bolt upright, already afraid. Over the months her fear to some extent left her. She took my visions and long silences, away from the world, for granted.

The first time I left the day for the world of the shades after she arrived, we were both on the ramparts looking out to sea. It was winter and misty, but I saw fire spreading over the surface of the water, ships burning. I think I stood there, mute, eyes unblinking, and screamed. Then I came to myself. Naomi stared at me, head to one side, then all she said was, in her broken tongue, 'Ah – you dream?' Someone, my mother or Polyxena, had managed to explain something about my condition to her, I suppose. She only touched my cold arm and led me inside. That was a period, as I say, when I had many visions and Naomi was good to me at that time.

ELEVEN

Thessaly

AND NOW, twenty years later, this woman Naomi stood against the wall, as I and the Queen of Sparta made our meal. I'd nodded a covert invitation to her to sit down but she'd shaken her head and elected to stand and be a slave. She, a slave, would not sit down with a queen. I had heard many Greeks also hated Helen, especially the women who had lost their menfolk in the war. And both Naomi and I were afraid Helen would put us back into the hands of our old tormentors. But what else did she know, could she guess?

No wonder the food was sour in my mouth. No wonder Naomi left the room for a moment, feeling the breath of that cursed house of Mycenae in her face again. I expect her memories, like mine, were returning, and I believed she blamed me for beginning to write down my story on those long rolls of papyrus brought at such vast expense from afar. She would be thinking the act of writing had called Helen down on us, like a curse. And perhaps she was right. Perhaps beginning to write this account of the past was like a summoning, such as women do for husbands, missing sons, or to call lovers to them.

There had been many times when Naomi must

have regretted having been made my child-slave and having had to share my bitter fate. She would be regretting it again. She knew I would give her money and let her leave if she wanted to, but that was not the point. She had a man and a child here and wanted no more upheavals in her life. She wanted things to stay the same. From the wall behind Queen Helen's back, she raised both her hands to her chest, shook them up and down, made a pleading, mendicant's face. I stared. She was insolently mimicking how women approach the fortune-teller in the market-place. She had guessed, as I had, that Helen had come to find out her own future, wanted her fortune told. Naomi ought to have been beaten for it.

So, I thought, Helen had come from my brother's farm. There he lived, peacefully at last, with Hector's widow, that poor woman, first widowed, then bereft of her child in Troy – who could think of Andromache without weeping? They cannot have welcomed Helen's visit. They had not my reasons for pretending to be someone else, but the attention of princes, or queens, is always dangerous, more so in their position. What had Helenus told her, I wondered? Not enough or not what she wanted – that was why she had come from him to me, through bad weather.

There was no bread. I called for Naomi. How could I beat her, I thought? I did this rarely, without enthusiasm, and when I did she would turn round as I brought the whip down and sneer at me. How could I beat her for mocking the woman who had brought us all to ruin? Or that was what the ballads said. She brought the bread. We finished our meal, the food bad and the wine sour in both our mouths, I suppose.

Across the table, in darkness lit only by torches, Helen was still beautiful, painted as she was and well over forty years old. But she had led an easy life, not rising early, overworking, bearing many children as most women do. Yet something had happened to her skin. I could see under the cosmetics it was puckered in places. Paint could not quite hide it. She would flinch, these days, from the glances of men who would once have fallen into her eyes – stood still, amazed – killed a brother for her. I believed as she had aged she had come into the hands of a doctor or a magician who had put warm wax or some heated compound of herbs on her face, promising it would take away the lines. Either the heat, or some corrosive substance in the mask had scarred her. And what of those damaged feet in the gold sandals? What had caused that? Was it an illness? More magic gone wrong?

We sat by the fire. 'You blame me,' she said. 'You have not forgiven me. Do you really think I caused all the trouble that has come to you?'

I shook my head. 'There were other reasons. But it would have been better if you had not come to Troy with Paris.'

'I was in love,' she said, quite proudly.

I responded almost automatically, telling her what Hecuba, my mother, had told all her daughters and I had told mine. 'Love is for slaves.' Of course, it is. Beaten for not working properly, a slave would say, 'I'm in love.' It is not fitting for dignified women and girls to behave like that. A family's condition depends on marriage. For a royal woman to become besotted is worse, for a queen utter folly – how can she carry out her duties when her mind is preoccupied by a lover?

Helen only said, 'You have not been in love.'

We were both silent as the door opened and, with snowflakes blowing through the entrance, Helen's three, tall manservants came in carrying bedding, a roll of carpet, or a hanging, a silver basin and ewer, a painted pot of herbs into which, I supposed, she would put spills or tapers, and light them to scent her bedchamber. I noted she had brought no female servants, not even one woman attendant; her manservants were tall and young.

As they went in procession to Helen's room I was seized with despair, so that my silence seemed to me something I would never break. The memories which were always a sad background to my life but now, after so many years, had become like a tune heard at a distance, with notes one cannot quite follow, or like a scent so faint one knows it before being able to say exactly what it is – those memories came crowding back. With them thoughts perhaps even more bitter – what had she made of me, this woman? What would I have been, how would I have lived if it had not been for that war in which she played such a significant, and damaging, part? I might have been a happy woman, confident that my brothers and sisters were well, seeing my parents die in dignity, burying them and mourning them with proper ceremony. I might have lived in a beautiful city with my husband and children. Instead, broken and abused, I had been only too grateful to spend my years hiding on a mountain farm, respecting though not loving a husband who respected, but did not love me. Without Helen my eldest son would not have been in exile for seven years. Often enough I'd thought my life worthless, decided I would be better throwing myself from a cliff, and dying below on the rocks by the sea. But that is a luxury a woman with a growing family cannot afford. I could not allow my children to be split up, perhaps neglected in another person's house or cruelly treated by a stepmother. Now, looking at Helen, I heard the crackle of Troy in flames and the screams of mothers as the Greeks killed their children.

And there sat Helen, still, in the dim light as beautiful as she had ever been, even if sunlight would have told a different story, still with those curving, ever-smiling lips, that blue, inturned gaze. To me she seemed like a dog who from boredom drags from a cupboard something hidden by the owners and pulls it proudly into the big hall in front of the company. The hosts, saddened by memory, embarrassed before guests, must then give an explanation – that is my brother's staff he broke when we quarrelled for good, it's the box of herbs for my complaint, the dress of my dead child, the shirt of the boy who left and never came back. And the dog wags its tail and waits for reward.

Helen, settled in her mind as to her sleeping arrangements, becoming used to the house and to me, realising, no doubt, that I would do her no harm, exuded ease. Charm flowed round her like waves of light. But she gave out no light. She left me in agony and darkness. She must have had that effect on Paris, and all the men who loved her. They would be always trying to get closer to the source of that light and abolish the darkness she herself had created for them. They would try, but never succeed. The fire we sat before, large flames licking up from dry wood, was dimmed by her presence. She took the heat from it. I found I was making the sign of Hecate, to ward off ill fortune. It is just a joining of each thumb to the little finger on both hands. I had learned not to use the sign during my years of exile. Now I sat, my fingers making the two little circles in my lap. The woman seemed oblivious of any effect she might have on me. She watched her men go through the house carrying her things, smiled her half-smile as if to say, 'Good. There we are, then. Now things are arranged as I like them.' It seemed barely human. Perhaps this was why Helenus, with no cause to thank her, and his wife Andromache with even less, had dealt with her gently. They knew she was too strange. Ordinary things could not be asked of her.

So – 'I was in love,' she told me.

I found my voice, but it came from far off. 'Couldn't you have resisted it, when you began to see the consequences?'

I heard her say, 'No – I could not,' and I believe this was true.

TWELVE

Troy

THE FIRST, inevitable result of Helen's abduction, as the Greeks called it, was the arrival of Menelaus. The city laughed harder – here came the cuckold to get his wife back. Our men, of course, had some sympathy for him – no man relishes the idea of being left by his wife – but our own customs were different from those of the Greeks. With us a man did not own his wife, so if she left, it was not supposed to be a matter (as with the theft of a horse) of curses, blows, law-suits or the seizing back of the property. The man had to accept the loss of his wife and return her dowry when she asked for it. So part of the laughter in the streets was therefore connected with the curious habits of the Greeks in their domestic lives.

The arrival of Menelaus was not taken so lightly at the palace. The arrival of the wounded husband was unwelcome if not unexpected. My parents and the advisers would have to deal with one of the two most powerful rulers in the Greek mainland, a chief voice among the other Greek rulers and a very angry man. There could be no question on our side of putting pressure on Helen to return to her husband or to give back the treasure the couple had brought away from Sparta with them, though some would have been glad to see her hand back that treasure. And not a few would have been relieved to see her leave voluntarily for Sparta with her former husband.

Menelaus came in shortly after the messenger bringing news of the arrival of his ship. Behind him came eight or nine helmeted men with spears, shields and swords swinging at their sides. He himself was armed. His red hair underneath a large winged helmet hung unkempt at his shoulders and he had shaved off his beard. He was pale and his eyes were red-rimmed. It was plain he had hardly slept for many nights. He was an unnerving sight as he entered the room with his hand on his sword, a hand which never left the hilt all the time he was there.

My mother greeted him from her seat, using the proper language, and invited him and his followers to sit. She ordered servants to bring refreshments. Menelaus stood as these formal preambles took place, his eyes not meeting my mother's and his hand twitching on his sword hilt. When she had concluded he looked at her, stared at my father, seated beside her, and demanded, 'King Priam. Will you fetch my wife from wherever she is?'

My father responded, again with the only formula suitable for the occasion, 'King Menelaus. You are welcome to my home. I give you honour.' He cut the courtesies short, however, and responded, 'I cannot do as you ask. She has renounced you and is now married to my son, Paris.' A king's word should have been good enough, but Menelaus, obviously barely restraining an impulse to cry out, 'You lie!' instead breathed in hard and muttered, 'I'll find her.' Whereupon he seized a servant from the door and, trundling the man out by the shoulder, left the hall and the palace with his men racing after him.

Citizens and slaves going about their business stood amazed as the tall, red-headed man, in full armour, pushing the servant in front of him, shouting, 'Lead me to the woman!' ran down the paved streets to Paris' house, actually no more than three hundred yards from the palace. His warriors sped behind. Once there he let go of the servant and rushed through the entrance, across the courtyard and through the open front door. He went into the main hall at a run. It was empty. He found Helen and Paris in the garden. The houses, built on a hillside, had little land behind them, but Paris and Helen's house had a courtyard with a well, a fig tree, an apple tree and a bed of herbs.

The day was very hot. Helen sat on a cushion at the well's edge trailing one white hand in the water, while with the other she tugged, teased and smoothed by turns the curly head of Paris, who was leaning against her knees. As Menelaus charged in she had just taken her other hand from the well to smooth Paris' hot brow. (Clemone, my half-sister, told me all this. She heard it from a servant – everyone knew quickly what had taken place in that house that day.) Menelaus had scattered the few servants who had tried to prevent his rush like so many chickens kicked aside in a farmyard and as he appeared in the doorway, his men behind him, Paris of course leaped to his feet. He was unarmed, wearing only a linen tunic. What Menelaus thought as he gazed at Paris' handsome face, his large blue eyes under the dark brows, his straight nose, gently curling brown hair and shapely body, manly, yet with some feminine grace, no one can know. If he had even really believed that Helen had been abducted, the scene he had just broken in on must have been a shock to him. Whatever he believed, the temptation to kill Paris must have been strong. Paris said later he was sure at that moment he was a dead man. But whether Menelaus had believed or allowed himself to believe Helen had been taken from him against her will, or whether he had always known she had left him for a lover, he did not draw his sword. He wanted Helen, not Paris' life. He told his warriors to seize her. They dragged her up from the well's edge. She stood passively, eyes wide, between two armed men.

Menelaus, at that point, might well have escaped from the city with her, reached his ship and carried her off without interference, but there was a yell behind him suddenly and there was my brother Hector, stocky, wearing the workgown in which he had entered the palace just after Menelaus left (he had been away on one of the farms). He had a raised sword in his hand. Behind him were others, equally hastily equipped – my brothers Chromius and Deiphobus, Abas, and a couple of squat Carians from the countryside. Some had swords, some not, one carried a pruning sickle. Though ill-prepared for battle they looked dangerous, and Menelaus and his men, including those holding Helen, got out their swords. There might have been a serious fight with terrible consequences for Hector and the others had no armour and the courtyard was small, leaving no room for manoeuvre.

Hector grasped how bad the outcome might be if there were a fight. He took a risk, put down his sword, stepped forward swiftly and grasped Menelaus by the arm. 'My lord,' he stated, 'you cannot force the woman to come with you. Be reasonable – what would be the point? What good is she to you now?' There was something in his tone, they said, which was sympathetic. It was not enemy to enemy. It was the voice of a man speaking to another man about a woman. Hector said only one more thing to the Spartan king. 'Do any of us,' he asked him, 'wish to be remembered as warriors who died fighting at home in a courtyard?' He meant, though he did not add ' – Over a faithless woman?'

Menelaus, who had been standing rigid as Hector spoke, staring all the time at the lovely face of his wife, now broke away. He said coldly, 'I have been mistaken. I believed the woman left against her will. I came to rescue her. Now I see the true state of affairs I will leave her to your brother and welcome. But I shall not go until the property she took with her is restored to me.'

'My dowry,' Helen said.

'You came to me with no dowry,' Menelaus said. 'Your dowry was your beauty, all knew that.'

'My father would never have let me marry without a dowry,' she told him.

'A dowry was agreed,' he said. 'Two farms, flocks, gold coins, many other things – but it was never paid and I did not insist. You know that.'

'The gods will witness,' said Helen, casting up her eyes, 'I took only what was mine.'

They said at that moment all present believed Menelaus would raise his sword and kill his wife before anyone could stop him.

Hector said, 'This should go to judgement.'

'Whose judgement?' responded Menelaus. 'Your

council's? Who do you think they would declare for?' It was as if he had suddenly become weary. He straightened himself and said, 'Hear me – I will go now. You can keep the woman and the money and property she stole from my treasury – for now. But,' he declared and there was a great chill in his voice, 'I shall come back and I shall take both from you. That is my promise.'

It was, they said, a terrifying declaration from that great red-headed man, pale with fury and still holding his sword. All knew it was a solemn speech, one of those statements which, once made, a nobleman must honour, even if it means losing his life. So, his head tilted back, Menelaus said, 'That is my promise.' Then with one hard look at Helen, still between the armed men, he wheeled round and left, the other Greeks close behind him. They went straight to their ship, walking to the harbour with set faces. People on the road got out of their way quickly. One man, driving his waggon off the road fast to evade them, broke an axle.

In Paris' courtyard the frightened servants began to relax. Paris looked indignant, Hector grave. Helen smiled. Her hand on her husband's arm, she said in a courtly way, 'Shall we go in?' She added, to Hector and the others, 'Some refreshment? You have come from your work.'

There were those who claimed this response was a sign of good breeding. Hector, heavy and sweating, was embarrassed, as if he had burst in dirty and started a fight in the house, instead of having been dragged into a crisis not of his making. He mumbled that he had better go home to his wife, who was unwell. My other brothers, and the others, also excused themselves.

Later, at the evening meal, as our family, and the nobles and townsmen sat at table, Hector raged, 'She smiled at me! After all that – I and the others forced to drive her husband from the house – after that, she smiles! Would she have smiled at me if some of us had been killed?'

'And no word since,' observed Deiphobus, a cooler man than Hector, but intelligent. 'It would be more suitable if they were here dining with us this evening.' This was quite true. It was a matter for the family, the city, perhaps the nation. It would have to be discussed and Paris should at least have been there for the discussion.

The light was failing. Helenus and I sat at the end of the long table. I had tugged Naomi downstairs with me for the evening meal and now she sat on the floor by my knees, the dog alongside. Helenus and I were both feeding Naomi and the dog scraps from the table, meat and bread, which both ate voraciously. Naomi had been with me only two weeks then and was still famished. As she stared up at me, her eyes wild and her body tensed for any danger which might come to her, she seemed less tame than the dog.

'So he said he'd be back?' questioned Anchises, although this fact had been mentioned more than once already. He pondered.

'What man in such a humiliating position would not say that?' demanded Deiphobus, who had a mocking spirit. 'He'd been refused by his wife and was backing down from a fight – he had to issue a threat. Why should we concern ourselves with him? We already know he and his brother are wild dogs, forever trying to steal from us and attack us if they dare. Now, Menelaus is angry about the woman, and his brother is angry for his sake – but it won't make any difference. They attack us already. They'll continue to attack us. Nothing's changed.'

'I do not like it,' said Anchises, predictably. No one said what we all knew – that, as he gravely pondered the matter, his son Aeneas was probably at Paris' house, holding a goblet of wine, laughing, asking the musicians for his favourite tune, while his wife, the patient Creusa, waited at home with her women.

'So – as for coming back to take his treasure and his revenge,' Deiphobus went on boldly, 'we know they will – and we'll see them off.' There was a laugh, shouts of agreement. Encouraged, he went on, 'Who cares for them? They'll probably tear each other to pieces before we see them again. We hear rumours of attempts to form a Greek alliance, but that can only be an alliance of enemies. And isn't it true,' he appealed to Anchises, who had spies in Greece, 'that Agamemnon's cousin is trying to raise a rebellion against him? Menelaus'll have his work cut out defending his brother if that happens. Their father quarrelled with his brother and ousted him from the throne, now the cousin quarrels with Agamemnon – ' He paused and some laughed, but not all. Deiphobus concluded, 'What are they? A family without sons, always at war with each other.'

It was an energetic speech, and all true. The table – there were sixteen of us – settled into comfort, even complacency, as we turned to other matters. A disunited family cannot rule. A family without sons, in warlike times, will find itself at a disadvantage. What we were not reckoning with, of course, was the fact that, from those terrible, ever-threatened cradles in Mycenae and Sparta, could spring beasts, hardened by neglect and lovelessness and desperately seeking compensation from everyone for early woes. Few they might be, sonless even, but the damage they, men, women, daughters, sons, could wreak had little to do with numbers.

A harpist had arrived on his mule that day and was staying at the palace. When we had eaten he sang a tale about the creation of the world by a great goddess, then a ballad concerning a woman who protected her husband in battle by weaving a tapestry. Each time the husband was threatened, she would weave his escape into her web.

I looked down and saw that Naomi had pushed herself through the feet at the table and was sitting gazing at the man as he sang. I could only see part of her shoulders, her bald head and one bright, brown eye as she leaned forward a little, all attention. The dog was asleep on the floor.

THIRTEEN

Troy

W E CAME to the end of winter. I was sixteen. At our looms, the women gossiped. 'No sign of a child yet,' they said of Helen. 'However hard they try,' said someone, laughing. They spoke of marriages. There was talk of marriage between one of my sisters and the mighty Sarpedon, a neighbouring prince. I fell into a dream and stopped work. My mother, thinking my fits of prophecy and other disturbances might be coming, though violently, to an end, had begun, dauntlessly, to try to reclaim me for marriage. This was why Naomi had been given to me, why I was at the loom, why I was tired, for I had spent the morning learning accounts and helping my mother with her correspondence. A long letter in the Akkadian language – language of the Hittite rulers and the common language of diplomacy – had to be composed, memorised and then, with the help of small memory-joggers, scratched on a piece of slate, then incised on to wet clay.

The letter was going to King Suppiluliumas, the Great King of the Hittites. The slaves' bird-tracks were my mother's report on our Greek neighbours. The king was watching their incursions into territories he protected with an unfriendly eye. Hecuba also gave news of our harvests from which he would expect a share, as price for his friendship and protection. There was mention of a possible marriage between Deiphobus and one of his daughters in which my mother made it plain the princess concerned must be by his first, most royal wife, not some later consort. My mother wrote diplomatically that, although she understood that the Great King had many concerns (he was at war on both his eastern and western borders) a case might be argued for mounting a full-scale attack on the Greeks immediately. What she had in mind was driving Achilles from Miletus, further down our coast, and from the island of Tenedos, which he also held. She wished further to raid and burn some of the Greeks' own coastal cities and burn part of their fleet. She did not put the details explicitly in a letter which might be intercepted, but knew the king would understand what she meant.

'In his uncle's time,' she said to me, 'the Great King could have been depended on for firm action. But Suppiluliumas was beleaguered by other enemies. In any case, the Hittites were not sea people and thought more naturally in terms of land battles.'

The letter was composed, the tablets baked and a messenger sent off on a fast horse while they were still warm. I was especially interested in the reply for it contained warm regards to the Great King's second son – from me. This meant my marriage to him was being debated. I would bring only a small dowry, for I had many sisters, but the advantages of the marriage would be clear on both sides. It would solidify the alliance. That my parents had so many children would be considered a bonus – there was less chance of the spouse being left childless if the parents of the bride or groom were fertile and all their children had lived.

For my own part, I didn't worry too much about the matter. If I married and did not have to go to the oracle's cave, I would not be able to make a free choice of husband. I owed it to my family to marry who they wanted me to marry. It would be better if they chose a man I knew, because it would be easier to refuse the match if it seemed unbearable. On the other hand, the thought of a grand marriage into that great Anatolian empire was exciting. And for the rest, having been seen hitherto as destined to become an oracle, I was happy that any marriage plan for me was being considered. When I had understood, as a small child, I was destined for the cave and the blood-pit, I had panicked and wept for weeks. Helenus had told me he would do all in his power to prevent it, but we both knew that if that were to be my fate we could do nothing about it.

So, that afternoon, as I stared at the green and blue stripes I was weaving, pushing the heavy wooden needle through the weave (Naomi on a stool beside me, inexpertly carding wool with a big wooden comb) I dreamed. Then, the needle stopped, the voices of the others grew softer, then silent. Just before that suspension of sound, light, movement which always preceded a moment of prophecy, I half-saw Naomi beside me sitting with her piece of carded wool suspended over the basket she was to put it in and realised, in one flash, I was doomed to see now more than I should, or wanted to. Then I whirled into grey fog.

I saw the bay of Troy and the sea beyond the bay black with ships. I heard the sounds of disembarkation, men calling to each other, horses whinnying, the sound of piles of spears hitting the dock, the thud of boxes being thrown down. Then I saw huge camps, huts and tents, extending across the bay, chariots, horses tethered, fires with cauldrons suspended above them, armoured men going to and fro, shouting, calling. Then there were noises – screams, battle cries, the wailing of women, the terrible heat of fire, the smell of charred wood, burning clothes and flesh. My vision turned to flame. I could see nothing but red, as if looking into the heart of a fire, and hear nothing but the sound of crackling, cracking and burning.

They told me afterwards I left the loom, stood in the middle of the floor, arms raised, screaming out these terrible visions. The women had stood back in fear against their looms. Then my sisters came towards me and others began to rush in from outside, but no one came quite near enough to touch me. It would have been wrong; bad luck to all of us. But – it must have been just before I fell – this awful vision ended and I felt pervaded by a piercing sweetness, an almost unbearable joy, a sensation unlike any I had ever remembered. Then, apparently, I fell.

They said it was Naomi, who had at first had to be held back from rushing straight to me, who ran as I fell to where I lay stretched on the stone slabs of the floor. It had been she and my sister Polyxena who had half-carried me from the room to the ramparts that overlooked the sea. And there, water fetched by Naomi and a small breeze revived me.

My mother took the return of my visions as final proof I was destined for the life of an oracle. One airless night, she commanded me to go with her and a servant to the oracle on her hill. Although I remember setting off in pressing heat and walking in darkness to the cave, I can remember little of the journey. I had set out afraid the oracle would tell my mother to leave me with her for ever then, as we began to ascend the hill to her cave I fell into terrible visions, seeing the dreadful final events which were to bring me to my farm on the Thessalian borders. I was unable to go any further. As the women bent over me on the path, my mother, I heard, hurried to the oracle, was let into that terrifying place, found her quite mundanely eating a meal with her unsexed attendant and was told to take me home. 'I don't need her,' she is supposed to have told my mother. 'She'll be saved if she stays with you.' (Later, it seemed a false prophecy and later still, a true one.)

They brought me back, where I lay like a corpse for some days. When I revived, my first thought was happy. I was relieved for I'd believed the oracle would claim me. Meanwhile, no one knew how to interpret the oracle's words. My mother took it to mean she did not need me then, but would later. My lessons ceased, because if I did not marry I would not require the skills for governing a large kingdom. As an oracle I could have a husband or lovers and bear children but I would not have a household, and after infancy the children would be taken away and reared by others, perhaps members of my family, so that my gifts would not be weakened by the day-to-day cares of ordinary life. It was a distinction, but one I did not want. I had been reared in a great house and I wanted at that time to be head of a family, and a queen as my mother was. This I confided to Polyxena, but all she could say was, 'It is your fate. You must do what is ordained.' She added in a friendly way, 'Think of me. I may end up with Sarpedon, that great bear, or his brother.'

'You could refuse,' I pointed out. '*I* have no choice.'

Then huge storms came and raged for two months. There was thunder and lightning, trees fell, roads disappeared in the floods, ships were lost and wrecked. The rivers on either side of the city burst their banks. Cows and sheep had to be rescued. A nest of young willows on the bank of the Scamander were carried away to sea. The time for the ceremonies came – we calculated the time by a moon we had scarcely seen for thirty days, except peeping through scudding clouds. We celebrated with fervour and prayed for the weather to calm.

My arrival at the start of womanhood and my new position, as someone destined to take her place as priestess or oracle, meant I would play a part. I should make some explanation of our customs, though they are not so very different from those of our neighbours or of the mighty nations to the east, the Assyrians, Babylonians, the Philistines.

There are two main ceremonies, one in the autumn after the grain – corn in the better land, barley elsewhere – is harvested.

At the harvest, in villages in the rural areas and outside the cities, after the last ears are reaped, a cry of lamentation goes up for the land robbed of its produce, as if we had wounded our vines and fruit-trees by plucking and cutting off their fruits, slain the corn with our sickles and left the earth bereft, as a mother of her son. There is a great sacrifice in the temples and fields, we grieve for the earth and the death of her children, her fruits. Though we are responsible and will profit by it we must acknowledge

154

her loss, perhaps out of respect and also in case, grieved and wounded, she will refuse to grow anything the next year. In the fields we sacrifice an ox or a ram. In some parts of the country they sacrifice a red dog. These animals in days gone by were probably men or women and certainly after a series of bad harvests, or when disease has struck the crops or men, when nature seems to have turned against us, the sacrifice is sometimes still a human being. The ceremonies for the earth, the cries and lamentations, go on for days, the women being chief mourners. They cut their hair as if for the death of a person.

The spring ceremony is as important, if not more so, for that is when we must implore the goddess to bring the new season in gently, produce the right conditions for the planting and growing of the grain for ourselves and grass for our beasts. During the ceremony we mourn the death of the young god, the son of the mother, and cry for him to return to us. It is a moving and terrifying ceremony. We sacrifice, our rivers are dyed red and loaded with red flowers where they grow. The women cut their hair, even shaving their heads to show the measure of their mourning, and, in an effort to bring back life, men and women couple in the temples and fields and the children born from these unions are named the 'children of the goddess'.

The goddess of our people is Hecate, tripartite goddess, in her youth a maiden, then a mother, then an old woman and in these three parts she represents both the life of men, from birth through maturity to old age, and also the life of nature, spring, summer, winter, growth, ripeness and harvest. Hecate is our goddess but also ourselves. When we sacrifice to her we sacrifice to life itself, to ourselves and the land, crops and animals which keep us alive, and we acknowledge our frail hold on life and fear of death.

That year's ceremonies were celebrated with passion, for the unusual storms made us fearful. By the time of the ceremony we had had weeks of wind and storm, had lived under lowering skies by day and had hardly seen sun, moon or stars. If the land did not drain and the earth warm soon, we would not be able to plant our wheat and barley in time, the sheep and cattle, hungry by the end of winter, would starve for want of fresh grass and their young would die.

We conducted the ceremony in a storm. As we left the city the wind was high, the air misty with damp. Thunder rolled faintly, there was lightning over the hills to the north. We sacrificed on the hill, at the blood-pit and in the fields below Troy, where the sea was rolling in in huge billows. The spirit of the ceremony took over. We forgot wind and rain and screamed our pleas for the return of the god, earth's child, Hecate's child. I remember the dark, people running through field and mountain groves. As I stood in the grove by the blood-pit, dark, animal-masked figures all round me – I did not know them, was not meant to know them – I saw a great oak to one side struck by lightning. It caught fire and in the light of the fire I saw a man and a woman on the ground, coupling. I saw a man with a blood-streaked face, women sodden with rain, muddy, dancing in a circle, a boy banging a drum, the sound of piping. I fell to the ground and lay near the tree, watching its flames in the branches, smelling the smoke.

The ceremonies went on for only two days, for the

storms grew even worse and halted them. On the third morning, when I awoke, the day was clear and sparkling. I left the city. People were sprawled asleep in the temple, in the market-place, across the threshold of the gates, which had been left open. Even the most impious foe would not risk the curse which would come on him if he attacked the city at such a time. So I walked out in the sunshine. The air was warm, but my bare feet were cold as I squelched through the sodden pastures, where still-wet, dejected sheep huddled in groups. The horses had all been stabled for weeks, being too delicate to endure such weather. It seemed the ceremonies had driven off the storms.

I sat down on a little mound, among the willows by the river and let the sun warm me. I turned my face up to it and listened to the sea, quiet now, further off.

A tall figure came up over the ridge of land separating grass from sea and trudged towards me. At first he was black against the sparkle from the sea. As he came closer I made out the lean figure of a man of about thirty, black-bearded, with curly black hair, wearing a water-stained robe and small cloak over his shoulders in the Phoenician style. He had nothing on his feet. He seemed weary. He sat down beside me, without a word. There was salt crusted in his hair and beard. In my turn I said nothing. I could not have spoken. I had seen him before in the burning tree. I had felt his presence, known him, before I met him, on that afternoon when I collapsed by the looms. I wondered, perhaps, what his arrival meant, and then knew. He gazed out to sea, flat as a millpond now, though plainly it had put paid to his ship the night before. Then he turned to me, his dark eyes reddened with salt, and said something in a language I could not understand. I shook my head. In our tongue he asked, 'This is Troy?' It was only partly a question, more a request for confirmation. I nodded. He drew a deep breath of relief, but there was some sadness in it. He was still half in his memories of the day, or the night before, when the tempest had taken him. He had lost men, his ship or both, and was still, in his head, at sea, with his sails flapping in tatters, mast smashed, rudder gone, ship being battered hither and yon, perhaps lying on deck, clinging to whatever he could to avoid being washed overboard. He turned his face up to the sun, seeking its warmth.

What I felt throughout my body was that warmth and sweetness I had felt before. I suspect that seldom, after a baby leaves the breast, does anybody feel that contentment again. I knew, whoever he was and whatever the consequences, I must and would have this man to love me.

There was a thong round his neck and he put a strong hand to it, pulled it over his head and opened the salt-stained leather pouch attached to it, which had been hanging under his cloak. The Phoenician, a man of Canaan, as we would call him in our language, tipped the contents of the pouch into his palm and, picking out the largest pearl from the collection of about ten, handed it to me. 'I am Arvad,' he said.

The pearl glowed like the moon through pale cloud and felt warm in my palm. I said, 'It's beautiful,' and tried to give it back. He took it in his fingers, put it back in my palm and curled my fingers round it. Was he trying to buy me, I wondered? But I retained it, for I knew if I was to have him he would have to give me a gift. Then we waded hand in hand to the other side of the river and under a clump of willows, curtained on all sides by the overhanging, just-greening branches, he urged me to the ground, lay on me and took me roughly. Even as he did so I felt in him the haste and panic of men aboard a ship in a storm, the struggle, at first to keep a footing on deck, hasty glances at the sky to get direction from stars obscured by dark, fast-moving cloud, the final terror of losing control of the vessel, being overturned, crashing on rocks, being thrown into the turbulent sea.

Afterwards I said his name. And he asked, 'What are you called?' An ordinary girl's cunning made me say, 'Alba.' The whole world knew King Priam and Queen Hecuba had a gifted, afflicted daughter, prophetess or madwoman, and I did not at that moment want him to know I was the girl. I did not want to be exceptional, so I told him, 'I am Alba,' and he smiled and said, 'Alba.' I don't think even then he believed me.

I said, 'I must find you food and shelter.' I took his hand and led him to the city. It was sunny now, as if the storms had never been. There was still no one about. Going through the Dardanian Gate we met an old woman, mud to the thighs, carrying two chickens, more dead than alive, tied by the feet with a piece of rope. Inside the city few were stirring. People were still sprawled all over the temple flagstones. The market-place was sticky with grease in patches, bones and fragments of bread lay everywhere. A man, a woman and a dog lay tumbled in a heap beside a wall. A scatter of birds, feasting on the fallen crusts, flew up as we approached. A baby wailed inside a house, two children played with a crudely carved boat in a big puddle. They smiled and greeted us as we went past. There was a thin plume of smoke coming up from the forge, where the big, mute boy was probably trying to light the fire for the first time in days.

I led the Phoenician captain up the winding streets to the palace, where I could find him food. We passed the gates of Helen and Paris' house. They were wide open, the guards were missing and nothing stirred, though somewhere inside a man was striking some chords on a lute. I greeted Advenor, who was going into the stables with a bucket in each hand. He was in no mood for conversation. Hector's gates were closed and there was no one to be seen through the bars, just an empty courtyard where a dog roamed and drank from a puddle.

Inside the palace an exhausted old woman was kneading dough on a table and a couple of slaves with brushes were trying to sweep the debris – eggshells, bones, puddles of wine – from the great hall. The old woman glanced at me as I came in hand-in-hand with the Phoenician. 'This man, Arvad, a Phoenician captain, has been shipwrecked,' I said. 'Is there any food to give him?' My dog appeared, muddy, wagging his tail. He'd got lost during the ceremonies and had found his way back.

The woman got some old bread, hard as a stone, and produced half a jug of barely drinkable wine. We sat at the long table. Arvad unquestioningly took the goblet I gave him, dipped his bread in it and ate. At the other end of the table a huge man I did not recognise lay asleep, half naked and covered in mud. As Arvad ate I stared at him and he at me. Naomi stumbled in and pulled at the Phoenician's sleeve, staring up inquisitively. He broke off a piece of bread, dipped it in his wine and offered it to her. She took it and ate, but it was reassurance, not the appeasement of hunger she craved. She went to get wood for the fire.

Gradually the household revived. My father came in and I served him wine. My mother was with the oracle and would not be seen that day, perhaps for several days. She was queen, but priestess also, and in some manner, at some times, also the goddess herself, so after the ceremonies a period of cleansing and consultation with the oracle was her portion. When she returned to the palace there would be a strange aura about her and she would be treated differently for some days, until it seemed right for her to return to her usual life.

So I sat in silence with the Phoenician while others, also silently, entered the hall, were given what food and wine there was. Naomi lit the fire. A waggon creaked into the courtyard outside.

Then I led the Phoenician up to the little room I had once shared with Helenus and Adosha. There were some damp rugs lying in a corner, otherwise nothing but a stone floor, a tiny window through which a little sun came. There we made love again. 'Well, Alba,' said Arvad with some scepticism, 'I'll sleep now.' He closed his eyes and fell into a deep sleep. I remained awake for a while, looking at him. My heart was filled with fierce desire and hope. Yet I was not as happy as I might have been. A corner of my mind was dark with fear. Perhaps it was the ordinary fear of a lover, the fear that happiness will not last. Perhaps it was a deeper feeling. But I pushed the fear from me, denied it, fell asleep. I was unaware of Naomi coming in, but she must have done so, for when we awoke some ten hours later, at dusk, she was there, lying across the doorway, eyes open, staring up at the ceiling. By then there was the smell of roasting meat, and voices and sounds. Someone was playing a lyre.

When we descended, the great hall was full. The table was crowded, there were people on stools, people round the fire. Some sat or leaned against the walls. The musician's song was being half-drowned by those further away from him who were talking. There was even a tumbler turning cartwheels in a small space on the floor, while his companion passed through the company, his hand out for money.

Naomi nudged a couple of merchants from their places at the end of the table, pointing at me and gabbling what she had picked up of our language, interspersed with her own tongue, or that of her captors. As she worried at them one noted the Phoenician and stood. He greeted him and we both took seats. The merchant and Arvad began a conversation in traders' speech – that strange language with words drawn from the Phoenician, Assyrian and some from a forgotten language of earlier times, I suppose. It is a language common to seamen and traders from Scythia to the African coast. It surprised me for some reason that the men knew each other, though it was not so very remarkable. Phoenicia is a narrow strip of the Mediterranean coast, very beautiful by all accounts, and the men are merchants, seamen, often pirates. They voyage everywhere. They know all men and all customs.

I had found the man I had seen in dreams and visions, the man I desired but I had not from the moment of meeting been clear about whether he had the same feelings for me, or was just a shipwrecked sailor, stunned by ill fortune and taking what he could get – a woman, a meal, a bed – in the spirit of a permanent voyager, a man who makes port and trusts his luck among strangers. I did not know and I did not ask. I felt myself, yet I was changed. I felt disturbed to my very roots, yet I was calm. The fate I had not known was now revealed to me. I would not marry a king, or a neighbour or join the oracle in her cave, or bear a child to the goddess, conceived at the temple during the ceremonies – I would go with the Phoenician on his ship. If I bore children, they would be his. My life lay in Sidon or in Tyre.

I did not owe these perceptions to my prophetic gifts. They were the ordinary hopes of a young girl who had fallen in love. I had seen the fate of my people, and my own fate at the hands of the Greek king in trances and visions, but I was a girl. I denied the visions and pretended to myself they were not true.

Meanwhile Arvad, though his manner was modest, was soon at the centre of a conversation involving many people. The Phoenicians do not fight for territory. Their cities lie along a hundred and fifty miles of coast but on the whole they hold only enough land to supply them. They do not attack their neighbours – the Philistines, who share the coast with them, the Assyrian and Hittite kingdoms on their other side, or the peoples beyond the hills and mountains at their back – the Israelites, Moabites, Edomites and such. Instead, they are sailors and merchants looking out to sea, trading and plundering over a thousand miles north, south, east and west of their homes. Their merchandise is spices grown beside the Euphrates, wool from Greece and Sicily, purple dye from Cyprus,

Scythian silver, African gold, Egyptian linen and paper, as well as the ordinary commodities – corn, wine, figs, honey. Those who are not sailors work in metals – they are skilful craftsmen and of course have access to all the places where metals are to be found. Because of these voyages the Phoenicians carry from place to place another commodity besides cargoes – this is news.

Arvad told the company more of the new Hittite king's campaigns at sea, to wrest his territories in the east back from the Assyrians, and of his troubles with the savage Gasga people on his other border around and beyond the Black Sea. His words suggested that the new king was a bold and clever man, but would be hard put to stop the rot of empire begun in the times of his predecessor. Arvad himself had set out in the last days of winter with a view to ending up in the Black Sea, getting copper, silver and tin from among the Cimmerians (and rare furs from the Scythians, he added), but heard now there was trouble there and even when his ship was repaired, he might have to think again about the trading trip.

Hector said urgently, 'We need iron. Can you get us some?'

Arvad's face stiffened a little. 'It is difficult,' he said. 'You would do better to go to the source.' He meant the Hittite king. 'We traders dislike war,' he said, with a glance at my brother Hector. 'Though we see enough of it.' Hector nodded.

Arvad said he had left Tenedos where he had exchanged corn for Greek gold. It was then that he had been hit by the freak storm, wrecked on the short trip between the island and our coast. The population, he said, was not discontented now. Achilles had gone home but had left another Thessalian in charge, a reasonable man with no more than the usual taste for seizing the goods of others and sending them back to Greece. The Thessalians, though an army of occupation, had hung up their weapons for the most part, were forming unions with the daughters of the more prosperous citizens and some of them were taking to the plough. He gave this information tactfully, knowing our position.

Deiphobus burst out that we should launch an offensive and retake the island. I was surprised that without agreeing directly, Arvad seemed to support his view – these Phoenicians have to speak diplomatically, trading always among warring nations as they do. I think now we should perhaps have attacked the Greeks earlier, when they were divided – but war is all blunder and mistakes, and fate always has the casting vote.

Arvad then civilly broke away. He had left his wrecked ship and those sailors who had survived the storm in a bay beyond Troy. He said he must now return and make provision for them. Could he buy from us what he needed – supplies for the men and timber for the repair of the ship? There was no question of that, my father responded. He and his men were our guests. The men must come to the city where they would be taken care of. This gesture of kindness and hospitality proved that my father had seen in Arvad a man of substance, notwithstanding his worn and battered clothing. He had assessed him as someone it would not only be appropriate, but possibly useful, to assist. And with that Arvad took my hand and we left the hall together.

Naomi, who did not want to be left behind anyway,

saw it would be suitable for me to be accompanied by a servant, so she swirled a red cloak, an old one Polyxena had given her, round her shoulders, called for my own cloak, which someone ran to fetch and stepped after us with dignity. People had to move aside to allow the Phoenician, the princess and her small bald attendant to leave. It must have been a strange sight. The lyre player broke off as we departed. My dog trotted after us in a proud, orderly way, as if he had duties to perform.

We got horses and blankets and made our way down from the city, took the road to the harbour, then turned right and rode along the beach, splashed through the shallows of the river to the next bay. We rounded the rocks to where a ship lay on its side, stranded, black in the faint light from the sky. Its prow leaned into the rocks on which it had crashed. At first there seemed to be no one there but, as we approached, the dark outlines of men began to rise from the side of the boat where they had been sheltering. Others began to come down towards us from the caves above the beach. There were only eight crewmen, all that remained of fifteen who had set out from Sidon a month earlier. Two were Africans so black you could not see them well in the darkness. Arvad spoke to them and, wrapped in blankets, they began to trudge along the beach and back to the city, weary and discouraged.

Arvad and I remained on the beach, looking out to sea. I did not speak at first. It is a sad thing for a captain to wreck his ship and lose good men. He often blames himself for the loss, whether he is responsible or not. When I thought the moment good I told him who I was, which I do not think surprised him by then, and probably would not have done earlier. I told him the truth too, about myself, that I had the gift of prophecy but it was often a fateful gift, for I was not believed. I was inwardly nervous but betrayed no shame for I was after all a princess.

He must have seen that I was afraid he would reject me, for he only said that in his experience many women had fatal gifts but rarely explained them so clearly to others from the outset. For his part he respected and cherished the presence of the gods, wherever and however they manifested themselves, and so did all his people. He added, perhaps complacently, that once happily married to him, a power which had proved burdensome might adapt itself into a happier form.

I questioned this, even then, to myself, but said nothing of my doubts. He might have been right for all I know. I was never to find out. As I record this almost-forgotten story, I must admit I almost weep for my younger self. It is painful to see again, from the outside, those two figures agreeing their future, hand-in-hand, looking out over the dark waves of the Aegean.

For the three weeks it took to repair the ship I was completely happy. My mother came from her retirement, pale and thin, and agreed to the marriage. It was a strange turn of events, but she was pleased, and so was my father. Arvad and I lived sometimes at the palace, sometimes in a hut on the beach near to where the ship was being repaired. The weather was warm. We cooked fish the men caught over a fire. They wandered to and from the ship while carpenters rebuilt half the hull, put in new planks and masts, tarred and caulked and hammered. So we walked, talked, made love and decided our future. It was agreed that he would return for me towards the end of summer, after his voyage north to the Black Sea, which, he said, would be profitable if there was no war. He planned to go into the lands of the Cimmerians, nomads, he said, who travelled vast grassy plains with their flocks, and who were extraordinary horsemen and good breeders of horses. I wanted to go with him but he said he was uncertain of what he would encounter. It might be dangerous and my parents would prefer me to stay with them, just for a few months.

The contrast between those days and what followed after fills me, as I have said, with unhappiness, even now. If I had gone with him I would have seen Thebes, Memphis and many other great cities, had a happy life. After he left without me, ruin came to me, to all of us.

I have survived, salvaged a sort of calm, the life of a hardy farmer's widow, children grown, carrying hay to the stable, delivering a lamb by night in a field, by torchlight, breaking the ice of the well in winter to get water. Well, that life is better than that of many others of my people, but when I remember what I felt as I watched the Phoenician ship bound off, sails filled with wind on the spring day when Arvad sailed, I am filled with regret and sadness.

By summer we were blockaded, the city under siege. The Greeks controlled the harbour so no ship could come near it. By the next spring I was married, not willingly, to an ally's son, so that my father-in-law would keep his warriors fighting alongside ours. In short, we were at war, and the first sacrifices of war are the ordinary satisfactions of life. Each one has his own – a child, a hoard of silver hidden in a wall, a husband, a wife, a horse, a field, an orchard. When war comes, the silver is looted, the child or the husband dies, the wife starves, the farm is burnt, the horses stolen.

On my wedding morning I skulked through the countryside behind the city, looking out for Greek patrols with the dog, Smiler. I climbed the hill and on the other side, just at the boundary of the little farm which would have been my dowry, I got away from him as fast as possible, clapping my heels to my donkey's flanks and as I scrambled back up the hill I threw stones at the poor dog as he tried to follow me. Finally, he stopped running and stood stock-still on the path as I went over the brow of the hill. When I looked back over my shoulder I saw him standing there gazing at me, bewildered, still wagging his tail slightly, believing it was a game he didn't understand, that somehow, it would be all right again. I raced downhill, the donkey scattering stones all over the place. I didn't care if we both tumbled over the side or were caught by a Greek patrol. We had eaten the horses. We were eating dogs by then. I'd had to get Smiler out of the city. It wouldn't have been long before he would have been caught and eaten too. War isn't noble and grand. People hunger, quarrel and rage – and eat dogs.

I will not name my husband – poor man, he died in battle a week later. I was a widow before the first clothes I washed for him had dried. On my wedding night, my husband on top, puffing and blowing, I tried to forget the dog and, all the time, I thought of Arvad and held in my hand the pearl he had given me.

FOURTEEN

Thessaly

T HIS TALE of Arvad the Phoenician and of
my lost future with him explains why when
Helen, radiant with her memories, told me I
had never loved, I, hard-handed farmer's widow in a
rough country, just gazed at her – and assented. I had
no wish to tell her my little story. Hers was the great
fable, the one of which the ballads spoke. Because
of it the Greeks attacked and the Phoenician never
returned. Perhaps he could have risked his life to
rescue me, perhaps he went back to a wife in Sidon,
perhaps he died among the Cimmerians or the fierce
Gasga people – I have no insight. I doubt if I will ever
find out. Helen would not have been interested in my
tale anyway. She had come to me for a reason and it
was not to discuss old times and old loves, as women
do round the fire at night before it burns to the embers
and they retire, knowing the next day will bring the
crying child, the burnt meat, the broken jug, the irri-
table husband, the web spoiled on the loom. No –
Helen was sitting there by my fire willing me to tell
her fortune.

Naomi had come in quietly and was sitting,
straight-faced and straight-backed, against the wall
and it was partly to avenge her – for her capture by

the Greeks, for torture, rape, the Greek child she had
borne and strangled – that I told Helen what pictures
I had of her future, visions I felt my brother Helenus
must also have had, but had been too kind to reveal.
Or perhaps it was not just a malign impulse to wound
the woman who had wounded so many (she had not
dared show her face publicly in Greece after the war
for many years – the Greek women would have
stoned her for the loss of their menfolk) but just the
descent of the goddess, imparting the oracular voice
which cannot be resisted. At any rate, as I began to
speak, and before I lost any sense of what I was
saying, I caught my own voice deepening and taking
on that tone, both rhythmic and monotonous, charac-
teristic of the prophetic statement. Then I became
unconscious of what I was saying, as seers do. It was
from Naomi I heard, next day, exactly what I told
the Queen of Sparta.

'Helen – your husband is nearing death, as you
suspect. None of his excesses – wine, boys, the torture
of women – will arrest it. What he thinks of as a cure
is only accelerating his death. As soon as you are
without his protection the Spartans will turn against
you, headed by your own daughter and her husband
the King of Mycenae. You will wander from place to
place, finding no haven. No one will take you in. You
will wander from island to island, prostitute yourself
in the ports of Tyre and Sidon, wander on, end up
begging your bread in the streets of Thebes, being
pelted by little boys, abused by strangers, sleeping in
the corners of the walls, friendless and alone, and
your death will come swinging hanged from a tree,
far away from home.'

When I came to myself, I did not know what I had

said. Naomi was putting logs on the fire and she had in her hand a goblet of wine, which she gave me. At the same time she hissed, 'Send her away – or I go.' Then she retreated to the back of the room again. Helen gazed at me with horror, seeming limp and diminished, leaning back in her chair as if I had struck her a savage blow. When she saw I had finished she remained in that position for a little while, then very quickly recovered her self-possession, sat straight in her chair as before, smiled and began to speak.

She struck fast and hard. 'Well, Cassandra. You've done your best,' she said. 'You were always vindictive. You will *never* forgive. You will *never* pardon me for the part I played in the war – and how small it really was – and the part I played in your fate. And if you want a villain,' she said, almost parenthetically, 'then I will show you one, one you never suspected. My sister.' She continued, 'You, Cassandra, almost alone of your entire family, escaped. You have had a husband, children, bread in your mouth, a roof over your head. The others died, and you know how horrible their deaths were. You did not see your own child's head smashed against a wall, as Andromache did. You were not cut down at your own altar, as your father was, cruelly slain like your mother. You flinch now – no wonder. Did you live on after the war as a beaten slave, like the other Trojans? Remember – my family was destroyed too, after the war, but you, almost alone in all this, have lived in peace for all these years. And still you cannot give up your spite. Where some now mourn, understand and accept the inevitability of things, you still live in hate and blame, striking like a little brown snake in the undergrowth, knowing nothing but that it must inject its venom into something – or someone. You,' she told me, 'are low, contemptible, mean, unforgiving, impious, vengeful.'

I was tired, as those are who have given out a prophecy, and her words were hard, even harder because I recognised some truth in them. They echoed some of my long, bitter thoughts. Why had I survived when my family and friends had died? Why, when the remnants of my people lived on as slaves or wanderers was I still living in peace and safety? Why could I not accept what had happened? Not believe that fate, which makes of us what it will, had had a hand in the disaster, that whatever we had done we were only carrying out what fate had planned? Perhaps I should have taken vengeance on some of those who had conducted the war (Helen herself?) and died as a result, or taken my own life and joined the others in the afterlife. I had not. Perhaps I had been protecting the child which then lay in my womb. Perhaps that was not the real, whole answer.

I hung my head, tired, ashamed, self-doubting. Her words had struck home, whether she spoke truly or only to punish me for what I had told her. In any case, she had not believed me. It did not matter to me whether she did or not. Perhaps next day, I thought, I would tell her what I knew she wanted to hear – that she would soon find a new love, a new king, a new capture by a lover who would take her from a man she did not love and circumstances she did not like. That was how it had always been for her, since she had been little more than a child. Men seized Helen and took her away. Her beauty shaped her destiny. But who was the caught, who the captive, in the end? So I could tell her what she wanted, that it would be like that for her again, though, if I did, she would go away, which I dearly wanted her to do. Meanwhile I was afraid Naomi would carry out her threat, and leave me. Indeed, it was not beyond her to poison Helen.

Helen, like me, had lost a sister as the consequence of war. In that, at any rate, we were alike. She had said, 'If you want to find a villain I will show you one you never suspected – my sister Clytemnestra.' She had, of course, visited her sister many times during the seven years after the war, when Clytemnestra was alive and reigning in Mycenae with her lover.

'Tell me,' I asked. So that evening and for the whole of the next day, in the farmhouse with snow falling outside, she told me Clytemnestra's tale of the wars in Troy. As she spoke I seemed to hear Clytemnestra's own voice, seemed to be listening, with horror, to the actual tones of that dead, dreadful queen.

Part Two

FIFTEEN

Mycenae, Summer

E VERY TEN days or so a messenger comes from Troy. The siege has been going on now for six months, since spring – since my daughter died. 'Lady Clytemnestra – ' they always begin, on their knees in the dark, gilded magnificence of the great hall of Mycenae. It is a room I hate, huge, hung with loot, a room for men to feast in.

'Lady Clytemnestra – ' they say. Then follows a tale of defeat, or half-success, a request for more men, supplies, horses. The war drags on. If it had gone according to the Greek nobles' confident plan it would have been over by now, but our beached ships still lie drawn up, two-deep across the bay of Troy. Our cavalry is still harrying the other cities of the coast and the farms behind the city. Each day Trojans and Greeks clash on the plain in front of Troy. And Troy still stands. The Trojan warriors hurl themselves from their city, determined to make us board our ships and go away, while our force tries to beat them back and drive through the gates into the city. There have been many deaths and woundings. So far, from what the messengers tell me, however guardedly, I see the Trojans have the best of it, and they are not so distressed by the siege that they will surrender the city.

Here women, boys and old people are cutting the hay, picking what grapes and figs are ripe, getting the wheat and barley planted.

These messengers arrive at our great, high-walled palace, weary and travel-dazed after long journeys. It is two days from Troy with a good wind, one even with a wind desperately strong and a bold captain, but more likely three or four. They come, war-stained and travel-stained, telling me of battles, men dead and wounded. They always ask for more supplies of clothing, armour, weapons, horses, drugs, healing herbs and food. These I supply without question as fast as possible, though our own stores are becoming depleted and I shall be obliged soon to start buying all these things from traders and foreign rulers, who will ask high prices, knowing our need. The resources of all areas of the country, the Epirus, Thessaly, Euboea, Boetia, Messenia, Attica, Sparta, which we call Laconia, have, to a greater or lesser extent, funded the war we are conducting, apparently to take revenge against Troy on account of my sister's 'capture'. We aim to take Troy, establish control of the coast and gain access to all the mainland's wealth and trade. Not just the mainland rulers but warriors from the islands – Crete and Rhodes being the most significant – are involved in this venture. All have raided their own treasuries to build ships and equip troops. Some, like Nestor of Pylos, could pay for two wars and still remain rich. Others, from rocky islands, have used up all they have, gambling on victory, fame for the warriors, loot and new territories to control. By and large Greece is a poor country. We have too many mountains and too little water for easy prosperity. We are far from the trade routes connecting the vast empires across the sea. But we are ambitious and look outwards for our wealth. We have no advantages but our strength and resolution.

Peiros, a young man, died raving on his farm near Corinth the other day, a month after he had been shipped home to his mother, widowed a year ago. The young man's leg mortified and could not be cleansed. His mother came to me in tears. She has another son out there in Troy and pleaded to know if the men would come back before winter. Her son had told her the army might stay on all year, into spring if necessary, until the Trojan resistance was battered down by casualties and siege conditions in the city, and they surrendered or were vanquished in a final decisive battle they were too weak to win.

When she arrived, I was alone in my chamber, a cool wind coming through the window at midday. She was awed by my grandeur, my bed, inlaid with many kinds of wood, my carved ivory chest, the rich hangings on the walls, the golden comb, the silver bowls.

The woman wept. She feared to lose another son. The land could not be worked without men. 'They must come home,' she said, distressed. 'There will be sickness there in Troy. More will be killed. The land here will go to waste with no one to work it.'

I told her, 'This is war. It is not pleasant. All must suffer, the men at war and those at home. I have lost a daughter in this cause, you a son. When the men come home in triumph we will rejoice, too, whatever our losses. The future of our people lies on that rich coast. We must be brave.'

She was not comforted. I did not intend her to

be. She asked desperately, 'But, lady, will they return soon?'

I told her I did not know, which was true. I told her, 'If we knew the plan, the Trojans would soon get to hear of it. There are spies everywhere. We are women. We must wait.'

She, too, waited, as if I could add more to what I had said – some news or perhaps word of condolence for her loss. But I turned to my loom, where I had begun my fine and splendid web, and said, 'Go home, good woman, and do your duty. This is what we must all do, high and low. See, I am weaving a cloak for my husband's return. Do the same for your son. It will distract you, calm and comfort you during the long winter evenings if the warriors do not return. Make clothes for the children your son's wife will bear.'

So she went off, unhappily. As she left, she glanced up at my face, while bowing low, and I saw alarm when her eyes met mine. She was in that state of grief and fear which will often produce, even in the most mundane person, an extra sensitivity to what is truly happening and what is passing through the mind of another. What she saw on the surface was her queen, gracious and composed in a flounced dress, bare-bosomed after the Cretan style, in a tall head-dress, seated straight in a high-backed chair inlaid with ivory, by a window through which a cool breeze blew, though it was midday. Beyond the window a small courtyard, with a flowering tree. She saw her queen, tall, brown-haired, blue-eyed, thirty-two years old and beautiful, though not beautiful enough – no woman, twin sister of Helen of Sparta, could ever be beautiful enough, had never been, from the cradle on, never would be, even if Helen herself was dead and her bones in a burial mound. But the woman at that moment saw beyond all this grandeur to something which disconcerted, even frightened her. So the homespun woman met a queen in her pride and read in her eyes – anger, my anger, always continuing anger, the fury of a maimed wolf. It is never appeased. I do not want it appeased. I want no peace of mind, reconciliation, nothing of that – only for my rage to maintain itself, grow with waiting – until I take my revenge, as I surely will. No wonder the widow flinched. One day she will tell her friends she knew, she guessed, she suspected what the queen was like. Indeed, she will say, she almost predicted what would happen. That will amuse her – it will be nothing to me.

And meanwhile I am waiting for the next messenger, held up by unfavourable winds. He is due soon. Instead my steward, Pandion, comes in – a Greek name, but he is pure Cretan, small, very handsome, intelligent, with large shining eyes. In his hands he carries a clay tablet, damp and shining, in case I wish him to make notes or write a letter. He reports on his trip west into our lands bordering Messenia – says the lads on the frontier have become warlike, have armed themselves and are raiding the farms on either side, bullying the defenceless women, taking sheep and wine. There are protests that nothing is being done to protect them; they declare they will pay no tribute.

I shall, I tell Pandion, ask my husband's cousin to go there with a small force of troops and settle the matter. I appointed this man, Pandion, steward after my husband left for Troy, saying the old steward was too elderly and aching in the bones to cope with the kind of situations likely to arise when my lord was absent. This was untrue. The old steward was too loyal to Agamemnon so I had to get rid of him.

Pandion, only twenty years old, merely nods. He already knows more than he would ever dare say. He knows, too, that he knows too much. If he ever told any of it he would be lucky to escape with his life, let alone the money with which I reward him and which I believe he saves. No doubt he plans to buy land in Crete eventually and go back there to live prosperously with his family. These Cretans are very clever, as clerks and craftsmen, and we pay them well. I think he had parents and a sister in Crete and will go back to them. The native Cretans regard us covertly as barbarians, though we have ruled them for generations. They see us as crude in all our ways, lacking taste and scholarship and worshipping gods which provide no proper framework for our lives. They do not understand that although we lust for gold and domination we also lust for beauty. It is a passion with us. We are slaves to the frescoes with which they decorate our walls, their engraved rings, their vases, all they offer us. They make our images of the gods.

I myself hold no brief for the Greek gods, these dozen or so deities whose lives develop like characters in a saga – who said what, who married whom, betrayed, tricked another. I have no objection to them either. In our temple-rooms their scowling pottery images, larger than the usual images of the gods, stand in a shrine for those who wish to offer to them. Elsewhere there are the images of Potnia, the goddess, and the frieze of goddesses painted by some long-dead Cretan – it is of no real interest what or who is worshipped, except that I fear for the little pottery goddess – Potnia – in her shrine.

There is something too useful about this other, newer pantheon. They separate man from the cycle of life. They reflect all too clearly the life of the state, and government – the powerful leader, head of the family, Zeus, Hera, the subordinate queen to Zeus, the family, the children, the alliances, the quarrels. These are the gods of those who do not humble themselves to other forces. Their gods reflect them – they must be the gods and the gods must be them. This is why I fear for the little goddess. Of course, the people have not wholly adopted this new religion. In time of crisis it is to them that the people turn – to the females of the pantheon, Athena, Demeter and the others, for they are really old goddesses of beasts and trees and plants. Even my husband, Agamemnon, did so. At the behest, he said, of a goddess, he sacrificed our daughter to the wind at Aulis so that his fleet could sail for Troy. Desperate to set sail, he believed then that the forces of nature, sea and wind, could be placated with a sacrifice. They had sacrificed beasts in plenty, but still the hostile north wind blew. So they took a human being, my daughter, and impiously killed her without her mother's knowledge.

It is for this crime that Agamemnon must die. He deceived me. A messenger came from Aulis, the small haven in Boetia where the fleet had assembled. The message from my husband told me falsely that he had arranged a good marriage for Iphegenia to that mighty madman Achilles. I knew my daughter, being fifteen, should be married and did not object. Achilles was rich and would be kind to her, as kind as any prince to his wife, perhaps kinder. And we needed Achilles for the war.

I told Iphegenia to go, saying, if she did not like the match, she must return. I packed her waggon with splendid goods. She put her own small things in a bag – some jewellery, a small chipped statue of a goddess she had had since childhood, a fine linen scarf, woven for her by her sister, dyed in the best Tyrean purple dye, that dark red-blue we prize. She set off, a tall, strong girl of fifteen, accompanied by her women servants and some armed men. But the threat to her was not robbers, nor jealous neighbours. It was her father, though I did not know it. And so I and her brother and sister kissed her and sent her off down the long road from the palace. Half a mile off, where the road bent, taking her out of sight, she turned and waved. This was the last time I ever saw her. Even now, I try not to look down that road – and if I do, I weep.

A week passed, then another and there was no message. At Aulis there were a thousand men, some hundred noblemen, fathers and sons, the rest being their kinsmen, their tenants and their sons, and even a few reliable slaves who had been offered land if the Greeks took Troy. With them they had horses, chariots, mules, carts, provisions – and ships. In the narrow straits between Euboea and the mainland fifty-seven ships, the biggest fleet, surely, ever assembled, shifted at anchor, beaten by wind and waves as they had been for a month, waiting for the wind to change. Not one day of that month had passed without the whole force examining the skies at dawn and dusk, looking for a change in the weather to see if at last they could set sail for Troy. But the wind stayed north. The camp stretched round the bay. The men were crowded into tents or roughly constructed shacks, some slept in the rocks – no one could have believed they would be there for so long.

No provision had been made for the delay. They had set out from their islands, their farms, manors, palaces all over the mainland, imagining that in a few days they would be in Troy. That high spirit had changed, becoming dangerous. Men who expect to fight, and do not, are like men who expect to take a woman who evades them. They rage or become bitter. Thus Agamemnon was faced with a mighty expedition going sour. The men were packed together at close quarters, in a state of discontent. They drank, quarrelled with each other, became apathetic and cynical. Stationary troops are vulnerable, too, in other ways. Messages from home reach them – their wives or parents speak of difficulties, of missing them, of crying children wanting their fathers. They begin to long for home. If they do not worry because they get messages, they worry because they get none. They fear disaster and the unfaithfulness of their wives. In short, all the matters which did not concern them unduly when setting off overwhelmed with the desire for riches and glory in battle, suddenly came back to mind. It's a short step then to declaring they must go home. The expedition breaks up.

Agamemnon consulted Calchas, the oracle, and Calchas told him the sacrifice required would have to be the most serious a man can make – the sacrifice of his child. So he sent for Iphegenia, saying she was going to be married, and one night, they told me, with the wind blowing clouds over the sky, using a flat rock by the sea as an altar, Agamemnon, my husband, her father, slew Iphegenia. I hope they drugged her. I hope they did not wake her, then pull her screaming with fear across the beach, force her across the stone, slay her as she struggled and pleaded with her killers – with her father, who held the knife. I hope she never knew who the man was who cut her throat. I hope she did not look into his face as he brought the knife down, knowing who he was, and, though unbelieving, have to believe what was happening. Poor Iphegenia. Merry, thoughtful, dreamy Iphegenia. Her father killed her to get a favourable wind for Troy.

The wind changed at dawn the next day and the fleet left almost before she would have been cold, but they burnt her body on the shore that night, the smoke from the pyre being the prayer they made. For a wind.

Agamemnon took the rights of a father over his children where the rights of a mother should have prevailed. When he slew my daughter he killed half of me. I shall never forgive him. I shall take revenge. It is my right, my duty, and it will be my final consolation.

Although I have pretended to accept this, I shall kill Agamemnon when he comes back to Greece, if he does not die first in Troy, as I hope and daily pray he will.

This is why I await the messengers so keenly. They may bring me the news I crave, that of Agamemnon's death. In the meanwhile I weave my web – that fine, brave cloak I shall give him if he returns. That done, I shall kill him.

SIXTEEN

Mycenae

HELEN TOLD me more about events in Mycenae during that first summer of the war. Her sister was queen, Agamemnon at war. Clytemnestra had taken a lover, her husband's cousin, Aegisthus.

A messenger from Troy came to Mycenae in autumn. Finding the queen presiding over the autumn sacrifice in one of the barley fields below the fortified palace, he sat down by a wall in the field to wait.

There were hundreds of people, some of whom had come long distances to the palace. At noon, as the sun hit its height the messenger saw Clytemnestra, in a purple gown and cloak, bring the bronze knife down on the white ox as it lay in the barley stubble of the sun-drenched field, held down by six strong men. It bellowed and thrashed in terror as she bent over it and with a firm hand slit its throat, pushing the knife in deep, drawing it along, using both hands effortfully across the broad, white-furred throat. The blood leaped up into the queen's face like a fountain, the animal's coat was spattered as she continued the stroke, bending over, showing some grace even in the difficult feat of despatching the animal as speedily as possible. A botch, a half-slain creature, would be a bad sign. Then she straightened, before the ox was completely dead, raising both arms to the sky, one hand still holding the bloody knife and, as the animal twitched its last, the watchers gasped, then groaned, then turned aside to weep. Children cried. Clytemnestra then seized a handful of her brown hair on one side of her head and sawed through it with the knife. Then she did the same on the other side. She flung her hair, wettened with blood, on to the fire men were lighting beside the carcass, where it made a little, bright flame. Pipe music began. Around the field stalls had been set up, wine was ladled from large jars. Mixed with borage, it was a potent brew, bringing waking dreams and making everyone a little mad.

The king's cousin, Prince Aegisthus, lord only of a patch of grass and stones, two horses and a house little better than a hovel in Messenia, joined the queen, who stood now, the knife lowered, still looking at the sky. He was a tall, very handsome man, raven-haired, clean-shaven with the same long face and dominant nose as his cousin. The pair began a solemn, high-stepping dance in the field and slowly the women joined in, making a circle, moving with linked hands round the dancing couple. Others began to dance, the music grew louder, pipes and drums joining in. The music grew faster and still louder. The circle round the two dancers moved more quickly – after some time the music stopped and the prince ran from the circle, breaking it. The queen followed, with her bloody knife. Where they went after that no one knew. Later they returned to the celebration.

After dark, to the sounds of the music, cries and shouts from all directions, the queen and the prince again left the festival hand-in-hand and walked up the hill to the palace. They moved proudly, heads erect, followed by others – courtiers, warriors, palace servants – and the messenger. Clytemnestra's face was still streaked with the blood of the sacrifice, her lips fatty with the slivers of the beast she had consumed, her gown stiffened with blood and fat, though the colour concealed the stains.

The ceremony, as all knew, had been more strained, more nervous, less full-blooded than it sometimes was before the men went to war. The great figure of Agamemnon, hair flowing to his shoulders, was missing, so were many other men, including the most powerful and influential. The quality of the ceremony had not been, as it usually was, like a full flood of water, roaring downriver, raking away banks, carrying with it branches and debris swept up in its flight. It had been a narrow, fast-moving stream, full of bitter water. All sensed this. On such occasions the celebrants thought and felt as one. All knew the festival had begun in fear and anxiety. The mourning had been for the earth bereft of its grains and fruits but also, in anticipation, for the absence of men in war, for their deaths and coming deaths, and for the steady diminishment of the lives of those at home. And hovering over the ceremonies had been the figure of the queen, husbandless, and the ambiguous figure of her consort.

When the ceremonies were over and the goddess consoled and appeased, people also knew that, if the army decided to winter in Troy, they would be faced with maintaining the nation without the help of the ablest. The tasks of pruning, mending walls and farm equipment and slaughtering the beasts which could not be kept through the winter would all have to be done by the old, the women and children. Then they would have to manage spring planting and lambing alone. If the war was won, the prizes would be great, but until it was there would be hard work and grief of many kinds for all.

At dawn the queen sent for the messenger, a young man she did not know from the Epirus. He was small and dark, in his twenties, but looked tired and his face bore lines the queen thought had probably not been there when his wife sent him off with the troops to Troy. His eyes had already taken on the shadows of war. He might have fought before, but not in such a long and bitter campaign. Often, the queen reflected, it is the length of time spent away which makes the real change to a warrior. And from his expression as he entered the room she deduced the army would not be returning for the winter. This young man, Dionos, hadn't the air of a man who had come to deliver a message, then return home. He was prepared to be back in the lines in a few weeks, facing a campaign with no foreseeable ending.

Dionos began with respectful salutations from Agamemnon. His message was that victory was not far away. The Trojans were suffering privations inside Troy and their troops were weakening. The messenger would tell her of a battle – the Trojans had not come off badly, but each battle, thought Agamemnon, further weakened and reduced their strength.

It had been a cloudy dawn, Dionos told her, and the Greeks had been in their camp near the sea just starting to rise, in a mist which made it hard to see – so much so that the coming of dawn had been hardly noted or felt. And when it came, the Trojans had fallen on them in strength in a surprise attack. They were desperate, probably, Dionos said. Spring had turned to summer, summer to autumn and still their enemies were there. The farmers within a range of fifteen miles of Troy had harvested grain and fruits under constant fear of attack. Often the results had been seized almost before their sickles had gone through the sheaf. The army had also been raiding the farms for meat. They faced starvation. Clearly they felt they must rid themselves of the enemy army before winter began.

So some five hundred Trojans – who could have thought they could rally so many friends from along the coast? – in a long line, filling the plain between the two rivers, advanced through the mist, which kept them hidden, and muffled to some extent the sound of their approach. They knew their own terrain better, too, Dionos reported, and thus it was that they were only three hundred yards from the Greek camp and coming up over the treacherous little rise just before the descent to the sea, when they were first spotted. Shouts went up. The dogs began to bark.

The desolate business of soldiers rising, uncomfortable, surrounded by other men, the anticipation of another day of numbing boredom or a crucial battle which might turn the war, suddenly turned into a terrifying emergency. They put on armour rapidly, then, stumblingly, mustered and formed a rough line to face the oncoming Trojans. They came over the hummock in the ground in what the soldiers called the 'Trojan leap', a mighty bound from the back foot, made with shield extended and sword raised, which brought a man who seemed to be out of range of a spear-thrust in an instant too close – too close, almost, for a sword-thrust. They were on the Greeks in an instant, while some were still donning their armour by the ships. Half the line consisted of men who had run out wearing no armour at all. Mighty Ajax was in only a tunic, even his feet bare. Agamemnon had a helmet and spear but no shield. And, the messenger said, the thin faces of the Trojans under their helmets were grim. They were men bent on murder, each desperate to finish the war before winter set in, starvation in the city became famine, sickness struck.

They broke through the Greek line and only seconds later were fighting desperately by the ships. The casualties were severe – forty Greeks killed or badly wounded. Agamemnon and five others found themselves struggling in shallow water, backed up against a beached ship, while ten Trojans, including the redoubtable Hector, rained blows on them. The only Greek to survive unwounded had been Agamemnon.

Achilles and his men, all armourless for they were bivouacked away from the main camp and had to come faster to the emergency, found themselves on the plain to the rear of the fighting, cut off by the mass of the Trojan army. Achilles lost five men, cut down by swords, in five minutes. They had been beaten back to the banks of the river Simois, then, just as, pale and red-eyed, Paris was about to bring his sword down on Achilles' head he, Paris, had suddenly smiled. 'Not today, Achilles,' he'd said and rapidly run, followed by the others, to the help of his brother Hector further down the beach. Achilles then stopped his men from going after them, said the messenger, though they had a good chance of catching and killing Paris. There had been a fierce argument between Menelaus and Achilles about this that night. 'He

spared me,' Achilles had said. 'What was I to do –
plant a spear in his back?' Menelaus had remained
furious. Achilles, seated by the fire, had simply turned
his face to the stars and said, as if to himself, 'Strange
thoughts and feelings come over a man in battle.'
That silenced Menelaus, though it did not reduce his
anger.

Meanwhile, Achilles and his men could find no
way of getting back to the main body of Greeks without being cut to pieces by the Trojans between them
and their allies. Lacking Achilles and his Thessalians,
the Greek army took more punishment, for the Trojans, with the air of men who scarcely cared for their
lives, pressed on, unbeatably. Someone cut the tethers
of the Greek horses and opened the gate of the compound in which the others were kept. Then finally, as
if they sensed their collective strength suddenly
ebbing, the Trojans turned, seemingly without a word
of command, rapidly stripped what they could of the
dead Greeks' armour and raced back to the city,
Though not, reported Dionos, before firing some of
the Greek huts and burning them to the ground. They
could have burnt the fleet, he said, but left the ships
alone, no doubt in the hope that the Greek army, after
this defeat, would give up the campaign, embark, and
go home.

The condition of the Greeks after this battle was
dreadful, the messenger said. There were deaths,
there were injuries which would end in death, more
than half the escaped horses could not be found. The
troops were demoralised. The death of companions is
terrible; the knowledge that the Trojans could raise
so many allies and fight like tigers was frightening
and discouraging. There had been a strong party –

the influential King Nestor and Diomedes, Prince of Argos, among them – for returning home and remounting the expedition the next spring. Agamemnon had pointed out that this was precisely what the Trojan attack was intended to make them do and that the chances of mounting such a powerful expedition again, after the first had failed, were slight. He said the enemy had made its bid and, if the expeditionary force turned tail and fled, that bid would have been successful. They had used up their strength, he said. He advocated determination, standing firm and acting like men, holding on and continuing the attacks until the siege and its consequences took their toll.

This was the messenger's account. 'Men fight better when they are defending their homes,' Clytemnestra said to him. 'Though, again, they may collapse rapidly when they hear too many women crying for the dead and see too many dying of starvation.'

The young messenger was disconcerted by the queen. She had heard his account without any expression of dismay and had remained unmoved even when her own husband was mentioned. Her remark was delivered in a neutral tone, neither triumphant nor even pitying. She had hardened her heart to endure the pain of war and the loss of her husband, Dionos concluded. He continued to the next part of his message.

'Since the arguments of Agamemnon won the day, though narrowly, he now requires you to send half the barley, half the vintage when the wine is made –'

She broke in, 'You must tell all this to my steward. Whatever my husband requires will be sent.'

He had to say more: 'He requires Pholkos the blacksmith and his brother.'

Clytemnestra nodded.

'Also, thirty horses.'

She nodded again. 'I will send my steward to note all this.' She left the room and woke Pandion, the Cretan, who was lying with a girl in his room. They had been roaming the countryside with the others at night, she assumed, making love, dancing and laughing in hills and fields, hedges and ditches. Though a little stupefied, Pandion was on his feet almost as soon as she called to him. He was naked and streaked with mud.

'I regret coming to you so early this morning,' said the queen, 'but the messenger from the camp in Troy is here. He was stopped from delivering his message yesterday by the ceremonies and now he tells me he must go on and deliver his news and requests to many others. He has instructions concerning sending much of the harvest and other supplies including horses to my lord in Troy so you must record them. After you have done that, come to me. We shall have to send to Egypt for grain. And we shall need thirty horses quickly.' The Cretan nodded. 'And the city will need to find blacksmiths – you must tell me who there is among your people, if there is anyone.' The Cretan nodded again and, picking up his robe from the floor, put it on. The girl was now staring up, frightened, from under her rugs. She had probably not known where she had arrived the night before, or very much about her lover. Now she was trying to piece together what was happening.

Still befuddled with wine, Pandion's head was clearing. Plainly Agamemnon's demands for supplies were large. Grain would have to be brought from abroad, horses – how many? – would have to be found. Plainly there had been a defeat. He asked, 'Does this mean that the army is not coming home this winter?'

'I have not been told,' she replied and left the room.

'Was that the queen?' asked the girl after she had gone.

'It was,' he told her.

'Where are her children?'

'One dead – a daughter – one sent away – the boy – to stay in safety with a foreign king. The other, Electra, only fourteen and a hater of her mother.'

The girl shuddered. 'She frightens me.' She was from a farm and no more than fifteen years old.

'She's the queen, not your mother,' responded Pandion. 'Now – go back to sleep or get up and go out. I'll have no time to amuse you today.'

The girl rolled up on her side and muttered, 'She frightens me,' but she then went back to sleep.

SEVENTEEN

Thessaly/Mycenae

HELEN, HAVING related all this, said now, 'And here is a tale you will not have heard in the ballads – which are for men. This is the tale of a woman betraying a woman, a sister's treachery to a sister.'

Like a woman in a trance, she took on her sister's voice once more, that deep, expressive voice, the voice of Clytemnestra.

Aegisthus, my husband's cousin, Regent while he was absent (though Agamemnon did not like it) and my lover (though Agamemnon did not know it), was concerned about the demand for a large proportion of the harvest of Mycenae, as well as the huge number of horses. Late one night he lay on my bed. He was anxious.

'Plainly they've decided to winter in Troy,' he said. 'But if so, will even these supplies last? I doubt it. There'll be requests for more. I believe he's securing the loyalty of the other nobles by feeding their men and giving them horses.'

I agreed with him. We had known for months the expedition was short of food. There were a thousand men to feed and they'd been there for half a year. They'd planned, when supplies ran short, to live off the land, but a thousand extra mouths to feed is a burden no countryside can support for long. In addition the farmers for miles round Troy were withholding supplies, even putting up armed resistance to Greek foraging parties. Roving bands of Trojan troops, after the same supplies, were often there to assist them. A sheep was expensive when it cost the life of a man – sometimes it wasn't worth fighting for. The farmers frequently refused the high prices Greeks offered for supplies, preferring to give or trade at much lower prices to the Trojan bands, for the city. The countryside was always full of foragers from both sides, often fighting each other for the contents of a waggon of hay, a couple of hens and a sack of barley. It was not war, it was not noble, but there was no choice. The farmers fought to protect their granaries. They hid their supplies, digging and camouflaging grain-pits in the forests, driving off their flocks if they thought a raiding party was on the way. Convoys of food, though, managed to make their way to Troy, prolonging the siege. It was infuriating, but there was no way of dealing with it. To have punished the farmers would have been like goading an already angry bull and what army needs an entire countryside turned against it, every child with a dagger in his robe, every path concealing a pit a horse can drop into? The Trojans' neighbours, from Lydia to the east to Lycia to the west, right down the coast, also refused to sell supplies to the Greeks or, if they did, charged insupportable prices. The burden of supplying the army therefore fell on the Greek states themselves, and the major part of that burden on us, in Mycenae.

There had been, too, a quarrel between Achilles and Agamemnon – over a girl, a Trojan, my husband had taken from Achilles. Achilles, on whom all were relying for victory, who had already, years before, captured Miletus, then Tenedos single-handed with his savage Thessalians, had retired from the war, refusing to fight. Agamemnon, furious at this rebellion by a subordinate, kept the girl – Achilles continued to refuse battle.

'Let him stay in his camp forever. Let the army strip the land,' I told Aegisthus. 'Let them take all we've got. Let us spend all we have buying supplies from elsewhere. Let Agamemnon at all costs stay in Troy.' He did not argue, for once Agamemnon had gone I had made him Regent. We were lovers. We were building up our own forces to resist Agamemnon if he returned alive from Troy.

Aegisthus' father had been king in Mycenae forty years earlier. He had been overthrown by his brother. All his children but one – Aegisthus – had been killed in the cruellest possible way by their own uncle, father of Agamemnon and Menelaus. He had then made himself king. Aegisthus, only remaining child of the deposed king, had lived in exile and bitterness, never forgetting that his cousin Agamemnon occupied a throne which should be his. After the sacrifice of Iphegenia and the departure of the fleet, he came to me. The commander of the small troupe of men left to guard the palace and keep peace in the realm died – I made sure of it. I then appointed Aegisthus in his place, sending word to my husband that his cousin had offered me help while he was away, pledged loyalty to the nation in its hour of need in return for a large concession of Trojan land when the war was won. I pointed out that the commander of the troops was dead. I, a woman, could not take on the burden of acting as an army commander and was terrified of attacks from inside Mycenae, or from outside, during his absence. There was also the prospect of slaves getting out of hand while their masters were away. I needed the backing of a male relative of his own, and was confident his cousin meant him no harm.

I had no word back, yes or no, although Agamemnon must have disliked the situation. Of course he mistrusted his cousin, but so far had no positive reason to do so – Aegisthus had so far lived quietly on his stricken farm. He had associated with no potential allies, sought no proud marriage with their families. Nevertheless, we both knew that at any moment my husband might decide to put an end to the Regency, perhaps in the easiest way, by making sure Aegisthus died, poisoned by a bribed servant, or stabbed one night by a returning soldier promised a price for doing the deed.

Meanwhile in secrecy Aegisthus and I coupled like beasts, our pleasure heightened immeasurably by what other things the act meant to us. Through it I was able, a little, to forget Iphegenia's death. The knowledge that this infidelity was the beginning of revenge that would end in Agamemnon's death was intoxicating. On his side, Aegisthus knew our union was part of his campaign to become king, a revenge for his father's disgrace and death, and for his own years of deprivation. Seeds sown so many years before were germinating. The harvest would not be long. We were no girl and boy, gladly melting warm flesh with warm flesh – our union was cold, full of pain and woundings, for we were both carrying years of grief and bitterness to our bed. Each act of love was an affirmation of hatred, ambition and revenge. We scratched and bit and made love in unnatural ways. Publicly we kept up appearances. I played the faithful wife, Aegisthus the loyal kinsman. A few who were close to us knew the truth – they must have – and some others may have guessed, those who had sufficient understanding to read the signs.

I knew my daughter, Electra, was spying on us. At fourteen years old she pretended to be sweet and innocent. Underneath she loved her father with no natural passion and therefore hated me immoderately. If she could find evidence to betray me to Agamemnon she would do so. But Agamemnon must have had more spies in the palace. He might already know his wife was unfaithful to him, and was biding his time. Or he might soon find out.

Two weeks after the last messenger, another ship landed at Pylos. The new messenger informed me that the Hittite Great King had sent a letter to the Greek camp telling Agamemnon that out of courtesy to him and his brothers – whom he named 'Great Kings', although they were not, that title was for the rulers of great empires like Assyria and Egypt – he would not be supplying troops to assist the Trojans in their war. The truth was probably that Suppiluliumas was so troubled with his own enemies, he needed all his warriors for himself. Nevertheless, Agamemnon said, this news meant that there would be no skilled reinforcements for Troy. In fact, it was possible that the Great King, believing Troy would fall to the Greeks anyway, was prepared to withhold support from the Trojans as a friendly gesture to the future rulers. At all events, my husband said, this letter had settled the question of whether or not to stay on in Troy and finish the war. With Hittite reinforcements of trained troops the Trojans might have driven him out. Now, he said, what the Greek troops could not accomplish, the siege would. My first consignment of supplies had arrived, he added. The rest must come soon before winter storms held up or even wrecked the ships carrying them. He needed also gifts – iron axes, gold rings and silver vessels – to give his fellow captains. I opened the treasury and took out what he wanted and sent Pandion off straight away to the port to purchase what was necessary from incoming traders. 'Let Agamemnon have everything he wants,' I again said to Aegisthus.

At night on the same day a second messenger crept through the guards and the dogs and knocked quietly on the door to my apartments. He woke my woman, who woke me and I went out to him. I knew he was a Trojan, but he did not tell me so and he spoke Greek as we do. Nevertheless, I knew what he was and at first suspected he might be planning to kill me. He was very frightened. He handed me a message, written on a scrap of paper such as the Egyptians use and very stained with what looked like water, old, dirty and with some lettering on the back I could not make out. On the other side was a message, written very small in what I recognised as Akkadian lettering. At the top was a name in Greek I recognised and which much alarmed me. I had to get a slave out of bed to read it.

I went downstairs to the great hall, not properly cleared of last night's feasting with local landowners, which had gone on until late at night as Aegisthus and I flattered them, poured them wine, listened to their stories. Tables and stools lay about, covered with dirty goblets and scraps of food. I stood on the bare floor, a cloak clutched round me in darkness. I dared not make any light for fear of attracting the attention of the household. I dreaded the scrap of letter in my own hand. The messenger sat on a stool, staring into the fireplace and trying to control his fear. Many a messenger has been put to death in sudden rage by a ruler who dislikes the message he brings, or in cold blood by one who wishes the news he brings to remain a secret.

The slave arrived, a bent man of about forty, a diplomat from Calcemish first caught on a Phoenician boat and whose identity we had denied when representations were made for his return. We said he was dead. He looked apprehensive and became more so when I told him if he revealed anything of what the message contained to anyone else he would die, and slowly. In a low voice he read out what the letter said. I watched him scan the message before he began to read. As he did so he paled and began to shake with fear.

'Read it,' I ordered, and he began, in a low voice. 'This is from Helen by the hand of Sinon of Troy, a friend. It says "Sister – our position here is grave and I fear the future. People are beginning to die and we have word there will be no reinforcements from Suppiluliumas. I fear to be widowed in the fighting, but more I fear capture by those who hate me when we are defeated. Will you get word to my husband Menelaus that I will gladly come back to him but first I must know he will take me back without harming me. I depend on you for my life. Get word to me if

Menelaus will take me back. Do this in the name of our father, Tyndareus. Help me." '

I believed the letter to be authentic. Perhaps Priam and Hecuba had been her accomplices, knew of Helen's plan to leave Troy safely. With Helen gone the war could end. But whether Helen was truly operating secretly or part of a Trojan plot did not matter to me. What counted was how it would affect my own plans. The slave ceased to read and the messenger stood gaping at me. Well, the Trojan must have reckoned on death from the outset and I suppose the slave knew before he began reading that his chance of seeing dawn that day was small. Neither of them could be allowed to live to tell the tale. I snatched the paper from the slave, pulled my cloak round me and began to scream for the guards. They raced in as I yelled there was a Trojan plot to murder me and the two men were dragged out and quickly butchered outside the palace. I heard the sounds. Next day there would be punishments for those who had allowed the assassins to get into the palace.

Aegisthus came in then, with some of the women and I told my tale of the spy, the bribed slave and the attempt to murder me. I kept the paper in my hand inside my cloak.

Upstairs in my bedchamber I told Aegisthus the real story. He gazed at the paper in amazement, holding it in his hand. We talked in whispers. 'You think Menelaus would take her back?' he asked.

'I think so.'

'So do I,' he said. 'Do you want to help her?'

'That's another matter,' I told him. He nodded.

It was partly, as far as he was concerned, a test of faith for me. If Agamemnon died in the war he could almost certainly marry me, the widow of the king, and take over the kingdom. But he never quite trusted me to kill Agamemnon if he returned and anyway, there was danger in the action – a general returning surrounded by battle-hardened troops can be hard to kill. Even if he dies, after the killing the troops may turn on the murderers.

'It would be better if he died in war,' I said.

'The risk is – that he'll come back victorious.'

'That I know.'

'But your son?'

'Twelve, sickly and away at the court of King Strophius, Orestes is no threat.'

In darkness we talked over and over the subject. Was the message what it purported to be? If Menelaus took Helen back would the war still continue? I knew I must ignore the message. I could not risk the war ending as long as there was any chance Agamemnon would be killed in Troy. If Agamemnon returned unharmed, the risk of bungling his death existed – and if that happened, Aegisthus and I would both die.

As for Helen, she had made her bed, I thought, and must lie on it. I had no hatred for her, but I could not let her upset my plans. She would have treated me the same.

'Destroy the message,' Aegisthus urged.

I agreed. There was no choice. It is a hard and bitter thing for any ruler to do, to refuse a chance to end a war. In fact even then I did not destroy the paper.

'I'll hide it,' I said. 'We may need to use it later.'

'Why?' he asked passionately. 'What use will it ever be?'

The truth was, it gave me power over him. As long

as I had the paper, I had power to end the war, bring my husband home unharmed and reconcile with him. I knew I would not do that, but Aegisthus did not. As long as the paper existed Aegisthus could not be quite sure of me, and that was better.

I told him, plausibly, 'We may need the message from Helen for reasons we can't anticipate now. It would be foolish to destroy it. What harm can it do, hidden? What harm to you? If Agamemnon's killed, he's killed. If he's victorious, you take his kingdom anyway – and the new kingdom he's won for us. But,' I said, 'we cannot be sure one day it may not suit us to try to end the war, so we'll keep this paper. What we must be aware of,' I warned, 'are Helen's further efforts to persuade Menelaus to accept her back – once she thinks this message went astray she may find other ways of trying to seduce him.' This thought at least diverted Aegisthus from his plan to get rid of the message at all costs. 'The women here are praying for her death,' he said.

'They fear for their men. The women of Troy will be praying even harder,' I said.

'You've no love for your sister.'

'Perhaps not.'

'Better to destroy the message,' he urged again. 'If word gets out you had the means of ending the war and failed to use it you'll be hated too.'

'A message no one can read delivered by a dead messenger?'

'Still dangerous.'

'You cannot rule without danger,' I told him. That much at least I had learned from Agamemnon.

The matter was causing a division between us. I

turned to him and made him love me. We could not afford to be enemies.

EIGHTEEN

Thessaly

I STARED aghast at my visitor, chilled by this dreadful story, delivered by Helen in the deep-timbred, calm, yet terrible voice which must have been her sister's. I was not only terrified by that voice, which made it seem as if the long-dead queen were in the room with us. Part of my horror was knowing that if Clytemnestra had chosen to intervene in her sister's case, Troy would not have fallen. History would have changed.

I wondered what these two sisters were – one, for love of a man, began a war. The other, for hatred of a man, let the war continue, a war which otherwise might have ended after six months. To disguise my feelings I bent and put another log on the fire. Yet, as I straightened up and looked at Helen, I think my voice was unsteady as I asked, 'She had a message from you asking her to construct a reconciliation between yourself and Menelaus and she did nothing? That was in the first summer of the war? She did nothing?'

Helen, oblivious to all I was thinking and feeling, continued, implacably self-centred, 'I did not want to leave Paris. I loved him with all my heart. But I was afraid when I saw such a mighty army. I could not believe Troy would hold out against Agamemnon and Menelaus. I knew them, remember, all too well – ' Her voice trailed away. 'I feared them so much. I believed only my sister could have negotiated my return.'

'When you heard nothing from her, knew she was not speaking to Menelaus on your behalf, couldn't you have used someone else as intermediary? Why did you not speak to Priam and Hecuba? Or even Achilles might have helped you. He was losing his taste for the war.'

'I waited,' Helen told me. 'I couldn't believe she would not help me. I took the delay to be the kind of pause which takes place when people are in delicate negotiations with each other – I knew Menelaus could not take me back without loss of face; that the Greek alliance might want to continue the attack on Troy whether I returned or not. A formula had to be found. I would have had to act in a certain way – you know these things, Cassandra,' she appealed to me. I nodded. 'Then it was nearly autumn. Then winter. I sent another message, asking her to speed the matter on. That ship sank. The message never arrived, though I did not know it then. And by the end of the year I began to give up hope. By then the war had gone too far. Too many were dead or dying. It would not have been possible to return to Menelaus – he would have been forced to kill me, or exile me on some distant rocky island. I could not have returned,' she repeated hopelessly, as if recalling what she had felt then. She smiled. 'Your prophecies always said Troy would fall. You can hardly believe that if my sister had arranged my return to Menelaus the outcome would have been different. We were all agents of fate, slaves obeying cruel orders.' She paused again. 'I should never have trusted a woman to help me, still less my sister.'

'You tried to escape, however – ' I said.

'I do not want to remember – ' she told me.

There must be many things she did not want to recall, I thought, and asked, 'How is Troy now?'

'Rebuilt,' she said carelessly. 'I saw it a few years ago. They rebuilt without expense, just took the old stones and used them for new, low buildings. The temple's still destroyed. They've left it there as an example to all who challenge Greek rights.'

'Rights,' I said bitterly.

She shrugged the pretty shrug I remembered. 'I suppose these days you'd call the city a trading post – low buildings, hens and goats in and out of everywhere, few inhabitants. The harbour's functioning, of course, that's where the wealth comes from.'

'Are there slaves?' I asked.

'Slaves – of course there are slaves. Of course they're all – ' Trojans, she had been about to say. My people. She had spoken on without considering what feelings the words might arouse in me – my city reduced and ruled by the enemy; my people, slaves. She managed to check herself and said hastily, 'There was no one I recognised, Cassandra, of course not. I would have told you. This is – you are lucky to be alive and well, and have lovely children.'

'You are rich in Sparta?' I questioned.

'Mycenae is richer. They call it the city of gold.'

'The city of gold,' I repeated.

NINETEEN

Troy, Summer

AND SO the Phoenician, my Phoenician, left in spring for his summer trading and three weeks later I was standing, as I often did, sleep being difficult, on the ramparts of the city looking to the horizon to see the dawn come. I was thinking, I suppose, that I should have followed my instinct and left with Arvad, not letting the conventions of marriage settlements and preparations deter me.

The women had been at their looms for weeks, weaving my wedding clothes and the gifts I would take with me on my marriage. A great cloak of red and silver was being made for me. It came to me that morning, I would never wear it.

My mother had been to the treasure rooms below the palace to choose a scanty dowry – there were many girls in our family to provide for. She sorted out golden cups, a bracelet of lapis lazuli, linen sheets and woollen blankets for the bed, a coronet of gold and an ancient hanging, once my grandfather's. In addition there was my grandfather's patch of land, dating back to the days when the family lorded it over the fishing village and a few acres which were then the territories of Troy. This smallholding was just on the other side of the hill from the city.

There I would sit, my back against the tumbledown wall of the farmhouse, thinking of the marriage which would take me far from here. I dreamed of voyages, taking me to Pharaoh's great new capital on the Nile at Memphis, or beyond that to the wealthy kingdom of Saba, where Ethiopian queens reigned and spotted leopards roamed. I dreamed of Thrace, Tyre and Sidon, Babylon, Hattusas – the world. Little birds were carrying twigs for the nests they were building in the gnarled apricot and apple trees of the ruined farm while I dreamed of a tall-masted ship, of journeys, cargoes of ivory and ebony, blue linen, corals, silver, copper from Thrace, gold from Egypt, amber from the Slavic lands beyond the Black Sea. Ethiopian gold and tusks of ivory, wheat, honey, spices and the iron of Anatolia where the Great King ruled –

They tried to get me to the loom to weave, but I was distracted. I quarrelled with my sister Creusa, Aeneas' wife. She said, 'Cassandra, you cannot voyage with your husband. That is a dream. A woman stays at home with her children.'

'I shall leave them with Arvad's mother,' I told her, 'or take them with me.'

'Do you think *he* will allow that?' she asked.

Creusa was heavily pregnant. Aeneas neglected her. It was unfair to have an argument with her but I was continuing the debate when Hecuba came up. She took my side: 'Cassandra is a princess,' she said. 'Allow is not a word her husband will use to her.'

Creusa looked sceptical. One of the women gazed at her and teased, 'Have you been taking lessons from the Greeks, Creusa?'

'Even the Greeks can't make a woman do everything they say,' said another. 'Think of Helen.' But

214

all knew that Helen's mother came of some strange old stock, was held, as was the tradition, to have been a goddess. Helen had not been reared according to the custom of the new Greeks. This was why both she and her sister, Agamemnon's wife, somewhat awed their own countrymen – even their own husbands, perhaps, though those brothers would not, being proud, have wanted to admit this.

Hecuba took Creusa away to rest. She was weary with pregnancy and her husband was making her unhappy. He still spent most of his evenings with Paris and Helen. Creusa was much alone. Before they went, my mother ordered me from the looms. I was useless. Naomi then took the opportunity to slip down into the town where she was conducting a precocious affair with a wealthy fish merchant.

Although I pined, the land was prosperous. The storm damage was cleared away, the drowned beasts buried, the weather became good, planting went well and the harbour was busy with ships. A time when, as the people said, all ewes had twins. My father, though, was anxious. Our request for help from the Hittite Great King had not been met. The king sent regrets, declared he thought for the time being an attack on the Greeks would be unwise. It was diplomatically worded, but a refusal just the same.

Meanwhile I did not sleep and had taken to roaming the ramparts early on, had become a dawn companion for whatever watchmen were on duty. On a fateful day I stood beside that night's watchman, with my brother, Troilus.

'When will he come for you?' he asked. 'You'll have to sleep before autumn,' he added in the sympathetic way of all brothers, 'or you'll be ugly when he returns. He might take a look, change his mind and set sail, never to be seen again.'

'You'll be pleased enough to visit me in Tyre,' I said.

'I'll be the first,' he grinned. 'Before any of the others.' He had always wanted to roam. A year ago he had been forbidden to go to Ethiopia, where our father's cousin was married to the queen, Candace. Now his eyes were sparkling.

'How wonderful that will be,' I said. 'Troilus, what do you think . . .?' But as I spoke I looked at him and my voice trailed off. He was staring far out to sea in disbelief. 'No,' he said. 'No – it can't be.' His voice cracked.

The sea reflected what little light there was. Far, far out on the horizon we could see a set of small black dots, which might have been birds had they not been so close to the water or might have been porpoises or dolphins, had they not been so evenly spaced. Peering through the darkness, we thought desperately that they could not be creatures of any kind. There was only one thing those shapes could be, but that was unthinkable. Finally I said in a low voice, 'They must be ships – but they cannot be. No fleet could be so large.'

We stood, chilled for a little while, taking in the sight, dreading it, unwilling to rouse the city until we were quite sure. And finally I said what we both knew, 'A Greek fleet,' and Troilus said flatly, 'It must be,' and was off along the ramparts like the wind, crying 'A fleet's coming! A fleet is here!' He ran into the palace shouting, heading first for the warriors' room, then for the chamber of my parents. While I, who had so often cried out in my visions of this arrival, now stood quite still, in the cool spring wind, looking out to sea.

The first person to arrive was a woman wearing only a cloak. She was in no doubt of what she saw, stared across the sea, raised her arms and cried, 'Oh, goddess, what are you doing to send this fate upon us? Where have we been at fault?'

Then came Deiphobus, dressed, carrying his sword. 'It is the Greeks,' he said, as if to himself. A woman with a crying child came up – Andromache. Then my brother Hector, her husband, in armour. He put his arm round his wife.

Now cries were coming up from the town. More people disturbed by the cries of others arrived on the ramparts. Meanwhile in the harbour, nearly a mile off, the arrival of the fleet had been spotted. Small figures were congregating on the quays. A sail was hauled up. Some people were running to the town. The captains, preparing to leave quickly, had despatched men to collect their crews. A laden waggon jerked out of the city gates and along the road to the quay. It was piled high with bundles. A woman sat on top, combing her long hair. Beasts were being tugged by their bridles across the quay and driven aboard ships. Inside the palace the shouting went on. There was complete panic.

Now, in the harbour, the captain of an Egyptian ship was fighting, on his own deck, with the skipper of a fishing vessel who had been trying to get out of the harbour ahead of him. Hector cried, 'Deiphobus! Get a fast horse and some men and go down to the harbour to control things – those sailors will wedge each other in, block the harbour and sink each other before any vessel can get out. We'll lose all the ships to the Greeks!' Not long after, Deiphobus, standing up in the stirrups, was galloping down the road to the harbour, overtaking waggons, people on foot with bundles and some with nothing at all, all trying to flee the invasion.

Throughout all this I stood by the palace wall, my face against the stones. The war had come at last. And what chance now had I of marrying the Phoenician? Hecuba found me in all the confusion. Hector was giving orders to the men, people were pushing past to see the oncoming fleet. Down in the harbour Deiphobus and his men were enforcing order with swords and spears. Hecuba seized my arm firmly. 'Come with me, Cassandra. I need you.' So, still mourning for my future, I followed her inside the palace. In the great hall the looms had been thrown at one end in an untidy heap and slaves were pulling up the flagstones where they had once stood. Helenus, in full armour, raced past me with a despairing look. Clemone ran in, a slave behind her, carrying wooden shovels. Armed men went to and fro as the slaves continued to haul up heavy flagstones. A small child stood and cried, knuckling his eyes. Two farmwomen entered and fell on their knees to Hecuba. 'We must shelter here, lady,' they said. 'But shut the gates, we pray.'

'Later,' Hecuba said. 'First those who want to escape by sea must go. The country people must enter the city up to the last moment. Then we will shut the gates. Did you bring food with you?'

'As much as we could.'

My mother's face was strained. 'Eat as little as you can. Save the rest,' she said. 'There may be hunger, later. Tell this to everybody.'

'You have seen this before,' I said.

My mother shook her head. 'I have heard what it is like,' she said. She paused. 'A siege.' She spoke the word as people speak the word 'death'.

Priam and Paris came in, arguing, Anchises behind them. 'We must attack them as they disembark,' Paris cried.

'We'd be massacred,' Priam told him. 'They must have a thousand men, all warriors, aboard. What have we – some two hundred and fifty, just woken, taken by surprise. And if we're all killed, the city falls to the Greeks. We must get reinforcements from the countryside, from along the coast – from wherever we can.'

'We could pick them off as they leave their ships,' Paris argued.

Anchises said, 'They might overwhelm us. This is very serious. Somehow Agamemnon and his brother have united the Greek kings. We are unprepared.'

'Why?' Paris asked furiously. 'Where were your spies? Perhaps we should have listened to Cassandra. My sister appears to have had a better idea of what was to happen than my father's chief adviser.'

'No one could have predicted Agamemnon's being able to make a coalition of that pack of warring dogs.'

'We should have *known* – '

'We could arm the slaves and the women for a battle by the sea,' Hecuba said calmly. 'It has been done.'

Anchises said, 'No, lady, if we lose a battle on the beach the war is over – they'll take the city. It's too dangerous.'

'Is our city's motto – has it always been – Do not

attack the Greeks?' Paris cried furiously. 'They have come for my wife! Hector! Where's Hector?'

The noise in the room was great, as slaves hauled up the floor tiles and broke the packed earth with whatever tools my mother had been able to supply. My step-brother Connates came in with breastplates, and threw them in the entrance with a crash. There were cries outside, the rattle of waggon wheels, the neighing of horses being forced into the traces – my mother was plainly sending out waggons to get supplies from nearby areas. There were shouts and more crashes of armour from the men's room. From the women's came the cries of children woken early and still unfed.

My sadness was that I could not join wholeheartedly in the struggle for survival, the preparations for siege and battle. I knew the outcome, had known it for years. So, of course, had Helenus, apparently now down in the town helping the smith to get his furnace burning hot, collecting any scrap of metal for melting, organising the collection of armour, swords in need of repair (how ill-prepared we were for this crisis). Both Helenus and I were to spend much time from now on in a struggle we were convinced would end in defeat. My mother swept me up. She said, 'Cassandra – I have need of you. There are letters to write, matters to organise. I need your help.'

I followed her from the room. 'Where's Hector?' cried Troilus as we passed. No one knew. In fact he had joined Deiphobus down at the harbour trying to sort out the confusion. It was important to get our own ships out to evade enemy capture.

By now the situation was near riot, as the captains tried to get from the harbour and people desperately tried to get aboard, offering coins and jewellery for passage away from Troy. One small, overladen fishing boat had already foundered under the weight of passengers and their goods taken on board by a greedy captain. Another fight aboard a ship began. The crew of a Phoenician trader and some Trojan soldiers were fighting aboard the Phoenician craft to see which vessel would leave first. Deiphobus had leaped from deck to deck to reach the ship and break up the fight.

Clemone was left with a whip to keep the slaves digging the pits for the storage jars. The disadvantage of slave labour in time of war is that a slave has nothing to lose at such a time. One captor is much the same as another. The slave may feel a change might be for the better. In the confusion a slave may escape. He may find advantage in siding with the enemy or subtly undermining his master's interests in the hope of his defeat. He may be bribed. He may be revenging himself for an injury – the injuries of servitude are many. And there is always a possibility of a slave revolt at a time of crisis. Consequently it is not unusual at such times for the masters to order the deaths of slaves.

We entered the room my mother used as an office and I saw her eyes rest speculatively on Naomi, returned from the fishmonger, who had followed me in, like a ghost. Naomi lifted her eyes to Hecuba's. What thoughts travelled between them I still do not know. Roused by the alarm from whatever nook she had been sleeping in – she was by no means the loyal attendant who sleeps across your threshold each night, nor did I want her to be – she had run to the palace and found me. She was obviously ready for orders. She had the advantage of not being surprised by this sudden overturning of the old certainties of a world at peace. In her short life she had seen more trouble than the rest of us. As she felt my mother's eyes on her she must have known she was between life and death, for in an emergency a clever slave can be more dangerous than one in whom the spark has died. Somehow, without words, if she did not assure my mother of her loyalty, she at least convinced her she would be more useful alive than dead. My mother went to her and put her hand on her head. She promised her freedom, when the Greeks were beaten. Naomi fell to her knees and thanked her.

Then my mother and I began to work. The hubbub in the palace continued. The Greeks must have been coming nearer and nearer and we both knew that before nightfall we might be defeated or under siege. There might be a battle and many deaths. Whose pyre would we be building tomorrow? Would we be conducting funerals for our dead, or leave them lying in the open, as we were led off into captivity?

Hecuba broke off from one point in her dictation, breaking the flow of my stylus as I wrote on the clay. She said bitterly, suddenly overwhelmed by the thought of what might be to come, 'You've been ready enough to alarm us for many years, Cassandra. What a pity your vision failed at the most crucial moment.'

The remark was unjust; it was foolish. But today my mother looked old. She was now a few years over forty, had married my father at the age of fifteen, taken over duties of priestess and queen and borne many children.

She was always calm and confident, but this shock invasion had taxed her sorely. The prospect of war bore heavily on the warriors, but it may have been that at this time her part of the struggle was more complex and more demanding than theirs. And she had not told me, then, that Hector had taken my young brother Polydorus to the harbour and entrusted him to a captain bound for Thrace that morning. He would be looked after by King Polymnestor of Thrace who had married one of my half-sisters. She had just sent her youngest son away from home with barely the chance to say farewell.

My mother sighed and continued with her dictation. That morning, as the Greek fleet came closer and closer to our shores, horsemen left with messages for our neighbours – to inland Phrygia, my mother's country of origin, to Paphlagonia by the Black Sea, to Macedonia, hundreds of miles off, but likely to send contingents to combat their Greek neighbours – and to all the nations and cities of the Aegean and Mediterranean coasts. Few would welcome the conquest of the wealthy regions around Troy by the Greeks. The question was whether we could impress them with the urgency of our case and persuade them that if Troy fell they might be next, as the hungry Greeks slowly devoured the whole region. Or would they do as people will, imagine we could defeat the Greeks without support or with the help of others, not themselves? Or think, even if Troy fell they would be able to accommodate their new, ferocious neighbours?

My mother, using all the subtlety at her command, had to call in old debts, make promises of future concessions, hint at marriages between her children and potential allies, finally, leaving them in no doubt of their fate if we, the most powerful city of the Aegean coastal region, a crucial spot for the Greeks to seize if they wanted to mount a full-scale attack on the mainland, were defeated, fell to our enemies.

The most important of these messages was to tell the Great King of the Hittites, Suppiluliumas, in his fortress at Hattusas that we had been attacked. We had to gain the help of this powerful ally. We wrote also to Rameses, Pharaoh of Egypt, reporting on the state of affairs.

We sent messengers on mules, in waggons, even on foot, when we dared take no more horses, to all the neighbouring farms and homesteads. We appealed for supplies and begged the farmers, if they had any care for their futures, not to trade with the Greeks and to hide what food and livestock they could from the raiding parties they were bound to send out. One such message went to Adosha's parents.

We noted on tablets the quantities of wood, oil, grain, metal and medicines in the city. I made lists, noted instructions, wrote and wrote.

My father came into the room, crying out that all his horses were being taken from the stables by messengers. Was he to fight the Greeks on foot and leave the chariots in the stables? My mother said she had only commandeered what horses she needed, but wasn't it more important to tell our neighbours what was happening and get reinforcements? Without her knowing it, as she spoke, tears flooded from her eyes, for her son, I suppose, or perhaps for all her sons, about to go into battle, or for the city – there was much to weep about on that day. My father sighed then and sat down on a stool. She recovered herself, said, as if nothing had happened, 'Are the preparations for battle made?'

'The harbour is slowly clearing. The army is

almost ready,' was all he said. Then wearily, 'Now, shall we go to the battlements to see our former guests invade our shores?'

And so they went to the ramparts, I following them, Naomi following me. The whole city was up there, men, women and children, the men in armour, or part-armour. The tradesmen, fishermen and some farmers from nearby who had heard the news had arrived with billhooks, slaughtering knives, whatever they could find. Most of the women had knives. I saw one with a child on her hip and an axe in her other hand.

The Greek fleet was still moving over a calm sea in bright sunshine, but now they were near our shores. There was little wind – they had men at the oars. From the ramparts we could make out the shapes of men, horses and chariots on deck. We could see tiny flashes of sunlight coming from bronze helmets.

In the harbour the last of our ships was struggling out. A boy was bringing five sheep across the plain to the Dardanian Gate. A thin stream of waggons and flocks, people on foot with bundles, was still coming into the city through the Scaean Gate.

There was silence on the ramparts, but for the sound of sobbing. From below came the bleat of a sheep, from the sky the cry of a bird. Otherwise, as the small ships approached, there was no sound but the steady hammering of the smith on the anvil. He and his slave could not be spared for a second, even to see the reason for their work. A ship, heavily laden with animals and people and their bundles of goods, sailed slowly round the headland out of sight. The harbour was almost empty now.

We could count the Greek ships. Fifty – the biggest

fleet any of us had ever seen. There might be as many as thirty warriors aboard each ship, with their baggage, chariots and horses – making one and a half thousand warriors, a huge army, outnumbering us by some six to one.

In the silence we all heard the two great gates of the city shut. There was the first dragging sound as they were scraped along flagstones, the thud as the two doors banged together, then, after a pause, the louder crash as four men pushed up the heavy wooden crossbar on one side and let it drop into the socket on the other. Then came a series of minor thuds as smaller bolts were shot. Always, before this, the gates had been shut at night and opened at dawn. The sound of the gates closing at night meant reassurance, that all in the city was well and would be until dawn. When we heard the gates opening at dawn, it meant a new day had come safely to us. We had never understood until now that those regular openings and closings of the gates were the sounds of a city at peace. Henceforth the gates would open and close at any time, to protect us from Greek attack, to let our men out to battle, to let them in as they fled from the enemy, to allow in supplies under heavy guard. The grating of the gates on the flagstones, the thud of the crosspiece going into its socket, would no longer mean safety but emergency or crisis. We would learn to wake up at night hearing the gates open, return to sleep, uneasy, wondering what news would greet us in the morning.

So the gates shut. I saw a straggler looking for refuge pushing a handcart towards the city. He glanced up as he heard the gates closing, panic-stricken, unable to believe it had happened. Even as the Greek ships grated in and began to drop anchor, he ran to the gates. I did not see what happened to the man or his cart. My eyes, the eyes of all, were on the ships – the gangplanks were down, the disembarkation of men, horses and baggage was beginning. On the foreshore stood a pair of tall, helmeted figures, too far away for us to be able to identify them by their features, but near enough to make out the wild red hair of Menelaus streaming from under his plumed helmet, the pale locks of his brother, Agamemnon, blowing from under a helmet crowned with bronze horns. They both looked at the city, saw us, and then, arms outspread, mimed delighted laughter. Others joined them and advanced in a line. Achilles was recognised by some, others pointed out Ajax, Nestor of Pylos, Diomedes of Tyrins. These leaders of the Greeks, and Idomeneus of Crete and Ulysses were all fully armed, carrying shields. They had jumped from their ships on to the shore of Troy and now stood on the plain, mocking us. We watched from the ramparts of our city, behind closed gates. The humiliation of this was much felt. The warriors muttered; women wailed, complained, turned to the men and cried 'Shame!' One beside me said, 'Give me a shield and a sword. What are we doing standing here watching an invasion?' Yet we all knew, in our hearts, there were too few of us to mount a successful attack on the Greeks and that an unsuccessful one might give the city and the nation to them at one swoop.

My mother's hand was on my shoulder. 'Come, Cassandra,' she said. 'We have seen it now. Let us go back to work.' The sun was high, the ships were at anchor, the Greeks were getting their supplies from the boats. Sickened, I followed Hecuba back to her office. In there the tablets of fresh clay were stacked high, the records from the storehouse lay to another side. It was cool. A fly buzzed. It felt as if nothing unusual was happening. I had known for years this was to come, yet now it had. It was so different, so extraordinary, my mind would hardly accept it.

My mother passed her hand over her eyes, leaned back in her carved chair, said, 'Now we must go to the treasure-house to make sure the record is accurate. This will be an expensive affair for the city.' She gazed at me, not seeming to be looking at all. She asked, 'Where have Paris and Helen been all this while? Shut indoors, I suppose. There will be bad feeling about Helen now. Well – we must start.' She began to read off lists to me. Later we stood down in the treasure-house, where heaps of rugs and woven hangings, the chests of clothing, the boxes of gold, jewellery and the elaborate old shields and swords all lay. There was scent of spices, of myrrh and frankincense. There was an ivory tusk from Africa in a corner. There was a big box of coins, strings of amber and lapis lazuli. We found some elaborate gold earrings and a necklace in a small ivory box. 'That was to have been part of your dowry – a surprise for you,' declared my mother.

And I said, 'I don't think I shall be wearing them now.' There was a silence. Then we began to count.

During the afternoon I went down to the lower part of the city, where I had not been all day, to intercept a messenger to my aunt, Queen of Lycia, with a forgotten request for salt. I found armed men everywhere. Even as the messenger left the gates, a contingent of men arriving from the west along the white, dusty path to the city, was spotted from the ramparts. So the gates were left open, with armed men inside and out, to protect the arriving force from Greek attack. A cry went up as they galloped in – Sarpedon, the Lycian, his brother Glaucus and some ten other warriors were there. I ran to Sarpedon, whom I knew well, and he reached down brawny arms and whisked me up into the saddle. How they had arrived so fast, after a message sent only in the early morning, I did not know. They must have mustered at great speed, then ridden like the wind from their fertile lands.

Hector arrived, having heard the cheering. He called for wine and food. We sat feasting in the temple, where the priestesses were offering a lamb in sacrifice. Sarpedon and Glaucus sat on either side of me – I felt like a girl being stolen by two bears, as in an ancient story – they were passing a wooden bowl of meat between them, over me. Both suggested to Hector that I should marry them as a reward for their assistance in the war. It was a joke, but I knew if the war extended itself, the marriages would become, like the giving of gifts and money, one more bargaining counter to ensure loyalty. If I had been under any illusions about the permanence of my own betrothal, the morning's work with my mother would have dispelled it. Everything she did spoke of urgency, desperation, crisis.

The day wore on. After the horror of the Greek arrival a surprising calm reigned. Men roamed the stalls set out in the city market. In the temple priestesses prayed and sang continually. Later, my mother would offer sacrifice. Families who had come to find shelter in the city arranged themselves and their bundles in corners of the warehouses, in the already crowded rooms of houses round about. Warriors made themselves comfortable in the temple. The market-place was full of penned sheep. There was a goat tethered to every available post. The heat seemed to mount as the blacksmith hammered on. Children cried, or laughed, or played in the dust. A small boy strutted along with a sword trailing in the dirt. There was heavy traffic in and out of the houses which offered food and lodging to travellers and everywhere was that mixture of boredom and tension we would learn to know so well. Suddenly at war, we did not know what to expect, what the next hour, let alone the next day, would bring. It was collectively, like those times when the child of a family is gravely ill. People are quiet, anxious, considerate of each other and kind to the other children of the family who do not fully understand what is happening.

The tradesmen and women were gloomy. They saw hard times ahead. The seller of fried fish, a jovial man, made a joke of it. 'Come on, soldiers, women,' he cried. 'Hurry up and buy. There'll be no fish tomorrow. I'll be frying old shoes and caps.'

'Don't worry,' Hector told him. 'They'll be gone in a week.' There was an uneasy laugh. Troy is a small city compared with others – it is no Tyre or Sidon, Babylon or Memphis, yet as it is a port and trading centre, many people come to the city from many places, bringing strange items and telling strange stories. The men of Troy are seafarers. The men and women of Troy were not naive. Few believed Hector's brave statement. The Greeks had been harrying the mainland for years, their ships had attacked even our fishermen, who had taken to going out in convoys. Now they had put aside their own quarrels to attack us with fifty ships and over a thousand hardened, fighting men. The city was besieged. No one believed Hector and perhaps he did not expect them to. He spoke to encourage.

'Well, prince,' the fish fryer responded. 'I'll believe you. But I won't kill the goat yet.' For the victory feast, he meant.

Then a woman, looking very distressed, rushed to Hector and grasped his arm. 'My child's sick. What can I do? He's burning hot.'

'Keep him away from the warriors,' Hector said grimly.

'What can I do? I can't go out to collect herbs for the fever with the enemy so close.'

'Talk to my sister,' Hector said and pushed me to her. She looked at me suspiciously. She was a countrywoman and had heard, no doubt, I was mad.

I went to see the child. The family, a man, a woman and three children, were living at the back of the forge, in a hut used for storing firewood, heaps of which now lay stacked on the ground outside. Mercifully the child was up and playing. She had been disturbed by the journey, no doubt, and other fears had made her mother think the girl sicker than she was. Nevertheless we would need to collect herbs for medicines from outside the city, under guard if necessary. We would have to do that for everything we needed – food, fuel for cooking and water. The city cisterns would soon run dry.

I went back to the palace and found my parents talking in the great hall in low voices. They were sitting opposite each other on stools, holding hands across the divide between them. I interrupted, 'I should take out women to gather herbs. But we will need guards.'

'Later,' my father said.

I trailed to the ramparts. A crowd was gathered there, watching the Greeks setting up camp. Fires had been lit. Two men were bringing in a cart with a dead cow on it. A sheep was already roasting on a spit in the middle of the camp. They were hauling trees from beside the river, cutting planks for their huts and making a corral for horses. How long would the clump of willows by the Scamander, where I had met Arvad, endure, I wondered, as their need for wood for shelter and cooking grew? I still hoped he might come back for me in autumn, as he'd promised, or earlier, seeing my danger. Yet, if he did, could I leave my family and country, when they were in such trouble? They needed me – I supposed they needed me. Yet they would blame me easily when there were defeats. As usual, when humankind is unhappy and looking for someone to blame for the misfortune, the prophet becomes the scapegoat.

The soldiers moved about, unloading cargo, riding in and out of camp. We heard the high, distant scream of a girl, some captive they had seized while reconnoitring for food and supplies. We stood silently watching the Greek force settle into camp. I thought of Adosha, wondered if she had listened to my warnings, made so long ago, and if the messenger we had sent had reached her.

We saw the small figures of soldiers on horseback bringing in a string of captives. On the ramparts women wept, some men, too. There was a council of war now in progress in the great hall, but I stayed where I was, craning to see if I recognised one of the captives. I did not. They were very far away. But someone else did for I heard a woman scream, there was a babble of words about a red scarf and a child, and someone cried out, 'Oh shame!' Next to me an old man, hands on either side of his head, rocked to and fro with the humiliation of the scene.

Then Helenus was beside me in full armour. Though tall, he was not fully grown. His thin shoulders did not fill his corselet, with its overlapping leaves of bronze. He wore greaves on his legs. He carried his helmet.

'Are we going to attack?' I asked.

He shrugged. 'I do not know.' Then he said in an undertone, 'Did you tell our mother about the tunnel in the sanctum where we used to hide?'

'I did,' I told him. 'She knew of it and plans to unblock it secretly if she can. It lets out on the hill in the woods near the cave of the oracle. It might be a chance to get water and food, carefully, when we really need them. The city's filling up. This will have to end soon. We can't hold out for long.'

He nodded. The city seldom lacked water, even in the driest weather, for there were rivers on either side. We would be unable to get water from them now, without running into Greek soldiers. Helenus' words emerged with difficulty from stiff lips. He was very frightened and trying not to show it. He whispered, 'If only you had left with the Phoenician.'

'He may come, in time,' I said. 'When word gets out what's happening. Messengers went in many directions this morning. Sarpedon and Glaucus are already here. I expect you've heard.'

'It's because of their arrival we contemplate attack,' Helenus said. 'Hector thinks we could see the enemy contingents off before they get established. This would take luck, though, and planning. Others think it better to wait for other reinforcements to arrive.'

We stared at each, of course.

I said tentatively to Helenus, in a low voice, 'Perhaps we have been wrong – all those years.'

He looked at me with little hope in his eyes. 'We have to behave as if we were wrong.'

There came the screech of one of the city gates opening to let in a fugitive, probably. Then it grated shut. Helenus and I, not knowing if tonight he would have to go into battle, gazed at each other sickly. Then he muttered, 'I must go back to the council – find out what they have decided.'

There was no battle that day, or the next, or the next. The city waited while the reinforcements arrived. Lycians came from my aunt's country, also Mysians, Phrygians and many others. The people in the city cheered as the gates opened and closed, letting in contingents of soldiers, supply waggons, refugees from the farms seeking the protection of the city. The anvil beat out its perpetual rhythm. My mother, hollow-eyed and always counting, supplied the soldiers, the refugees, the palace. The Greeks continued to make their camp, not attacking the troops of soldiers as they arrived, merely picking off refugees if they could, unless we sent men out to protect them.

We had begun to dig out the tunnel by day, because at night the sounds would be audible to Greek spies roaming round the walls under cover of darkness. Inside the sanctum priestesses prayed continually. Two old warriors posted outside guarded the spot, for the tunnel had to be kept a secret, even from our own people.

It was a strange time. The silence of the city was chilling. Women and slaves were exhausted with the preparations for war. The fighting men were keyed up, but inactive, waiting only for the watchmen to signal an approach. We all knew the conflict would be terrible when it began.

For nights the conferences went on until even the sound of the forge ceased. I sat on the floor, with many others, and was sometimes so tired I dozed, hearing the voices of the men going on and on, discussing strategy, prospects and the rest.

Now a city which had previously housed five hundred people accommodated six hundred civilians and five hundred men at arms. There were groups of soldiers, or families in all the gardens of the houses higher up the city, except for Paris' house, where it was felt to be too dangerous for Helen. There were people in every doorway. Forcing your way past soldiers down the steps into the lower city you could pause, see below, crowding the square, in every doorway, a mass of people, soldiers from all nations, in all garbs, sitting about, families in little groups, sometimes under an improvised shade made of a cloak or skirt, mothers suckling babies, fathers mending shoes, children carrying water, a seething mass of people getting in each other's way, trying to cook, eat, wash in small spaces.

Sarpedon and his Lycians, eventually numbering a hundred men, chose to camp outside the walls behind the city with their priestess (and harlot), her flute-player and her drummer, who played on a Babylonian drum. The priestess was called Vina. She was a tall woman of about thirty, who looked none the worse for being the wife of a hundred men by night and, by day, their cook and housekeeper, as well as their seer and, I imagine, friend.

We had no way of disposing of any waste, human or animal, now. This had formerly been carried from the city in waggons and put in pits we dug. Now we began to create a reeking mound beside the Scaean Gate. Excrement, the remains of the beasts we were smoking and salting and every kind of detritus was flung over the walls on to it for we could no longer spare the slaves to take waggons of refuse from the city, risking the Greeks seizing horses, waggons and slaves. Many slaves had in any case run off and no one tried to stop them.

On the third night after the Greek landing, there was another council. There were almost a hundred people in the room. My mother said if the war did not kill us, the smell and flies from the midden would drive us into surrender eventually. This mundane remark reflected her real anxiety that the war would be lost because conditions in the city became impossible. Dirt, hunger and thirst would do more damage than the enemy. No one listened. There were too many other factions, too many other points of view in the council. Some, even now, were advocating nego-tiation, not war. My father was for strong resistance. Hector, too, maintained a series of battles coming thick and fast would get rid of the Greeks. We now had enough men. Though still outnumbered, skill and courage, he said, would bring victory. 'Any soldier,' he told the council, 'fighting for his own homeland is worth two invaders.'

Anchises, ever-cautious, pointed out that we had

been at peace a long time, while the Greeks had been continually at war, with each other or abroad, and were battle-tried. In spite of our increasing readiness for war he still advocated making terms with the Greeks by a complex mixture of bribes and threats. One of the more important pieces in this game, he said nervously, was Helen, Paris' wife, who would, he said, have to be returned to her former husband as a pledge of good faith.

A surprising number of people advocated peace, even at this late stage. The merchants, with the harbour idle and the Greeks blockading the countryside and commandeering the goods of anyone foolish or ill-informed enough to try to enter the city from the landward side, saw their livelihoods at an end for the duration of the war. The fishermen and those dependent on their catches felt the same. So did many of the farmers.

On the other side were the young men, warriors, my father and many older men. 'They plan to destroy us,' Hector said bluntly. 'They always have. They have taken Miletus. They have taken Tenedos. They plan to take this whole coast. They must have Troy because without it they will never control the coast. We have bribed them away once and they have come back with an army. We must fight them now we have the men to do so.'

Anchises said, leaning on his stick to make himself look older and wiser, 'Let us again persuade them to leave. At worst they will come back next year, when we have had better time to prepare. At best they will go away and tear each other to pieces like the dogs they are. In the course of a long life I have learned that many problems are solved by doing nothing; time, not action, provides the answer. I know too that war seldom solves anything.'

My father said, 'Anchises. You and I are of an age and I know there is much in what you say. But there are some difficulties, some enemies which do not go away.'

Hector jumped in, pressing Anchises. 'If you are in the mountains to the east and a wolf runs at you, what do you do – ignore it or kill it to save your life? These Greeks are wolves. They will not leave. If we bribe them, contrive with them, make treaties with them, we only give them encouragement. They will come after us again, even stronger and more confident next time. We must tackle them now. Defeat them once and for all.'

'Spoken like a brave young man,' Anchises observed tolerantly.

Hector grew angry. 'Don't count my youth against me. Reflect, Anchises. I and my brothers – and, indeed, your own son – have grown up under the shadow of Greek piracy and their attacks on our neighbours. We have known nothing else since we were children. Our experience has always been of the Greeks coming closer, ever more threatening. And of our retreating from them. Now they have mounted an expedition against us, the biggest we have ever seen. They are outside our city, slavering for our blood and our gold. And still you suggest compromise. This fight, as I see it, will not come too soon, but almost too late. We should have seized Tenedos back from Achilles last year, before he took root there. If we do not fight now, I tell you, we will be here next year, the Greeks around the city again, stronger again, and with the confidence that comes from knowing we fear them. Your understanding of the Greeks is drawn from the time when they were not so determined to destroy us. You think that somehow those days can be brought back. I tell you, they cannot.'

His words swayed the council. Huge Sarpedon observed calmly from the stool where he sat, overwhelming it, 'We have come here with troops and supplies because you appealed to us in this terrible crisis. But if you make some accommodation with these villains you may not be able to count on such ready support the next time. The desire for peace in older men and women is valuable, preventing pointless and hot-headed acts which do no good. But any desire, yielded to over-often, can destroy a man. Here, it is not a man, but nations, which will be destroyed.'

Archos was a merchant from the town, a cornvendor, owner of two ships now sailing about cargoless and without direction under captains he was inevitably beginning to mistrust. He was the man who had suggested murdering Agamemnon and Menelaus when they came on their visit two years before. He stood up now, rapped his staff on the floor and cried, 'Whatever we do, let us get it over with. While we talk and do nothing we're being ruined. The harvest will go to the Greeks unless we clear them out by one means or another. Trade's at a standstill. The city's crammed with soldiers and paupers. In the blink of an eye we'll be digging into our reserves just to pay the cost of survival.'

Pandarus of Lycia, a merchant as well as a warrior, nodded beside him.

'For some of us,' Troilus observed, 'the price of falling to the Greeks may be less than for others.'

'What do you mean by that?' exclaimed Archos' son.

Troilus said, 'A merchant who knows his business is usually able to survive and prosper under any rule. His concern can be more with the resumption of trade than the outcome of wars or negotiation.'

Archos was now holding back his son, who was trying to attack Troilus. There were exclamations from the witnesses. Anchises said, 'Stop! What use is this?' But Archos, grasping his son's arm with one hand, spoke over Anchises' voice and said loudly, 'Let no one call me a traitor. I stand for Troy. You will recall I suggested killing the Mycenaean brothers when they came here to spy out our land, consume our goods and ask for favours. Then you told me I was a villain. What do you think now? Secretly, you'll be thinking, "Oh – if only we'd let Archos pay a couple of assassins to do the deed then." But it's too late for a knife in the back in the dark. Unless Troy makes up its mind now, ruin will come through indecision. And – yes – if the Greeks took the city I would try to preserve my trade. Who would not? Who would rather starve? Or be a slave? Only a hypocrite would say anything else.'

The talk grew more agitated, more animosities emerged, parties were formed supporting one course of action or the other. It was well into the night now. I fell asleep in a corner. I awoke when Deiphobus came in off watch, a man arriving from the fresh air in a room where others have confused themselves with long talking, and stood in his armour in the doorway saying, 'I observe we have no conclusion. The Greeks you will like to know are nicely settled in their camp on our shores. I can't see my brother

Paris here, or his wife. Have you discussed sending the woman back? That would at least get rid of their pretext for this attack.'

My father shook his head. My mother said, 'She would not agree. Nor would Paris. Honour is involved.'

Deiphobus took off his helmet, shook his head to relieve the pressure it had caused and exclaimed, 'Honour! Honour – I've watched this long, weary night, after the long, weary day we have all endured, and what I have heard is the sound of Greek dogs barking on our shores. Greek horses neighing. Snatches of song – Greeks singing songs on the shores of Troy. And I've heard something else as I watched and listened – the sound of music and laughter from Paris' house. What is he celebrating? Who are his guests? Why is he not here?' And he turned to look significantly at Anchises whose son Aeneas, not being present, might rightly have been suspected of being at the party in my brother's elegant house.

Anchises said, though he had spoken differently earlier, 'It is known that Paris would never allow Helen to leave. She will not go. She loves him and fears, I have no doubt, the wrath of Menelaus.'

Deiphobus said furiously, 'I have heard that music and laughter and so have many others in this city. Our allies, men who have come to fight for us, will have been curious about these people who feast and dance, while they are expected to go out and fight for us – for her. No doubt they will have been told who rejoices while they gird themselves up for battle – the king's son and his consort over whom the war is being fought. I wonder what they think. I am loyal to my brother, I love him, but this – ' He clenched his fists and turned his face to the ground to hide his expression. There was a silence.

'Your brother's wife,' Hector muttered defensively.

Deiphobus raised his head. 'My brother's wife,' he said softly. 'Before that, the wife of Menelaus. Before that, another man's. And after this – who knows whose wife she may become? She is a woman blessed, and cursed, by beauty which comes from no human source. I have felt it. Which of us here has not? Which of us, let us all be honest, has not in his heart envied Paris his wife?' There was a kind of shame on all the men's faces, the shame of a pointless, never-to-be-satisfied desire for another man's wife, the shame of returning home, seeing their own loyal wives and sweethearts as if they were lowly, undesirable creatures foisted on them by an unkind fate – and being ashamed of that feeling. Helen's gift to all men was shame. She carried it in every fold of her garments. It drifted from her, like dust, everywhere she went.

Deiphobus then gently said, 'We are asking other women to be widows to preserve her marriage to the Prince of Troy.'

Pandarus, a trader, so no friend of war, said delicately, 'There is perhaps a case for appealing to Paris . . .'

'To bundle his wife out of the city like a thief?' Priam said hotly.

'If he and she could be persuaded,' Pandarus suggested. 'I believe under the laughter and gaiety she is afraid – afraid of the consequences of this war, perhaps, but more afraid of Menelaus, who might, she thinks, kill her if she returned.'

'I don't believe,' Hector said, 'that the return of Helen would persuade the Greeks to go. They have achieved a rare agreement among themselves to mount a joint and costly expedition. If they return they may never get the alliance together again.'

Archos said, 'If she were returned with the gold and treasure she brought with her –'

'Much of it spent,' Hecuba said grimly, sensing that the coffers of the palace were under threat.

Pandarus bowed and said, 'Madam. Many of us would be prepared to make up the deficiency, if we could secure peace. Will you go to your son, as a mother, and discuss the matter of his wife's return to her previous husband?'

There was, as I have said, ever the case where Helen was concerned, shame and dishonour in the room. Some warriors felt their own fear, being offered the chance of escape from battle; some merchants and others recognised they were trying to evade a war for the sake of profit. My mother was being forced to ask her son to give up his wife, my father to consent to the effort by his silence.

And still there was no battle plan.

Next day a band of Greeks attacked a waggon of barley being escorted to the city by our soldiers. A young man, son of the potter, died of a spear-thrust. Fought off, the Greeks wheeled round and rode away. The body was loaded in with the barley and brought back to the city by Aeneas, cursing himself for having taken too few men with him to guard the waggon. The potter lost a son bidding to become more skilful than himself. My mother heard the news, then, heavy-hearted, she went reluctantly, without much hope of a result, to the house of Paris and Helen. To persuade Helen to leave.

It was mid-morning, but slaves were still clearing

away the remains of the party, sweeping tiles with water, removing dishes. Paris and Helen were asleep. My mother had asked a servant to fetch Paris from his bed but it was Helen who came to greet her. Hecuba then decided, she told me, to tackle her unpleasant mission directly. I realised that, queen and priestess though she was, trained, and inured, therefore, to the loss of her children, knowing from the moment they put her child into her arms after birth that she might have to sacrifice it, boy or girl, to war, dynastic marriage, even to the goddess, if it were so decreed, there was still in her much of an ordinary mother's feelings. Helen, through her escape with Paris, had put Hecuba's sons' lives at risk in battle, her daughters in danger of death or slavery. Not only her own family were endangered, of course. The trouble fell on all the Troiad, of which she was queen. She must have been angry to her very bones. But she told me later, as she stood there on the tiles of the great hall, watching the beautiful, majestic progress of the still sleep-laden Helen towards her, for a moment she was almost disarmed.

Helen put both her hands into my mother's, murmuring, 'Welcome, Madam.' She seated her, with great courtesy, and ordered wine. As ever, she charmed. Hecuba said she forgot the growing shortages, the over-crowding, the grimness of Troy, even the potter's dead son, for whom they were now building a funeral pyre behind the city. It was like a dream, she said, where one scene changes into another and the dreamer accepts it without question. On the one hand, a young man's body was being taken out behind the city to be burned. On the other, here was a beauty, smiling gently in her sumptuous palace. It was only imagining, suddenly, the mother, father, sister and brother, all known to her, crying over that still-limp body, which made her, she said, speak to Helen even as firmly as she did.

'Young Saron, the potter's son, died today,' she began.

'I grieve for him and his parents,' came the sincere response.

'A band of Greek warriors killed him to seize the waggon he was guarding,' my mother continued.

Helen said nothing.

'There will be many more such deaths,' Hecuba continued against the silence. 'Death for petty things, such as a bucket of water or a sheep, deaths in battle, deaths from starvation and sickness, for if we are besieged there will be sickness, as there always is. Your sister-in-law Creusa expects a child. I wonder if it will live?'

Helen's smile, by then, my mother said, was still in place but had become more rigid. She was not, however, going to help my mother in the direction she was going. 'One of such deaths,' my mother continued, 'might be that of your husband, my son.'

At this, my mother reported, Helen's hand flew to her mouth and she drew in her breath sharply. It seemed she could contemplate any death, any disaster, with equanimity unless it involved her lover, or, presumably, herself. My mother went on, 'A shocking thought, for both of us, but we must face facts. War is war; men die.'

'I could not live – ' said Helen. 'I could not live – '

My mother then leaned forward and told her, 'A great love – a truly great love such as you bear my son – must sometimes be served in a hard way.'

Helen burst out, 'You are asking me to return to Menelaus? To save Paris?'

'To save all of us,' Hecuba said. She added harshly, 'What do you want – Paris alive without you or Paris dead, having spent his final moments with you? That is the choice.'

Helen wept. 'The Greeks would not leave. Menelaus will kill me. He would not give me an easy death. The city can overcome the Greeks. We will vanquish them, make them go home again.' She spoke rather like a child. Then she controlled herself and stood. Her manner changed. 'Lady,' she said, 'you have come to me, the wife of your son, without his knowledge, to tell me to return to my past husband, who hates me and would kill me. What will your son think of what you have done when I tell him?'

'He ought to think his mother is trying to save his life and the lives of his brothers and many more,' said my mother, also rising. Bitterness had come into her voice. 'But he loves you so much and I don't suppose he will think that.' Now she begged, 'Will you not consider what I have said?'

'Lady – I carry his child,' said the beautiful woman standing surrounded by all signs of wealth, to my worn and anxious mother. I doubt if my mother had had more than three hours' sleep a night since the landing of the Greeks.

My mother, the priestess Hecuba, whose aspects reflected the phases of the moon, instinctively disbelieved Helen's claim to be pregnant.

Her only uncertainty was whether Helen believed it herself, or not. She was forced to congratulate her, expressing her own delight and that of the family, and then she withdrew, unhappy, disillusioned and ashamed.

Returning, straight-backed and very pale, Hecuba went instantly to her chamber. After some hours I took her food and wine. She was lying on her bed. She told me then of this interview with Helen, adding, 'Yet, perhaps she is right. She might return to Menelaus, he might kill her, and still the Greeks would not leave. If this war is a long one she will be hated by both sides in the end.'

I told her the grave news. 'Hector believes the Greeks are mustering for the attack. Our men are preparing for battle.'

She stood up. 'Then the women must prepare for casualties,' she said firmly, and we went to the temple to assemble what we would need.

As I began to walk down to the lower part of the city I met Advenor wrestling with two prancing, yoked horses and taking them down to where the chariots were kept beside the main square. He instantly sent me back for another. I dragged the reluctant beast after me as I descended, not without a glance at the barred gates of Paris' house, as I went. Hector's gates were open. Armed men lounged about under trees in the compound outside it. Hector's little son was supporting himself by clinging to the big knees of a warrior, looking up and laughing at him.

Down in the city there was the rattle of armed men moving about. The chariots were being dragged out and harnessed up, the charioteers examining the harnesses with great care. From the temple came the sound of flutes, drums and singing. A group of

Scythian bowmen had arrived and they sat in a corner, wearing their pointed hats, and trousers, curved bows cradled in their laps, staring at the scene with blank and fathomless expressions. One of them appeared to be a woman. A market man beside me spat in their direction. It appeared they had arrived just before dawn, then one of the men had grabbed a young girl sleeping in her own doorway for coolness and instantly dragged her off and raped her. They seemed to feel this was a harmless act and it had been impossible to tell them as they spoke no language we understood. In the end the girl's father had given the perpetrator an enormous thrashing with an oar, but this beating had not damaged the man as much as it should. 'He stood up, laughed, spat, and though he was covered in blood not so much as his little finger was broken,' said the market man disgustedly.

Meanwhile, there in all the confusion, I saw Paris, bare-headed, helping my half-brother Chamois calm the white horse of my nightmares, so that he, Chamois, could get it into the shafts. Then I knew Chamois was doomed. A capped Phrygian came to assist. These allies, some thirty of them, had been billeted in an old fish warehouse. They complained of the smell. Neighbours complained of their musicians playing late into the night, keeping children awake. Beside the temple a gang of twenty short men with clubs, wearing only breechclouts, were clustered round a black stone they had brought with them, in which no doubt their collective soul lay.

Buckets of water were being carried all over the place. I looked at each mug dipped by child or soldier with the dread of a miser. Why were children, horses and soldiers always so thirsty? Our cisterns would not sustain a week of this. When the fighting commenced women would have to brave the battlefields and go to the rivers for water. At that point I hated the Greeks, who fought abroad, while their own civilians – women and children, old people – were living safely at home.

Hector, my father, Sarpedon and some others stood in a corner of the square, discussing tactics. Clemone passed me with a huge bundle of torn rags, saying, 'Help us, Cassandra.' Polyxena appeared and tucked a shaking hand in mine. Helenus came and took my other hand. He bent and kissed me.

'It's not farewell, Helenus,' I told him. 'We know that.' For we would have known, surely, years before, of our own deaths and had no doubt seen our own fates and each other's.

He smiled. 'That's hard to believe at this moment.'

'You're in full armour, yet you're not with them,' I said.

'They don't want me now,' he told me. 'I grew tired of Hector shouting his dispositions, his instructions, embracing the warriors, wishing them luck and always ignoring me.' His tone dropped. 'They'll want me soon enough,' he muttered. Helenus, due to his gift, had been robbed of that surging spirit which makes a young man feel all he wants to do is fight and win, that he is immortal, only the enemy can die. He had no pride of manhood, that sense of honour and heroism which gets men into battle and keeps them there. He was already in the state all our warriors eventually came to – weary, rallying each day a courage they no longer felt they had.

A guard rushed down the street into the square and cried out, 'They're on the move!' I went to the temple. The women were arranging pallets on the ground for the reception of the wounded, and as they did so they chanted. At the altar the priestess held up a struggling white hen and cut its throat with a curved knife. The musicians played on, a long stream of music of worship, knowing that soon they would be beside the open gates, drumming and playing our men forward. There was little I could do here or anywhere now, except, by my existence, demoralise the combatants by reminding them I had predicted defeat. Helenus and I went up to the palace again. Halfway up, I gazed down. Adosha, at the gates, was tugging at an armoured boy, trying to get him out of a crowd of soldiers.

From the ramparts, we watched the gleaming lines of Greeks a thousand-strong moving forward under the sun, light glinting from their armour.

In front, blind Calchas strode in a long robe, his white hair streaming, both arms held high to the heavens. There was a boy beside him to guide him as he walked ahead of the army, uttering incantations. Behind him marched three long lines of men on foot, each line one hundred men strong. To the rear was a fourth long line of chariots. There were bowmen behind the chariots but plainly they could not be useful. They would find it hard to shoot effectively over the lines of their own men in front. More spearmen marched behind.

Polyxena's small chilly hand was in mine.

'Where's Achilles?' I asked Helenus. 'Do you know what he looks like?'

'Paris knows him and says he's not there. He's tall, very strong, like a giant and easy to pick out,' Helenus said. 'Hector's dread is that he and his Thessalians are holding back ready to come up at the last. His camp is over there.' Helenus pointed to the left. 'Where you see the plume of smoke from a fire. One of our men who has very keen eyes, says the women are washing clothes in tubs there, and cooking all manner of things, while the Myrmidians, Achilles' Thessalian troops lounge about, unarmoured, so far as he can tell. It's mysterious.'

The Greeks were within six hundred yards of the city wall. As Calchas was led away by his boy to the side of the battlefield, Agamemnon raised his long sword and yelled up at us over the sound of our battle music, 'We shall see you inside the city at nightfall.' There was a chorus of laughter and shouts from the Greeks.

'Have you come for your wife, Menelaus?' shouted one of our guards. 'Do you think she's grateful?'

Then came the grating of the gates and yelling as our own soldiers and chariots came out pell mell. The musicians stood by the gates, playing wild music. Our Scythian contingent drew up in front of the city and began firing arrows into the Greek ranks from the backs of their small horses. Then suddenly they raced to the rear of the Greek army to fire into their ranks from the back. They did enormous damage in a very short time; it was like magic. The rest was disaster. Our chariots crashed into our own foot-soldiers, a mess of men hit the left flank of the Greek troops, leaving the middle and the right unaffected so that the Greek troops were able to turn and rush in large numbers to the aid of their comrades. This left the Trojans encircled and outnumbered three to one. Meanwhile the Scythians, who had done great damage, could no longer shoot arrows into the mêlée for fear of hitting the wrong men. They had retreated to the trees by the riverside, where they sat, nudging each other like children, grinning and pointing things out, interested spectators, rather than participants. Nevertheless, the troops were fighting over the bodies of many casualties they had caused with their deadly arrows.

Hector was standing in his chariot, tackling with his sword a Greek who had leaped into it. The Greek fell. Menelaus and Troilus were standing in a mass of men, barely able to lift their swords against each other. Trojans were being forced back, slipping in blood, stumbling over dead and wounded, towards the open gates of the city.

On the ramparts we watched in horror. I saw a Greek cut the reins in Chamois' chariot, then, as the white horse broke free and bolted, the warrior was in the chariot, hacking at my half-brother like a butcher. All around me were cries and lamentations. Polyxena sobbed, 'Make them stop. Make them stop.'

'Where's Paris – where are the others?' I asked Helenus.

'Listen,' he said. The other gate was being opened and soon there came Paris, bare-headed in his chariot, Aeneas and all the rest running or galloping across the front of the walls to surround the Greeks. The Greek bowmen, in the rear, away from the fighting began to loose arrows at the Trojans encircling the mêlée, at which the Scythians as one man – and one woman, I suppose – stood up casually, jumped on their little ponies, galloped wildly behind the line of Greek archers and began intrepidly loosing off shots fast and with terrifying accuracy at them. I suppose in a few minutes these fifteen men had put paid to double that number of Greek bowmen. The remainder just took to their heels and ran back down to the Greek camp. The Scythians, once more unable to fire into the main fight, rode off, dismounted and sat down by the river again.

Paris, in the meantime, spotted the man he wanted to find. He thrust his chariot, horses rearing and slipping, into the battle and pushed through to the centre where Menelaus, red hair streaming, stood in his chariot. Around both chariots men were fighting on foot. Above the grunts and groans, the screaming of a horse wounded and thrashing on the ground, Paris, grinning horribly, yelled (we could hear it from where we stood): 'Have you come for your wife, Menelaus?'

They told us, Menelaus replied, 'I'll fight you for her. Then when you're dead, the rest of you.'

Paris reared his spear arm back.

'Put on a helmet,' yelled Menelaus, raising his shield.

'I prefer the sun,' shouted Paris, looking up deceptively and, as Menelaus' eye automatically followed his, he hurled his spear. It caught Menelaus in the right shoulder, stuck, then fell. Menelaus raised his left arm and hurled his spear, which missed Paris, then both men jumped from their chariots and were lost in the mêlée. Apparently they fought on foot with swords until Menelaus, attempting to bring his weapon down on Paris' bare head, had it wrenched from his hand by Troilus, even then fighting off the onslaught of the mighty Ajax, a terrifyingly huge man, hairy as a bear – but, they said, slow, so often a nimble man could evade his massive sword-blows. After that Paris threw away his sword, also, and the two men, both husbands of Helen, grappled in the dust and blood on the ground among the fighting men, like brothers who have fallen out over a puppy. The Trojan ring closed in, became engulfed in the fighting. That was when Helenus left me, running off shouting, 'I am needed now.'

Meanwhile, from where the rest of us stood it was hard to comprehend anything in the mass of struggling bodies. Here, suddenly, a corpse was being stripped of its armour by a Greek – then the Greek was felled by the blow of a club. Here was the shocked look on a young man's face as a blow from tall Agamemnon struck him. He did not know, as we did, that it had gone right through his helmet and split his skull. The blood was pouring from his helmet. He put his hand to his wet cheek, looked blankly at his fingers, red with blood, then fell dead. I saw the Greek, Diomedes, his expression a fierce grimace, stripping a Trojan body of its armour in the throng, rising, a helmet in one hand, to fell an attacker with one sword-blow. The squat mountain men in their breech-clouts only, who had embarrassed the Trojans and been mocked by the oncoming Greeks, were leaping away from swordsmen with uncanny speed, dodging in and out of the fighting men, bringing down their clubs on the enemy. In close fighting a club can be just as effective a weapon as a well-wrought sword, and a helmet is no protection against a heavy blow. I watched one rescue huge Sarpedon, toe to toe with an equally big Greek, by reaching up and bringing the Greek down with a mighty thwack on the head. Sarpedon then finished him with his sword, as he lay on the ground. I saw a horse trample a felled man; heard the screams and groans of men and horses; saw Hector and Nestor fighting hand to hand.

Then Agamemnon, all streaked with blood,

climbed on to his chariot, shouted for a retreat, and charged through the men, his horse bleeding from a neck wound, followed by the others, who broke from the battle and, fighting all the way, retreated to their ships. Even as the troops fought back towards the sea, Trojan women ran out to fetch in the dead and wounded from outside the city gate. Others ran for water, with backward looks at those bent over the prone bodies.

Then, there was Adosha, standing beside me with her baby, Hector's child, in her arms.

'I saw you below urging Vanno not to fight. Why have you come here?' I asked her urgently. 'I told you to hide. Go back to the country.'

'My husband's here,' she said. 'And two of my brothers. I saw Vanno fall under Menelaus' chariot.'

'It's too cruel, standing here,' I said. 'Watching, unable to do anything. But you must return – your parents need you. Save yourself and the boy.'

'You don't know what it's like out there now the Greeks have come,' she told me, bitter that I did not understand. 'We dug grain pits in the woods, but they burned my father's feet over the fire until he told them where they were. They took all we had until harvest, and two pieces of silver we had hidden. They took the horse. It's only a matter of time before they come back for the rest. They always suspect you have more. They punish. They rape. They kill. Troy's our only hope now. We had to come. To protect the city and ourselves.'

I said desperately, 'Adosha – you reared Helenus and me. You heard all our nightmares. Now they've come true. Leave – go anywhere.'

But she said with a shrug, 'Even Greeks can be beaten.'

I looked into the eyes of my brother's child and thought, poor baby.

The tally was fifty of our men dead, five mortally wounded, eleven more standing a chance, good or bad, of recovery. We left the Greek dead where they were. The groans of the wounded and dying we ignored as our own sick men required our attention. Later, under cover of darkness, the Greeks would come to our walls and take away their men. At that time we allowed them to collect their dead and wounded. Later we became ruthless and killed their injured as they lay among the dead. We slew their helpless men and they killed ours. However we always allowed the dead to be taken away for a pious burial. War makes villains and hypocrites of us all.

The little men with clubs had lost seven of their number. They carried their dead off up the hill behind Troy and, on the evidence of a boy scouting about at the time, they ate them. Encamped there in their hidden spot, they came out to battle with the Greeks over and over again. Later, when there were only three of them left, they disappeared, loaded down with captured armour and Greek necklets, and were never seen again.

Paris came back into the city covered with blood, a hank of red hair in his hand. Apparently he went to his house and flung himself on to Helen's bed. She had taken poppy-juice as soon as he went off to battle. Waking from her drugged dreams she saw the hair and shrieked, 'Is he dead?' Paris' comrade who had followed him, blind with fatigue, into the bedroom, not understanding where he was going, recounted later that he hardly knew from her voice whether she was pleased at the prospect of Menelaus' death or frightened by it.

Adosha was running round the city looking for her brother Vanno. She had seen him in his over-large armour falling under Menelaus' chariot wheels. He was not in Troy. Now she thought him dead – alive, captured – then dead again. He was alive of course, a slave. The bright youth was to be snuffed out, to be replaced by the beaten man.

Below, the city tried to patch itself together, help the wounded, prepare the dead, while in the palace the great hall was full of men just out of their armour, some not even washed. Arms and legs were bandaged, sometimes only with rags, faces were cut and bruised and all were exhausted. But there was an air of grim triumph – the first battle, and we had seen the Greeks run! The hall reeked of smoke and sweat and the smell of cooking meat. Clemone and I were turning two sheep on the spit in the fireplace, for fighting men must eat. My mother had taken most of the slaves to attend the wounded or cut wood for the funeral pyres which would be lit on the plain behind the city at dawn.

Helenus was by the fire polishing a breastplate. He turned it over. There was a long streak of blood inside. 'I stripped it from the man I killed,' he told me.

'I had guessed,' I replied.

'We beat them,' he boasted. 'Did you see them run? Hector says tomorrow will finish it.'

My brother Troilus clapped him on the shoulder and gave him his goblet of wine. Paris – was dancing!

There was a laugh from a group of three men, one with a splinted leg, one with a bandaged head. The other had blood, not his own, spattered up his legs, to the knees.

I thought, Helenus is my twin; he is too young for all this; he knows better than to say this will be over tomorrow – he has spent his childhood fearing this war and knowing the outcome. But I cut him a slice of cooked meat from the outside of the sheep which we were turning and said only, 'Eat – a warrior must eat.' It broke my heart to see him wolf it down. Aeneas sat staring into space, reliving the battle in his head. Hector was looking grim, Paris stopped his dance. His eyes darting strangely round the room, he said, 'Well, men. I shall kill the bastard Menelaus, tomorrow.' There was a cheer.

'The meat's nearly ready,' said Clemone, my sister. 'And the men are looking at you strangely. The prophecies. Helenus is all right – he's fighting. But you'd better go. They'll feel better if you, who have prophesied defeat so often, aren't here.' It was a cruel comment but true. I went despondently and alone to the battlements. I looked down at the Greek camp. Their fires were all alight and there were cries, and the distant hammering of their anvil, as the smith repaired battered and broken armour. I wandered the darkened ramparts, the scenes of battle replaying themselves in my head.

And so the summer wore on. There were more battles, more deaths. Our men grew wearier, more determined, battle-hardened. The city became near-unworkable, full of soldiers and refugees and filth, short of supplies of every kind. The midden mounted, and stank. Women were killed getting water. The plain below the city became baked earth. No blade of grass was left by trampling feet. The trees around the rivers, the copses everywhere were cut down by both sides for firewood to cook with and keep the anvils going. And the funeral pyres. Almost every evening the darkness was lit by them. They burned from dusk to dawn. Nearly every dusk they were rekindled to burn more corpses. Everyone grew thinner. Thin children played at war, death and injury. Advenor broke his heart when we began to eat horses from the stables. Our barley and oil were now being measured out by the cupful. The levels of the big storage jars in the palace were dropping.

When the reply came to our message asking for reinforcements from Hattusas, the Great King's answer was disappointing. He could spare no troops he said, and held out no promise that he would help us later on. This was bitter news. We clung on, hoping of course that our enemies would give up and go home before the winter storms began. Anchises was certain of this. 'They will not stay,' he assured us. 'They have the harvest to get in, their ceremonies to conduct at home. The princes must return to keep order on their estates, which are being run by youths and women. They must conduct their spring ceremonies and plant – then they may return.'

Hector said, 'They may decide to forego all that, let their land go to rack and ruin, their wives turn unfaithful and their slaves run off, in the hopes of capturing this city, with its wealth, its harbour, the command of the trade routes through the Taurus to

Assyria and Babylonia. And as for their women,' he added, 'perhaps they would rather have ours.'

There was a silence in the council. All thought of their own womenfolk, then their minds turned to Helen, Paris' fatal bride, our unwanted guest. There must have been a hundred weary men, some injured, in the torchlit hall, all thinking of this one woman. For months now she had barely been seen. She was unable to leave her house, which had become for her a kind of gilded prison. If she left her gates men spat on the ground as she passed and women hissed, 'Murderess!'

TWENTY

Thessaly

W<small>E WERE</small> two women, past youth, sitting at a dying fire. A dawn wind was getting up outside, blowing inland from the sea.

'They call it the city of gold,' Helen had reported, speaking of her son-in-law's kingdom, Mycenae.

'Gold', 'murderess', 'gold', 'murderess' went the words in my head. I threw another log on the fire but, defying the laws of hospitality, said, 'It's late. I must retire soon. I keep country hours here.' 'Gold', 'murderess', 'gold' – I heard. The impact of so many memories so suddenly aroused had worn me out. I did not need to sleep, but I needed to be alone, out of Helen's presence, to think.

I asked hypocritically, for I did not care, 'Are your son and daughter well?' I neither loved nor hated them, though I had reason to fear them. Who, with less cause, would not fear the children of parents such as theirs? Orestes, the king, was Agamemnon's child – and Clytemnestra's – and Hermione, his wife, was the daughter of Menelaus – and Helen. Two brothers had married two sisters – the children had then married each other, a cousin marriage. To inbreed, in such a family! If they had been animals any stockman would have destroyed them before he permitted it.

I remembered Orestes, mad, naked, foaming at the mouth, running over our hillsides, with the men of the neighbourhood chasing him with sickles, old swords, wooden clubs, bent on catching and killing this dangerous madman. I didn't know who he was then. I had opened my stable door for him so he could go inside. When they came to ask if I'd seen him, I lied and swore I'd seen him take the perilous path down the cliff to the sea. I didn't tell Helen that. I doubt if Orestes remembered what happened.

Helen told me, stiffly, the king and queen of Mycenae were well. It appeared to me there was a difficulty, or worse, between herself and her son-in-law and daughter. I had the strongest instinct that soon Orestes would die. That would end the horrid line of Pelops, who had fathered Atreus, who had in turn fathered the dreadful Agamemnon and Menelaus, and whose other son had fathered Aegisthus, Clytemnestra's lover, the man who had cuckolded and assisted in the death of his cousin Agamemnon. That whole line of bloody, violent, incestuous men and women, killers of anyone who stood in their way, was due to end, not before time. Those people killed as easily inside their own families as outside. A streak of madness ran in their blood. Perhaps I had felt some pity for poor Orestes, while he was raving, but I had none for him now he was sane and sitting on his father's throne at Mycenae.

The logs burned up, casting light into my quiet room. Helen looked about her, then back at the fire. 'I envy you your peace of mind, your quiet life,' she said. She feared her own future. She had denied my prophecies, but she was afraid anyway.

After a pause, she said in a melancholy tone, 'What

we have seen – Oh, what we have seen, Cassandra! I shall never forget that winter of siege in Troy – the hunger, the smell – and how I was treated.'

I said brusquely, 'I'm tired. I must rest. Forgive me,' and left her sitting alone by the fireside. As I walked out I heard her silently crying out to me, 'Don't leave me. Don't leave me alone.' Perhaps she had never had any idea of herself except as an object of love to others. If she was alone, unloved, she felt she did not exist; solitude was to her like death. But I went to my room.

Naomi was there soon after me. 'What are you going to do? She must go. Have you told her she must leave? Will she betray us to her son-in-law – or Menelaus?'

I shook my head. 'She's not interested in anyone but herself. She's worried that Menelaus will die and without his protection the Greeks will take vengeance on her. They won't have forgotten. The widows and orphans, the men crippled in that war – they'll remember. If she were as beautiful as before she could find another protector. But not now – and I believe her son-in-law and daughter have rejected her. They don't want her in Mycenae. Perhaps Orestes fears for his throne. He won't take in Helen whom so many people hate, so she's searching for a new king to save her. She must be a queen.'

'I know that well,' Naomi interrupted, 'and if I had a king, I would give him to her myself to get rid of her. If only you had told her that a new princely lover awaited her, instead of prophesying her future as a beggar and outcast – if you'd told her a wonderful, new life lay ahead, she'd have been off at dawn tomorrow.' She stared at me fiercely. 'I've been talking to her menservants. They have no orders. They've been at Pylos. They've been in Mycenae, they've been over the mountains in the Epirus with your brother. They're wondering when she'll turn for home. They say, the two Spartans among them, she's running from Menelaus; he's mad and may kill her. They're frightened for themselves. Supposing he follows her and finds her here? Do you want to see Menelaus at your door?'

She stared at me angrily. I could not reply.

'If she doesn't go soon, we'll be snowed in together – you, me and Helen. What a prospect. Just looking at her makes me feel mad. What memories doesn't it bring back, all too much to bear. She's a danger to us. You should kill her before she leaves here. I hope you sleep tonight. I won't.' Naomi departed then, with a threatening look. She was herself planning to leave, I know. Helen's presence was a threat to her, as well as me. The doings of the mighty often involve the deaths of slaves and servants.

It was not fear, though, which kept me awake that night, or even the sensation of having this alien visitor under my roof. Some might say, to avenge my family and cause them to rejoice among the summer fields and hills where they were now united, I should have taken a knife and killed Helen. But how could I, seeing a wretched future for her, deliver the blow which would set her free? And her fate was set. No one could do anything about it. What prevented me from sleeping that night were memories of that autumn and winter when the Greeks did not go home and the siege deepened – and I took the long journey east to Hattusas.

TWENTY-ONE

Troy, Autumn

WE WERE hungry that autumn – fishermen could not go out to fish the coast, which was patrolled by Greeks. We could not reap the harvest we had planted. Farmers were robbed to feed the Greek army. Any supplies coming in were liable to be seized before they reached the gates. Only the courage of our countrymen, facing all dangers to reach us, saved us from complete starvation. We endured, waiting for the tunnel from the temple to the hills to be dug out. We would be able to make sparing use of it then, so long as the Greeks did not spot it.

There were now over fifteen hundred people in the city. Our stores were dwindling. My mother added to her duties by going, each day, to supervise a dole of flour and oil to citizens and soldiers. Meat on the whole went to the soldiers; the children gnawed on the bones. Each day there were skirmishes. Because it had begun to rain the troops often fought in mud on that naked plain between the city and the sea, once a pasture of tall grass filled with our sheep and horses. We were worn with hunger and grief. At night the anvil played its one constant tune, and the soldiers sang.

At the house of Paris a kind of frenzy reigned. The

music was louder, so was the laughter, but it had an edge of hysteria. The citizens hated Helen. Now they began to hate Paris, once their hero.

Yet another conference took place. Oh, the weariness of these meetings, analysis of the battle before, strategy and calculation. At first, after victorious battles, there was a kind of exultation in the air, jokes were swapped, men laughed, the defeat of the Greeks seemed near. Now they were growing tired, there had been too many deaths, the war had gone on too long.

This new conference took place one afternoon, the room, as ever, crammed with soldiers, some still in armour. That day the Greeks had chased our troops back to Troy. Now they were laughing not far from our walls. They cat-called and made obscene gestures if they saw a woman. Sarpedon, the huge Lycian captain, was furious. He turned on Hector: 'Where were you? I was cut off, with four men, facing Diomedes and his followers. We barely escaped – had to turn and run like boys caught robbing a neighbour's fig tree. I looked behind me and saw Diomedes, leaning on his sword, laughing at me.'

Hector said, 'I was surrounded.'

'Not that I saw.'

'We were attacked when they saw we would go to your aid.'

Sarpedon sighed. 'Maybe, maybe. It was a disgrace, though.' He looked round sharply. 'Where's Paris? He should be here.'

Aeneas answered for his friend, 'Nursing a blow on the shoulder from a man of Rhodes.'

'Well, I've been talking to my men, and we want Helen to go back to her husband,' Sarpedon said bluntly. He was no diplomat. 'You're his friend – you go there to drink his wine and dance to his music. Tell her. Tell her to go.'

Aeneas flinched, but said nothing.

'My brother is her husband,' announced Hector, with dignity, disliking Sarpedon's tone.

Sarpedon gave a crude laugh. Hector's ready temper began to rise. Meanwhile my father and Anchises were arguing tactics. Archos, the merchant, was suggesting abandoning the city silently by night and fighting a guerrilla war in the countryside. 'We're pinned down,' he said. 'It's against nature to wage war like this.'

We had all grieved when it was plain the Greeks were prepared to winter in Troy, almost despaired when it became plain that the Hittite Great King was prepared to consider himself neutral, sending no reinforcements to us. Now the war was static and views about how to change the situation many and various.

At that point a woman, a corn merchant from the town, came in. She shouted, 'Hear me! Hear me!' A mixture of authority and demand in her tone silenced the mumbling discussions. A rough ring formed round her, though my father, mother and Anchises did not move from their seats. Archos craned over their shoulders. The woman, Rhoda, addressed the crowd. She said, 'We've had enough. We're starving. People keep flooding in to take what little food there is. My daughter's child died last night. There's no trade. Our savings are gone. It's all right for you, the warriors. You who have money and land behind you, who fight for glory. What happens to us, starving slowly, watching our sons die in your battles, our babies die of hunger? What's next, do you suppose? I'll tell you – disease. We have famine here. Disease follows famine as night follows day. What shall we do then? I tell you – give up the city before there's no one left to defend it. Make terms. The Greeks will let us live if we give in.'

The crowd began to hurl insults at her. Deiphobus shouted, 'So you'd give in to them, would you?'

'Yes, I would,' the woman bawled back. 'I've got a granddaughter to bury. She won't be the last of my family I bury, if this goes on. Unless I die first. Who cares about surrender? Negotiate – life's what matters, not victory, not at this price.'

'Silly woman – why don't you leave the city?' someone called.

'And get captured and taken to Greece as a slave?' she shouted back.

'If we give up the city that'll happen anyway.'

'Oh no,' Rhoda shouted. 'Oh no. Not to me. I'm a skilled woman. The Greeks would need me to sell corn, mill and bake. All men need bread, believe me.'

My mother stepped forward and took her by the arm. She said something quietly to her, which appeared to calm the woman. I was swaying by the fire. I heard my voice, my prophetic voice, start to speak. 'I see the mountains,' was what I heard myself say. Others heard the rest. Then the familiar cold and blackness engulfed me.

I awoke with Polyxena bending over me, bathing my face. Rhoda, her face stiff with horror, was nevertheless chafing my hands. As my eyes rolled round I saw a ring of faces round me. My eye caught a young man still wearing a dusty helmet, a bearded old man, his narrow eyes hostile. And Hector, impatient and furious. Polyxena was hauling me to my feet, Rhoda was on my other side. They helped me from the room and laid me outside on the flagstones.

Aeneas was bending over me. 'Idiot,' he hissed. 'Can't you control your fits?' He looked at Polyxena. 'Can't she control these fits? Do we have to be subjected to this at such a time?'

Polyxena said in a low voice, 'It is a gift.'

'No doubt,' he said, 'but not one we need at present. This shouting, roaring about defeat – visions, pictures of the city in flames – what good is it?' He turned. I heard his rapid pace away from me.

I asked, 'What did I say?'

'The usual thing,' Polyxena answered. She was trying to be kind, in spite of herself. It was plain I'd horrified the assembly – interrupted a council of war with terrifying visions of defeat. My own head was full of images of fire, soldiers rampaging through the dark streets, the screams of the wounded, blood running over the stones. I was desolate. I closed my eyes, my head swimming. I would have to go away. What use was I?

I heard Rhoda saying, 'She told us what we feared to hear.'

Polyxena was twelve years old. She muttered, 'Lies and nonsense. And you should not be talking of surrender, either.'

'You're just a girl,' scolded the woman, 'carried away by talk of fighting and victory.' Then she, too, went away.

'Leave me alone, Polyxena,' I asked, and she did. I stumbled to my feet, went to the city walls and leaned across. It was dusk. A cool breeze blew. Below, at the shining edge of the sea, lay the Greek fleet. By the ships, the Greek army was lighting fires.

Small figures moved to and fro. Sounds came to me, a horse's whinny, a shout. At this time of day before the war, our ships would have been coming calmly over the waves into harbour, while below the city walls horses and sheep would have been standing in the grass as the light faded.

My mother came up to me. 'They've found another spy in the town,' she said; and even as she spoke I heard screams, then a silence.

'What have they done?'

'Cut out his tongue.'

The big beam across the gates was flung back, the gates scraped open, there was a shout, then they closed. A small figure below began a lurching run, down to the Greek lines. The figure weaved a hundred yards or so with buckling knees, then fell and lay writhing on the ground.

'The tunnel's nearly finished,' Hecuba told me. 'It goes a quarter of a mile in the direction of the hills. If we use it carefully we can get in supplies by night, perhaps send out small raiding parties to surprise the enemy.'

'Good news,' I said. Then, pausing, I told her, 'Mother, I remember speaking of the hills just now, before I lost my sense of what I was saying. I think it was a message that I should go to the Great King at Hattusas and ask for his help. We have had his message that no reinforcements will be sent. We fear he has agreed with the Greeks to support neither side in this war. But we're weakening and breaking up. Someone must go and persuade him that if he lets Troy fall, sooner or later he'll have to face the Greeks himself, when they attack him. Someone must tell the

Great King what is happening here, appeal to him in the name of our old friendship. You know this.'

She nodded. 'Suppiluliumas, unlike his father, is not a wise man. He's heavily pressed. He relies on us to repel the Greeks alone. The decision is short-sighted, disloyal. He might be persuaded.'

'I should go,' I said. 'You cannot spare a single man who can bear arms.'

She had known I would say that. She sighed. She was very weary, I knew.

'And,' I added, 'if my visions persist I'm likely to become almost as unpopular as Helen – people are beginning to reject even Paris. They'll begin to falter if they see Paris as a destroyer while I – I become a voice eternally crying defeat. They must stand by the royal house. I will be better out of the city.' What I said was true. It was also true that I could not bear the wounds and the deaths any longer, or the constant, lowering hunger, the exhaustion, the imprisonment in the city. It was not that I wanted to risk my life, just that the price of keeping it seemed too high.

'It's a long and dangerous journey to take when all the while your visions tell you the war is lost to us whatever you do.'

'Perhaps it's our only chance.'

She nodded. 'Wait until the tunnel's open – you can be the first person through. Someone will have to go with you.'

'Naomi.'

'You need a better escort than that.'

'We can't travel in state. The Greeks are all over the countryside. And you can spare no men. Give me that half-Hittite slave Advenor employs in the stables. He'll know the country. We'll promise him release if we get there. But I must go soon or the snows will come and I'll be stranded in Hattusas until spring.'

My mother looked at me sadly.

'Your sons face death daily. The whole city faces death if we lose the war,' I told her.

'I know,' she said. 'That is why I cannot dissuade you. You must go.'

The distance from Troy to Suppiluliumas' high capital is six hundred miles or so as the crow flies, but the traveller setting out from Troy at that time would normally strike south and follow the route along the coast before turning east to penetrate the mountainous areas of the Hittite kingdom. This makes the journey longer but easier, and safer, since the first hundred miles of the journey is, or used to be, through friendly country. The rest of the journey is along the caravan route leading through Hattusas and right to the Taurus mountains. It is protected all the way by Hittite forces. We would take the longer route – Naomi, I and the slave, whose name, so far as we could make it out, was Nisintas. Naomi protested when told he was to be our only bodyguard. She knew him. 'You can't understand what he says, but that's deliberate, in my opinion. He mutters and stumbles in his speech because he doesn't want to speak to anyone. He sulks. His only virtue is that he's a hulking brute and that could turn against us. An offer of freedom when we reach Hattusas may seem less certain to him than hitting us over the head in some remote spot before we get there. Or he could just run away, leaving us with no bodyguard.'

I told her we could not make the party any larger.

With the countryside full of Greek patrols, my only hope was, at each step of the journey, to pretend to be a young woman accompanied by two slaves, going a short distance to visit her family. Any suggestion that I was King Priam's daughter would endanger us all. The Greeks would give a good price for me. And no troops could be spared to guard us.

Naomi was not satisfied. 'Once we're up in those mountains, he could sell us,' Naomi told me. 'You haven't been a slave. I have. I am.'

'You and he could form an alliance and hold me to ransom,' I told her.

'How can you say that?'

'No one else can be spared,' I repeated. 'Even this Nisintas is needed in Troy because of his strength. Naomi,' I said emphatically, 'it is not right for you to argue with me. I am your mistress. You are a slave. And if I can't persuade the Great King to help us, we will all be slaves. Do you understand?'

'Yes, Madam,' she said, in no pleasant or subservient way. She knew we could die on the journey, one way or another; she was angry; she knew I needed her. Politeness was not her first concern.

Thus we set out, the first people to go through the newly-opened tunnel, walking often at a crouch and in silence, because we were not sure how much could be heard through the ground over our heads, fearing any sound might carry up to a party of Greeks patrolling the darkened countryside. The air was thick and damp-smelling as we stumbled along, dreading that at any moment the roof of this untried tunnel might give way.

Nisintas carried torches. Hecuba, my mother, came with us. My aunt, Queen of Lycia, was to meet her at the other end of the tunnel, with her famous champion, an African, big as a giant, who could fight two men at the same time. My aunt also brought money. Our funds were running low for we had no income through trade or taxes. We were now fighting our battle on behalf of all the coastal regions, and for the inland nations too. If the Greeks took Troy, the whole region would belong to them. This, aside from family feeling, was why the Queen of Lycia came in person with money and her famous warrior. They would set him at Agamemnon, in particular, hoping that if the leader were killed the alliance would crumble.

We emerged gratefully on the hillside, pushing concealing brushwood away from the opening, climbing out, breathing in the night air. We were concealed by a clump of trees – oak, larch and wild fig. Through the branches we could see a sky full of stars. It was strange to breathe the clean air of the countryside, after the crowded, stinking city. A startled bird woke and began to sing. In the shadows among the trees stood my aunt, the huge African, Veribel, and the oracle herself, bent, in a red robe, her face painted white. It was an awe-inspiring sight. My aunt was so like my mother they might have been twins; the tall, black-faced man's countenance was barely visible in the darkness; the oracle was tiny and bent, her face a white mask. My aunt stepped forward and embraced first my mother, then me. She had consulted the oracle before we arrived. 'Good omens for the journey,' she whispered. Nisintas was scrutinising the African. He must seldom have seen anyone so dark, or so much more powerful than himself. There was little time for speech. If a Greek patrol caught us they would have had a notable prize – two enemy queens, the Trojan oracle, a princess and two prime fighting men.

The oracle came to me. She knew I dreaded her. She whispered, in that strange, man-woman voice, 'You will return – but you already know you will.'

Then, with no backward glances, we set off to the left, heading for the coast road, which we found not long after. We walked half the length of the straits which lay on our left, hearing the waves on one side, the stirring in the forest on the other. We each had a bundle of clothes and food. Nisintas had a big club also. We were moved by the quiet after the noisy crowded city; the air seemed very fresh. As to the rest, I think we all knew we might die on the journey but had lived with the thought of death for so long now that it made little difference. In any case Naomi and Nisintas had been slaves since their youth and their lives had never been worth anything at all.

Dawn came up over the wooded hills on our right. When it was full light we stopped just outside a fishing village. Nisintas went ahead to be sure there were no Greeks there. Then we entered the main street. There were huts and small stone buildings on one side. The sea, and the shore where boats were beached lay on the other. Clear dawn light fell on an empty village. It was very quiet. All the doors of the low houses were shut. There was no one round the boats, no women washing clothes in the washing troughs, or carrying water, no children coming out to begin their day. We stood there, looking for a human face, when a door opened and out came a small, self-important man, barefoot in a robe with a pointed Phrygian cap on his head. This he seemed to wear as a mark of rank. In a bad Greek accent he said, 'Welcome.'

I spoke to him in the language of the country people, saying, 'I have left Troy because of the war, to join my mother's family among the Phrygians. These are my servants. We could not buy horses before leaving. They were all needed for the war. Do you know of anyone who has horses, mules or a waggon for sale?'

He had a crafty air. I did not like him. He did not trust me. He told me, 'The Greeks took the horses a month ago.' It was impossible to tell if they had, or if the village had hidden what animals they had.

'We would pay a good price,' I added. Our journey would take us a month on foot. If we took too long and if the snows came early in the high fortress city of Hattusas, we might be cut off there till spring. He regarded me cautiously.

'Your servants?' he enquired, looking at Nisintas and Naomi.

'Yes,' I replied. I knew he wanted me to identify myself, but I dared not. He could have been a friend of the Greeks, either bribed, or just a man who preferred to stay friendly with the strong. 'Look,' I said, 'these are dangerous times. We need to be mounted.'

'You speak our language,' he said.

'Evidently. Can you help?'

Then a young woman ran out of the poor house from which he had come. She bowed deeply to me and whispered to the older man. I thought she had recognised me. If the short man, her father, chose to call out and get help in capturing me, we would be in serious trouble. Behind me, Naomi was muttering to Nisintas, who stepped forward, ready for a fight. But the man bowed and said, 'Lady, we have two horses left, both broken-down animals, too poor for the Greeks to bother with. You can have them for a price. I would give them, but times are hard now. Buy them, mount up and get away as fast as you can. Greek patrols and foraging parties come here regularly.'

So we got two mounts, an old horse and a mare with cracked hooves. We plodded out of the village. By now a small crowd had assembled. In more formal times, I would have ridden one horse, Naomi and Nisintas the other, but to put too much weight on one of these sad beasts so I could ride alone would have been folly. Nisintas rode the mare; Naomi and I got up on the horse. And so we travelled on.

There was another village further up the coast, but it was burned out, and by the signs of it, only days before. We had all seen the Greeks riding out in the mornings and returning at night with their booty – a sheep, a girl, a boy, a load of hay for their horses. Here was the reality of their expeditions – the low stone houses, more like caves with their roofs gone, the stones blackened, the population dead or fled, the narrow street empty of all life.

As midday approached we became more wary and headed uphill into the trees, found a place near the river running seawards, ate and fell asleep. The horses grazed nearby. We woke near dusk, with the sun slanting through the trees above us. It seemed very strange to come from sleep and find myself on a hill with Naomi sleeping nearby, her head on her pack and big Nisintas sitting blinking about suspiciously, his club across his knees. I said, 'There'll be a moon. We should travel by night until we're almost out of

277

the river-country, in case we meet a Greek patrol or are recognised and sold to them as captives.'

The country people, farmers and fisherfolk, were mostly on our side, but they and their families had to live in these disturbed times. If it was between betraying us or seeing their village burned and people killed, what would they do? It was better to travel by night when the Greeks, fearing ambush in a countryside unfamiliar to them, always returned to camp.

We built a small fire to warm ourselves, for though it was still hot in the daytime, the evenings were colder. I sat, thinking little, except of the journey ahead, while Naomi talked to Nisintas. Under pressure from her he seemed to be speaking more fluently. Evidently he had gained a grasp of the demotic speech of Troy during his years of slavery. His silence was, as Naomi had told me, only because he preferred it to be thought he could not speak or understand. Naomi, who found it impossible to endure life if not in communication with those about her, was talking incessantly and asking him questions. I began to pay attention to their conversation. It wasn't very reassuring. To begin with, Nisintas was no more a Hittite than I was, nor had Hattusas been his home – which meant the promise of release from slavery when we arrived was no very strong inducement. It emerged the big slave was the son of a Babylonian woman who had abandoned him to his father, an Assyrian merchant. This man traded to and fro between Assyria and Hattusas across the Taurus range far to the east. Nisintas had certainly been in Hattusas and had links there. He'd been captured ten years ago by mountain brigands, who had attacked his father's caravan, killed the father and sold the son off to a man buying slaves for the Hittite iron mines – even at that age Nisintas must have looked strong. Then somehow he'd been sold again to a farmer on the plains between Hattusas and the sea. The farmer had a sideline as an ironsmith in winter, so for a few years Nisintas had been a farm labourer in summer and an apprentice at the forge in winter.

By this stage, eavesdropping on what the two slaves were saying, I had become fascinated – also appalled. Here was a slave who, by his own account, understood metal-work and no one in Troy in time of war knew this. He'd been sweeping out stables and lifting bales of hay for years.

He described the business of a forge – iron requires brick-lined furnaces and rapid work with the boiling metal and also demands higher temperatures and more work than bronze. He showed Naomi a horrid pit six inches long on his arm, where the hot metal had stuck. 'Nearly lost my right arm,' he said gloomily. It was apparently while he was an invalid that he had begun a relationship with the youngest daughter of the farmer. When the outraged farmer discovered his daughter sleeping with a slave, he sold him off in the slave market at Hattusas. From there he had been brought to Troy in a caravan and sold again.

At this point Nisintas began to complain about Advenor, the guardian of our horses. Naomi interrupted by asking, 'If you hated horses why didn't you say you knew about working in metal?'

He gave her his glum look and responded, 'Why should a slave say anything? There's nothing in speech, for a slave.'

When we set off again, in darkness, down the hill and back to our route, I knew Nisintas had no special interest in being freed in Hattusas. There were no friends and family to greet him. He was with me under compulsion and as Naomi said, if it seemed a good idea to kill us, or sell us, or run off, he could easily do so. His frame of mind was unguessable now and, I suspected, always would be, to me at any rate. He was a slave and usually a slave can only be understood by another slave.

So we went slowly along the coast, on our bad horses, clopping by night through quiet hamlets, where dogs barked, sleeping in caves or under trees during the day. I awoke one day and from the bushes in which we were sleeping I saw five Greeks ride past. One I knew to be Diomedes. He looked tired and had a big, unhealed gash running down one cheek.

The moon was coming to the full. The nights were clear, the landscape was silver, as in a dream.

Outside Brusa, which I calculated was beyond the reach of Greek patrols, the mare finally became so lame we had to lead her. My mother had said we would be welcomed at Brusa and helped to equip ourselves for the tougher part of our journey. We would get good horses and a waggon there. 'Mules would be better,' advised Nisintas. 'They're not so dignified, but only horses trained to those hills can manage them. These lowland animals could go lame, fall over the side of a precipice. You could purchase a horse for your arrivals, lady,' he added encouragingly. 'Ride it into towns – and lead it through the mountains.'

At Brusa we found prosperity. The area lay fairly much outside the range of the Greeks at that time and the city walls were thick. The Queen of Brusa, as she styled herself (certainly her family had held the area for countless generations) was, though, not a happy woman. The gates were shut when we approached in mid-morning, and there were bowmen on the ramparts. I approached without fear, though Naomi quivered. I said, 'What threat do we pose, even from a distance – two women and a man leading a lame horse? What they fear is twenty Greek horsemen, well mounted, with plumes flowing from their helmets. The Queen of Brusa is my mother's father's second wife's child. She has the land and city through her own mother, Laodice of Brusa. She is also called Laodice.' I had been drilled in all the diplomatic details of treaty, alliance and family before I left Troy. In addition to the family connection Brusa was a major city on the caravan route. Many Trojans had visited the city for trade purposes, and Laodice had sent twenty-five soldiers for the defence of Troy. She would help us – or so I thought.

Naomi was not reassured (rightly, as it turned out). Meanwhile Nisintas walked behind, leading the lame horse and sulky as ever. I had to shout up at the ramparts. I named myself, because I had to and I thought it safe. We were instantly let in and whisked through cobbled streets full of traders and citizens to the great hall of the queen's palace. Laodice was sitting on a large, carved, ebony chair at the head of the room, her two consorts beside her. The fire was lit and half a sheep was roasting on a spit; servants were going to and fro.

The queen was a small, dark woman, wearing a long purple dress. Her consorts were Eldom, who I believe was her brother or half-brother, and a youth called Syr or Sor, I was not clear which. They have the habit in those parts of selecting annually a young man to be consort of the queen-priestess. In spring, at the end of a year, he is slain in the fields, to bring life to them. Sometimes, if he pleases the queen, they kill a surrogate, but the consort rarely survives more than a few years before it is his time to die. Sitting around the feet of the queen, on the floor, or on stools, were six or seven children, from a boy of about fifteen down to a little girl of four. Laodice had on her lap a curly-headed child of eighteen months, who stared, big-eyed, at us as we came in.

I advanced and bowed respectfully, while Naomi and Nisintas sank down against the walls at the back. Laodice invited me to sit. A chair was placed opposite her and the two men. Laodice's brother-consort Eldom was a thickset man, with full lips above a black beard. The other consort was slender and liquid-eyed with a charming, but wary, proud air. His lips were reddened. He had in some senses the greatest position in the kingdom for he was their fortune and their fate. On the other hand, his life was at the disposition of the queen and her priests and priestesses.

'So,' Laodice said, smiling. 'A guest. I welcome you. An even greater pleasure in times when few travel.'

I told her, as courteously as possible, but fairly briskly, about my mission to enlist the aid of the Hittite Great King to rid all our coast of the Greeks once and for all. I added news of the war in Troy and praised the courage of the men she had sent, all of whom were, when I set out, alive and uninjured. (In fact, the troops from Brusa were not skilful or brave.) Though it was midday, the smoke from the fire seemed to thicken and the room became darker. Through the gloom I saw her smile. 'I wish you well

with your mission,' she said. 'It is most important.
— You must rest here and we will give you every help
to continue the journey.'

'I am grateful, and thank you,' I responded, 'but I
know you will not take it amiss if my stay is brief. It
is late in the year to be travelling east, and my journey is urgent.'

She told me she quite understood. 'These Greeks,'
her brother said ferociously, 'are as bad as the plague.
They kill, they interrupt normal life. Our subjects on
outlying farms tell us they cannot pay their taxes
because the farms are continually robbed. Sometimes
this is true.'

'Any more young warriors you could send to Troy
would be welcomed,' I told him. 'There's strength in
numbers.'

'The young men we have here,' he told me, 'are
needed for the defence of our own city. We have sent
all we can spare.'

I pointed out that if Troy were fully manned and
supplied, the Greeks could be beaten and their city
need never be attacked. I mentioned other allies who
had sent more warriors – and braver, though I did
not say so.

'What do you expect?' he replied. 'The Greeks are
at their throats – they're not at ours – so far.'

I glanced at the queen, and though she sat smiling
pleasantly I could see she agreed with her brother in
not wanting to send more troops to Troy. They would
let us fight the battle for them, trust we would win
and, if we lost, hope to be unaffected by the Greek
presence on the coast. If they needed to they would
try to make treaties with their new rulers. I did not

want to offend them by suggesting this was the case. I assured them that I understood their position.

The queen then offered me the use of a room in which to change my travel-stained clothes. When I arrived there I found scented water in a bath set into the floor and, on a marble table, a dress of fine white wool and a new cloak, dyed with costly purple dye. A female servant stood by to attend me. I bathed and changed and went back to the hall for a meal which we ate from silver dishes. Later, the queen, her consorts and some of her officials gave me a tour of the city. As I have said, it was a wealthy city. From the ramparts one looked out over the sea, on one side, and on the other long, glowing, reaped fields, where rich crops of corn and barley had stood. Beyond, forests lay. There was to be a feast, they said, in my honour that evening. They were treating me with every courtesy – but I had begun to mistrust Laodice.

At the feast, with musicians playing, torches round the walls and all the dignitaries of the city present, we spoke of Troy and their own city, their trade, the state of the kingdom at Hattusas and the nature of the Great King, Suppiluliumas. Some called him weak; others said he was not weak, only beset by the problems of maintaining his vast empire, a thousand-mile stretch of land, controlled by conquest or treaty, from Troy to Babylon. There were the attacks on his territory from the Gasga people by the Black Sea in the west and the Assyrians to the south. He was a ruler with many difficulties, said these people of Brusa, who seemed to take a gloomy pleasure in telling me how little I had to hope for from the Great King.

I had felt disappointed, even uneasy, during my

conversation with Laodice and her brother-consort. I felt the same again now, as these well-dressed, prosperous men and women told me my journey was hopeless. I suspected these people had long been jealous of Troy – of our friendly relationship with Suppiluliumas, our riches and power, the beauty and strength of my many brothers and sisters. My parents had given me all the information they could about my journey but they had not told me of this envy; perhaps they were unaware of it. I got the impression that although it was in my hosts' interests that I should gain military support from the Hittite king, they quite enjoyed the spectacle of the daughter of Priam and Hecuba travelling with only two slaves to plead for aid. At the same time, they were treating me with honour. Nevertheless, in the wealthy hall at Brusa I remembered the perpetual hunger and war in Troy. At least the city had not fallen to the Greeks, which had been my great fear while travelling. Such news would have got to Brusa like wildfire, been brought by the beaks of the very birds in the sky.

I was glad to retire. I found Queen Laodice's servant in my allotted room and, looking out of sorts, Nisintas, who was sitting in the middle of the floor. I was about to send him packing to the slave quarters, when Naomi pressed my arm in warning. She it was who stepped forward, asking the queen's servant to leave me, which the woman did, with a doubtful glance.

'What is this?' I asked, ready to lose my temper.

Again, Naomi touched my arm, this time glancing towards the entrance to the room which was covered only by a hanging. She was indicating someone might be spying on us.

I went over to Nisintas, saying, 'Why are you here?' He looked at me sullenly, then at Naomi, who had begun to give him orders which he obeyed. She went up to him and whispered, too low for me to hear. She seemed to be doing most of the talking. Then she took me to the window. 'I told him to stay in your room. They're discussing whether it would be wise to capture you and offer you to the Greeks as a token of goodwill. Some think it would be too dangerous – if Troy were to win the war the reprisals on your behalf would be terrible. Others would rather take a chance on a Greek victory and ingratiate themselves now with the future victors.' I stared at her. She was quite serious. When I had been strolling about the town with the queen and prominent citizens, Naomi and Nisintas had been talking with the servants and slaves, who knew everything.

I looked out into the darkness, wondering what to do. We desperately needed horses, a waggon too, if possible, and supplies of food. A welcome at Brusa had been part of my mother's plan for the journey. I sank to the floor with my hand over my face. It was not a dignified thing to do, especially before slaves, but suddenly I recalled the spring, before the Greeks came, that time with my beloved Arvad, and my dreams of the future. I remembered the arrival of that great, threatening fleet. I should have been married, embarked on Arvad's ship, happy, voyaging to Memphis, Babylon, Saba. Instead we were at war. I feared for my family. Now I was taking a long and dangerous journey to Hattusas – when I knew, had always known, the city would fall anyway. This news of treachery crushed me. Even if I escaped the ill-will of the Queen of Brusa would I not find more danger and treachery, for one reason or another, along the road to Hattusas? I was young, tired, full of despair. Beside me now, Naomi hissed urgently, 'Nisintas found all this out from Prince Syr's slave. Syr talks to his slave, being of low birth.'

I looked at Nisintas, still sitting on the floor. He turned his ox-like gaze to me. Nothing was to be read on his face.

'Perhaps the slave lies,' I said hollowly.

She shrugged, knowing that if I did not accept the truth I would doom us all. I had to believe it. Nisintas had no reason to lie. He had never wanted to go to Hattusas. My capture would mean nothing to him, except that he would not have to make the arduous journey. He would still be a slave – slave in Brusa, slave in Troy – what difference would it make to him?

I could still hear the noise of the feast. The queen's servant came in again, with a bowl of water, a jug of wine, silver cups. 'The queen is coming,' she announced. I didn't like the sound of it. I kicked Nisintas up, saying 'Back to your quarters, slave. You deserve a beating.' He shambled off. I slapped Naomi's face a couple of times and sent her to wait outside the room. She put up a fuss, blubbering, pleading and apologising.

The queen entered, small, but straight-backed, a golden comb in her well-arranged black hair. Two stools were brought and we sat down. 'I come merely to bid you goodnight, lady,' she said in her soft, pleasant voice, 'and to hope you will honour us with at least a few days more of your presence, though I know your journey is pressing.'

'I should be happy to stay a little longer in your magnificent city,' I responded. 'You are very kind and your entertainment is generous. I shall have much to tell of Brusa when I reach Hattusas.'

She nodded her thanks, then stood. 'I trust you will sleep well,' she said, 'and look forward to your company tomorrow.' She left with great dignity, turning in the doorway and gesturing towards the silver jug. 'I hope before you sleep you will enjoy a cup of our wine, which you generously praised at the feast.'

'You make me most happy,' I responded.

After a bare interval Naomi returned, crawling on the floor and weeping for forgiveness. The queen's servant's back was turned as she arranged my bed coverings. From the floor Naomi shook her head at the wine and made a face. I nodded. It would be unsafe to drink it. If they meant to capture me they might have drugged the wine. I was beginning to understand that Naomi had seen a side of the world about which I had only heard. She knew the savagery, powerlessness, the enmities, adulteries and treacheries of the long caravan trails through deserts, forests and hills, far from any law. As a little alert child-slave she had learned much then which was useful now in these hard times.

The maid was now offering me the goblet. 'Later,' I said. Still she offered it, saying something about the queen's gift. I turned from her, saying I would now prepare for sleep and would drink it before I retired. I dismissed her and she had to go. Naomi then put out the torches and threw the wine from the window.

We sat silently in the darkness for a while. Naomi was against the wall to the left of the entrance to the room. I lay on my bed wondering what to do – I had no ideas and I was very frightened. Naomi wanted a decision but was too afraid to speak to me.

Then there was the faint smell of a musk-based scent in the atmosphere, the odour I associated with Syr. At first I had thought it was some natural scent from his skin, then realised he perfumed himself. He must be in, or near, the room, but there had been no sound. Then in the darkness, I saw his figure, naked except for a breechclout. I closed my eyes, pretending to be asleep. He might be about to kill me, or rape me. Or perhaps he was only curious, wandering the palace on bare feet, with what thoughts circulating in his head no one could imagine – to be god, queen's consort and sacrifice, all at once, is to be in a position no other person could understand. He might have been a little mad.

He left the room as soundlessly as he had entered. I waited until I thought he had really gone. Then I sat up. Naomi came over. How he had not seen her I don't know, though I know that in those days she could make herself as small, grey and still as a mouse when she chose, another of the gifts she had learned as a child, no doubt.

Her eyes were wide. I shook my head, baffled, but at least Syr's visit had made me decide to leave the city as soon as possible. Syr had come to the room, for what purposes I did not know; he could return at any time to fulfil those purposes, whatever they were. I did not trust Laodice or her brother. But the city gates were closed and I was not sure if the guards would open them at night for us without consulting the queen. A failed attempt at an escape could precipitate a crisis. I whispered to Naomi, 'Can you fetch Nisintas, without being spotted?' She drew in her breath with a hiss, nodded and sped off.

Nisintas lay massively across the threshold all

night. As far as I can tell we all three slept. I do not know if Syr came back, but if he did he must have seen Nisintas and decided not to enter the room.

Just before dawn I rose and went quietly through the palace and out to the market-place. I bargained for a waggon, a team of two mules and a ragged little horse the coper told me came from the hill country. I also bought rugs and blankets, and food. In this way we could be independent of dubious hospitality of any kind. I did all this speedily, astonishing the sellers with my readiness to accept a price. I feared the arrival of someone from the palace, who would report back what I was doing. The only hope was to leave quickly before the decision to treat me as an honoured guest or sell me to the Greeks was firmly made. Additional servants, or slaves, might have given extra protection, but there was the danger they would turn against me. I had developed a little more confidence in Nisintas, but I was still not sure of him and I did not want to add more doubts about servants to the other anxieties of the journey.

I had hoped that in a few days we might meet a caravan going east to Hattusas, and travel with it in relative safety, but it was late in the year for such a journey. Any caravan going that way would be risking the weather, or accepting that it might be wintering in Hattusas and few would wish to do that. For the rest, I hoped to take the queen by surprise when I announced myself ready to go. I thought it unlikely she would actively forbid me, a princess of Troy, to leave her city in broad daylight. Anything she did to harm me would be done in darkness.

I informed her I was leaving that morning. She did attempt to persuade me to stay, pretended to be hurt by my leaving, hinted at a change of mind, suggested if I would stay a little longer we could discuss her sending more troops to Troy. Perhaps, she suggested, it was unnecessary to undertake a difficult journey to Hattusas to ask for an army which might not be given, if she and I could arrange for a band of thirty or forty young men to accompany me back to Troy to fight in the war. It was all very seductive. There was no reason to believe, untrustworthy as she was, that she had not truly decided that Troy's victory over the Greeks might serve her and her people better than Troy's defeat. Nevertheless, I thought it better not to gamble on Queen Laodice's change of heart. I told her my errand to Hattusas was urgent because of the danger of early snows in the mountains; I would return to her city on the way back. With the need for politeness and the formalities involved, it took half a morning to bid Queen Laodice and the two princes farewell and I was uneasy all the time. Eventually it was over.

TWENTY-TWO

The Journey to Hattusas

WE LEFT Brusa before midday in bright sunshine, heading eastwards along the valley, wishing to avoid not only the roaming Gasga people who were overrunning the area but any skirmishes between the Hittite regiments trying to keep them under control. I rode the horse, the two slaves were in the waggon.

We made good progress on the narrow, white valley road, surrounded by fields and vineyards in which even now they were culling the last of the grapes. In the few hamlets we passed they were busy at their wooden wine presses, or drying fruits for the winter. As we progressed, the people seemed less afraid of strangers. Children stared at us, but without fear or indeed undue curiosity. They were used to stranger parties than ours – Hittite contingents in armour galloping through, waggons containing anything from fish to metals from the mountains. They had seen columns of chained slaves and savage tribesmen from beyond the Black Sea, leading animals laden with furs.

We did not stop. The sun shone. In spite of my

horse's uneven gait I was in the half-excited, half-apprehensive, always interested mood of a traveller. Troy seemed very far away. So, strangely, was any sense that visions were lurking in my head just beyond consciousness, ready to surface. It was as if my gift had withdrawn itself when we left Troy. According to one's nature, one either acts or dreams, I suppose, but circumstances can make an actor of a dreamer and the other way about. My fear was that when the prophetic gift returned, it could have greater force and cost me a higher price for having been subdued for so long. But for the moment I was a cheerful traveller, on a warm day of autumn – nothing more.

In front – I wanted to keep an eye on them – Naomi and Nisintas sat on the waggon, apparently on friendly terms. Nisintas had driven mules before and the animals seemed docile. We made good progress. Ahead of us lay the journey across the long, upland plain towards Hattusas – grim travelling, perhaps, but on well-kept roads, safely patrolled by Hittite soldiers.

We camped in the hills that night. Wrapped in rugs, I saw the stars above me, then knew no more until dawn. The others were still asleep. I got wood, built a fire, set barley to boil. We would need a good breakfast today. I sat under a larch, looking down into the silent valley, over which birds swooped. We ate the barley hot with chunks of cold spiced lamb. After a cup of wine well-watered with cold water from a stream we packed up the waggon and set off.

For a person born and bred in low coastal country, there is something intimidating about being high among hills and mountains for the first time. All

around were grey rocks, clumps of trees, a little veg-
etation on which an occasional goat pastured, and,
because the land was less easily cultivated, few
people, no villages. In several hours' travelling we
saw one boy driving a couple of sheep from nowhere
to nowhere. It was a good road; the air was chill.

Towards nightfall, as the shadows came down over
the hills and the track, we passed a wedding party
with torches, drums and pipes, a girl in a long dress
and amber beads, a young man wearing the pelt of
an animal over his shoulders. The head of the animal,
huge and doglike, hung down his back. A crowd of
revellers was round them. Where they had come
from, or where they were heading, could not be
guessed. I greeted them in the Akkadian tongue, but
they just stared at me. That language is used in those
parts, but perhaps more among the nobility and merchants and for religious purposes. Then we passed
them and camped that night on a straight stretch of
road, all bundled together in the waggon for safety.
Once the mules woke and began to whinny, but when
we peered over the sides of the waggon, there seemed
to be nothing there.

'Wolves,' Naomi said with a shudder.

'No wolves here, at this season,' Nisintas said
shortly. Then we slept again.

Nevertheless, when we rose and got on the way
again, into the rising sun, I realised, though I was in
good spirits, we could not go on travelling in such a
small party through this wild, uninhabited landscape.
The vast plain we were crossing was controlled by
the Great King who had regiments everywhere, but
territory like this where men can appear from behind
hills and disappear again, is country for bandits, just

as the sea is for pirates. I would have to find an answer at the next city, Gordion, which I had been told lay ahead at the junction of two rivers.

The next days were gruelling. The temperatures dropped, the days grew shorter, the long plain stretched ahead remorselessly. I thought we would reach Gordion after three days but on the fourth night we slept on the roadside, as usual, in a bleak pass with steep hills on either side and travelled the deserted road all through the next day. There was still no sign we were nearing a city – no sign, indeed, of anything but a herd of wild goats which blocked our path. The old male goat, head down, was about to run at the waggon and two mules, until Naomi stood up and bellowed furiously at him.

In the waggon that night, too, we heard voices in the hills to our left. Naomi said they were spirits. I feared they were bandits. The sounds went on all night, grumbling conversation, the odd shout. We dozed, Naomi and I waking occasionally and both groping in our clothes for our daggers, while Nisintas slept, still grasping his club. Were they some local spirits? Was this the place where no person familiar with the region would ever stop? Or were they robbers, waiting to strike us? It was a bad night, and next day a cold, determined rain fell on the silent pass, and still the track stretched ahead with no sign of a city ahead. My horse was tiring, for want of proper pasture, though the mules were all right. They could live on the scrubby, lifeless grass along the trail. And so we plodded along, cold and soaked, the rugs over our heads and shoulders offering little protection.

I began to fear the worst. There was no city ahead, we were lost, on the way to nowhere and with our food running short. We could go on through this inhuman landscape, or turn and hope to return safely to the plains before we starved. But if we returned now it would be too late to get to Hattusas before the snows.

Then, from nowhere on that road, a band of Hittite horsemen galloped past us. They must have come down from the hills behind. They were little, wiry men in dun-coloured trousers and boots. They had round, bronze breastplates and practical-looking pointed helmets with earflaps. They rode sturdy little shaggy horses. We tried to stop them, but they were past us and round a bend in the road in a flash. It was an encouragement, though. We must be on the road to somewhere.

Further encouragement came. The rain stopped, the air became clearer and a pale blue sky emerged. Then we found ourselves travelling beside a broad river. There was a hamlet, where I saw a woman in a green-dyed cloak, and a child with a wooden toy by the roadside. I took these things as sure signs that we were near a city. Then, on the horizon, were great walls seeming to have been carved from the hillside rock. Gordion was a forbidding city, if you were not looking at it with the eyes of hope, as I was. Then suddenly other travellers appeared as if by magic – a woman pushing a cart containing a heap of big, unfamiliar-looking green vegetables and a bawling sheep on its side with its feet tied, a couple of young men, one riding a donkey, the other walking, a waggon driven by a man in a sheepskin with three soldiers in the back, a man carrying nothing but a lute.

This appearance of other individuals made me

realise the state we were in. The waggon was inches deep in water. Naomi and Nisintas were slumping. I was drenched and freezing. (Our clothes were far too light. It is impossible for lowlanders to believe how tough garments must be to protect them in those regions.) Suddenly self-conscious, I realised we were reaching an important Hittite city on an important mission and I was wet, exhausted, dirty, riding a tired, plodding horse with its head down. And so we reached the giant stone portals of the city and passed through its great gates.

The streets were broad and level, stone buildings lay to either side. A vast temple with two great statues of the weather god and sun goddess stood directly inside the city gates. From inside the temple came a roaring of voices. I never fully understood that religion, except that it revolved around the god and goddess and their two children, named by more than one name. They had ceremonies in spring and autumn, as all do. Their king is also a god, but often consults local oracles or village witches to answer problems or find out what course to take.

I rode up to a cluster of soldiers, standing around doing nothing, as soldiers often seem to, and asked for the palace of Estan, prince of the kingdom. My mother had told me he was named after Estan, the Hittite war-god. She had told me all she knew of the names and natures of those that I must approach in this city, but it was far off and information scanty. One man she had asked, who had met Estan, called him honest and methodical.

I had no royal appurtenances, of course. I was sixteen years old, riding a useful, but undistinguished horse and, for a cloak, I wore the sole blanket we had managed to keep dry. Everything else was wet. My entourage was two damp slaves in a mule-cart. But calculating, I expect, that no one but a noble-woman would have dared make the request, two of the soldiers fell in and led the way to Estan's palace.

I was awed by the streets we went through. They were crowded, wide and full of buildings larger than anything I had ever seen before. This solidity of stone, lacking beauty or grace, was a visible sign of power and wealth. And if this city was subsidiary to Hattusas, the capital, then what could Hattusas itself be like? Here were temple after temple, chariots in huge numbers. Here women wore jewellery which we would have locked away in treasure chests; wealth was everywhere.

We entered a vast portal with stone lions set on pillars thirty feet high. It must have been a quarter of a mile, through many courtyards, to the palace itself. One was surrounded by buildings, where clerks went in and out; another was full of carts, waggons and chariots; one was a whole market-place, where vendors sold fish, meat and strange vegetables.

We went through more great pillars to an atrium where a soldier went off and spoke to an official in a long robe and pointed hat. Not long after I was ushered into the presence of Estan. He sat at a long table, surrounded by some robed men. On the table were scrolls of papyrus, inscribed stone tablets and beside him, while everyone, it seemed, was speaking at once, stood a clerk with a frame containing soft clay on which he was writing rapidly with a wooden stylus. At Estan's end of the table was a heap of sand, which he was, as I came in, sweeping flat with his hand, obliterating some sketch he had made, and preparing to redraw it.

Estan himself was a small, thin man, with sharp eyes. I needed his support, since he would, I felt sure, send a messenger to Hattusas ahead of me, concerning my visit. However, I was not presenting myself well. Dirty and ill-clad as I was, I had been offered no chance to change my clothes; nor, apparently, had Estan bothered to prepare a meeting of nobles, as I expected. I was being brought into a conference as it was taking place, rather as if I'd come to deliver a roll of cloth, not as an emissary from a far-off city under siege.

However, he greeted me very cordially, though I saw curiosity under his polite manner. He left his table and gestured me towards a central fire burning in the room. Chairs were brought. Two people followed him to the fire – his clerk, who took a position behind him, still carrying his clay tablet and stylus, and an elderly woman with grey hair, wearing a long brown dress and cloak, who sat on one of the chairs.

Estan did not say who she was. I was ignorant of their customs. The woman could have been his mother, sister, or his first and oldest wife. She had a keen but friendly eye and wore very costly earrings containing thumbnail-sized red stones set in gold. I believe the stones were rubies. I spoke to him in the Hittite tongue, of course, and there seemed no point in concealing my mission, since I guessed, as soon as I had left the palace, he would launch a man on a fast horse with a message for Hattusas.

These encounters between dignitaries have their rituals – an exchange of compliments is followed by an exchange of information, and, finally, an intimation of the point of the visit, usually guessed by the host during the preliminaries. The visits from the Greek kings had not taken this form, but they felt no need to observe the normal rules, if, in fact, they knew them.

I outlined the state of affairs in Troy, although I knew they must have other reports. I mentioned my encounter with Queen Laodice at Brusa and said I thought her mind might be turning towards alliance with the Greeks. I added that I considered this to be grave news for the Great King, who of course wished to maintain his influence in that area. I did not need to point out that aid to Troy from Suppiluliumas would soon help her to work out where her best interests lay. All this time Estan turned his neutral, restrained face to mine. His eyes met mine firmly, as did those of the woman.

I was afraid that during the long days of my journey, events would have become much worse in Troy, and knew that news might have reached here before I did. Mercifully, Estan had nothing to tell me. Nor, of course, could he make any offer of assistance – that was a matter for the Great King to decide. He did not seem unsympathetic, though. Where Laodice had plainly been trifling with the notion of alliance with the Greeks, Estan was against them and expressed what looked like sincere distress about our difficulties. It would not have been diplomatic to mention Suppiluliumas' previous refusal to send troops, but I began to hope there had been a change of policy. They might already have received news the Greeks could win the war and have suddenly appreciated the danger enemies planted on the mainland could represent for them.

Estan said bluntly, 'You have taken risks in coming here alone, with only two slaves, as I think you said. A truly Trojan measure. You must have an escort for the rest of your journey.'

The woman then spoke: 'We have heard of you, Cassandra. Is it not true that you and your twin have prophesied the fate of the city?'

'I have, I know,' I said. 'But not all prophecies are true.'

She gave me a shrewd look – these people were very direct – stood up and said, 'Will you come with me? You must stay and rest.' I received the impression she was Estan's mother, a figure of some power. She led me from the vast hall across a court-yard, up a huge flight of steps, through a vast portico. She pushed through a tapestried hanging. 'Your apartments,' she said. 'Your woman will be sent to you. The other slave will be looked after.' There was a set of interconnected rooms, well furnished and with hangings of unusual, bold design on walls and floors. The ceiling was painted blue. None the less these high, rich rooms were dark, dark because of leaden skies overhead and because a sombre pall lay over this palace, and the city itself.

There she left me. I walked through the first room into the bedroom, gazed down from the window to a courtyard below, where fifty bowmen were practising with their short, arched bows under the grey skies. They were quick, nimble men, and well trained. With fifty such men and a troop of well-trained cavalry, I thought, we could take the Greeks by surprise, and finish them.

I longed now to be back in Troy, whatever its woes. I ached for the familiar stones of the city, for my parents, Helenus, all my brothers and sisters. Then, for there was nothing else to do, I was in the hands of my hosts, I took off my damp clothes, got under the bedcovers and slept.

When I woke it seemed to be some hours before dawn. Naomi was shaking my shoulder. In her other hand she held a torch. 'We must be off,' she said. 'There's an escort downstairs. They've put food for you in the chamber beyond. And clothing.'

'It's dark,' I said.

'You don't have to tell me. They woke us up. The queen's waiting for you.'

She threw a cloak over me and I went shivering into the other room, where the queen, an attendant with a torch on either side of her, told me, 'King Suppiluliumas has asked to see you in Hattusas today, if possible. We would have wished to entertain you longer, but this is the Great King's command.'

'I am grateful for this attention,' I said, and I was. The fact of my arrival as a suppliant from Troy seemed to have made me, and my mission, important. We had been at war for six months with the city under siege. We had sent messages appealing for aid to the king which had been refused. My arrival in person altered nothing, I sometimes thought, but I did not realise that the great world does not work like that – a message is just a message, the arrival of an individual adds effect. We had crept from Brusa like fugitives, travelled here in some hardship. I had not realised that the very fact of this journey, undertaken with such difficulty, and some risk, by Priam's daughter, somehow made the matter in hand more significant.

Before long I was in a chariot and Nisintas and

Naomi in a horse-drawn waggon with soldiers. There were horsemen bearing torches ahead of and behind us. The city gates were opened and we set off through the darkness.

We travelled slowly at first, because of the dark, but when dawn came we were heading up through mountains at a steady pace. The sun rose ahead, over high, forested hills.

We stopped at midday. Naomi produced food, and we ate apart from the soldiers. Nisintas approached just before we set off again, head down, looking fearful.

'What is it?' I asked.

He seemed unable to speak. Naomi became formal. 'He requests, humbly, to know whether he understood you to say, and your good mother the queen, that it was your intention to free him at Hattusas. He says he is sorry if he was mistaken.'

'Certainly. He has been faithful to his trust,' I responded.

Nisintas stared me full in the face. He began to smile.

'He thought you were going to sell him everywhere we stopped along the road,' Naomi told me. 'That's all he's been used to in the past. Then he realised he'd revealed he was a smith, and thought if you didn't sell him on the way, you'd make him come back to Troy to work in the smithy.'

I had certainly entertained the idea, but felt it would bring bad luck to break the promise to free him, which had been given in solemn circumstances, at the outset of an important journey, in the presence of the oracle. I said, 'If he wants to come back as a free man, he's welcome to do so. We have need of him.'

'He wants to see his old lover, the farmer's daughter,' she explained. 'If she's married with many children, he'll return to Troy.' They had worked the whole thing out between them.

Nisintas was listening. His smile faded. He probably thought I would change my mind about freeing him at the last moment. So then and there, before we set off on the last leg of the journey to Hattusas, I made a formal statement so that the soldiers could hear, declaring him a free man. I don't suppose it made any sense to the soldiers. I had to make up some words to give the situation as much dignity as possible. Slaves are seldom freed unless they are prosperous captives ransomed by their families. If they are freed it is because the owner says they are free, and the whole community behaves accordingly. Here, far from home, I had to invent a ceremony.

And so, late that night, we set off again, travelling without stopping and before dawn next day reached our destination.

There is no sight in the world I have seen like the vision of Hattusas, massive on the skyline as you approach it. They tell me there are greater cities, more charming and beautiful, set in more hospitable landscapes, but I cannot believe that, in its sombre way, anything could be more impressive than the appearance of that place in all its might. It covers four hundred acres of high mountain, a vast area overlooking long, fertile, upland plains. The huge palace is on even higher ground and the sea is almost two hundred miles away. I thought of this distant sea as we went towards the city. For those who have lived with the sea always beside them, inland life seems strange and unnatural.

Before we reached the massive ramparts, I looked back only to see Nisintas, who had up to now been slumped in the waggon showing no outward sign of having been recently freed, suddenly jump over the side of the vehicle and run like a hare down a slope. It was hard to believe such a big, heavy man could travel so fast. There was a cry from the soldiers in the waggon but I signalled to them not to stop him.

Then we were rolling through the straight, gravelled streets of Hattusas, a trumpeter on a horse blowing a call to clear the way, the citizens staring. And what citizens! There were curly-haired Assyrians in long robes, the pigtailed Hittite men in their short girdles and cloaks, round-faced men with narrow eyes, black hair in fringes and wearing furs. And soldiers everywhere!

Though the traffic had to give way to us, it was a slow business: ox-carts had to pull to the side of a road jammed with waggons, long strings of horses and carts piled high with goods and children. We got mixed up in a whole caravan of horses, mules, armed men, merchants, a string of slaves. Most of this traffic was heading east to the Taurus mountains to get back to Assyria, Babylonia, Phoenicia, before the snows. In Gordion I had wished myself in Troy. But I was young, part of me was loyal, to family and country. The rest wanted what youth wants – love, pleasure, change. I suddenly saw how easy it would be, after my meeting with Suppiluliumas, to go east with them before winter – and find Arvad. I need not return to my beleaguered city.

And then, we were at the palace of the Great King.

TWENTY-THREE

Thessaly

I WOKE before dawn the morning after Helen's arrival. The light woke me, that glow which shines through the air as snow drifts down and is thrown up from where it lies. I watched the soothing fall from my bed. Drowsily, I thought Helen could not leave now. She would stay in the farmhouse until it melted. I could not get rid of her. I could order her out, of course, but it would be a harsh host who ordered a guest out into a snow-storm. At least the delay would mean I could try to find out if she intended to betray me to her son-in-law.

I got up before the servants woke, lit the fire in the big room, then pulled on a sheepskin coat, pushed my feet into the leather slippers worn in Thessaly in winter, and went out to feed and water the horses. As I did so, Helen's stable-servant woke. I left the rest of the job to him and stood in the courtyard, snow blowing round about me. The stone bench at which I had set out to write my tale was coated lightly with snow. For a time I had been able to write in tranquillity, but that time was now over. I had begun to record my message to contradict the Greek version of my own and my family's history. I had written in order to remember, and in remembering, perhaps to find some kind of reconciliation. All that had ended with Helen's arrival. I did not know when, or if, I would ever conclude my tale.

Perhaps, as Naomi suspected, the very act of making those black sparrow's footsteps on my thick, brown papyrus had called up the Spartan queen. More likely, I thought, breathing the sharp, clear air, as the snow blew around me, the time for peace was over. I had a sense of urgency, I felt events pressing about me. A new cycle was beginning. Helen's arrival had not caused it. It was a symptom, a signal like the first arrow in a battle, which will be followed by a hail of others. The way in which matters reveal themselves to such as me, blessed and cursed with foresight, is a mystery. All I recognise is that moment when change is imminent. I knew the little world in which I had sheltered for twenty years was about to break apart. I stood in the falling snow, as if entranced, and bade farewell to the old Cassandra, farmer's wife, mother of children, woman in hiding.

Yet the day-to-day life went on. Up came the farmyard cock with his three wives, all old friends reared on the family hearth, all hoping for a handful or two of corn. A man would have to be sent to the hillside to find a ewe for slaughter and I would have to decide, if the weather continued to be severe, if the flock should be rounded up and brought down to walled fields nearer the farmhouse. But in my mind I heard the warning horns blowing from ship to ship in fog as a raiding fleet came towards our coast, heard the crew calling to each other across the water, the crunch as the ships beached. For this was what would happen. It would not be too long.

Inside the house Naomi was stirring oatmeal over

the fire. Cakes of lamb mixed with onions smoked on a griddle. 'You'll want the men to bring the sheep off the hills,' she said.

'I won't,' I said. I knew I should not put the sheep in pens where they would need to be fed and watered. I had so little confidence in the next day, now, I thought there might be no one to feed them; they might be better off fending for themselves on the hillsides. 'But drive the old ewe with the shut eye in for slaughter,' I told her.

'I planned to see my man today,' she told me. Her boy ran in and stared at her as she complained, 'Things are not as they used to be. It began with your writings on the paper. It raised Helen, like casting a spell. Where will it end? I don't like your looks. I feel trouble all round. Why can't the woman go away? What's on your mind? I'm too old for all this. I thought my troubles were over.' She looked at me, as if I were deliberately rushing towards disaster.

'You're alive,' I said. 'You must want to see your man badly to walk four miles in snow. Stay, take care of the boy. Get a skin from where they hang. They should be ready now. Start making him a jacket and then finish the blanket on the loom. You may have to move quickly. Or not – I don't know.'

'I knew it!' she said triumphantly. 'You're mad – dwelling on the old story. You've gone mad. And brought Helen down on us.' As ever, foretelling brought blame.

'Do as I say, Naomi,' I said. 'There can be no harm in making the boy a jacket – or finishing your work.'

'Too old for all this,' she said again.

She was about thirty-two. Old age was a long way off. I repeated, 'Do as I say,' adding, 'or seek refuge with your man if you like. You are free, as free as a slave can ever be. Come, Naomi, stay with me, if only for a little while. You were not born the luckiest woman in the world. Even slavery brought you a worse fate than a slave ought to expect.'

She stared at me. The old Naomi revived. 'If that's how it's to be,' she said, 'I'll go over the hill today. With the boy. He can stay with his grandmother until matters are more in order here.' Then Helen came in, and with an obeisance just this side of insolence, Naomi withdrew.

'Will you eat?' I asked Helen. The scarring of the once-beautiful face was more noticeable in daylight. She seemed to move with some difficulty. She sat down by the fire, saying, 'No, sister. I have no appetite.' She looked into the flames. 'You have many children?'

'Four,' I said. I was stirring the pot on the tripod. I shouted for a manservant, who came and took it away. I gave him the lamb patties also – servants would feast this morning.

'I have only a daughter,' she went on. 'And do your children love you?'

Love – she'd used the word again. She used it too often. What it can have meant to her I do not know. I think in her mind she was always on a dais, with people looking at her, desiring her, admiring her, loving her.

I responded, 'I do not know if my children love me. As you know, among the kind of people we are – I was reared to be – loyalty and good faith are the most prized virtues. What do you mean when you say "love"?'

She only sighed. I told her, as a farmer's wife will,

of my husband's death, of my young sons and daughters. I spoke of Penelope, married to the harbourmaster at Pinios, ten miles down the coast; of Iris and her husband Telemon; of Phaon, the youngest, aboard his brother-in-law's ship; of Dryas, the local smith. I did not mention Diomed, my eldest son, now twenty. To distract her, I said, 'Your daughter is queen in Mycenae. You must be happy, a queen and mother of a queen. When you have a grandson he will rule both kingdoms.'

'Are you bitter?' she said.

'One day I will tell you how I saved the life of your son-in-law,' I replied. The snow was still coming down softly outside. 'It seems we're trapped here together,' I remarked. 'That's very strange, isn't it? We've not seen each other for twenty years. There's little affection on either side – how could there be? – yet here we are. I must go to the loom. You will have to entertain me with tales, as women do. This blanket is worth a lamb, or some hens to me, at market.' I wished to wound her. I continued, 'We are poor folk here, you see. You will have to gossip to me, tell me stories, as I weave. Such terrible stories! But they are all we have to tell, aren't they, Helen, these tales of violence and betrayal? Tell me – what did you think when you discovered your sister had deliberately ignored your appeal to approach your husband, try to effect a reconciliation, and get you safely out of Troy? And how did she pass the time in her palace at Argos, while we died in Troy?'

'Like you,' Helen said, 'with weaving.' She spoke grimly. For once there was something in her speech which commented on a life and a state of mind not her own. Her links to her dead sister must have been very strong. 'Weaving,' she reported and told me how Clytemnestra had spent that long winter, when I went first to Anatolia, seeking the support of the Great King, then returned to Troy. And again I heard the voice of Clytemnestra of Mycenae.

TWENTY-FOUR

Mycenae

M Y HUSBAND had spies in Troy, men and women who got messages to our generals down by the sea. One of these was Sinon, actually the son of Priam by a Greek woman, considered loyal by his family, but in fact an envious man. He was jealous of his brothers, especially those born of his father and Hecuba, favoured sons like Hector, Paris, Deiphobus, Troilus, those who would inherit command of land and sea and make advantageous marriages, if Troy survived.

The rage of the dispossessed, or those who feel they are, is fertile ground for treachery. Agamemnon's cousin, my lover, was such a man. Of course Agamemnon promised Sinon the city when the war was won. How many promises of that kind had he made – six, a dozen, twenty? But Sinon believed him, so, living in Troy as a warrior and taking his share of the fighting against the Greeks, he nevertheless crept out at night to deliver messages to the Greek camp about what was happening inside the city. He was particularly useful, since, as a warrior, he took part in the councils of war in Troy. Sinon came to me, in Mycenae. But now he could not return to Troy. He had left the city ten days earlier on a moonless night, telling the gateman he needed to go to a farm three minutes from the city to see his pregnant wife, an excuse he had given before, bribing the man with coins he had of course got originally from Agamemnon. He slid into the Greek camp, demanded to see Agamemnon, was admitted and found him fondling the slave girl he had stolen from Achilles. His general Ulysses was there, also with a girl, another captured Trojan. This lamentable history of looted and quarrelled-over girls, which had, of course, resulted in Achilles' withdrawal from the war, was in my view proof that the army was deteriorating. They had been too long from home and victory seemed as far away as when they had landed.

Sinon told Agamemnon and his general, that small, quick-eyed, strong man, that he had learned from casual conversation with the innocent Polyxena, Cassandra's sister, that Cassandra had gone to appeal for regiments from Suppiluliumas. That secret could not be kept for long – they had pretended she was ill for a few days, until she'd escaped from the areas controlled by the Greeks. This information, which Sinon considered so important, made Agamemnon laugh. 'We had assurances, many months ago from the Great King that he would not intervene in the war between ourselves and Troy. What difference will the arrival of that young woman, a girl mistrusted by her own people because she fills the city with cries that Troy will fall, make in Hattusas? Suppiluliumas sends no troops because he cannot. The arrival of the girl – if she does arrive and does not die on the way – will mean nothing. What is he to think when a young woman, foreteller of Troy's doom, arrives to ask for his soldiers? That she is a fraud, an hysteric, who makes prophecies in which she herself does not believe? Or that she believes her own prophecies but insanely comes to beg for his soldiers so that they will die in Troy with the Trojans? But we'll cut her off on the way back, never fear, and parade her body under the walls of Troy. Or I'll take her for myself.'

This treacherous man, by now traitor to both sides, told me that after this statement Agamemnon fell silent, thinking, then began to smile. He dismissed Sinon, after giving him a ring, saying casually, 'This must be a new form of diplomacy. I must send for my own daughter and ask her to ride to Hattusas to argue for me.'

'I cannot go back to Troy again,' Sinon said in alarm.

'Why not?' demanded Agamemnon.

'I shall be suspected. How long can I keep on creeping out at night? One day the gateman will betray me, I shall be seen –'

'The man who wants to be a king – so brave,' Agamemnon told him contemptuously.

'Small chance to be a king, if I'm detected and killed.'

'This is war. Death is part of it.'

'I cannot go. Let me stay and fight with you.'

'Return,' said Agamemnon, 'to Troy.'

Sinon muttered, 'There's death in the city.'

'What?' cried Agamemnon.

'A man and a woman died,' Sinon said. 'It could be plague. I don't want to return.'

'Two deaths do not make a plague.'

'Don't dismiss the news too lightly,' interposed Ulysses.

'Two dead in a starving city?' Agamemnon said incredulously.

'Well, we shall soon find out,' the general continued quietly. He added, 'Should I not go to Hattusas, in case Cassandra has gained some concessions from Suppiluliumas? And I might meet her as she was coming back and capture her. I could send her to you and continue the journey.'

Agamemnon laughed. 'Afraid of the plague? Or do you want to be the first to get your hands on Cassandra?'

Ulysses shook his head. 'She might succeed in her mission. The Great King might have second thoughts about sending reinforcements for Troy. He has no great love for us. Depending on circumstances he might find he can spare a regiment. Cassandra might persuade him. Who knows?'

'I can't spare you to chase Cassandra or go to Hattusas and back. Stay and fight.'

Sinon had not left Agamemnon's hut, for he had to persist in his argument about not returning to Troy. Over previous months he had supplied numbers of troops, casualty figures, details of strategies contemplated or decided on by the Trojans, and he thought now the information about Cassandra's trip to Hattusas would be enough to earn him the safety of the Greek camp. But Agamemnon again ordered him out. 'Return to Troy,' he ordered.

Sinon dared not go back. Instead he took ship directly back to Greece and true to his habits came first to me with information, expecting me to pay. First, he gave me news of the quarrel between Agamemnon and Achilles over the Trojan slave Briseis – how often she shared his bed, what gifts he gave her.

(Fool! I knew of it already, and if I had cared, like a peasant woman betrayed, about the fidelity of my husband, I would have gone to Greece, killed her, put on armour, fought with the warriors.) Then he told me of Cassandra's journey to Hattusas and for that I did pay him. Also for his claim there was plague in Troy. If there was plague there, the Greeks might be able, at last, to capture the weakened city. Or, and it would take little, they might get plague themselves. When sickness strikes armies, the victory can often go to the side which loses fewest men to it. I let Sinon go and went back to my loom, weaving that light and beautiful cloak I would throw over my husband's shoulders when, if, he came home.

My dark, slender daughter came into the room. 'News of my father?' she asked eagerly. 'How is he? How fares the war?' Electra loved her father. Her marriage had been planned to the son of the King of Rhodes, to keep him loyal, but Agamemnon continually put off the wedding, and now said he wished it to take place after the successful conclusion of the war. I believe he did not want to give her to any other man. He believed his daughter was his just as he believed his wife was his and his kingdom was his. I, and even my deplorable sister, came from a different tradition, where the worship of the goddess prevailed, in regions often ruled by queens. I hated Agamemnon, hated the gods he had set on his altars beneath the ground. He believed he owned everything. He had killed one of his daughters and now clung, unnaturally, to the other. A madman.

I had to conceal my relationship with Aegisthus from Electra. She suspected it, I know, and would have told her father, if she ever had evidence. She knew I disliked her, but maintained towards me a kind of ostentatious, dutiful obedience, a syrupy respect, as if she tried to move my heart towards her. An onlooker would have believed her a loving, pious daughter, but I knew the bad blood of my husband's family. She would have killed me if she could. I told her the war went well, her father was a hero, I prayed for his return. She looked at me from under her eyelids. ˉSuch a look! Pretended affection and respect, masking spite. I got rid of her and went back to my weaving.

Agamemnon would not believe sending an owned daughter to the Great King would have any effect, but I thought otherwise, that Cassandra might indeed get soldiers from him. Age-old ties of obligation and respect existed between Hattusas and Troy. Cassandra's arrival, with reports of the war dragging on, and the Greeks dug in for the winter on their shores, might convince Suppiluliumas that the issue was in the balance. If he could not count on Troy to fight us off without his assistance, he might well send troops.

As for the plague, I yearned to hear of Agamemnon dying, dried out, in pools of his own faeces – yet, if Troy was weakened through sickness, he could take it, and return a hero. I prayed for his death, cast spells for it, would lay hands on the most powerful sorceress in Greece to assure it, if I could.

There had been no more messages from Helen. I did not envy her life in Troy. For the rest, I wished Cassandra well in her mission. I secretly offered sacrifices of blood, hair and bone to Cassandra's goddess, Hecate, and prayed for her success.

And so we went towards the shortest day of the year. Aegisthus was away putting down troublesome raids on our borders caused by those taking advantage of our lack of men. The land wasted without men to work it. I offered sacrifices to Hecate. My daughter Electra went about the palace like a ghost, watching, spying, mourning her father's absence, the madman's daughter.

But the Trojans still fought on, deaths, wounds and plague notwithstanding.

TWENTY-FIVE

Hattusas

IN THE great ceremonial hall of the palace of Suppiluliumas I stood on vast, cold flagstones, speaking of Troy. The king sat beside his wife on a throne with lion-heads carved into the wood. The hall filled with incense, like smoke. Huge walls were draped with costly rugs. Great stone images stood against them also.

Suppiluliumas was small and strong-looking, cleanshaven, with braided hair. But the rest of him was all majesty, pomp and all the things which cloak the individual in power and make him more than a man, and inscrutable, as a man, to others. I had expected this. I had seen my own parents don that royal mask, sometimes deliberately, sometimes not, and had noticed that, although they were still my parents, at those moments they were much more than that – other than themselves. So it was, or more so, with the Hittite king and queen. Suppiluliumas wore an embroidered robe over trousers. His consort, in a gold coronet above plaited, henna-red hair, had on a long, gold gown. She had a round, expressionless face and small brown eyes. They sat at a higher level to me on their thrones and they were very still. They did not give, and did not want to, any impression that they were ordinary people. They were not ordinary people.

I knew the Great King could decide to do anything with me: kill me, which was unlikely, unless some oracle decreed it, or keep me as a guest, a slave, a consort. I could do nothing but speak as appealingly as I could about my country's plight and plead, as cleverly as I might, for assistance. He already knew my case – the messenger from Gordion must have brought that information earlier. Nevertheless, from my knees, my voice sounding very small and light in that huge space, I made my appeal humbly and finished speaking.

Suppiluliumas' hollow voice came booming at me, 'We will send two regiments in spring. Can the city hold until then?'

I crawled towards him, on hands and knees, as my mother had instructed me to do. I reared up, my arms round his knees, and thought irrelevantly the movement was like that of one child trying to topple another from a stool.

'Thank you, Great King,' I said, raising my eyes slowly to him. Plainly he did not like this. I dropped them again.

He said a deadly thing, 'They say there is plague in Troy.'

I could not feel my lips as I responded, eyes on the ground, 'I know nothing of it. All was well when I left.'

'I must have reports of this. You will return with fifteen of my warriors as an escort. Fourteen will remain to fight; one must ride back immediately, before the snows, with a report on this matter. The others must not live inside the city if there is disease there. If there is sickness, no further troops will be sent while it continues.'

I again glanced up at him briefly. His eyes were like black stone, obsidian, reflecting nothing. I looked down, stood, and backed away from him until I was a long distance away. Then a court official took my arm, turned me round and hurried me off, through lightly-falling snow, across the great courtyards and through the huge buildings of Hattusas. He handed me over to a woman with plaited hair under a veil of the thinnest material I have ever seen. They had brought me to the women's house. I was scarcely conscious of this. As I had been taken through the palace I had heard nothing but 'plague in Troy' in my ears. Now, I reeled, and had to steady myself against the woman's shoulder. She kindly took me to a room, where a great pool of hot water steamed. There I bathed, an army of other women standing near me. They seemed to be of many races. As I was washed they talked, asking me questions about my family and the war, asking me, also, if rumours of plague in Troy were true. I knew I had better answer them coherently – these were the Great King's relatives, no doubt, wives, aunts, daughters, possibly his mother. I did not know how influential they might be. They dressed me and food was brought – I was still in a daze. Preparing myself for and going through the interview with the Great King had tired me greatly. It was so important. Hearing of plague in Troy had been a dreadful blow. Moreover, I was not speaking in my own language. I was also conscious that the all-powerful king might change his mind about the armies, although this was unlikely – he had given his public word – or might arbitrarily decide to do something else with me – marry me himself, marry me to another person, just detain me until spring.

These women would report on me, I thought, not just on my state of being and apparent character, but on my looks, which they had had plenty of opportunity to examine. It would be very difficult to escape being a wife of Suppiluliumas if that was what he decided. Behind all these thoughts was another – anxiety about the plague.

The women took me to a large, grand room where we ate a meat, dressed with many spices, that I had never tasted before. There was also a peculiar soft grain, and strange vegetables and fruit, then a sweet-meat made of nuts and honey. There was great wealth here evidently – the women wore fine fabrics and jewellery of gold and glittering stones. There must have been fifteen or twenty women at this meal, some evidently of the utmost, foreign refinement, others near barbarians. For example, one was a doe-eyed Babylonian, I thought, while another was a Gasga chieftainess with terrifying eyes, bold and blue as a winter sky. Another, I felt sure, was of the Greek tribe, a young woman of fifteen, red-haired, who avoided my eyes or any speech with me. In the end, the others drifted off and I was left with two women. One was about thirty-five and of great importance, judging by her dress of silver and gold and her noble bearing. The other was some ten years younger, with piled-up hair, a heavily-beaded dress and a big, embroidered cloak. Her eyes were ringed with kohl, her headdress elaborate. These women both addressed me as 'sister' and treated me with respect. I was not, however, easy in my mind. In these kingdoms the channels through which power flows are complicated and many run underground, making it dangerous not to understand who people are and what they want. These women could have been anyone, from the king's mother and chief wife to powerful sorceresses. It was impolite of them not to explain who they were. I thought it was deliberate. They wished to investigate me.

'You will be leaving us soon, sister, before the snows,' said the older woman.

'The snow is here,' I said astonished.

She was amused. 'You have not seen it as we do in winter, day after day, piled as high as two men, until spring comes and melts it.' She laughed again at my expression. 'You will never have seen the world turn white.'

'We hear you are gifted with second sight. Do you tell fortunes?' the younger woman enquired eagerly.

'I regret it does not come on command,' I had to answer. 'I have not the gift of those oracles to whom you ask a question and they will straight away give you a true answer.' I added, though, not wishing to offend, 'I will try, if you wish it.' I hoped that the effort, to see perhaps if the younger woman was to bear a son who would be a king, or if the older woman was to die or win a great victory, or whatever they wanted me to foretell would not submerge me in that other world where I could only tell the real truth that came to me. For so often the truth was hard and alarmed or displeased the listeners. Sometimes I have the good fortune to be in control of my gift, able to predict truly, but suppress the bad and emphasise the good, in someone's future, just as a fortune-teller will. But more often, I can only say what I am told to say. And bad news would not endear me to these women of Suppululiumas' court. Bad news never makes friends. Some might ask, could I not just lie, as a fortune-teller does in the market-place? But to know true prophecy and lie is dangerous. The god or goddess who gave the gift may, if it is abused, take revenge.

An offer to tell a fortune is in my experience never refused. The older woman stuck a small, smooth palm out at me. 'Shall I take off my rings?' she asked. My eye was stuck now into the heart of the carved ruby – it had a bird's, perhaps an eagle's, eye inscribed on it. It was most beautiful. It was also somewhat evil.

Touching her small, warm hand, I felt, or knew now the woman was the mother of the king. She must have borne him when she was no more than twelve years old. There would have been other sons, by other women, yet her son was king. Her efforts on his behalf had probably been formidable, as she was. I then saw her own mother, magnolia-skinned and almond-eyed, taking the ring from the jeweller who had engraved it, blinding him, so that he would make no more. Her mother had been a princess from very far off – the land of great emperors, where plants grew in great ponds. This I told the king's mother. I was glad it was a small vision, a mere trickle. Then it ceased. I had spoken little, but I had spoken truly. When I released the queen's hand both she and the younger woman smiled. I had under-estimated their subtlety. They were not interested in their futures, only in my authenticity. But was it a trap? It was known I had said Troy would fall. Would they tell the king? Would he decide that if I was a true prophetess, then it was pointless to commit troops for our salvation?

'What do your priests and priestesses say of Troy? Do they speak of the war?' I asked boldly.

'We go to the old witches, village people,' the young woman told me. 'They say strange things, nothing clear. The old woman from Carchemish says it is a war which will bring eternal fame to all who strive in it. This prophecy puzzled us.' It was plain they saw Troy as a very minor part of their empire.

'Does the Great King know this?' I asked.

'He went to the old woman a month ago. She lives in a hut by the river Euphrates, from which she will not move. So the Great King visited her. She is said to be one hundred years old. Certainly she can remember much, or seems to. She repeated the other foretellings. She said, over and over, "Troy will never be forgotten." '

I reflected that the rulers of such great empires have few desires that cannot be satisfied. Death and being wiped from the memories of men are the two enemies they cannot vanquish. This is why they make big statues, huge cities that will live after them. This prophecy, of eternal fame through Troy, would help our cause. I said nothing about this, though.

In vision I saw the other woman with a child. 'You will bear a son,' I declared. She gave me an enigmatic glance. 'Perhaps,' I temporised. 'Or perhaps I am mistaken.'

'Perhaps.' She smiled. I think she knew she had conceived a child. The atmosphere was less suspicious, more friendly. I imagined myself dealing with two amiable lionesses. I could pat and stroke the huge beasts, amuse them perhaps, but never without the fear that they might, on a whim, kill me. Emboldened,

I asked the question I had planned to ask the Great King before he spoke of plague in the city.

'I need iron, my lady,' I said. 'May I have iron?' I was pleading for speartips and swords. I had the idea that compared with those of iron, bronze swords would seem soft as clay.

'Iron would be of no use to you. You could not smelt it,' the queen's mother said. 'You could not repair it unless you had a smith who knew the proper way to handle the metal. Have you such a man?'

I shook my head. 'Could you send us one?'

'I will think about it,' was all she said.

I spent the night with several other women in a stifling room, where braziers gave off strange, lovely scents. I was dizzy with it in that heat, covered as I was by the hide of some huge, coarse-furred beast.

Next morning Naomi and I left in a chariot, with fifteen horsemen in armour mounted on fast ponies. Naomi had spent her night among the Hittite slaves. Galloping terrifyingly downhill, I asked her, 'Any word of Nisintas?'

'They gossip about him,' she reported. 'He's a hero. All are excited about his journey from Troy with you, lady. It seems he came back to find the farmer's daughter widowed – but her oldest child was his. She welcomed him. And the farmer is in need of a strong back for his forge. Nisintas is a happy man, now.'

'I was hoping he'd come back as a smith,' I said.

She shook her head. 'Is there plague in Troy?' she asked. Slaves hear everything.

'How do I know?' I asked. 'They say so – it may be a rumour.'

326

And so we went on, day after day, across the plain, sleeping a few hours wrapped in furs, in the snow, then off again, by torchlight. The journey, at Hittite military speed, was very fast. In a week we were at Brusa, into which we clattered late one night, and were given a royal welcome, with no fear this time of poison or assassination.

Laodice denied rumours of plague in Troy had reached her. I spent an easier night.

We left Brusa at dawn next day. From a bend in the road the queen's consort, Syr, broke from some bushes, naked and smeared with body paint and mud, and stood in the road, tears running down his face. He pleaded to come with us to Troy. His life, he was babbling, wasn't worth a potsherd at Brusa; the king and queen were mad. His conception of himself as a sacred part of the nation and people was much damaged by their perverted behaviour. The night before they had painted him with indigo and gold, allowed him to be used in ways he found wrong by two Greek captains and he had realised then he was within an inch of his life. They were collaborating with the Greeks. If the alliance went any further he sensed, he said, they would sacrifice him, not for the traditional religious reasons, for fertility and prosperity, but to try to ensure a Greek victory.

Syr said they'd lied when they said there was no plague in Troy. They had heard rumours, but the queen feared the news would cause us to delay or even cancel our return. She desperately wanted to be rid of us before we discovered her collaboration with the Greeks. She'd been forced to conceal the two captains when we arrived.

I was cast down by the news – I had no idea what

to do with this man. He was highly unstable, probably drugged, and had almost certainly been ruined by his life in Brusa. For all I knew he might also be a spy. At best he would be another mouth to feed in what I began increasingly to fear was a city not just at war, but also plagued. I did not want to stay arguing with him on the road. Desperate to get home with the troops, and to find out what was happening I urged, 'Go back to where you came from.' But he told me he came from Brusa itself – until two years ago he had worked for his father, making barrels for salted fish. So I gave him a tunic I had planned to give one of my brothers and left him on the road. He was young, he had a trade; Troy was at war; we had no food, winter was coming, there was nothing I could do for him. We sped on.

At dawn next morning we came over the rise and looked down on the city nearly a mile away. There would be no point in re-entering the city by the tunnel on the hillside. Each time it was entered or left increased the risk of discovery and, besides, with a contingent of armed men, we had no fear of capture. We paused on the hill above the plain and looked down.

Beyond Troy lay the sea, the Greek camp, their ships. In that area the small figures of almost a thousand Greek warriors moved about. Then there was the city and, beneath us on the plain behind it, the black smoke of several funeral pyres arose. A crowd emerged from the city, surrounding a waggon, drawn by two horses. Whatever there was in the waggon was covered by straw matting, but even from a distance there was an indication of human shapes. A truce had been declared to allow funeral ceremonies for the Trojan dead. There were so many pyres, I thought desperately. So many must have died. The meadow where once sweet grass and flowers had grown, and our flocks had grazed, was now covered in blackened circles.

The captain of the Hittite soldiers was biting his lip. I said, 'You see the funeral rites and you can see how many must have died. There may be plague in the city. You will not want to come any closer.'

He said, 'My orders were to stay at a distance if there was plague.'

'Better to remain here and set up your camp. We can communicate through messengers.'

'If we're to fight with you we might as well bury your dead with you,' he replied, adding grimly, 'in any case, we may end up on your funeral pyres – we might as well inspect the arrangements. We'll ride down together.' And slowly, as if approaching our deaths, we rode downhill under grey skies, the wind whipping round us.

We had of course been seen by that crowd of two hundred mourners. All were sadly thin. Many were weeping and on some faces tears ran through grime. They looked towards us as we approached. Deiphobus ran towards me, smiling, but the bones of his face stood out. His arms and legs were thin, his tunic grubby. Behind him came my mother. I had searched in vain for other familiar faces and saw none. The captain of our troupe dismounted and greeted my mother. Deiphobus was embracing me, laughing. 'We thought you might be dead.'

'I thought you might be,' I said, weeping. 'Who lies in that waggon?'

'The uncle of Aeneas. And young Crachis, the inn-keeper's boy – and the sister of Adosha, only fourteen,' he told me. 'Crachis died of wounds, the others of disease.' He added, 'Thirty fighting men have died since you left, including Democoon, and old Clytios, who insisted on putting on armour and going into battle. Fifteen citizens have died of the disease. And Creusa lost her unborn child.'

He paused. That was when my mother came to embrace me. 'Your father lies ill,' she murmured.

We stood for the long hours of the fetching of wood, the pouring on of oil, the ceremonies, the weeping, as those tragically light bodies were piled on the communal pyre. Anchises' brother was in his ceremonial robe. There was the light, undergrown body of Adosha's sister, there was the boy, Crachis – in the end they just looked like rags and bones, huge dolls with false hair tumbling round waxy faces. Where there are too many bodies the meaning of funeral ceremonies seems to disappear. It is disposal, not mourning, especially when the faces of the mourners are almost as sunken as those of the corpses, as ours seemed to be, and when they have so little energy to express their grief or, perhaps, such grief has become a state of mind.

I held the hands of Adosha and my mother, and we all wept. Anchises was not there to mourn his brother. He was ill. Creusa, too, was ill. Aeneas stood on my mother's other side, still in armour, grim and silent. My mother was thin. Her eyes were sunken. She could not ask me how my mission had gone, though, even with my father ill and at this solemn moment, she must have been concerned to know.

'The news is good,' I told her briefly and heard her sigh. 'How is my father?' It was a heart-stopping

330

moment which lasted for a long time. Would she tell me he was dying? A cold wind blew across the plain, bringing dead leaves with it.

'He may recover,' she told me steadily.

The Hittite soldiers stood respectfully at a distance, awed and frightened by the mournful scene. I knew they must be apprehensive about the future. They had looked forward, as soldiers do, to seeing a strange part of the country and to battle, with the prospect of booty for the brave and lucky. They were finding disease, exhausted, dirty warriors, indications of defeat.

Ten men galloped up – Greek cavalry. 'Go away!' cried Deiphobus. 'Let us bury our dead in peace!' But they made a wide circle round us and rode slowly round the pyre, the waggon and the group of mourners, encircling us to prevent us from breaking from the pyre in search of food and water. The Hittite soldiers were astonished and the two groups of men, Hittite and Greek, regarded each other curiously. The Greeks' armour was dented; their faces were gaunt. They looked hardly better than we did. Aeneas took the lighted torch and hurled it through the air. It fell on the wasted body of his uncle, in his elaborate robe. Deiphobus lit around the bottom of the pyre. It flared. Adosha screamed. The lost lives of the dead went up into the sky, the bitter smell of their burning bodies blew east on the wind. The Greek soldiers rode round and round.

'Plague has reached our enemies,' Deiphobus muttered to me. 'Before, we thought defeat inevitable as we weakened day by day. Anchises was urging surrender. News of their sickness made us decide to hold on. And we were awaiting your return.'

My mother and I, and Deiphobus, supporting Adosha, stood and gazed at the burning pyre. The centre now flamed and there was just a glimpse, through flames, of black things, no longer bodies. We all wailed for the dead. Under the eyes of the slowly circling enemy, we sang their resurrection in the paradise of the mother.

Then Hecuba took my hand. 'Come back now,' she said. 'You look weary, and you must tell me of your journey.'

'Should we not wait?' I asked. It was customary to stay with the mourners until the bodies were consumed.

She smiled a weary smile. 'The ceremonies grow shorter,' she said.

Deiphobus went to look after the Hittite soldiers, while we walked back to the city. Smiler, my dog, bounded from the open gate. He, too, was very thin. My mother said nothing, but I knew they had fed the dog with scraps, which however undesirable should have gone to the people.

Hector came out to embrace me, and my brothers and sisters and many others. We went into the city. Once it had smelled of woodsmoke, bread baking on hot stone, of fish, of the heavy scent of apricots in season, of fermenting wine or incense from the temple. Now it smelled of dirt, disease, hard grease and underneath, of faeces, urine and sickness. The courtyard of the temple as we passed was full of prone figures. There were groans. Two women were hauling out the body of a youth, naked but for a breechclout, every rib showing, one leg only a bandaged stump. His face was greenish. He might have been dead, or only nearly so.

There were no stalls, there was no smell of food. There were few people about. I did not know then that during famines people lie down, at home, in a kind of daze. Hunger keeps itself secret. Two thin children sat on a pavement, blank-faced. Thin women watched as we passed. A skeletal man in armour leaned against a wall. The big mute young man, the slave, pitifully reduced from what he was, stood at his forge, hammering out a sword, a grim expression on his blackened face.

Anchises came down the steps of the street leading upwards, hand outstretched. But he looked very bent, weakened, seeming much older. 'You've brought soldiers,' he said.

For what? I thought privately. So that they could starve, or die of the sickness too? He told me later that the day before Achilles had been seen taking his men away in a ship. 'His rage continues. Now he's completely abandoned Agamemnon. We shall mount the attack soon,' he promised.

'How is my husband?' asked Hecuba.

'No worse,' he said. 'Creusa also lives. Perhaps it is best the child died,' he added. 'There is no food for any of the children. Helen brought Creusa a peach, a little withered, but still a peach.'

'Generous as ever,' commented my mother. I had never heard such bitterness in her voice. My sick father, I discovered, was living on gruel made of barley. People were boiling twice-boiled bones for soup, children chewing leaves which had blown into the city. People ate wheat husks, grape pressings, half rotten, half-fermented skins and pips, bad for all, lethal for the weak. One thing was certain – no one else in that city had a peach, wrinkled or not.

As we wound up to the palace I saw that trees in the gardens of the wealthy had been cut down, for fuel, I supposed. Paris and Helen's house was shut. Behind the gates fierce dogs leapt up, ready to kill intruders. As we passed I saw my mother looking deliberately ahead, unwilling to acknowledge the closed palace, the dogs, the couple hiding behind their own walls. I thought at first the palace was closed merely because they were hoarding food in there and feared attack from starving people. Later, I realised there was another reason why they hid. They feared if they opened their gates someone would kill Helen – a soldier, a bereaved mother or wife.

I missed many faces, the faces of those now dead or too ill, like my father, to be present. Meanwhile Deiphobus brought the Hittite captain to a meeting of all the warriors where the result of my visit to Suppululiumas was told to everyone. All agreed the city must hold out, if possible until spring, when the promised reinforcements would arrive. It was important that news of the reinforcements should not reach the Greeks. They must be led to think the fifteen soldiers were the only Hittite warriors coming.

That night Helen tried to leave the city, disguised as an old woman. She was brought to the great hall of the palace before dawn. She stood in rags, the old shawl she had thrown over her head to hide her face falling away from her blonde hair. That surpassingly beautiful face was tear-stained and desperate. She sobbed. My mother said, in a voice like ice, 'Do not cry. You cannot leave now. You cannot go back to

Menelaus and trade our secrets for your safety. Too late to go now, Helen.'

She was led off by Paris, gasping, 'I am a prisoner in this city, a prisoner.' I would not wish to see Paris' expression then on the face of my worst enemy, nor have that enemy feel as he must have done. I have already said how, wherever she went, Helen brought shame to others.

Unhappily, because of my return and the news I brought, though it was too late, the hall was full. Hector was there of course, as was Sarpedon, who had fallen asleep, and many of the Lycians, and Troilus and Anchises – this degrading scene, in short, took place before the weary and incredulous faces of many of Troy's greatest warriors – men who risked their lives almost daily in a war begun by Helen's flight.

The shame on the face of Paris, as he led off his sobbing, foolishly disguised wife, was pitiable. Both Hector and Troilus dropped their heads as they passed. Anchises, sometimes a foolish man, had been turned into a realist by tragedy, by hunger and by the earlier fear of my father, the king's, death. Unusually, he said nothing, but his face was filled with disgust. Into the silence, a grey-bearded farmer, Colaxes, captain of a band of Lycians, spoke. His son had died a month before, in great pain, of wounds delivered by Menelaus.

He said, 'We have witnessed something here of which we must never speak. This foolish woman Helen, cause of this war, might have offered herself back to her former husband by representations made to the King of Sparta in a decent manner. Then, if Menelaus had agreed to take her, and withdrawn his men, the war would have ended. Instead, she acted like a thief in the night, without any thought of the consequences. No doubt she thought that if Menelaus rejected her, she could sneak back again in her disguise without anyone knowing. She deliberately risked her own capture by Menelaus, who could then have continued the war, with the benefit of all the information she could give him. This,' he said, looking round, 'is the nature of the woman for whom we fight and die – foolish, near-treacherous and degraded. I do not want it known that it was for a woman of this character my beloved son died, and for whom my remaining son will go on fighting. And if we allow tonight's events to become public, the Greeks will mock – how they will mock – and our own citizens will despair, when they discover Helen was attempting to flee the city. We must swear never to reveal this disgrace. Tomorrow we go into battle again,' he added. 'We have the Hittite warriors now, plague has struck the Greeks, but we don't know how badly. We have a promise of reinforcements. We must not flag because our own warriors are bitter and weary.'

'Paris will be in the forefront of the fighting, that's for sure,' Hector promised.

Sarpedon staggered to his feet, putting a wine-skin to his lips and taking a big draught. 'He could be killed a hundred times and not redeem that woman's honour,' he said. 'But then, she's only a woman after all, making up in treachery for what she lacks in strength. The battle's not about her after all, is it, friends? It's the cursed Greeks and their cursed ambitions. That's it, isn't it? Come on – that's what we all know.' He lurched to the door and left.

Helenus said, 'He's not drunk.'

I said, 'I know. He's a gallant man.'

336

Next day in the early morning I joined the women of Troy on the ramparts as the gate was opened and our warriors went out. Beside me a woman said, 'Four more deaths last night in the city.' Another said, 'Let's hope there were five among the Greeks.'

But they had already mustered down by the sea, still a thousand strong, so it seemed to our distressed eyes. Now they came towards Troy heavy-footed over sodden, trampled ground. Our lines advanced to meet them. The Phrygian bowmen let fly.

Returning after so many weeks away, I saw clearly not only what had happened to my own people but to the Greeks as well. As they came closer, I saw huge Diomedes had lost his former carefree look, that of a cheerful young man, itching for a fight. Ulysses' face was grim. Agamemnon was the grimmest and most terrifying of all. His nose was like a beak, his face long and sallow. He had the air of a man about to avenge himself for the worst crime in the world. It was obvious the advance was not only slow because the earth below their feet was damp and heavy. They were tired now, like wrestlers who have fought for hours – and still their opponents will not yield. Many must have wished now they had never seen the shores of Troy.

On the ramparts of Troy we women stood, gaunt-faced and anxious. Almost all had some relative, husband, father, brother, some dear friend among the warriors. Once our troops, and theirs, had advanced singing; once the armies had shouted at each other; now the battles began in silence. One woman sobbed helplessly, for no real reason, except, perhaps, that she could bear no more. Adosha, with one brother dead, another captured and perhaps dead, stood with the ashes from her dead sister's pyre still visible in her hair. In her arms she held her son, Hector's child. That Hector's wife, Andromache, holding Hector's other son, stood to my right seemed not to matter at all. Perhaps it was enough that both children, unlike so many, were still alive.

We must have stood a hundred times at the top of the city, watching spears hit home, swords clash against each other, watching men fall. This time, though weary, we had some hope, something new to think about. There were fifteen Hittite soldiers, fresh men on fresh, tough horses on our side. Perhaps they could turn the battle for us. Perhaps even now we could turn resistance into victory.

Hector got the charioteers to attack from right and left, just as the lines of marching men were within arm's reach. Trojan chariots swung in on the Greek force as hand-to-hand fighting began. I saw Ajax, always recognisable by the vast boar's tusks he wore on his helmet, stumble and fall as a chariot veered into him. A Trojan was on him in a flash, bludgeoning him across the head with his sword. I watched our carpenter, old Harmon's son, go down by a big spear-thrust from Menelaus. Diomedes was leaping among the Trojan troops. Then down the hill came the Hittite men, on their little horses, at great speed, smacking into the battle at force, scattering Greek and Trojan alike. Their curved swords rose and fell. They were well-trained fighting men, they were fresh. And this put heart into our own troops. The battle, as if by magic, pushed down and down towards the shore, as the Hittite cavalry turned and wheeled, their swords flashing. That a mere fifteen men could be accomplishing all this astonished us.

We could see our own men right down at the beach now, fighting among the ships, a confusing tangle of small figures, struggling together, with the Hittite horsemen among them, rearing reluctant horses into the waves. Below, women with jugs and basins were running to the river Scamander, filling their vessels and racing back to the city. To the left I saw a party of four or five women, with bundles, a baby, trailing children they were urging on over their shoulders. They were leaving, taking the road east, unwilling any longer to starve and hope for victory. They would risk being picked up later by Greek patrols, risk finding themselves roofless somewhere else – anything to escape Troy and the fighting.

Just to the right of the road I saw a girl holding a flaming brand, trying to urge a boy on to an unsaddled pony. She pointed towards the beach holding the torch aloft, while he hesitated, argued. Suddenly she jumped astride the horse herself and, bare legs kicking into its sides, was charging down to the beach. Her plan, and it was clever, though very dangerous, was to set fire to the Greek ships, where they lay. It was a decision the council had long debated – whether to leave the fleet alone, and hope the Greeks would re-embark and go home, or burn the fleet and cut them off. But the girl had made her own decision.

We watched as she rode through the edge of the mêlée of warriors and men fighting in the water, urged her horse into the sea and hurled the burning torch into a pile of something on the deck of the nearest ship. It caught. It burned. Then a warrior reared up, caught the horse's head with one hand, thrust a spear into the girl with the other, then wrenched her, using the spear as a lever, into the water. On the ramparts, a groan went up. A knot of women formed round one woman, as she screamed. The girl's mother, or sister, I supposed. Andromache went to the woman, to comfort her and praise her brave daughter.

A trumpet blared now. Hector had given the order to retreat. 'Why?' Adosha cried. 'Why?' As our troops plodded slowly away from the beach, unopposed in their retreat, we saw why. There were dead, or wounded, across the pommels of each horse, in chariots carried between men. Men leaned on each other's shoulders. As they walked they took off helmets, wiped blood from their faces, with slow, fumbling gestures. Spears trailed, swords dangled from their hands. The Greeks, worse hit than our men, did not pursue.

We rushed from the gates to help. I ran past Hector, whose face was a bloody mask under his helmet. He could not see and was supported by a limping Aeneas. Adosha, still holding her child, grasped a collapsing boy who was shaking from head to foot. I put my shoulder under Deiphobus' arm, my arm round his neck, and helped him back to the city. One hand held his sword, which trailed on the ground. His other arm dangled uselessly. His eyes stared; he did not know where he was.

The Hittite soldiers, with their burden of corpses and wounded, were also staring straight ahead, shocked after battle. Sarpedon carried a bleeding, twisting man in his arms, speaking to him steadily as he came through the gates.

Long hours passed as we tended the wounded. With Naomi, I took water from man to man. Injured men filled all the houses, the temple and the warehouses on the lower level of the city. They lay on floors of houses, in workshops, in gardens, higher up. Inside the city, already with its burden of sickness, were sixteen dead warriors, fifty gravely injured, a hundred warriors with slashes, cuts and broken bones, some of which would, in other circumstances, have been considered serious. Now Aeneas' damaged knee, which might half cripple him, the mighty gash which had cut through Hector's helmet into his head and many other woundings were considered minor injuries. We concerned ourselves with the belly of a man ruptured by a spear, a shattered spine caused by being pushed back against a ship, while a Greek warrior hacked at the victim with his sword, a man's chest pierced by a spear. The uninjured – men, women, old men, even children – unbuckled armour, tried to staunch the blood, washed, wiped, bandaged, tried to comfort.

Hector was sitting against a wall, holding a red cloth to his head, talking in a mumble to my father and Anchises. A slave was supporting my father as they spoke. The Hittite captain stood by, with a stony face. 'We could not have gone on. They were turning,' Hector said.

'Tomorrow, then,' the Hittite said grimly.

Hector nodded. 'Tomorrow.'

I did not see the girl with the torch among the wounded.

Next day the Greeks built their funeral pyres, then turned to building a rampart to defend their camp. They moved slowly, but steadily it went up. This rampart, made of earth brought in waggons from beyond the river, was ten feet tall and five feet thick, with two gaps for chariots to go through. Beyond it was a moat some five feet deep. Sharpened palings were embedded in it as in pits to catch fierce beasts.

We should have prevented the Greeks from doing this, but fighting right down by the beach in such an exposed position could have cost us many more casualties. Weakened by sickness and the last battle, we had to allow them to fortify their camp.

They were now dying behind their wall, both from disease and wounds just as we died behind ours. We daily saw the smoke from their funeral pyres on the beach rising from behind their ramparts. It was Anchises who said, at a council meeting, 'This proves they fear our attack more now. We are besieging them as they are besieging us. Now we are all prisoners.'

It was not strictly true, of course, for the Greeks were not in their own land and had only to get into their ships and go home.

Meanwhile, Achilles had evidently returned in a storm from Tenedos, for no ascertainable reason. He had not come to fight, anyway. He had already created for himself a rather handsome wooden dwelling some distance from the main part of the Greek camp, unprotected by the rampart. He now made this the centre of a fenced compound – but refused to come out and fight. His countrymen, the Myrmidons, who were of course under his direct orders, were not fighting either. He was not on speaking terms with Agamemnon. The Greeks were furious. He and his friends, chief among them being Patroclus, exercised in the compound outside his dwelling. They feasted and played games. It was a grave insult to Agamemnon, for not only could the Greeks see his pranks – we, the enemy, could watch him too.

He was a perverse and quixotic man, admired by both sides for his courage and gallantry. Hector, a man of exactly the same kind, said, 'The cause of his sulks is the Trojan girl, Briseis no doubt. And his hatred of Agamemnon's pride. He wishes to prove Agamemnon is not general over the whole expeditionary force. And I think, too, he sees himself as too great a man to want victory over a sick and starving city full of women and children. What heroism is there in that? It's not beyond him to offer to join us, mark my words. He's his own man, not Agamemnon's. He fights when he wants for whom he wants.'

And then – Achilles returned to Tenedos again.

Meanwhile the smoke from our funerals rose, day and night, in the fields beyond the city. Often the Greek cavalrymen rode round and round the site of the funerals. This made our bitter grieving worse – as we burned the dead, their murderers rode about at a distance, watching.

We had, of course, a means of entering and leaving the city secretly – the tunnel my mother had caused to be opened. The Hittite troop, with some reinforcements of our own, were camped on the hills at the tunnel mouth. It would be understood by the Greeks they were keeping clear of the city to avoid plague. Because they were vulnerable to attack from Greek forces though, we had a signalling system, a fire which could be lit to warn us if they were about to be attacked. But this never happened. The Greeks were weary and restricted their efforts to the city, knowing better than to attack such skilful and ferocious enemies.

Through the tunnel mouth supplies could be brought into the city, never enough, but something to relieve the famine. Through it, too, we could receive rare messages from the outside world.

The winter wore on. The shortest day came and went. A black and terrible sacrifice took place on that day. We had no beasts left to sacrifice, so the old custom, seldom used, was revived, and a Greek boy slave from the city, a pretty youth of about twelve, though very thin, was killed in honour of the goddess. Anchises held this would please her and bring us victory. Those who wished to attend the ceremony, about a hundred or so, came from the city under heavy guard that night. It was overcast, there was no visible moon, a bad omen, there were few painted faces, the only sound was of a mournful flute and one drum, beating slowly. Throughout the ceremony our soldiers had to circle the crowd every step of the way, up the hill to the sacred place. They waited among the trees while the ceremony was conducted. As my mother, in the grove by the blood-pit, the oracle beside her, brought down the knife, the boy cursed us all in Greek. His voice, in one thin, high scream, cut through the sound of the drum as he delivered his curse in the names of Artemis and Clytemnestra. His speech was so fluent and so terrifying, it was plainly inspired. It made our thin blood turn to water.

A darkness came over me. Free of visions for so long, even as the boy died, crying out his curses, I saw Troy burn again, the Greek king dashing the head of Hector's child against a wall, blood running over the stones of the city, survivors in chains, setting out in a mournful convoy across the Aegean for Greece. Adosha said my mother also screamed as I lay on the ground, writhing and shouting out my vision. She was crying out, 'Oh, goddess, take this curse from me – ' and few knew whether she meant the prophecy or the prophetess. Others, too, were raving and yelling. As soon as I fell, Naomi flung herself across my prone body, Adosha said, while Helenus ran forward at speed, in his armour – he was on guard – and helped to pick me up. Then he and Hector turned and, with my body across Helenus' saddle, and Hector running beside the horse, his sword drawn, they rapidly carried me back to the city. They feared the wrath of my fellow citizens, ground down by siege, horrified by a sacrifice gone badly wrong. The people would have killed me, said Adosha grimly, if Naomi had not sensed the danger so quickly and attracted the attention of my brothers before the crowd had rallied.

We were in the little room we had occupied when Helenus and I were children. 'There would have been two sacrifices last night,' Adosha said, 'if that skimpy creature hadn't been nimble-witted enough to make a fuss and save you. Especially as the first sacrifice went so badly.' She pointed at Naomi, who was putting a couple of sticks on the brazier. She must have acquired them in the grove the night before. While the sacrifice took place she had been collecting wood and hiding it in her clothes. It was bitterly cold. We were short of fuel and Naomi made her adherence to her own childhood religion, involving the magical box of laws, written on stone, and the god who was the wind, an excuse for believing in nothing.

There was a macabre satisfaction in Adosha's warning voice, as if she had not forgiven me for being such a disturbing child when she was my girl-nurse. Or perhaps she shared the views of my fellow citizens, after the terrible foretellings she heard me utter that night. She had lost two brothers, after all. She warned me, 'When the spring ceremonies come, if the Greeks have not left, they may decide only you will serve as a sacrifice. There'll be no need to bless the planting or the lambing or pray for a good harvest. There'll be no planting. There are scarcely any sheep left. Victory will be the blessing we seek from the goddess and who better to secure it than you?'

'If my death can secure victory, if I am the sacrifice they require, then so be it,' I said.

Naomi's defiant sneer on hearing this shocked even me, who knew her so well. Adosha smacked her face, reproving her for her impiety at the same time. 'That was a fearful curse the boy delivered as he died,' she scolded. 'We must show all reverence over serious matters. If your mistress can sacrifice herself for the city, surely you can behave properly.'

Naomi took the reproof and looked sombre. Yet I knew, underneath it all, she was an unbeliever. Of course, I was not. I had felt the great wings of a hostile Artemis in the grove that night, beating about in an atmosphere thick with her hatred. How to lift this curse I did not know. Unless it be by my own willing death.

TWENTY-SIX

Thessaly

WENTY YEARS later, I thought of my readiness
to sacrifice myself for Troy. Would it have
made any difference? I doubt it. The fates are
not generous enough to make life so straightforward.
Would that they were. Even now, I suspect, they were
urging us forward from war to the fatal moment when
Agamemnon was to die. I thought of this as Helen
gave me her sister Clytemnestra's account of the
events leading inexorably to that moment. The dead
queen's voice, burning ice, came into the darkened
room. I shivered. It was as if she were there with us.
But she herself had been dead for thirteen years.

The blood of the spring sacrifice in Mycenae that year
ran over unploughed fields where grass, asphodels
and poppies grew wild. We had not ploughed in
autumn or in spring; now we could not plant our
grain. Many of the fields had been fallow the year
before, or, if they had been planted, by menfolk before
they set out for Troy, the crops had not been properly
tended or harvested. Saplings were sprouting
unchecked at the margins of the fields, weeds and
wild flowers sprang up where ploughs should have

347

made furrows. Earth was already beginning to seize back her land. We were, of course, hungry and would become hungrier. Harvests had been poor, stock eaten instead of saved for breeding. The women had sheared as best they could the previous year, but had little time for weaving or even mending clothes. The spectacle of the under-tended farms, harassed women and overworked, neglected children distressed me greatly, whatever my other thoughts and plans. Unfarmed land, ungathered harvest and stricken farmers are a chilling and shaming sight for any ruler.

Meanwhile messages came from Troy demanding reinforcements. In Argos Aegisthus, in his role as a loyal relative, rounded up all men between the ages of fourteen and forty-five, no matter how their mothers or grandchildren clung to them, no matter how sick they claimed to be. The force that had gone out, high-hearted, in search of a quick victory, wealth and slaves, had lost many to plague and battle. Now we were down to the old, the young, the sick and the cowards. We had ground the ears; now we had to grind the husks. Many houses were now bereaved. All were anxious. The news of sickness in the camp at Troy caused as much fear as the war itself. The people were gloomy and disheartened.

I was, of course, urged to offer great sacrifices for victory, conduct impressive ceremonies throughout Mycenae. This I did not do. The spring ceremonies are for goddess and land, because we depend on them and they on us. I could not offer for victory at that time, even if I had wanted to, because rebirth and regeneration are in direct opposition to war, which is an act of man. It would have been impious to unite them. Desperation – and the people were becoming

348

desperate – has to be controlled, or madness takes over.

By now most families in Mycenae and throughout the rest of Greece had received news of a death – son, uncle, husband – from disease or on the battlefield. I, unluckily, had not. Good men died. The bad ones stayed alive. Agamemnon and Menelaus remained obstinately unwounded and free of disease, as if under the protection of some mad god who deflected sickness, arrows and spears from them, while the innocent perished.

I knew when this war ended the country would be full of injured men and of women telling each other, 'My son fell at Troy,' 'My husband died of a spearthrust at Troy,' 'When I was a girl, before my father died in Troy – ' Meanwhile the country was going to seed. Men were dead and maimed, women sad and weary, and the palace coffers emptied as I despatched more arms, horses and provisions and bought in corn and barley both for the army and to prevent want from turning into famine at home. This waste was what those brothers, my husband and Menelaus, had produced.

I went to Pylos and visited Nestor's queen. She took me to the temple of Artemis and I consulted the oracle there. This oracle, a young handsome man, looked into the future and after a few sentences fell to babbling in a strange tongue. I knew he saw, but would not say what he saw. When I bade him farewell he would not meet my eyes. I was a guest in Pylos, so I could do nothing about this and went to Sparta straight away, leaving Nestor's queen, the Queen of Pylos, terrified – by what she guessed of me and by what the oracle had not dared tell me.

It was a hard journey. Everywhere I went it was the same sad story – broken walls, overgrown fields, unpruned trees and vines going wild – little stock, burdened people – widows, orphans – hunger. The roads were strewn with rocks and pitted, and in places blocked. In other spots they had been washed away by the winter rains and not repaired for want of man-power. In Pylos they had told me Achilles' old father was barely holding off a Thracian band who wanted his farm. It was said that Achilles and the Myrmidons were on their way back to Thessaly to help him. I rejoiced to hear it. With Achilles gone the Greek army would be beaten. Though I did not know if the account were true; rumours flew everywhere.

When I reached Sparta, Sostris, the Regent there, an old man with a withered leg, told me late at night as we sat by the embers of the fire in the great hall, 'The bandits are all but uncontrollable. I can do little. If only Menelaus would return. I fear the future.' He brightened up, though, as he said, 'If they win, Menelaus has promised me Lycia.'

'If all the men who had been promised Lycia were together in this room,' I told him bluntly, 'the crowd would be so large we would have to stand.' There in Sparta I also saw Helen's only child, my niece Hermione. This girl was intended to be the bride of my son Orestes. She asked me about him – young as she was, I thought she was in love with him. The marriage was planned of course, to confirm the alliance of our states, Sparta and Mycenae, and keep our wealth inside the family – sensible, but in this case probably unwise, for Orestes and Hermione were double cousins. I did not think my husband or his brother sane; a farmer would hesitate to breed animals like that. I told Hermione that Orestes was at King Strophius' court – not adding that I believed my husband had sent him there in case of a Trojan victory. I and his sister would be killed or enslaved but Orestes would be protected by Strophius.

I had not come to Sparta to see the Regent, or Helen's daughter. I had come for the Old Woman, the most famous oracle in Greece. Even before I visited the palace I went to the cave in the rock below the citadel and persuaded the Old Woman there to come back to Mycenae with me, promising her much gold. Sostris said wearily, 'You are taking away the Old Woman. If you want her, take her. Consult her about the outcome of this war. She will promise victory because she thinks if she does not, she will die.' I did not want to know about the war, though I did not tell him that. He was a man afraid. If Menelaus died, if the Greeks lost the war, the Trojans would seek him out and kill him. He had two sons in Troy, also.

'If your sister went back to Menelaus, would the war end, do you think?' he asked.

'It's too late now,' I told him. 'This has gone on too long. Too many have died. The army would not leave Troy now, whatever Helen did. And I believe Menelaus would not dare to take her back now. His own people would turn on him.' I believed this. I had prevented Helen's return when it might have ended the war. Now it was too late for her to come back.

Then I left Sparta, spring still bringing flowers and new grass to the neglected land. I took the Old Woman, wrapped in many blankets, back in my chariot. She was indeed very old, only skin and bone, and almost bald. They said she'd been captured from Troezen, when Helen's brothers seized back their kidnapped, ten-year-old sister after her abduction. But I think the Old Woman originally came from further away than that. At any rate, she had been old, very old, almost twenty years ago. Menelaus had inherited her from Helen's father as a kind of wedding gift and had her installed in the caves to prophesy. She was famous as a seer. If she said the Greek army would win the war, I thought probably she was right.

Aegisthus was away on patrol when I returned with her. I let her rest: then, that night, I called her to me when I was alone. Alas for her, she told me horrors. Her words beat black and red waves into my head; a foul tide. She had delivered her prophecies in an old, weak voice, but now added, in a tone like a girl's, 'Now you will kill me, lady. I am old. I hate your world. You are already cursed, so kill me – you cannot make your own fate any worse. I am old, I wish to go home, to be at peace in the fields of the goddess. I do not wish to see any more of this – so kill me now.'

Her words washed to and fro in my bursting head. 'Kill me,' she said again.

Yet there was a moment, as I plunged my dagger into her thin, chicken's breast, when she and I were equals, when I almost loved her. When she was dead I felt calm again. Perhaps she was right, and I was indeed cursed. Perhaps I would go in death into the shadow-land where the dead moan and gibber in darkness, like chained madmen, I did not know or care.

We none of us know what happens after death and it is better not to care. I had been sent, a princess of Sparta, to Agamemnon at the age of sixteen at the same time my father had married Helen to Menelaus.

Two sisters married two brothers. I had gone to my husband and borne what he could do to me, what he was, without flinching. Until he killed our daughter. He had never broken my pride till then. I was the daughter of a king, and the queen of another. I could endure anything because I was a queen. Then – Iphegenia. With the blow he struck to her, he murdered both of us, her in body, me in spirit. And secured his own death, too, for then I decided to kill him. If that cursed me, then I was cursed. But the old laws by which we have lived up to now say a mother's rights over a child are greater than a father's. And in killing his daughter, Agamemnon had not only committed murder but flouted that ancient law. So – who had the right to curse me? Where would that curse come from? I, the mother, was taking vengeance on the man who had taken the life of my child.

I stood there with the Old Woman like a rag at my feet – she had little bone or blood left in her – until Aegisthus came in, dusty, in armour. I went to him with my arms out. He took me here, on the floor, beside the body of the Old Woman. He burned out all the terrifying words she had used to me, the horrible pictures she had raised. As I screamed in orgasm the fear left me. I knew I would triumph.

TWENTY-SEVEN

Troy

THE SACRIFICE of the Greek boy slave brought no change of luck. We would have to endure the winter, hoping Suppiluliumas would send the reinforcements he had promised. We were cold and hungry; the sickness continued to take its toll. What I remember is how silent the city became. There was the sound of the anvil, the prayers in the temple, the cry of a child but otherwise nothing but the screaming of gulls over our towers and ramparts. We would gaze up at them, knowing they were free to fly where they wanted, over the sea, over the fields, over the Greek camp on our shores. The children, ragged and dirty, played less. And when they did play, their games were all fightings, chest-clutchings, hideous coughs and writhings – then death.

Six of the Hittites died too, including their captain. It is a sad thing to die in an alien land among strangers. The remains of their little force still guarded the entrance to the tunnel. They would not enter the city. It stank of sickness they feared to catch. They were weary with fighting and sick of living outside the city, involved in a war which had nothing to do with them, facing death miles from home.

This was when they married me to the husband I

mentioned, because his father, too, was tired of committing troops to a battle further off, tired of the reports of deaths of his own people. That was when I led my skeleton of a dog out to make his own way in the world, blanked my mind in order to give my body to my new husband, rose next day, heartsick, to look out to sea at the Greek camp behind their rampart.

Then Achilles returned. Why he had come, what had been said to persuade him, I do not know. The sight of his many troops setting up camp again was like a black cloud settling over us. As we watched, as ever, from the ramparts, Paris stood with his arm round Hector. 'He's come to fight this time,' Paris said.

Hector did not reply.

'He's fated to lead a short life,' Paris went on. 'Perhaps this is the end of it.'

I tried to conceal the tears in my eyes. Andromache's child lifted a thin arm, pointed, and said, 'Ships – ships.' Poor child, he had learned the word by seeing them from a distance, I doubt if he would have recognised one if he had been standing beside it, on the beach, in the fresh air, touching the wooden hull.

For many days Achilles did nothing but amuse himself. Then his friend Patroclus, bored, perhaps, with this inactivity, went into battle, wearing Achilles' own armour. Hector killed him.

Achilles' grief was overwhelming. Some days after Patroclus' funeral he recovered. His mighty grief gave way to rage on the same scale.

From the ramparts at dawn we watched Achilles'

355

tall figure running at speed from behind the Greek rampart up to the little rise outside the city walls. He was naked to the waist, bare-legged and barefoot. He raised his spear and called, 'Prepare to die, Trojans.' Hector's spear was against the wall. He seized it. This great, bronze-tipped weapon thudded down beside Achilles. We saw Greeks on the ramparts gesticulating, saw them calling him back. His beaky nose was raised towards us. His hair, brown as a horse's, flew about in the wind. He cried, 'Thank you, Hector. I shall cherish the spear. I shall kill you with it, too.'

'You can try. You must be fresh enough, since so far you've done no fighting,' Hector called down. 'This we can all understand. Most men fear battle. And yet – most overcome it.'

Achilles smiled. 'I like you, Hector. I shall regret your death. I'll marry your sister when you're dead,' he called back. He gave a great roar of laughter. 'And your mother too, most probably. Hector, brother-in-law, son, prepare to die.'

By now other spears were being flung at him. There was a flight of arrows, and Achilles turned, still laughing, and ran back. A chorus of yells followed him.

Hector was angry. 'I shall kill him, that madman. They say he's a satyr, too. He seduces or rapes whatever moves. No woman is safe, or man. His best friend was, they say, his lover. He was disguised as a girl when a child, to protect him. That may have saved him from being murdered, but damaged his mind. He knows no law now, not men's law, nor women's. He's like a perverted animal.'

'This is rumour,' said Paris. 'But one thing is cer-

tain, he fights like an animal. Do not dare to attack
him without others round you.'

'I'd attack him unarmed, with my bare hands if I
could, though he had a sword and a shield,' muttered
Hector.

I knew that Achilles was more than an animal,
more than a man, was imbued with some strange
spirit, like the gusts of spring wind blowing from the
sea which were catching us now – like a lion, like a
river in full spate. I had seen him kill my brother
Hector so often in dreams and visions. Now, blackness swept over me anew. I lifted my arms. I prophesied this and much else, or so they told me.

Then the citizens turned on me. They had not
forgotten what had happened after the sacrifice of the
Greek boy. Now, tired, hungry, bereaved they turned
on me. They beat me until Hector stopped them, of
course. Then they had me carried away. When I came
to myself I was lying on a stone floor, alone, in darkness. I guessed from the smell of oil and herbs I must
be in an empty store-room below the great hall. I was
in great fear because my visions were still with me,
though coming with less force, and I was alone, in
utter blackness. Later I felt my way round the walls
and across every inch of the floor space. I found there
was nothing in the room, not a stool, blanket, jar of
water. There I lay for a day, hungry and thirsty, feeling, or hearing muffled feet overhead, hearing thuds,
sometimes a voice. I knew eventually they would
bring food – Naomi, Polyxena, someone would smuggle it to me – but when would I be released?

My parents and Anchises had married me for stra-
tegic reasons, and now imprisoned me for the same
cause. I could not be allowed to destroy belief in

victory. People who had suffered so much had only to lose courage to be defeated. It might have been better for me if the promised troops had arrived from Hattusas, but they had not. In fact it was too early (the Great King had promised troops for the spring) but people in their desperation were beginning to suspect we had been let down, or that I, perhaps, being mad, had been mistaken when I said Suppiluliumas had offered reinforcements.

I must have lain there for ten days. A guard brought me scraps of bread, and water. No one else was allowed to come near me though I wondered, sadly, why Naomi had not contrived to smuggle me some food, or a lamp, or a blanket. During that time the plague ran its course and began to ebb away. I was wretched – dazed, in pain, at first, from the beating. I could not tell day from night. I dreamed of my lover, Arvad. I thought bitterly that if my family were prepared to treat me so cruelly, I might as well have left Hattusas while I had the chance and gone east over the mountains to that sunny Phoenician coast, where I might have found my lover. It was destined that I would not, I suppose, but I was young. I believed and did not believe in my fate. Meanwhile, I endured captivity. We Trojans were reared to endure. While I lay there imprisoned, Achilles killed my brother Hector.

Lying in darkness, I heard the great howl of lamentation go up. I knew – I saw that long battle between the two strong men, while the warriors on both sides stood silent, watching the two heroes battle. I saw my brother felled, his blood draining into the dusty ground. I lay in my grief like one dead. I willed my own death on. What use to be alive when one such as Hector had died? I willed death with my remaining strength, but of course it did not come.

At that time, too, Naomi was captured.

TWENTY-EIGHT

Troy and Thessaly

URING THE war we thought chiefly of the warriors who would win or lose the war for us. Now I must recall, for the sake of justice, all who died, whether fighting men or not. I must remember the women who died collecting food and water, the slaves and children who perished of sickness and starvation in the siege. I must remember the many deaths of those who never held a sword and about whom no ballads will ever be written.

Naomi was caught after scavenging ten eggs and a little sack of barley from a hamlet ten miles off. A troop led by Diomedes merely swept up her thin body as she crept towards the city gate at dusk. She was captured for a clutch of eggs and the makings of four loaves of bread. Naomi told me about this in Greece not long after my good husband, asking no questions, had got her back from the slave huts where I'd found her. It took her weeks to lose that grim, gaunt face. Then, one day in the fields, as we were resting at midday during the reaping, she'd told me her story. By then the war had been over for nearly two years. As we spoke beneath a tree in the barley field, my eldest child slept beside us on a blanket.

The Greeks took her back behind their rampart,

she said, and put her to nursing their sick and wounded. Initially she was chained with the other slaves, the Trojans and those they had captured from all along our coast. She was desolate, but she was better fed there and promptly formed a relationship with a soldier of Achilles' troop, Strephon, by name. Her captors were from the hill lands of Thessaly, far from the prosperous coastal regions of Mycenae, Pylos and the rest: they were fanatically loyal to their leader and were regarded as uncivilised by the other Greeks.

'Strephon was a boorish, rural kind of man,' she reported. 'No worse than many. In any case, what's a slave to do? From Strephon I got a necklace taken from Miletus, also clothes and food – and I needed them, for you know how ragged and hungry we had become. I was unchained. I mourned for you, in prison like that. If I'd been there I could have pleaded for you, smuggled you things, but there it was. I was a captive of the Greeks, you of the Trojans – war is war. I was better off a prisoner of the Greeks, I have to say. In war you live from day to day.'

'I remember,' I told her.

She shrugged. 'A slave's like a bundle, anyway, always passed from hand to hand. I knew some of the captives, of course. It was a relief to get away from the foetid air of the city, to be near the sea. Yet it was still imprisonment and the fear of dying was no less.

'Agamemnon himself questioned me on the day I was captured. I was dragged that evening to his hut, hands tied and knocked about with the butts of spears. He was sitting on a wooden chair with the girl, Briseis, who had been captured at a city conquered by Achilles, Lyrnessus, further down the coast. Agamemnon had insisted on taking this very beautiful girl from Achilles, who much resented this, as all know. As leader of the Greek confederacy Agamemnon was already claiming that he was entitled to most of the spoils if Troy fell but Achilles was now challenging Agamemnon's leadership and entitlements. Agamemnon had to keep the girl in order to keep his ascendancy over Achilles who was loved by the Greeks, as Agamemnon was not.

'By the time I saw Briseis, she'd been through the hands of Achilles, and probably Patroclus, for those two shared everything, and then ended up with Agamemnon, joining him in his bed and his nightmares. She was speechless. They said she'd tried to walk into the sea and drown, but they'd dragged her back. The day they questioned me, Agamemnon was despondent.

'They knocked me about a bit,' Naomi reported unemotionally, 'trying to get information about Troy. I said I was a slave in Advenor's house, I knew nothing, only that Advenor's wife hated me and did not allow me to leave the house. I'd heard no gossip and no reports.

'Word of your visit to Hattusas, Cassandra, had reached Agamemnon. That was what he was most interested in – the prospect of reinforcements. It was plain they thought the city was lost, unless further troops arrived. Starvation would finish the war for them. Nevertheless, Agamemnon was miserable. Of course I said I'd heard nothing of reinforcements, only seen the Hittite troop you returned with. I tried to make him think the rumours about further troops were just rumours in a city full of them – I didn't have to say much, for at that stage, as you know, Troy itself thought you had erred when you said Suppiluliumas would send reinforcements. Still, he frightened me, Agamemnon, with that long, grim face. We used to call Achilles "The Madman". He was a boy, Achilles, all enthusiasm, and desire for glory and good times, all temper one minute, good humour the next. I cried for him when he died, in spite of his being an enemy. Agamemnon was the madman. You know.'

'I know,' I agreed, as we sat in the hot barley field trying to catch a breeze from the sea.

'Yes, you do,' Naomi said. 'Well – shame came to all of us then. It's a pity women can suffer all the pain and humiliation men can – and one more shame as well. Anyway, Agamemnon threw me out of his hut when he thought I could tell him nothing. My fear was that one of the other captives would tell the Greeks I was your personal servant and was always about the palace. There's no honour in situations like that,' Naomi explained. 'It's dog eat dog. We were pitched in the open air. No shade, no shelter. We stole each other's food if we could. Then Strephon took me to his hut in Achilles' compound. He patted me on the head once, Achilles,' she said proudly. 'That was,' she added, 'after Hector's death. Before it, they said, after Patroclus died, he did not eat, drink or sleep for a week – he was roaming the compound and the Greek camp day and night, tears running down his dirty face, weeping and raging, mourning his friend.

'The day after my capture and my interview with Agamemnon, Hector died. I was washing clouts – bandages, blood-stained rags – in the sea. I knew there was a battle. I was tired, so tired of battles. Then the screams of joy. Two warriors were dancing,

363

embraced, beside me on the shore. More arrived crying out, "The war is over! The war is over now! Hector's dead!" They hugged each other, feasted all night. At midnight I woke and crept out. Achilles was naked in the sea, lifting his arms to heaven and weeping. Such distress!'

Naomi stared out across our quiet fields, seawards – she gazed as if seeking Troy. 'Such distress,' she said again. 'And now brave Achilles, too, is dead. Hector, Troilus, Paris –' She broke off, nearer to tears than I had ever seen her. Then she recovered herself and continued. 'They told me he would not bury Patroclus until he was avenged – by Hector's death, of course. He raged for a week, then one night, he slept. They said that the morning he went out to kill Hector he washed himself at dawn in the sea. He was filthy, by then. He came to the council, stood up and declared he regretted not having joined the fighting earlier, the dispute between himself and Agamemnon over the girl had been foolish, the other disputes between them were just as paltry. The death of Patroclus altered everything. Patroclus must be avenged. It was, they said, handsomely done. Many wept for him in his grief over Patroclus, and for his noble behaviour.'

'Which ended in my brother's death.' I was bitter.

'True. But better to die at Achilles' hands than in the hands of those other curs,' she said.

Imprisoned, hearing the lamentations, I remembered the guard telling me, as he threw me a bit of bread, 'Hector is dead! You will be next!'

'It is all I desire,' I had said, but he banged the door shut without hearing me.

In the barley field I said to Naomi, 'Better to die

364

at Achilles' hands? Are you espousing the cause of the heroes? After all you've seen? You surprise me, Naomi. Death, in the end, is death, however it comes. These heroes are half in love with it.'

From across the fields where he was scything barley in the hot sun my husband, Iphitus, called out, 'Woman! The boy is asleep now! Come and reap – am I to do all this by myself?'

Naomi sighed and stood up. She said, 'I saw dead Hector from the Greek ramparts by the shore as Achilles dragged him day after day round the plain of Troy. Even the Greeks were weeping. One shouted at Achilles, "Barbarian!" There was a silence throughout the Greek camp as Achilles continued his maltreatment of your brother's corpse. But no one, not even Agamemnon, or Calchas the priest, dared reproach him. By then, in his heroism and great grief for Patroclus, he seemed to be in the hands of a god. Untouchable. Also, each man feared that if he reproached Achilles, Achilles would strike him down.'

Iphitus cried out again, 'Are you going to gossip forever?' and I, too, stood up, picked up my scythe. I looked down at my sleeping son and said to Naomi, 'We must not speak of these things.' Then I crossed the field and began to reap beside my husband.

TWENTY-NINE

Troy

AFTER HECTOR'S death they released me from my prison. My eyes blinked in the unaccustomed light as they led me, filthy and starving, to the ramparts to see my brother, his heels pierced and thongs threaded through, being dragged behind Achilles' chariot round and round the plain of Troy. Achilles, 'The Madman', whipped up his horses, tugging at the bit until the horses' mouths were sprayed with blood and foam. This was the third day of this cruel spectacle.

Next morning, from the ramparts, we saw Hector's body still attached to the chariot, lying by Patroclus' cold funeral pyre. At that distance, the chariot looked like a child's toy cart lying in a corner, Hector's body like a rag doll beside it. My father arrived with gifts and ransomed Hector's body. Then came his funeral. As his body burned on the pyre behind Troy, the Greek soldiers stood silently at a distance. Ostensibly they were there to guard us, but we knew they came to honour Hector as a brave and honourable man. The ceremony was all but over when a Greek messenger galloped up to them from Troy. They turned and with all speed, and evidently alarmed, raced on horseback past Troy back to their camp.

The Ethiopians were coming. We wondered, standing at Hector's funeral pyre, about the sudden retreat of the Greeks, then the long column of fifty mounted men came towards us. There were a hundred infantrymen behind them. We were amazed by the arrival of those soldiers. One of the black men had a lionskin over his back, the other that of a huge, spotted beast, a great cat. Its feet trailed down behind him to the ground. Its head lay on his back. We were aghast, not knowing what this could mean.

Another of them, young and pale-skinned, came up to my father, leading his horse. 'Uncle,' he greeted my father and embraced him. In his grief my father, his face smeared with the ashes of Hector's pyre, did not recognise him. It was Memnon, his nephew, his brother's child. This man was married to Candace, the Ethiopian queen, and lived in huge splendour in her palace at Saba. These Ethiopians were of two races: the 'burnt-faces' as the Greeks termed them, came from the more southerly part of the country, the paler ones from the north, nearer Egypt. The country traded in valuable wood and in gold and ivory. It was fertile and immensely rich.

Naomi told me later the Greeks were terrified of these 'burnt-face' men. They thought they were dead, and being already dead, could not be killed in battle. They would be invincible.

The Ethiopians had come at the instigation of the Pharaoh of Egypt, who at that time had control, though it was dwindling, over the kingdom of Ethiopia. This arrangement had been urged by Suppiluliumas, reluctant to commit too many of his own troops to Troy, but ready to put pressure on an ally to do so. Behind war is always the pull and tug of alliance, self-interest, trade. In this case Pharaoh, wanting Hittite iron and wanting to please the Hittite king, had promised assistance from the kingdom of Ethiopia. Memnon, the king of Ethiopia, was young and wanted war and booty; he was also a relative of my father's. So it was that these men, with their long spears, the pelts of strange animals slung over their shoulders had arrived from the west, halted outside the city, but found the gates shut (the city was empty but for the wounded) and had come to us as we watched the smoke from Hector's pyre rising up into the blue, blue sky.

We took it in turns to sit all night with Andromache, who was in a most pitiable state, sometimes lying on her bed, then agitatedly rising, to pace the room, weeping, unable to bear that bed she would never again share with her husband. Sometimes she was silent, her face a mask of misery. Sometimes she wandered wildly from room to room, moaning, weeping, clutching at her head. Sometimes she clasped her arms round her body, bowing over, groaning, like a woman in the final stages of childbirth.

'He was a hero, never to be forgotten,' I told her. 'And you have his son.'

I thought when my mother asked me to stay with Andromache, that my dead brother's wife might refuse to have me near her, might curse me for my prediction of Hector's death. She did not. She even said, in the normal voice people can produce from time to time when they are in agony, 'If we had listened – if I had listened – I could have kept him from the battle that day. Don't you think so, Cassandra? I could have detained him.'

I could only say, 'I don't know. I don't know.' Then she broke down again, flung herself against the wall, and facing it, supporting herself on her arms, wept, 'He will be forgotten. Hero? Yes. But how long is a hero remembered?'

'Forever.'

She shook her head. 'For a few generations, no more. He is dust, in the ground and in people's minds. I do not want a dead hero,' she then wept. 'I want a live Hector, a coward Hector, if need be. Remember him,' she sobbed. 'Remember him.'

'He will be remembered.'

Towards dawn my mother came, as so often, with a strong draught for her. She collapsed into a heavy, drugged sleep, from which, poor thing, she would awake all too soon to remember her husband was dead.

Just before dawn the city gates were flung open and, in the half light, an army such as has never been seen before left our gates. The Trojan allies, desperate to avenge Hector's death, were given heart because of the newly-arrived Ethiopians. The spectacle of fresh cavalry and a hundred infantrymen, many black, bearing their long pointed shields and long spears, terrified the Greeks. These Ethiopians wore no helmets, only the skins of the ferocious beasts of their country, as a kind of magical protection to them.

The Greeks stood by their rampart, in ranks. Their bowmen were aloft on its wall. As the Trojan forces grimly advanced, none of the Greeks turned and ran, though each must have feared that he would die in battle that day. The tall figures of Agamemnon and Menelaus were in the centre as our troops moved forward. To the right were Achilles and his Myrmidons, in a solid phalanx. Diomedes, Ajax and Nestor were to the left. As our troops swooped down, blind Calchas, their prophet and magician holding aloft his staff, offered up a prayer, a curse or a spell, I don't know which. He too, old as he was, held his ground until the very last moment, then was pulled back by the mighty arms of Ajax.

For four long hours, until the sun was high, the struggle continued. The Greeks died in large numbers by their rampart. Many were driven back into the stake-filled ditch. They retreated through their gates, across the causeway, over their moat, fighting every inch. They formed up at either end of the wall, to protect the ships.

From the tower above our ramparts Trojans began to signal frantically to the faraway troops, who were in desperate combat. Finally Paris, in his chariot, who had retreated to muster his men, observed the wild signals. 'Ships!' they were crying. 'Ships.' It was an approaching fleet, ten or twelve ships heading for Troy, where no fleet came. They were Greek reinforcements. By the time Paris spotted them, the ships, under sail, and rowing, were also within sight of the Greeks on the shore. The battle became more urgent on our side – if there were reinforcements they must arrive to find the battle over, the Trojans on shore to greet them. But the Greeks, relief at hand, resisted more strongly. As the ships came closer, Paris, who, with Aeneas, had taken over command since Hector's death, gave the order to retreat. The warriors were exhausted. There was no point in fighting on, at midday, only to be attacked by fresh forces which might number some three hundred men.

Without those reinforcements the Greeks could have been defeated that day. But Paris had waved his arm signalling retreat. The chariots wheeled. Sarpedon, furious at the order to return to the city, hurled his spear futilely at Paris' retreating chariot. He and the Lycians gathered for a time to argue furiously – but they had no choice. They were forced to leave, for the entire Trojan army, including Memnon and the Ethiopians, was retreating. There were too few Lycians to stay alone on the open plain. They would have been massacred.

Back in Troy, the men sat in silence with their heads in their hands. They had so nearly won the battle, even the war. Later a quarrel broke out. 'We could have fought on,' said Memnon bitterly.

'Not worth the risk,' Paris said.

'The risk of your life?' Memnon enquired. Paris leaped at him and had to be pulled off.

The Phrygian bowmen played dice. Sarpedon and his men had retreated to their camp behind the city. The Ethiopians sat, discouraged, in the square, ignoring the admiring girls who eyed them.

Later, Memnon sent a cadre of Ethiopians covertly to the lines by night to burn the fleet, but they were all captured – and by that stage, the Greeks having seen them wounded and falling like ordinary men, no longer believed these troops were immortal.

Poor Andromache still mourned. The city prepared for fresh battles against a reinforced enemy. The priestesses offered sacrifice. And the oracle came

from the hills. She predicted victory. And then she wept.

THIRTY

Troy

THEN CAME the Amazons and the last battle in Troy.

We saw the Amazons at dawn, from the city walls on the other side from the sea, fighting a furious battle with forty Greeks, who had gone out to forage for wood. They were small women on small, rough, upland horses, wearing trousers and Hittite helmets with flaps over their ears, and they had curved Hittite bows on their pommels. They killed two Greeks with their curved swords, drove the rest back, almost to the walls of our city, at which point the Greeks turned their horses and disappeared, leaving their waggons, and two more men, both injured, behind. The women then rode into the city laughing. One was holding a wounded arm, another had a Greek helmet and shield across the pommel of her horse. We had crowded up on the walls to watch. Now we rushed down to greet them. Others sped out to claim the waggon and its contents. Two sheep found there furnished what was to us a feast.

While they were cooked, a council of war took place in the great hall. My mother produced bread, and the last of the wine, apologising for such scanty hospitality. A new mood of hope prevailed. Both the

Ethiopians and the Amazons had arrived to reinforce us – their supply waggons were expected shortly. We had enough troops to defend the passage of these waggons into the city. And we detected confusion in the Greek camp, indicating that their reinforcements, though more numerous than ours, were perhaps raw warriors. Our own reinforcements were men and women of calibre. We had already seen the courage and ferocity of the Ethiopians in battle and the determination and speed of the Amazons putting war-tried Greeks to flight. Perhaps – we hardly dared think it – now we could push out the Greeks, reclaim our lives, our city, our countryside.

How can I describe what had happened to Troy? The once fertile plain between the city and the sea was flattened, denuded of all grass. All the trees by the river had been cut down. The river banks were crumbling, so many went up and down them. They were littered with rags, pieces of harness, broken sandals, split planks. Further off, for miles around, there were no trees. The countryside was ravaged, the farms empty, many burnt. The livestock had gone, the fields were overgrown. Grass grew in the docks.

At the council of war on that important evening, my father spoke of Hector. Priam was an old man now, not fully recovered from his sickness, bereaved of his oldest and best-loved son. He stood erect, but his voice was weak.

'We welcome our allies and the chance they bring to defeat our enemies. But we must remember the heroic Hector, who fought and encouraged when there was no help, when defeat seemed almost certain, disaster almost inevitable. He is dead now, but it was he who prevented defeat, day after weary day and had he not done so, there would be no battles now to fight. Troy would have fallen.'

It fell to Memnon to translate this to his countrymen and to acknowledge the virtues of this man – his cousin – whom he had never met. I translated for the Amazons, mostly mountain women from the area between Hattusas and the Taurus mountains, who spoke a version of the Hittite tongue. A group of them did not even speak that, but some dialect of their own, so their comrades had in turn to translate for them. In looks these women were different from each other, some being fine-boned, with emphatic noses and very dark eyes and hair like the Hittites, others from deep in the mountains being more squat, round-faced, with brownish hair and ruddy complexions.

To our intense interest, two of these mountain women carried short, straight swords made of iron, the iron being very little dented or buckled, as swords of bronze usually are. These weapons were very strong. Of course, everyone wanted to test them, but the women were very proud of their swords and only reluctantly let others handle them. They were also extremely costly, worth at least the price of a chariot and two fine horses or a heavy gold necklace.

The captain of the Amazons, Penthesilea, was short in stature, with large, direct brown eyes and an open stare. She had a big scar on one cheek, which looked like an old sword-slash and thick black hair, in pigtails. She must have been about thirty and, apart from the sword-slash, very beautiful.

That council took a long time; multiple translations were necessary.

Memnon's general, a black Ethiopian with gold bracelets right up his left arm, seemed convinced we should attack next day and finish the war. Anchises, characteristically, counselled patience and after much debate my father sided with him.

My mother spoke, saying, 'This war must end soon. We have no food left. Many of our people are already dead. Others have had to leave the city or starve and we do not know what has happened to them. We daily risk our lives for food, water, herbs for medicine. The baggage trains promised by our allies from Ethiopia and Hattusas will help us but not for long. We cannot continue like this. We must fight and win now, or Troy will fall from starvation. And the sickness could come back.'

The discussion went on. At one point a sentry came in, grinning. He stood in the doorway and shouted, 'Listen! They're drilling their new troops now, in darkness. You can hear Agamemnon's curses from the ramparts. Those men are the dregs – the scrapings of the barrel.' There was a laugh. This information helped the council to make up its mind to stage an early attack, before the Greek reinforcements had found their feet.

Paris and Aeneas were not pleased at having to submit their judgements to these extraordinary new troops who, from their speech, appeared to have fought all over the known world, from beyond the Black Sea to the Euphrates. Hitherto only Sarpedon, among the allies, had had any real influence on the Trojan strategy and now Sarpedon was making a friend of Memnon's general, by name, if I have it correctly, Tewodros. He cordially invited Tewodros and the Ethiopians to share his campsite outside the city walls, which was becoming more dangerous as the Greeks grew bolder. Tewodros agreed to this plan.

Being there in greater numbers, they thought, it would be easier to prevent Greek foraging parties from getting into the back country. Their horses could then be tethered there under guard in the fields behind the city. We were short of fodder for what horses remained. Many had been killed in battle. Others had been killed because we could not feed them. All too often we needed them to feed us.

Since my imprisonment I had been as subdued as possible, knowing that in the view of my own people, I was half-way between prophetess and curser of my own city. I assisted with the preparation of the feast. When it was ready I helped to serve it, then took a stool and sat at the back of the room, which was filled with warriors. Helenus, who understood, came over and sat by me, wordlessly. Now we were both thinking of Hector. He said, 'If the reinforcements had come only a few days sooner, Hector might have lived.'

I answered, 'I think he was destined to die.' We wept together, while the clash of spits, the feasting, the talk went on.

Then a watchman ran in, saying there was a noise, and some lights on the road. Memnon thought it was probably his Ethiopian baggage train and he sent a troop out to protect it from marauding Greeks. Not too long after, we saw the convoy coming up the road in darkness, eight mule-drawn waggons, loaded with arms, provisions and bedding, women and children walking beside it, with smaller children seated on top. Strapped on top too, were huge drums, the ends of brightly painted carved wood. We also spotted a small contingent of Greeks on horseback by the riverside, but, on being charged by Memnon's men, they fled.

The city gates swung open and the convoy entered Troy. The food they brought had to be disposed of – and it was a blessing. The more able-bodied wounded had to be moved for the temple was needed for some of the new arrivals – about thirty women and fifty children, from babies to ten- or twelve-year-olds. Their gods and the drums were set up on the temple floor. There were families in all the big houses. The great hall of the palace was full of little groupings, on rugs or skins, surrounded by bundles of clothing and domestic items they had brought with them. A few hours before dawn one woman gave birth, swiftly and soundlessly, to a baby daughter.

King Memnon and his army had of course disappeared to their camp with the Lycians, leaving the women and children in the city. The Amazons contemplated all this confusion ruefully – they had left their own children behind in the mountains to the north. They took themselves off to camp with the small Hittite force on the hill where the tunnel ended.

The Amazon leader, Penthesilea, and her lieutenant, one of the ruddy mountain women, stayed behind with the small group of generals for the continuing council of war. These generals were Memnon's general Tewodros, Paris, Deiphobus, Troilus and Helenus. The question was whether an attack at daybreak was a possibility after all this confusion, and if it was, what strategy should be employed. It was important to attack the Greeks before their reinforcements could become effective, but our own had not fought together, did not know each other's strengths and weaknesses and how to deploy themselves most effectively. In spite of this it was decided to attack at morning; the Amazon women would stand with the Phrygians to the rear, on the small eminence outside the city, as they were the better archers. They would join the battle only when it became too dangerous to shoot arrows into the mêlée. The Ethiopians would take the centre with the Hittite soldiers. The others would dispose themselves to right and left, while Sarpedon and the Lycians held back, ready to strike at the last moment when the battle was fiercest. I was sitting beside Helenus, silent. 'This is the final battle,' he said. 'I wonder which of us will survive.'

Later, unable to sleep, I stood on the ramparts as the watch paced up and down. Down in the Greek camp, the fires still burned. They must know, too, this might be the last battle of the war. The Amazon, Penthesilea, joined me. 'The Greek leaders cannot sleep, either,' she said. 'Soldiers can, generals can't.' She pointed downwards, asking, 'The battlefield?' I nodded.

There was a mournful silence. I said, 'Once our foals pranced there. We were famous for our horses. Now it is only bare earth ridged with the tracks of chariot wheels, soaked with our blood – and theirs. It's in the wind we breathe.'

She nodded.

'You're far from home,' I said.

'You find us odd. Your women do not fight. Let me tell you the legend. Years ago in the mountains of Anatolia, savages, more like beasts than men, covered in hair, used to lurk in caves, high up in the hills. They would attack the villagers who lived below and one day they came down and killed all the men. As the men fell the women put on their men's armour, drove them off, these savage men, and killed them.

The Rarisha were no more. This, they say, began the tradition of women warriors. Later the Great Kings came and took us over, formed us into an elite corps. We serve officially under the king's mother. We are paid, we get good booty, with which we can buy land at home and if we die, our dependants are taken care of.'

'And your menfolk?'

'They farm the land. The older women take care of our children.' She added, 'Fighting is a skill. It can be learned. When it comes to firing a bow, it is steadiness and accuracy, not strength, which count in the end, and in hand-to-hand fighting, speed, agility and discipline are as useful as brute force, wildly applied.'

'Do you not wish you were at home?' I asked.

'Most soldiers wish they were at home,' she told me. 'There are boys down in the Greek camp, now awake and staring up at the stars, wishing they were in their own beds, with their brothers, the dog on the floor beside them. Tonight Greeks and Trojans, both, are pining for their women and children, wondering if they will ever embrace their wives again, take their sons to the river to fish, wondering how their children will fare if they die tomorrow. If we win, I shall share in the booty of rich Mycenae. My children could be rulers in Argos, Pylos, Rhodes. You are the prophetess,' she said. 'Cassandra? They tell me you brought us here by going to the Great King.'

A dog began to howl down in the Greek camp.

'Yes,' I told her. 'But I'm not well looked on in Troy.' I did not tell her why; she had enough to think about.

'I heard that. Well – I must go and rest, if not sleep. I'll stay here until dawn, then go back to my troop.'

And, saying this, she pulled her cloak about her, retreated to the palace wall, lay down on the stones and, like a soldier, either slept, or went into that light stupor which is the sleep of soldiers before a battle.

I, meanwhile, remained on the ramparts alone, waiting for the sun. As dawn drew near others joined me silently. We watched the moon fade, the early light come across the sea's horizon. We prayed. As the sun came up the bent old oracle was beside me in her red gown, her face painted. I turned to look into her eyes, like dark pits. Neither of us, I knew, saw anything but the coming light, felt anything but the salt-laden wind from the sea.

As the sun tipped up over the horizon, there was a great sigh, then no more.

Naomi told me that down in the Greek camp they all stood, their faces for once turned from Troy, towards the sea, the sunrise, and their homeland. There were the tall figures of Menelaus, Agamemnon, Achilles, Diomedes, Ajax on the beach among their troops. Naomi said she felt all bloodlust, all desire for women, craving for fame, glory, for loot and dominion – all seemed to have gone, as each mother's son faced his home, watching the dawn of the day which might bring his death.

THIRTY-ONE

Troy

S TRANGELY, I spent the early morning of that
day with Helen. It was strange because by then
she was the enemy in Troy, and in Greece too,
as we found out later. Odd to seek out such a woman
at such a time. Other women were preparing food for
the warriors, making medicines, rolling bandages. My
mother and Polyxena were with Hector's widow. Yet
I sought out the woman who was at the root of all
these terrible events, a curious choice at such a time.
Yet was my position much different from hers?
Everywhere I went I met the sidelong glances of those
who remembered my prophecies and that my own
family had incarcerated me for them. I ought to have
considered my loyal duty to my mother – helped to
nurse the wounded, distribute food, deal with weaponry, with all the details of a city at war and perhaps
facing its last and most crucial battle.

I was seventeen years old. My twin brother, all my
remaining brothers, faced death today and so did I,
so did all of us.

Through this war I had probably lost my chance
of happiness in marriage. My own countrymen mistrusted and hated me and because I was young,
afraid, hungry and resentful, I went to Paris' house

to spend what might be my last hours, on this day of days, in Helen's company. It was not only that Troy hated her and mistrusted me. It was that Helen hated this war and so did I. We were fit companions.

A guard let me in. Even in that house the deprivation had made its mark. Certain hangings, certain vessels normally on display were missing. Had they been sold for food, stored against looting? The great hall was dusty and neglected. There was little water, even here. Down in the city, the Ethiopians' drums began to play.

Helen, trembling, was helping my brother on with his armour. Less than a week before I had watched Andromache nobly do the same for Hector, now dead. Helen had no dignity. She wept as she stood on tiptoe to put Paris' helmet on his head, then broke down completely and ran away crying, 'Go, go. Go now. I can stand no more.' It was shameful conduct, not expected of women in time of war. I kissed Paris and fastened his helmet, but he did not notice me. He was staring blindly at the doorway through which Helen had run. He was about to go after her when Deiphobus came in, fully armed, and said, 'Come, Paris. It's time.' Paris continued towards the doorway. Deiphobus burst out, as he would not have done if his nerves had not been stretched to their utmost, 'In the name of our brother, Hector, who died in battle only days ago, do not lose your honour, *do not go after that woman.*'

Paris stared at him in horror. Deiphobus, almost equally horrified, stared back. Then Paris moved towards him softly, like a man in a trance, saying only, 'I am coming, brother.'

'I should not have . . .'

'There's no time, as you say. In Hector's name, then,' and he put his arm round Deiphobus' neck and they left at a soldierly pace, bidding me farewell over their shoulders. As they went into the compound outside, I heard them start to sing.

The drums went on beating. I found Helen sobbing by the fountain. She babbled, 'I shall never see him again. I know it. Cassandra, what do you see – will he live? What will I do without him? Offer a sacrifice to Hecate, Cassandra. She will listen to you. She is your mother. What shall I do? What shall I do? Friend and lover. Friend and lover. Oh Paris. Oh Paris, my husband. What do you see, Cassandra? What do you see?'

'Nothing,' I told her. 'Nothing.' And this was true.

The drums beat faster. Pipes grew shrill. Down by our gates the oracle would be dancing, weaving patterns of victory into the ground. Women would be embracing husbands and sons. In the temple my mother would be offering sacrifice, the women behind her praying. The moon was full, the goddess was the old woman now.

Naomi told me later the Greek musicians were playing pipes and beating drums down by the beach before dawn. At dawn they had sacrificed a Trojan girl. The magician Calchas offered prayers to the god of war, and to Artemis, the mother of them all.

But my nerve had gone. I could not go to the gates to see the army out, or to the ramparts, to witness the battle. I stayed with Helen in that dusty room.

The battle began. As ever, the Phrygians stood on the small eminence in front of the city with their bows. This time they were interspersed with most of the Amazon women on their small horses. These two

384

units would go to work with their bows as the Greeks advanced, then ride into the fighting. Memnon's tough, fresh Ethiopians took the centre of the army with the Hittites, while the Trojans were on the right flank, Lycians and the rest of the Amazons on the left. In the middle of the Ethiopians, the chariots were clustered in ranks.

It was a near-perfect battle-plan. First would be the arrows, fired downhill into the Greek ranks. Their own bowmen, never good, could only cluster on the rampart, which gave them limited range. After that the chariots would race into the thick of the throng, with the Ethiopians, to take the main burden of the fighting. The soldiers on both flanks would then attack from each side. Sarpedon and his men would hold back until it was plain where our army was weakest. Then they would throw themselves into the battle.

The Amazons stood on the mound in front of the city half up in the stirrups of their horses, bows poised. The long line of chariots and warriors on foot advanced slowly. Almost at once the Greek troops made their first mistake. Over-confident perhaps, because of their superior numbers, they raced towards us at speed. Our own charioteers restrained their horses, over-excited by the noise of the drums and the tension of the men around them, making them walk slowly with the lines of advancing men. Now the drums on both sides were silent. The shouting, fighting, cries of encouragement from man to man were absent. Nothing was to be heard but the jingling of chariot harnesses, the thud of advancing feet, the whinny of a horse, the cries of gulls overhead.

The Greeks advanced with their chariots at a run. Faces were grim or fearful beneath their helmets. It was Ulysses who half pulled up, grabbed Agamemnon's arm, spoke urgently up into his face warning him. But still they came on rapidly until, suddenly, they were within range of our bowyers, but too far from their own archers for cover.

Then came the silent and deadly arrows from our side. The Greek line began to shatter. Many fell. A scream went up from our ramparts as Diomedes, the Greek hero, fell. Then the Trojan chariots took off, the Ethiopian and Hittite forces raced forward with the mounted Amazons. Paris was first into the Greek lines, his horse rearing in their faces. He swept past Agamemnon who gazed up at him in horror.

In the deadly struggle that ensued Paris and Deiphobus, avenging their brother, moved like men in the throes of lunacy, spearing, withdrawing bloodied spear to spear again. They did not tire. They made no mistakes. They cut down Menelaus who was dragged away by his men. The tall black men fought ferociously, many fell, but took more Greeks with them. The Hittite women, who as soon as battle was joined, had shouldered their bows, lifted their curved swords and sped into the battle, tackled, outnumbering them, King Nestor and his throng, cutting half of them down. Seeing this, Achilles signalled his Myrmidons, who raced to Nestor's assistance. Then Paris, fighting side by side with Memnon, spotted his brother's killer. Abandoning a joint attack on Ulysses and his small, tough Ithacans, Paris and Deiphobus ran to confront Achilles. Paris was hacking at those who surrounded Achilles. Furious, he was grinning like a dog, his perfect teeth exposed in a face covered in dust. Several of Memnon's men came up and the

Myrmidons and Achilles turned. 'Run!' Achilles yelled.

'So you run from us, do you?' called Deiphobus, exulting.

Sarpedon and his troops could control themselves no longer. They flung themselves into the fight.

It was midday, the sun high and hot, no sound but the occasional shout, a scream, the perpetual sound of metal on metal, men grunting and straining against each other under blue sky, all beyond any thought but finding their man and killing him. And slowly the Greeks were forced back to their own rampart. By now they were fighting in small bands, each one cut off from the other. The carnage among their novice troops had been so great they were retreating across heaps of their own dead and wounded. A chariot, driver dead, lurched about the field, the horses in a panic, rearing in their traces.

Forced back to their rampart and then across the causeway, they fought bravely but the Trojan troops, men inspired, pressed on. They were tireless. There was no resisting them. Sometimes it almost seemed they did not feel the sword blows. In the stake-filled moat men lay impaled and screaming. Our army pushed on, flooding across the causeway pursuing the Greeks behind their own rampart. There they continued the deadly work.

On the shore the Greeks, shouting, began to try to launch their ships for a retreat, under a hail of arrows from the Amazons, who had scaled the rampart and were firing down on them while the Trojan force, cutting and hacking, began pushing them right into the sea.

This took place as Helen and I sat by her well,

now low and muddy and filled with leaves from the unwatered lemon tree. We held hands and said little. Sometimes her clutch on me tightened fiercely, like that of a woman in childbirth. The city was silent.

The Greeks, in full retreat now, managed to launch six of their ships, though many fell in the attempt. Those who had scrambled in began to row, while others, wounded and unwounded, splashed through the shallows to try to get into the boats. Some staggered and fell into the water in the attempt. As our troops, fighting in the sea, dragged men from the ships, Greeks were elsewhere pushing slaves and booty aboard.

Slowly the ships laboured out, rowing with half the oars unmanned until they reached water too deep for any man, Trojan or Greek, to reach them. There, in clear sight of the shore the oarsmen slumped over their oars, while others crowded to the side, gazing towards the shore where some three hundred men of their number, stranded, were fighting double the number of Trojans for their lives. There was no attempt on our side to take captives. We slaughtered them like beasts and stripped them of their armour where they lay, some in, some out of the water. Bodies with gaping wounds bathed by the sea, washed about like dead fish.

The great figure of Agamemnon stood in the bow of his ship staring at this scene. In another ship Achilles was sobbing, one arm over his eyes – he had left three of his men behind in the panic, had tried to jump overboard to rescue them, and had been wrestled to the deck by his men.

*

So the great battle ended. A contingent of our men was left on shore to hold off the Greeks if they decided to return, though we thought they would not. We released the Greeks' slaves. Women came out from the city with waggons to collect the dead and wounded. Our soldiers began to go back to the city. A column of tired men and tired horses crossed the trampled plain. Some sat down in the dust, grey-faced and staring. Others moved to the rivers, to drink, to sit on the denuded banks, to sleep. Some raided the supplies of wine held by the Greeks on the shore.

Paris and Deiphobus, Troilus and Aeneas, lay together outside the gate. They said Paris, his arm over his eyes, wept, while Troilus stared up at the sky and laughed. They were surrounded by dancing figures.

The war had been going on for almost two years and suddenly it was over. No one could believe it, at first. But the guards on the ramparts reported that what remained of the Greek fleet was rowing raggedly out to sea. They were retreating. Their casualties had been too great, this last battle too decisive. The war was over.

Hours passed slowly in Helen's quiet garden while that last battle was waged. There seemed to be no servant, not even a slave in the house, only two big slavering guard dogs who came in and lay between us as if pleased to be in company.

Helen was silent much of the time. I don't know what thoughts were going on in her head.

'If he should die, if he should die,' she repeated. Then, 'Why are you here, Cassandra? Why are you not watching the battle or preparing food, nursing the wounded?'

'My people suspect me as they suspect you,' I said bluntly. 'And I know this can only end badly. I know my own fate and I'm tired. That's why I'm here.'

She sighed. 'If the Greeks win –'

For a long while we sat, heavy-hearted, by the well in her garden.

When the cry came, 'Victory!' from all over the city, she and I started, stared at each other unable to believe it. But the noise went on and on, a trumpet blew, Aeneas came staggering in, dusty, one arm useless, carrying a broken sword in his other hand. 'Paris sent me to tell you he is alive, lady, and the Greeks have been driven off to sea. We are victorious.'

He sat down heavily beside us at the well and stared, through red eyes, at nothing at all.

Helen was instantly on her feet and running from the house into the street, down to the town to find her husband. I followed – Aeneas' loyal wife, whom he had for so long neglected, would find him and tend his wounds. People were embracing each other, laughing, crying out with joy.

I joined the waggon, taking food and drink to the soldiers on the beach, hoping as well to find Naomi. The captives abandoned by the Greeks had been released, and were going back to the city, hand in hand. But there was no sign of Naomi.

They had piled the stripped Greeks into a big heap. Heads dangled, arms and legs stuck out of this mound of carcasses. Here was the new face of the enemy, not snarling from under helmets, appearing horribly through dust with a raised sword – just a pile of bearded fathers and beardless sons, one no more than twelve. He stared with sightless eyes into the afternoon sky. The boy should have been at home, leading goats. My half-brother Dymas, only a few years older than the dead boy, looked down at him and said, 'So that is the enemy.' Then he assumed a cruel grin and kicked a body lying at the bottom of the heap. He said, 'These are the dregs of their army. The big fish were quick enough to get away.' He took a swig of the water I handed him, wiped his hand across his mouth like a thirsty farmer, and threw his head back and shouted over the sea in the direction the Greek vessels had taken, 'Come back and finish the fight.'

I passed on with the water I was carrying, needed by some, not by others who had made free with the supplies of wine and food abandoned by the Greeks. Our guards were sitting, some even sleeping. There would still be warning if the Greeks decided to bring back their ships for a further attack but no one expected them to do so. Their defeat had been too decisive.

Helenus was there sitting among the soldiers. He was covered in blood, not his own, too exhausted to wash it off. He said to me quietly, 'It can't be over.' I shrugged. Few of us had slept, or eaten. We were all dirty, gaunt with semi-starvation, and beyond thought. A Lydian cousin, child of my aunt's husband, who had been a captive, chained to a stake on the shore, told me the tougher Greeks had bundled some of their women aboard the fleeing ships. There had been fury about this in the midst of the panic. Agamemnon had shouted, 'Save your comrades,' but he'd been seen jostling his unhappy girl Briseis aboard earlier. Those who had seen him do it justified their own acts by remembering his, and those who had not, did it anyway. Two or three captives had managed to leap overboard and swim back to shore – one told me he had seen Naomi among the captive women pushed aboard. So far she was still alive, but would I ever see her again, I wondered? This thought barely upset me at the time, accustomed as I was to death and separation. To know an individual might still be alive seemed in those days good enough.

A wild wave of joy and mourning swept the city. It is impossible to describe our feelings, so many years on. People laughed, though tears ran down their faces. Drunken soldiers embraced each other or girls, and then stopped, stared into space, remembering the dead. Only the little half-naked starvelings we called our children lacked these complicated feelings. They skipped about, being given food by the soldiers. They put on discarded helmets. They mock-fought with discarded swords, they ran in and out of the open gates, hardly able to believe that they could do so, freely with no angry guard or panicky parent's hand to snatch them back from the danger outside.

Beyond the open Scaean Gate, Sarpedon's brother and his fierce men sat mourning their brave leader. He lay in the centre of the Lycian throng, unwashed, untended, still in his much-battered armour. His brother Glaucus rose to greet me, tears running down his dusty face. He embraced me. 'You brought the reinforcements, Cassandra,' he said. 'For that we are grateful. But my brother has fallen. We have been here long enough. We will take him home for burial by our parents. In our grief we feel this war is not won. It may be your prophecies are correct. For our own magician tells us now – now we are victorious – that you were right. She did not say this earlier. She promised victory. We believed her then. Now she prophesies defeat. We can't understand. We do not know what to believe. But we know Sarpedon is dead and we can fight no longer. Unlike many we did not fight for wealth or demand brides for matches which would otherwise have been refused. We came early to your aid, we stayed and fought bravely, sacrificing much, including our lives. Now we have agreed to go.'

Their magician, the beautiful, red-haired woman, nodded directly at me, reinforcing her message that her prophecies were indeed true. She had foretold victory for her Lycians in the last battle and it had come. Now she predicted defeat. Yet we had triumphed. Troy was safe. Her message was strange.

A great cry came up from the city – shouts and cheers. The sacrifice in the temple was over. The women were screaming. As the Lycians stood slowly, picking up bundles and armour, and as Glaucus took up the body of his brother, I encountered again the deep brown gaze of the red-headed priestess of the Lycians.

'Farewell, and thanks,' I said to Glaucus. 'Your brother paid for our triumph with his life.'

Glaucus under his burden wept. He put a heavily-muscled, scarred arm up to wipe away the tears running down his face. As others came to bid them farewell, I bowed to the priestess, and went into the city. The musicians were playing. A girl was dancing with a soldier. Another waggon of wine came through the gate. Soldiers crowded towards it.

Adosha came towards me, leading her boy by the hand. In the other was a bundle of bedding and other things. She smiled and embraced me. 'You're going back to the farm?' I asked.

'It's over,' she said. 'I must go back to my father and mother, if they're still alive.'

We must plough, reap and pick what we can, prepare for winter. 'Take care of the boy,' I said.

'He's almost all that's left of my family,' she replied.

I kissed them both and went up the hill, past Paris' house. There was a stir inside. However, a soldier on duty shut the gates again. Helen still mistrusted Troy, and perhaps rightly. I went into the palace, where a feast was in preparation. I found my mother in her office, but she was lying in a chair, her feet on a stool carved of black wood, a gift brought by Memnon. Her hair was loose, her face drained. 'Go to your father,' she said. 'He is ill.'

I could find him nowhere in all that hurly-burly and rejoicing, as I searched for him in the city. In the end I discovered him by the black circle of Hector's funeral pyre. I stood a little way off, watching him as he sat on the grass near the remains of the fire where they had burned his eldest son. He did not see me. He took a handful of the days-old ashes from the black circle, dribbled them on his head, doubled over and wept. By another pyre stood a young woman, stock-still, perfectly quiet, staring at yet another circle of blackened earth and half-burnt wood.

As the celebration went on that night I thought of those two figures, bereaved father and sad widow, thought that Adosha should by now be home on her quiet farm. I should have recalled something completely different about that scene, not what was present, but what was absent. Would it have made any difference, if I had?

THIRTY-TWO

Thessaly

HECTOR'S CHILD by Adosha is still alive, but his official child, by Andromache, died on the night when Troy eventually fell to the Greeks, when they slaughtered us as triumphant lions slaughter the cubs from the old litter when they have killed the fathers. Yet Hector's son lives as does his widow, Andromache, and my brother Helenus. And others, too.

My own decision to remember and record my past and that of my people begins to heal my grief, up to now a carefully protected but still open wound. I have yet to tell the last, terrible part of my tale and then this process will end. At first, in spite of my forebodings, I think I had imagined that when my story was finally told, the history of my people related and my soul more at peace, I could then go reconciled, on the long trip into age and death. But even as I began to write my story, I sensed violence and horror again coming closer to Mycenae. I knew the remainder of my tale would be told, but not before Greece itself had been visited by the very horrors it had brought on Troy so many years ago. And I knew there would not be long to wait.

Meanwhile the snow had stopped. It was cold at

midday, with the land sprinkled in snow, but it was starting to melt – the stones of the track down from the farm were already exposed. My guest must leave. If she waited the snow might return. I told her, politely, that this was the case.

Helen was reluctant to go, not because she was enjoying her stay or my company (she did not refer to my prophecies about her future, but I knew she dwelt on them which could not be making her feel any more at ease under my roof). She delayed her decision to leave, I believed, because she had no idea where else to go. Naomi had told me she was unwelcome at her son-in-law's court at Mycenae. She did not want to go back to her husband in Sparta or he did not want her back. I dreaded that she would decide to return across the hills to my brother and Andromache. Her very presence could only be a burden to them. She had no understanding of what her part in the war had cost them.

I was at my loom in the corner while she sat composedly by the fire, her hand, as if out of habit, by her cheek, shielding the worst of the scarring, when Naomi came to me and whispered, 'Is she going? She should leave now.'

'I cannot compel her to leave.'

Naomi went to Helen and fell on her knees. 'Lady,' she said, 'excuse my speech – if you do not leave now you may be trapped here for weeks, perhaps months, by snow.' This was most probably an exaggeration. Helen stared at Naomi and murmured, 'Then, then – I will speak to them.' She fell to musing again. Naomi, with a hopeless and vindictive glance at me, suggesting I was making insufficient effort to dislodge my guest, left the room. But Helen, after some part

396

of an hour, did rise, crossing the room gracefully on her damaged feet, saying as she left the room, 'Forgive me but I must go and speak to my men.'

They apparently agreed with Naomi about the prospect of more snow. Whether they believed her warning or just wanted to be away from the farm, I do not know. At any rate preparations for their departure began.

Meanwhile Helen and I sat together. 'I shall be sorry to go,' she said. 'This is a humble place but it is tranquil. Such peace is rare in my life.'

'I do not think the peace will last for long.'

'Why do you say that? What would disturb it?'

I shook my head. 'I don't know.'

She smiled. 'Ever the old Cassandra,' she said. 'Always these terrible prophecies of disaster.' It was in this way she repudiated what I had foretold for her.

Her men passed to and fro, carrying back into the yard what she had brought with her. Helen, that great beauty who had perhaps doomed Troy as surely as if she had put a torch to it herself, looked sadly into the fire.

'You will repose here for many years – perhaps marry again – some local widower,' she suggested. 'A good life –'

Could she really envy me the life she imagined? Did she imagine I would be pleased to marry a local widower who would take rights over my home and land and most probably work me to an early death? 'Shall we trade places?' I offered. 'You remain on this mountain farm, perhaps even wed the widower, weave his wool and tend his children, scour his pots and work his fields? And I'll take your place in the palace as Queen of Sparta? Perhaps Menelaus would not recognise me after so many years.'

'Your appearance has changed little,' she said.

This was not true. The waning of her own surpassing beauty obsessed her. She must see herself as grotesque, others unaltered.

'It's foolish to pretend you envy me,' I told her. 'You are the woman celebrated by the ballads. You have enjoyed all the fruits of womanhood. You are the most beautiful woman in the world, still – and you pretend to envy me.' She was silent then. How bad life was for her in Sparta I could not guess. Menelaus was almost certainly mad, almost certainly hated her, almost certainly was dying. She must fear his death. It might not relieve her misery, only change its nature – without him the stored hatred of her people might emerge unchecked; her son-in-law would become ruler, taking charge of both kingdoms. He bore her no love, nor, it seemed, did her daughter. Did she imagine she might have to flee? This would have made my prophecy that she would die in exile more painful. She now returned to that prophecy as the servants packed food for the journey, even as I presented her with the small parting gift expected of me – I had so little, my gift could only be a small scarf, woven in fine wool, dyed with our local dyes, and depicting a white hind, crowned with a gold coronet, leading a line of huntsmen. This was a legend of the region.

As she put on the scarf she asked, 'Will you give me another gift – my future – the truth this time, not a rigmarole designed to frighten me and pay off old scores?'

I temporised. As I have said, there is always a

temptation to tell people what they want to hear, but to do so is impious and can be dangerous to those who abuse the goddess's gifts. I asked her, 'What did Helenus tell you, Madam?'

She scoffed. 'He saw burning palaces. He did not see me. I tried to persuade him. He said only that he could not see my future.'

'Burning palaces? Where?'

'Here in Greece. Burning ships and palaces, men fighting. I told him he was mad. Perhaps his visions were memories of Troy. And,' she remembered, 'he asked me to tell you of his visions of destruction. He said that he thought you would know. But tell me, if he could not see me in a vision what does that mean? Not death, surely?'

There was something she was not telling me. 'Did he say more?'

'Nothing that I recall. Cassandra,' she appealed, 'can you not see something for me? We were friends once. I was of your family. Do you remember how we spent the day of the great Trojan victory?'

I said, 'Helen, I have said, my gifts are gone.' But I felt the depths of misery underlying her gentle manner and the perpetual, yearning half-smile. She wore a soft blue gown, the smile played over that half-wrecked yet still lovely countenance, and underneath, there was turmoil. No one could resist Helen. I was forced to relent. I put both hands to my head, like the village fortune-teller. I said, in the low, sing-song voice of a local woman, 'Oh, I feel it now. I feel it, Helen. I feel the future – yours. Oh – alas – alas, sadly your husband Menelaus will die. Great King that he is, he is not immortal. We all must die. Helen – you will mourn him and then from a mist will come a king even greater. A great and handsome ruler, head of a strong kingdom. You will be his queen.'

She stood up radiant, exclaiming, 'I thought as much. I had intimations of that kind myself. I have, you know, some small gift myself for fortune-telling and prophecy. And you tell me what I learned from an Egyptian at my husband's court.'

'They are very skilled, I hear.'

She frowned. 'The Babylonian astrologer did not agree with what the Egyptian said, or what you have just told me.'

One of her tall servants came to tell her that the waggon was ready. We went to the yard. Within minutes she would be in the litter, the visit would be ended. We would be at peace again. And that was when one of my servants came down the hill outside, shouting and waving his arms.

'What's this?' I asked Naomi. 'What is he saying?'

'I don't know,' she said. 'He went up to search for a missing sheep. He thought it might have been caught somewhere high up.'

'He has seen strangers on the road,' said one of my servants, reading the signals.

On a clear day from high up in the hills, people as much as three miles off can be seen. I was startled. Whoever was coming could only be coming here. And who would do that at this time of year? Helen's visit had been exceptional enough. I could not credit yet another arrival. I looked at Helen, speculating that in some way she had brought others to the farm. Could it be her husband or son-in-law? Neither meant any good to me or mine. But one glance at her told me she was not expecting this visit. She was terrified, though attempting to disguise her fear.

I asked, 'Do you know anything of this?' She shook her head. I had the secret now, though. She feared her husband so much she thought he had sent men to kill her. There was no time to allow her any pride. If Menelaus had come for her he would find me, too.

'Do you think Menelaus has sent men to attack you? Does he know you're here? Have you told him where I am? What have you brought down on all of us?'

Naomi was at my side watching her face, as she replied, 'Nothing – it's nothing. He can't know where I am.'

'You told no one?'

'I left my son-in-law's court without saying where I was going. And I didn't really believe Helenus when he told me you were here. How could I? I couldn't believe it until I saw you. You've been dead for twenty years.'

The man from the hillside came up to me breathlessly, 'A party coming here to the farm – four soldiers, I think, and a waggon, and a rider on a horse. They're far off. It's hard to see.'

Naomi was beside me listening. She asked, 'Shall I shut the gates?' I nodded and she and two men dragged the heavy wooden gates across the entrance to the yard. They were seldom shut for we were too remote for trouble. Sometimes there were robbers in the neighbourhood; in winter there was the threat of hungry wolves. But the gates were rarely shut. Formerly we had closed them when we were slaughtering – since the death of my husband I had ordered the beasts to be killed in the fields and carried in dead. The men had puzzled about this but I had always hated the carnage, especially when things were mishandled and animals were clubbed about the courtyard by farmworkers. Or when a panic-stricken, bellowing bullock charged blindly about, gouting blood. That sight, small wonder, had always horrified me.

'Are your men armed?' I asked Helen.

She nodded, but evidently lacked confidence in their fighting ability, as did I. They were large and strong but they were no warriors. She and I knew, better than most, the faces of real fighting men. But she instructed her men to get out what swords and spears they had while I went with Naomi to find the billhooks and poles we might have to use as weapons if the necessity arose. I sent a man off to the house of Telemon and my daughter Iris. I said we might be in trouble. But their farm was ten miles away. Help would be slow in coming.

I walked back into the house with Helen. On the way I asked her, 'Are you sure you can't guess who these strangers might be? If you can, I urge you to confide in me.'

She shook her head. I believed she was telling the truth. Inside the house I prepared to receive guests. For all I knew the visitors might mean no harm. I hoped they did not, but I was not confident.

THIRTY-THREE

Troy

OF COURSE after six Greek ships laboured away under their burden of men, captives and booty, watchmen remained on the ramparts and there were men at the gates. The habits of war prevailed and we were still not perfectly confident the Greeks had gone for good. Nevertheless, that day we rejoiced. People drank and feasted. The soldiers made music all round the city walls. Children again played by the river. Denuded of trees as it was, the banks turned into bare earth by enemy feet, this playground nevertheless was a delight to children shut up for so long in the city. I saw two using a fractured Greek helmet as a bucket. Water poured through the bottom, which had been cloven by some sword with a thrust which had probably proved fatal to the wearer. On the sea-shore huge plumes of smoke came up from the funeral pyres of the Greeks who had been slain there. Deiphobus went to inspect the harbour and found inside one of the buildings two dead women, foully raped and left to die. They were strangers to all of us and all we could do was give them respectful funeral rites. The day was full of joy at the prospect of peace, sadness for the dead, and horror, as wherever we looked we were reminded of what we had endured. On the shore lay the huts behind the rampart the Greeks had built, the detritus of an army which had fled – cauldrons and spits for cooking, piles of clothing, bones, a midden and loot of every kind from an earring buried in the sand on the beach to heaps of armour.

The Lycians had departed, but the other troops stayed to rejoice and commandeer what they could. My father had posted guards all round the camp. What loot was to be found there, he declared, should be fairly distributed.

That night in the great hall we had a fire, over which we stirred a skinny goat, a stray we had found wandering as we scoured the surrounding country-side for food.

My mother collapsed and lay in bed with a fever. The exhaustion of war, and the loss of Hector, might, I thought, have killed her.

Nevertheless, the army was still mustered and a conference took place among the leaders about mounting an attack on Mycenae and Pylos, both, we imagined, weakened by loss of men and poor harvests. War is an unslakable thirst. We might not have started the war, but we had learned, some of us, to love it. We had victory, now we wanted revenge. Yet there were good reasons for attacking Greece. The Greek cities were still immensely rich, full of the wealth the Greeks had gained by trade and seizure. A successful raid would refill coffers emptied by the war. It would be wise to crush them completely in case they revived. And there was revenge – but if we attacked our enemies, it would have to be soon, before the autumn storms began.

I sat beside Helenus, as usual. His head drooped

as the men spoke on. Pandarus the merchant was for the venture. He saw himself as the new governor of Pylos. 'Now's the moment to strike them, once and for all.'

'Hector will be avenged,' Deiphobus said.

'Suppiluliumas will be pleased to extend his empire through us,' Anchises said.

'None of us will rest until Agamemnon and Menelaus are dead,' added Paris.

'More war,' Helenus muttered to me. 'Will it never end?'

'How can it?' I asked. It would have been unnatural, I meant, not to have tried to take revenge, and get compensation somehow for what we had lost.

Helenus took it another way. All those visions and nightmares from childhood onwards. 'Torment,' he said. 'And yet we seem to have been wrong. Do you think our efforts altered what should have happened? Can man overturn ordained fate by his own strength and heroism?'

'That can never be,' I said.

'Yet here we are, the victors, planning another war.'

Paris was urging on the laggards, those who were keener to enjoy the peace and to patiently reconstruct and recover what we could.

Though Pandarus was for the new venture, Archos was not. 'Let's get the harbour working again,' he said. 'Trade back to normal. Plant what we can for the winter. Lick our wounds, mourn our dead, consider attacking in spring, after the planting.'

'If we're restored by then, so will they be,' Paris said hotly. 'We must kill them all now, like cutting a snake in half with a spade.'

His words had the opposite effect of what he intended. Some thought Paris would risk anything to kill his wife's previous husband, and avenge his brother. They sensed he felt some guilt for the war and wished to wipe it out.

My father turned to Memnon, the Ethiopian king. Memnon said, 'We had planned to be here on campaign at least until winter. My troops are ready for battle. The Greek leaders are rich – why not get ships and sail for Greece?'

Archos said only, 'I have lost two sons in this fighting. One remains. I will have nothing to do with this business. Nor do I think this prince,' and he looked directly at Paris, 'is thinking first of this city and this nation.' And he left the room. He had given great offence to Paris, who stood staring angrily after him.

Helen was still in her guarded palace, now picketed day and night by a dozen mourning women who looked as if they were prepared to remain there. She dared not go out for fear they would attack her. She had appealed to have the women removed, but my father could do nothing. 'They have lost their menfolk in this war,' he told her, 'and you have not. Let them be and rejoice that your husband and my son has survived, a hero.'

Helen was already pressing her husband to lay down his arms and make a trading voyage elsewhere – to Egypt, Phoenicia, anywhere but Troy, now a prison to her. She dared not go out for fear of assault. All day the mourning women remained as soldiers and musicians and local people who had come in from the countryside to talk to my father on a multitude of subjects all passed that mourning group. Sometimes they wept, sometimes cried out, 'Come out, murderess, and let us look at you.' 'Come out, Helen, and I will send you where my son has gone.' There is no doubt they would have killed her if they could have laid hands on her.

But others sang and rejoiced all day. By nightfall the atmosphere was frenetic. The musicians played louder and faster, people danced in the streets, up and down the city, from top to bottom. Many, of course, were quietly at home, nursing the wounded or simply sitting or lying, numbed and exhausted after the struggle. Many simply slept as if they would never wake.

Polyxena and I could hear the sounds of triumph, but with Creusa, Clemone and the other women, we were taking care of our mother and of Andromache, who, after Hector's death, had shut herself in a room. She had been there for three days now, neither eating nor drinking. And there were children to look after, there was the amputation of a soldier's foot in the temple area, a woman was giving birth, bread had to be made. Slaves had died or run away, servants disappeared. The war was over, but peace had not yet begun.

When the Greeks attacked three hours before dawn we were not prepared. The celebrations had gone on all night. People, exhausted, were sleeping where they had fallen. The ramparts and the gates, as I have said, were still manned but that made no difference. It was not over the walls or through the gates they came.

The retreating army had not sailed for home, merely set a course which made it look as if they had.

Then, as the result of a back-up plan they must have made some time before, once out of sight, they veered west for Tenedos and took shelter behind the island, invisible, though only a few miles from our shores. There they had rested, eaten and repaired their armour. Then they again set sail for Troy and before dawn were anchored in a bay beyond the harbour out of sight of the city walls.

Their forces were much weakened. They could not have taken the city directly. But they entered through the mouth of the tunnel on the hill beyond Troy.

Later the Greeks told of a dream, or vision of the prophet Calchas, aboard ship as they left in disorder after their defeat. It was a dream of a huge horse, containing some of their own men, left as a gift from them for the Trojans, trustingly dragged into the city. By night, according to Calchas' dream, the soldiers inside released themselves and opened the city gates. The Greeks flooded through; the city was taken. Later still, this dream became the story told by the Greeks as true. That they came out of the belly of the city, that it was taken by a ruse, is true but the rest is not. For, how, after all those years of war, could we have trusted such a gift?

I was to discover not too long after who had revealed the secret of the tunnel in return for a promise of ruling the kingdom when the Greeks were triumphant. Naomi knew even sooner. She told me many years later how she was pushed aboard the Greek ship by her soldier lover during the rout. How the boat sailed for Tenedos. There on the shore the night before Troy fell, she saw the face of the traitor. She told me, 'He'd come across the sea, travelled across the isthmus, then sailed to Tenedos, where he found us. I saw his face. He passed where I was sitting on the beach at night – he had come from the Greek camp – Agamemnon's arm was round his shoulders. Agamemnon was saying, "Farewell, new King of Troy. I shall be there at your wedding." The night was bright as day. I saw the moonlight on his traitor's face as they put up the sail of his boat and, as the boat floated out, Agamemnon stood on the beach with his arms raised in comradely farewell.'

'What did he mean about the wedding, do you think?' I asked her.

'He had been promised Helen as his wife,' Naomi said promptly.

'Agamemnon promised him his own brother's wife?'

'He would have promised anything for victory.'

'And any man would have done anything to gain her,' I said. 'I wonder when this arrangement between Agamemnon and the traitor came about. How long before the fall of Troy?'

'It would have been when the reinforcements came,' she asserted.

'Our victory would not have been enough for him. He wanted more. He wanted Helen.'

We had time, later, to reconstruct the events. What follows is not what I saw, for in these situations no one sees everything. I say what I saw and what the survivors told me.

The party of men, about twenty of them, led by Diomedes, crept through the tunnel and into the body of the temple, where injured men and some of the Ethiopian women and children slept. They trod carefully between the sleeping figures but a soldier awoke, cried out and they slew him. Then a baby woke. They speared the child, moving on rapidly, but the mother, grasping for it, finding it gone, screamed out, then endured the unthinkable experience of having the body of the child, wrenched from the spear like skewered meat, flung on her, bleeding. As she screamed, another soldier put his knife to her throat. She went on screaming, and was killed.

People were waking, in confusion, crying out, or lying dazed as the enemy moved nimbly and quietly through their prone figures. The sleepers awoke from celebrating a victory; their antagonists were warriors, their edges honed sword-sharp by battle, seeking revenge. They moved silently, their faces blackened, killing where they needed to. Before anyone really knew what was happening, they were through the temple and at the gates. They killed the guards rapidly and six of them began to lever up the heavy wooden crossbar which secured the gates, while the others protected them with drawn swords.

There were men and women, now fighting to get to the gates and defend them. Paris came naked, with his sword, and attacked Diomedes, who had to turn to defend himself. The blacksmith, hearing the outcry had raced from the smithy and felled one of the Greeks with the hammer he had seized up. Penthesilea and Troilus joined the fight against Diomedes. A deadly struggle in darkness took place. Now came the battering at the gates from without. And, having heard that the struggle to open the gates had begun, six Greek soldiers started to scale the walls from outside. Scrambling over them, these Greeks then overcame the sentries on the ramparts and began to fight their way down the steps to join the group trying to open the gates. Two were killed and one wounded but the arrival of the other three proved enough of a reinforcement to help Nestor's son and the others to lift the bar. The gates screeched as a yelling band of armoured men, some fifty of them, in full armour, burst through the Scaean Gate. A small group raced through the city to the other gate, opened it, and in came a further fifty men.

In the end it was so simply done. A mere one hundred Greeks burst into the city in darkness, while we were off guard, tired after rejoicing, taking the first rest we had been granted for a year and a half. And it was over for us from that point on. The Ethiopian and Trojan forces managed to drive out the invading force at the Scaean Gate. They battled outside, while inside the city the second wave of Greeks fought on, inch by inch, to join up with their comrades.

Now the two armies joined battle for the last time. The mighty figure of Achilles could be seen trading sword blow for sword blow with the Amazon general, Penthesilea. All around, men struggled desperately. In the darkness Penthesilea's tiny figure could be seen, nimbly evading the mighty thrusts of Achilles' sword, but her efforts may have exhausted her, or she was unlucky. Achilles thrust her through the chest. She put one hand to her breast – and fell.

In the palace I, the prophetess, was at the top of the steps leading down to the city, wielding my brother's sword. I had been asleep in the women's room, when the outcry woke us. Babies and small children started yelling, women were shouting questions when suddenly, just as the first torch was lit, two Greek soldiers appeared looming in the doorway. The women seized what they had, even brooch pins, and prepared to defend themselves. I somehow ducked past them in the darkness, and ran into the great hall where stood my mother and father, bewildered. My mother was ill and shaking, one arm around white-faced Polyxena. Creusa was there, with her boy, and Andromache, with hers. My brother Hector's old sword, the one he had used as a lad, trailed from my mother's hand. It was dented and had a broken hilt, had been kept by my mother out of sentiment and never handed over to the smith for remaking as it should have been. She held the sword out to me.

'Find Helenus,' she said. 'Fight with him.' I shall never know why she gave me Hector's old sword to help defend the city. She embraced me, then, with dignity, she put her other arm round my poor broken father and I ran from the room, leaving the group, my father, young sister, my mother, my brother Hector's widow and her child, my sister Creusa and her child, all together in the room. All are dead now, of course, except Andromache.

It was dark, Greeks and Trojans fought here and there. Cries and shouts rose. I found Helenus by a miracle, it seemed, and together, at the top of the steps leading up to the palace and the city ramparts, attempting to prevent more Greeks from entering the palace, we fought. There were four of us – crippled Advenor, who had come from the stables when the noise began, Helenus and I, and Penthesilea's general, who had become separated from the main troop of Amazons fighting outside the city gates. She had been in the stables with Advenor, taking her pleasure, adventitiously, as soldiers do.

Now I was looking down into the blue eyes of Menelaus. His red hair was damp with sweat. He grinned.

Helenus, grasping his sword, gasped, 'You're on the wrong level, Menelaus. Your wife's below – with Paris.' The Greeks pushed up. Menelaus swung his sword at Helenus and missed. From above Advenor struck one of the Greeks inexpertly on the head. The man slipped and fell on the steps and lay in the blood gouting from his head. But in spite of what we did they were all warriors and we were not. They pushed us aside and ten men, Menelaus with them, ran in the darkness towards the palace. One of them struck down Advenor as he ran by.

Advenor lay still, on the cobbles outside his own stables. Helenus disappeared as did the Amazon general. She went to find her regiment, but by then they were mourning for Penthesilea, whom Achilles had killed outside the gates. I followed the soldiers. Menelaus turned, saw me, seized me and dragged me into the palace with him. But even as, grasping me, he confronted my family, the battle for the city was not yet over. There was fighting everywhere.

The Amazons, though, were departing. Penthesilea was dead – they must have known the war now could have only one conclusion. It had been outside the gates that one of Penthesilea's soldiers, fighting the mighty Ajax, had turned her head to see Achilles kill her leader. Then began the high intolerable wail, and this sound, piercing all other noises, brought the other women running. The terrible high-pitched mourning around Penthesilea's body began even in the midst of battle. The Greeks ceased to attack them. They parted ranks to let the women gather up their leader.

413

Soon the broken column of women, still wailing, stooped on their horses, Penthesilea's bloody body across the pommel of one of them, was making its way across the plain from Troy, back to the mountains, where they would bury her.

After her death at the hands of Achilles the great man had stood still, gazing at her fallen body. Thersites had bent to strip her armour. 'No!' roared Achilles. 'No!'

Thersites turned. In a voice of great scorn and contempt – for Penthesilea, for Achilles' seeming sentimentality – he said, 'It's a woman, Achilles. This thing is an enemy woman,' and he kicked the body in the side.

As Thersites once more bent over the corpse Achilles pulled back his arm and with his spear still stained with Penthesilea's blood, pierced Thersites through. Thersites fell to the ground, writhing with the spear through his chest.

A great 'Ah!' of shock and blame went up from the Greek ranks. Achilles got into his chariot, whipped up his horses and rode straight through their ranks with a terrifying, set face, and down to the beach and into the sea, still in his armour, the plume of his helmet blowing.

I did not know this, nor of Memnon and his troops chasing Achilles and his Myrmidons all over the plain of Troy nor of Memnon's suddenly sparing the life of the great hero, as he had him on the ground, ivory-tipped spear pointing at his centre. I did not see Paris, gallant in defeat, defending himself against Agamemnon on the steps of Troy as the first wafts of smoke began to waver up. I did not see Paris die, for which

I am grateful, nor did I see the deaths of my other brothers.

I was in the great hall. I had cut Menelaus' arm, before he disarmed me. It was with this arm he grasped me, his blood was staining my dress. Menelaus and the remaining Greeks, spears raised, swords drawn, surrounded in the darkness my parents, and Creusa, Andromache and their children. Polyxena had fainted when they pushed through the entrance, Menelaus dragging me. She lay on the floor. The smell of smoke began to enter the room. The Greeks were already burning the city.

Menelaus, as we came in, had peered through the gloom for his wife, and not found her. Terrible screams came up from the city, making the silence in this room more strange.

'You know where she is – fetch Helen,' he ordered. He pointed quite arbitrarily at Creusa, who, with a terrified glance, left the darkened hall still clutching her son. A Greek went with her to make sure she did not escape. I supposed she went to Paris' house. For me, everything was like a dream. I did not realise that the blood dripping down my dress was only partly Menelaus' – I had been wounded in the side. Mercifully, even now, perhaps because of my dazed condition, I cannot see plainly Menelaus snatching Andromache's child from her arms and swinging him round, battering his head against the wall. I know he flung the lifeless body into a corner, know Andromache broke from the surrounding ring of soldiers and went to the body, crying out, 'You have killed my husband, now my son. Now kill me – my life is over. Let me die. I never want to see another dawn. Menelaus – I beg you – kill me.'

Even as she uttered this appeal a soldier came behind her and snatched her cloak-pin. It was gold. The other soldiers stood restlessly – they did not want Menelaus to get Helen; they did not want to see the king and queen of Troy persecuted; what they wanted was to get into the storehouses and find the treasures of Troy, into the women's room, to find jewellery, the men's room for swords and armour. Even as my nephew was killed, his mother mourned and I feared for my parents' lives, I felt the need of these men for loot.

It is still unbearable to remember. Time has no meaning during events like this – these moments are very long and very short at the same time, no one in such a situation can believe what they are seeing is really happening.

Later, memory is a burden but, again, a kind of incredulity exists – did it happen, was the person I am now actually there, at that time, taking part in events? Did I do this or that? Should I have done something else? Was I, was I there?

I remember thinking Menelaus would go soon; go to his wife, his comrades. But he did not. Then I thought, he must know the war is over, that is why he does not go. It is over. The Greeks are victorious. We will die. I saw my parents, my father leaning on my mother, Andromache bent over her child in a corner, Polyxena stirring, panting on the ground. She seemed to be speaking, but I could not hear her voice. Menelaus still grasped me, automatically, as a man holds his cloak. His mind, I think, was entirely on Helen. I grew weaker as my blood continued to flow. He had not noticed that either, though I was beginning to feel pain and realised the chief wound was

416

mine. An infuriated soldier threw Creusa into the room. He shouted, 'Your wife is gone! And a man in armour ran up and seized the child from this woman's arms.'

Menelaus took a step forward, dragging me, smacked the soldier across the face with the flat of his sword. Creusa smiled up at him from the ground. 'My husband has the child.'

Menelaus went to her and kicked her, crying, 'Two more to find and kill.' He told the soldiers to take us to the temple and guard us. From the ground by Menelaus' feet, Creusa looked up at me, still dangling on Menelaus' right arm, and murmured, 'Right, Cassandra. Right.' Her eyes closed. I heard my mother saying to Menelaus, 'The city's on fire, oh Great King. Run, or you'll burn up. Run and find your wife.' And he did. He turned without a word, dropped my arm and charged out of the room. Andromache had the dead baby in her arms. She was smoothing his hair and talking to him. I went and sat by her.

Somehow, as the soldiers pushed and shoved, supporting each other we were urged down the steps to the city. Andromache still carried her dead child. There were dead sprawled over the steps. Beside them houses were ablaze. The Greek soldiers were staggering from doorways through smoke, laden with gold and silver vessels and handfuls of jewellery. Paris' house was on fire. Lower down I saw Paris himself, dead, in a heap of Greek soldiers. I heard the crackle of fire, women screaming and, close to me, Andromache crying. There were sounds of some fighting taking place in odd corners, in someone's garden, round a corner. In the nook where they put up the stall selling fish, struggling figures could be seen through smoke. Lower down still, on the patch of ground between two houses where children used to meet to play knucklebones or fire little bows and arrows, two big-helmeted Greeks were fighting, presumably for the pile of rugs and household ornaments lying nearby. A woman staggered by, screaming, both hands to her head, blood between her fingers, where the earrings had been pulled from her ears. Still we descended, Andromache leaning on me, holding her boy's corpse, Polyxena dragged between two soldiers, my mother guarded, supporting my father. The smoke was beginning to choke us. It billowed over the dead, lying everywhere. The forge was on fire, flames gushed from the entrance to the temple. Soldiers rushed out, one dragged a girl, another a heap of armour. Inside the priestess screamed.

We went through the Scaean Gate – the last time I ever did so – and that is all I recollect. Except for the dead body of the oracle lying like a heap of rags by one gate post. I am happy I did not see, as my mother did, Agamemnon killing my father. He dragged him into the flaming temple and slew him there. But my father would not have minded making his end there, with the temple as his funeral pyre.

And so my poor Troy, poor city, was broken, looted and burned. Alas for the city, alas, too, for those whom once it nurtured.

And there was more to come. In Mycenae, Clytemnestra heard the news of the Greek victory.

Part Three

THIRTY-FOUR

Mycenae

'VICTORY! AGAMEMNON has victory! Your husband is alive and triumphant!'
This was the message of the soldier from Troy when he arrived. He wore a stained blue tunic smelling of the fire in Troy, a deadly reek of wood, oil, burned clothing and flesh. As he told me the story of the entry through the tunnel, the battle in the city and the victory I thought – this soldier has come as a hero, battle-stained, riding from the port with the marks of his triumph about him. His story told, he took out an elaborately worked embroidered scarf, also smelling of smoke, dropped to his knees and presented it to me. I thought, looking at his streaked, triumphant face – good boy, good little hero – you have burned, raped and looted the enemy. Now see what is in store for you at home.

We were in my private room, but outside the hubbub was beginning. Women and servants cried out. I had been weaving, as ever, my cloak for Agamemnon, nearly finished now.

For days I had sensed bad news coming. For three nights, the first being the night they sacked Troy and killed the Trojans, I had been at my loom. Those days I spent, red-eyed, brain racing, awaiting the ill-tidings I knew would come. While I paced the ramparts at Mycenae, looking out across a smooth, blue sea, the girl, Electra, watched me as a cat watches a moth flying round the room. The sun was hot across the blighted landscape of Argos.

Harvest was coming and there was almost nothing to reap, or gather. The land was full of widows, orphans and maimed men. People could no longer understand why, across that sea, such carnage was taking place, why it should go on. Slaves rebelled, there were robberies from one farm to another, caused by desperation; Aegisthus rode the land, putting down trouble. As he went he secretly fomented discord. 'Your lord cares more for plunder than he does for you, perhaps,' he would suggest to the hard-pressed oldest son, no more than thirteen, on a poor farm. 'Will booty bring back your husband?' he would ask of a widow. 'I say this only to show how I share your feelings. Now your man is dead, you may think quiet prosperity would have been better than adventure.' 'I pity you,' he would say to a weeping father. 'Young men, raised by fierce leaders, can be seduced into reckless wars in search of gain. But who will look after you in your old age? Seeing your grief even I find myself forced to wonder why they had to take families' only sons for this war.'

Aegisthus' subtle words, thrown like seeds, only where he thought the ground was ready for them, had their effect. To desolation, hunger and bereavement, Aegisthus added discontent.

Pandion, my Cretan steward, was now beginning to understand much, and suspect more. His almond eyes expressed that knowledge, although of course he dared say nothing. He was involved, his life now in danger. If Agamemnon, when he returned, found out all that had been going on, Pandion, who must have known, would die. Yet, he would be wondering, had I a plan? And would it be of any advantage to him?

He had followed the messenger into my chamber, finding me with the unexamined scarf in my lap. He listened as the messenger told of the earlier defeat of the Greeks, the flight to Tenedos, the return to Troy, the entry through the tunnel, of victory and the looting and burning of the city. Paris, Troilus, Deiphobus, all the king's sons, he said, were dead. Agamemnon had killed Priam in the temple. What remained of his family were captive, chained on the shore at Troy, slaves waiting for passage to Greece.

I knew my husband would have raped Cassandra, the prophetess. I pitied the girl.

Electra stood beside me, as the news was given, sobbing with joy. The Cretan smiled, congratulated me. 'Queen of Troy,' declared the messenger, from his knees, 'I have brought much booty with me from your husband – the treasures of Priam he seized on the night of victory. The scarf is from the palace store-house. He particularly wished me to give it to you. Inside are the earrings Queen Hecuba always wore.'

I opened it with the tips of my fingers. There lay long, elaborately-worked golden earrings, fresh, I supposed, from the ears of the poor queen. How could I not pity her? All her sons were dead, she and her daughters would die in captivity.

I was obliged to send messengers throughout Argos, to declare a victory. One messenger, on the fastest horse we had, I sent to Aegisthus.

'Cousin Aegisthus will be returning to his own lands now, Mother, will he not?' asked Electra.

'Most certainly,' I told her. 'He has been a loyal friend.'

That night, I sat at my loom, the fine cloak almost finished, weaving my deep spells into every thread. I had had the loom taken to the great hall and sat in its vast darkness, one torch burning. On the floor lay the first instalment of the booty from Troy – silver and gold jugs and cups, jewellery, headdresses, some coins. A great black oval stone the size of a three-year-old child and streaked with dried blood, lay on its side amid the gleaming loot. Was that Priam's blood? Had he clutched at this ancient god, even as he died?

Electra came again quietly in the darkness. 'I cannot sleep. When will Father return? Will our cousin go back to his own land when he hears the news? Have you sent to tell him to return? Will he come back here? When will Father come? Shall we go to Troy? Have you sent for Orestes now? When will our family be reunited?'

Never, I thought of saying in answer to her last question. Never, because your sister is dead, sacrificed to get the army to Troy, so that this triumph which so delights you could be achieved. I wanted to imprison Electra far away, chained against a wall where I would not have to hear that insistent, unnaturally childish voice. I did not want my concentration disturbed as I finished the cloak. Aegisthus must be coming. And I had much to think of.

I said, 'Go to bed. Everything is attended to. I must finish this cloak for your father. The cloak of victory.'

'I can't sleep, after this joyful news. I have lain awake, night after night, fearing the next message would be of Father's death.'

And all the time, I knew none of this girlish talk was sincere. I knew she hated me. I knew if she could get Agamemnon's ear she would betray me. I said again, 'Go to bed. I need to finish the cloak. I am too tired to talk tonight. This war has exhausted us all. You do not quite understand – you are a child.'

'Not a child,' she exclaimed. 'I am a woman now.'

'Yes, indeed,' I said. 'We must soon think of your marriage, now this is all over.'

That jolted her. She wanted no marriage. Perhaps she thought to get rid of me, and herself marry her father. It's not unheard of, in aristocratic families, desiring to retain their power. Dowries remain inside the family, no hostages are given to rival clans. Was this what she had in mind? I think so.

So, 'Not yet,' she cried. 'Not yet.'

'Of course not yet. Now, go to bed. It may be days before the fleet arrives. You cannot spend the next two or three nights awake.'

All this calmed her somewhat. I sent a servant to follow her with a draught of wine in which I put a drug to make sure she slept. I knew Aegisthus would be back within hours, and I needed no eavesdroppers on our discussion.

Interrupted, I left the loom and called the Cretan. There was no help for it – I had to secure his co-operation. I could kill him, but his death, only days before my husband's return, would be incriminating. If he helped me, he could have what he liked. We owned Troy and the cities and land around it now. But I had two potential betrayers near me – my daughter who might not be believed, and the Cretan Pandion, who could be bought, as well I knew, and whose evidence might be damning. The servant I sent

425

to fetch him brought good news. Pandion had gone, stolen a horse, had been seen riding fast from the palace with a bundle in front of him – some of Agamemnon's booty, no doubt. He had intelligently solved my problem and saved his own life.

Near dawn, Aegisthus burst in. My worst fears were confirmed by his expression as he came. That handsome face was disintegrating with panic, melting like wax. 'Disaster,' he said. 'Both Agamemnon and his brother triumphant – and alive. The countryfolk are already coming here to give him welcome.' He was dusty, paced the room, attempting to summon a kind of male energy he certainly did not command at that moment.

'Pray he arrives soon, then,' I said. 'Sit down.' I gave him wine. 'Are you planning flight? Do you want to return to your stone hutch? Do you want to live there in exile with some cast-off Trojan slave forever? Do you want to rear children with her, little better than slaves themselves?'

'Agamemnon would reward me for my loyalty while he was away,' he told me.

I laughed aloud. He gazed at me fearfully.

'He would,' he claimed. 'He would give me Trojan lands.'

'He would put a spear through your throat,' I said. 'Do you think he's stupid? He knows you for his next enemy. If he didn't, Electra will make sure he does.'

'The child?' he exclaimed. He was incredulous.

'She is fourteen years old. Her eyes have been everywhere for a year. So have the eyes of many others.'

'The Cretan!' he exclaimed again.

'The Cretan is gone,' I said, 'but there are others

– servants, slaves, stablemen, my own women – how long do you think it would be before someone, for gain, confirmed Agamemnon's suspicions? Do you think the world is blind? I am Helen's sister – do you think my husband trusts me?'

He put his head in his hands. I guessed his thoughts. 'Egypt?' I suggested. 'Babylon? Hattusas, even, high in the mountains at Hattusas, in perpetual snow where no one could find you? Is that what you are thinking? Do you believe that a man shortly about to proclaim himself a Great King cannot, if he wants, lever you out of any crack in the rocks where you might hide? That he wouldn't send men out to ride for a year and a day, if necessary, until they found you and killed you? Did you not think of all this? Were you simply counting on Agamemnon's death in war? When we talked and planned what we'd do if he returned triumphant, were we just telling each other stories at night?'

He ignored me, saying, 'If I were far enough away, he would not bother about me.'

'So – beg on the streets of Memphis,' I said. 'Freeze in the snow outside the palace at Hattusas. Agamemnon is powerful. No one will take you in.'

But I needed him. I went to him, smoothed his sweating brow. Closer to him, I was more alarmed. His face was chalky. He trembled. His hand, when I took it, was cold.

He had been bold enough in my husband's absence. Bold enough in the bedroom, firm enough also to keep the country under some kind of control. He was not, I knew, a coward. His terrors came from the past. His father had been destroyed by Agamemnon's father. Aegisthus had secretly taken on his father's battle, planned to avenge him. But now he feared the same defeat and humiliation his father had endured. 'Do you want no revenge for what happened to your father?' I said gently. 'He is crying out to you now to take back what was his, and is yours by right. I love you. We are one. Help me kill Agamemnon, if not for your sake or mine, for your father's. Your parents are calling to you now. Can you not hear them? Look what we have, look what we have done. Do not draw back from the last step.'

And so I calmed him, so I persuaded him, so I took him to bed, and soothed him. He was steady now. All we had to do was wait for Agamemnon's return.

THIRTY-FIVE

Thessaly

W E HAD closed the gate and posted men, such as we had. We went inside to wait for the unexpected visitors to the farm. We were preparing food – there was no more we could do. Helen said, 'My sister pitied you.'

'Pitied me?' I echoed.

'When she knew you were in the hands of her husband,' Helen told me. Her thoughts were disjointed. These unexpected visitors had frightened her. She was a woman with many fears. She went on, 'We sat like this before – expecting attack. Do you remember?' She paused. 'It cannot be Menelaus, come to kill me.'

But I knew she was still uncertain. 'You haven't told him who I am? Assure me of that,' I asked.

'I have told you more than once, until I found Helenus I didn't know you were alive.'

'You could have sent a messenger secretly from here to Mycenae or Sparta,' I persisted.

'I did not.' She gazed at me speculatively. 'You haven't told me of one of your children – the oldest.'

'What do you know of my son?'

'Your brother said you had a boy, Diomed, at

Pharaoh's court. You haven't told me of him, only of the others. I wonder why?'

'What reason would I have? I forgot. He is so far away. It is many years since I saw him,' I answered, and was relieved when a cry went up outside. Better an attack from these coming strangers than this question from Helen, I thought. Anything was better than that.

Helen and I went out into the yard, I running, Helen moving more slowly on her damaged feet. I could see them winding uphill now. I drew in my breath in horror. A chariot of foreign make, pulling hard, surrounded by a galloping guard of soldiers – Egyptian soldiers, easily seen to be such by their weaponry and headdresses.

The visitor could be nobody but my oldest son, Diomed, now twenty. I had not seen him for seven years. I attempted to conceal my alarm from Helen. Why, I asked myself, had that person I most longed to see, who had been a thousand miles away at Memphis at the court of the Pharaoh for so long – why should he come now, at this most unfortunate time? There was nothing I could do to stop his unlucky arrival. A tall figure waved at me. I saw his face again, the same – older, changed – the same. 'Pull back the gates,' I said. And to Helen, 'It is my son.'

'I am happy for you,' she responded mechanically. 'I will go inside so that you can first greet him privately. Then, I long to see him, Cassandra.'

Naomi took me by the shoulder, hissing, 'Go out – tell him to turn back.'

But he was already running up the track towards me as I stood by the gate.

'Too late,' I told her and ran from the gate to

embrace him. 'Diomed,' I said, 'there is a woman within who must not see you.'

I could tell from his face he knew what I had kept from him for so long. Someone had told him. 'Who is she?' he asked.

'The Queen of Sparta – Helen.'

I gazed at him helplessly. I was at fault. I had not told him what he should know and my omission was largely to protect myself, not him. But someone had told the truth and I was not sure, knowing it, how he saw me, or indeed himself.

'My aunt,' he said. His face showed understanding.

'She is. She could betray us all.'

'I've come to take you back with me, Mother. She can harm neither of us in Egypt.'

I was very confused. He knew his own secret; he had considered it, absorbed it. He had come to conclusions and made a plan. Egypt? A departure for Egypt? Bewildered, I could only say, urgently, 'She is leaving. Hide until she goes. Go into the hills.'

I had lived for twenty years with this fear.

'Mother,' he said patiently, 'this is an old tale. They cannot touch you now. I'm a captain in Pharaoh's army. I can protect you from old history, these blood-thirsty quarrelling princelings. In any case, you must leave. That's why I'm here. There's another danger.'

'I know it,' I told him. But I pleaded, 'Do not go into the house until Helen leaves.'

But it was too late. She came out and moved across the snow-sprinkled yard, a courtly smile of welcome on her face. But as she approached, the smile turned into an expression of horror. Within ten paces of Diomed she stopped, her damaged hand flew to her face. Head thrown a little back she stared and stared at Diomed, who stepped forward and said, 'Welcome, Aunt.'

My son, tall, very blond, long-nosed, even at twenty a little hollow-cheeked was, in nearly every respect – face, colouring, stature, even his stance – the very image of his father, Agamemnon.

THIRTY-SIX

Troy

W E HAD been chained in groups near the
shore for a day without food or water or
shelter from the sun. I was with the Trojan
women – my mother, Andromache, Creusa and many
others. The Greek leaders, determined to inflict as
much humiliation as possible, had made no provision
for separating the royal women from the others, as
might have been expected. There were few men
among us, none of our family. We had seen Paris'
body and had to believe the rest were also dead. All
around us women wailed and children cried, mourning the past, dreading the future, anxious about those
they had not been able to find. There were perhaps a
hundred of us. We suffered physical misery, of course,
but, worse, hopes and fears chased each other in
our benumbed brains. Someone missing might still be
alive, we thought, or, what kind of death might
another have met? For ourselves we feared slavery,
the punishment of the Greeks and death. Some hoped
for rescue or ransom.

Night came, as my mother continued to try to comfort Polyxena, or rather, bring her to the stage where
comfort was possible, for she sat like a stone, while
Andromache chafed her hands. Creusa spoke, too

433

often, of that moment when the figure of Aeneas, fully armoured, had appeared through the smoke and seized her boy from her arms, then disappeared before the eyes of her astonished guard. Were either of them alive now, she wondered? Would they appear and bargain for us, rescue us? Andromache, always with the image of her own husband dead and of her son's lifeless body, torn from her arms by soldiers as we were dragged from the city, could not respond and found it hard to listen to Creusa's babble. All the time our eyes were drawn towards Troy, where flames leaped up in the darkness. Around us men stampeded to and fro, carrying loot, shouting. Horses whinnied, chariot wheels crashed. Creusa ceased to speak at dawn. My mother stopped trying to rally Polyxena. 'The coming day will be worse than this,' she said. 'Perhaps it is better if she feels nothing.'

Next day soldiers were still carrying the wealth of Troy to their ships. Behind, under a clear blue sky, the city still burned, a funeral pyre for husbands, sons, brothers.

The sun grew hotter and beat down on us. At midday, when it was at its height, Agamemnon came. None of us looked at him. I saw his big feet and strong, golden-haired legs planted in the sand. He looked down at my mother. 'I shall have your daughter,' he told her. She clasped Polyxena closer. 'Not that one – or not yet.' My mother's glance went to Creusa, then to me. 'Yes, I'll take the mad one first,' he said. 'Perhaps a man will bring her to her senses.'

I knew. I had always known. He had been in my nightmares for many years. Does knowing a thing is to happen make it any better? I doubt it – the reality is always different; the experience is what it is. You cannot prepare for it.

I looked up at his face. There was the beak of a nose and the hollow cheeks, the straggling, sweat-stained blond hair. And suddenly I saw death in that face, but not my death – his own. I could not credit this at first. When a man or woman's death is beginning, it manifests itself at first as a bruise on the countenance. Few can see it. I could. There, like the first tiny bruise on an apple, lay death on Agamemnon's face. He flinched from my gaze. 'Smile,' he said. 'Smile at your bridegroom.' It was not hard to smile, now I knew he would die.

'I dislike these strong looks, Hecuba,' he said. 'Do your women not plead, or moan, or ask for any mercy even for each other?'

She said nothing, but later, after he had gone, she asked, 'Cassandra, why did you smile? You seemed almost joyful. Can you welcome this?'

I cast my eyes to the sand. The gift of foretelling had been a source of pain between us for too long.

'Do you want to be his concubine?' my mother said, in agitation.

Creusa sobbed, 'Who will they give me to? Who shall I have to endure?'

Rape is of course the confirmation of victory; the final humiliation of the enemy is achieved when the victors take their women. The passion they feel as they rape is not for the women, it is hatred for their menfolk, the enemy.

The long afternoon wore on. Thirst was a burden. Children cried for water. Women fainted. Turning our heads to the left, we saw ships being brought from our harbour and from lower down the coast, from

Miletus. They were bringing vessels to transport us and their booty back to Greece. 'We shall sail tonight,' my mother said. A little further off two Greeks were quarrelling over one of Creusa's women. One felled the other, grabbed the girl and carried her off screaming.

At dusk a wind came, cooling us. Through the gloom a giant came, at first terrifying us. It was Achilles, with his men, bringing water. He went to Andromache, offering her the cup. 'You have been given to my son,' he said. 'He is not a bad man. He will treat Hector's widow well.'

Andromache's eyes were on the ground. She refused to drink from the cup he held out. 'You throw me to your son and expect me to thank you? You, who killed my husband? No son of yours, or any Greek, will have me long. I will kill myself, starve to death if I must.'

'Lady,' he said, 'war is war. Many die. Those left alive must go on living.' There was pity in his voice. 'I have arranged for my son to have you out of respect for your late husband. Do not throw my goodwill in my face.'

'After your leader dashed my infant son's head against a wall?'

'War is war,' he repeated. 'Some would not have slain Hector's son before the eyes of his mother, but none would have left the child alive. This you know. The choice is yours, Andromache. Neoptolemus my son is the lesser of evils.'

'No good can ever come to me again, made a widow and childless, and a captive to you.'

He began to lose his temper. 'If you dream of ransom, forget the dream. The Queen of Lycia has

436

offered ransoms for all of you. We have refused. Agamemnon says he wants the nest of vipers dead under
his foot.'

'Why not let my sister ransom us?' Hecuba said
bitterly. 'What harm can we do?'

'Trojan women,' Achilles said. 'The wolves are
dead, the she-wolves left behind. Your women
endured the long siege. The city would have fallen
earlier without you. In the end you fought in dead
men's armour. This innocent prophetess, a princess
and subject to her divine gifts, was seen attacking
Menelaus with a sword – a rare sight, a sight I wish
I'd seen. My lady,' he said to my mother, 'I am a
merciful man, though a simple one, but the others,
Agamemnon, Menelaus and the intelligent Ulysses
tell me you are women of iron. Are we to send you
to your sister, to plot and plan, rally, bear more Trojans to fight us? No, you must sink into unknown,
unremembered graves, far from here. This is what
they tell me and I see they are right.'

He began to walk away. Creusa was sobbing. He
turned – he was indeed a somewhat merciful man,
'You have less cause to weep than the others,' he
told her. 'Your husband Aeneas escaped the city as it
burned. With his father and your son. Your husband
is a man who could survive anything – he lives, as
far as I know.' I heard some contempt in his voice.

Creusa's sobs redoubled. 'Alive – oh, I give thanks.
Give thanks. He will ransom me. Aeneas will save
me.'

Achilles left. We were all thankful that Aeneas,
Anchises and the child were safe and we were happy
for Creusa, though a woman nearby, her head under
a canopy made of a piece of cloth propped on a stick,

called in a cracked voice, 'Spare a thought for others, lady, while you're rejoicing.' How clever Aeneas was, we thought. But I wondered, strong and clever as he was, how had he managed to escape with an elderly man, and a boy to carry?

The soldiers released us from our chains to go to the latrines. There, watched by a soldier, I sat beside a boy of about seven straining his guts out, his face all bones, his eyes showing the horrible blank patience of a child who no longer knows any certainty. I could not meet these eyes. I could not give one word of comfort to the child. I should have noticed the lack of soldiers round the tunnel mouth, I thought, and had not. We had rejoiced when we should have been on guard against a Greek return. Hector would never have trusted a Greek withdrawal. So I thought, as the child strained and I urinated under the eyes of a laughing guard. The victorious have one thought, the defeated many, and guilt at their defeat is never far away. The boy stared blankly ahead, the soldier shouted at him. He got up and walked off, head down, back to whatever was left of his family.

Later, as even the wailing of the women and children had begun to decline, from exhaustion, the soldier roused us, and we were marched, aching from our chains, along the beach and through water on to the ships. We sat on deck, soldiers all around. Creusa, who I think had been expecting sudden rescue or ransom by Aeneas, wept anew. She gazed towards Troy. She said what many must have been thinking, 'If we had given in when the Greeks invaded and made a treaty with them, submitted, on our terms, much loss of life and suffering might have been avoided.'

Hecuba must have been shocked and indignant, but said nothing. Andromache said only, 'I doubt that, Creusa. They would not have let us live.'

'They might have let my man live, at any rate,' said the woman next to us harshly. It was Raina, the inn-keeper's daughter. 'And my father. My daughter's gone, raped to death, burned – I don't know how she died. They might all have lived.' There was a silence. Wars are always the same: the nobles fight, the poor die; everyone knows that. None could answer.

'Is my daughter alive, Cassandra?' Raina now asked me urgently. 'Is she? You can see. Tell me!'

'Shut up, you women,' said one of the soldiers. He spoke Greek. Not all the women could understand him, but all knew what he was saying. There was another silence. A woman sobbed. Still the ships did not move. Perhaps we would be there till dawn, half-way between our old lives and our new fates in Greece. The waiting seemed eternal.

Then a soldier came up and dragged me to my feet. 'Where is she being taken?' my mother asked.

'To Agamemnon,' he said, pulling me away. My countrywomen heard the name and began to wail pitifully.

He took me to the hold and shut me in. It was very hot and dark, full, it seemed, of bales and bundles of loot. I sat down, lights flashing in front of my eyes. The hatch opened, feet came down the wooden ladder, Agamemnon was there, carrying a torch, which he put in a socket on the wall. Light filled the hold. I saw one bundle, made of the rug which had been on Paris' wall and bulging with items from his house. I shook. I kept my eyes to the floor. He would rape me, might damage me internally, might kill me. I only wanted it, whatever it was, to be over.

Then I found that Hecate, Queen of Night, ruled me. She was close to me, closer than a mother, as he said, 'I told your mother I would have you, and I will.' I saw the moon, a thin sickle, the rest dark. I heard him say, 'Your brother, Paris, the adulterer, is dead.' He did not want a calm victim. He wanted tears, pleas, bargains. 'I may yet ransom your mother. I may give your sister, Polyxena, to Ajax. I may kill you all.'

Something stirred within me, as he had intended it should. He was telling me, if I begged, or if I colluded in my own rape, he might show mercy. The glimmer of hope that I might persuade him to spare in some way those left alive, soon died. This was another part of the torment. Paris was dead, my handsome brother, consort to the goddess. 'He has slain my lover,' I heard a woman's voice say. Tears rolled down my face.

Finding I could not be made to speak, that I showed no feeling but for my tears, he slapped me violently on both sides of my face, so that my head snapped, first right, then left. The pain brought me partly out of my trance, but I said only, 'Do what you will to me, Great King.' He was not a Great King, never would be and he knew it. I looked up at him, just to check the death-mark on his face, which I could see, in the mind's eye, as clearly as if the blemish had been there, visible to all. The blue-black mark was spreading. He had little time left. He kicked me, picked me up by the throat and shook me as a child shakes a puppy. In spite of the pain I asked myself would it not be easier to give him what he wanted, the tears, entreaties, profession of intense fear and a willingness to do anything he wanted? To feign love, if necessary. But the goddess had her hand on me and, as he threw me down, pinioned my arms, entered me, I heard her music as he raped me.

After he had gone, I lay on the sacks, knowing nothing but pain. And shame – terrible shame. Aloft I heard Agamemnon shout, then the creaking of sail. We were getting under way, leaving Troy.

Later – it must have been dawn, for I saw light as the hatch flew back, Agamemnon returned. He was even more violent this time. He punched me in the stomach. I think he cracked some ribs. When he had gone I turned my head and vomited on to Paris' great hanging. Later the girl, Briseis, brought me food, which I refused. She supported me as I drank some water. I asked what was happening to the captives. She was cowed to the point of idiocy – I now knew why – and simply shook her head. 'Tell them, if you can, I am alive, and will live,' I told her. She stared at me, with huge terrified eyes. I doubt if she understood. I found out later that there was no one of my family left on board by that time. Before we set sail my mother, Polyxena and Andromache had been transferred to Ulysses' ship. They had been taken to Thrace. There, Polyxena and my mother both died. My mother was not even spared, at the last, the knowledge that although she believed her last son, young Polydorus, was safe with the King of Thrace where she had sent him, he was not. The king had killed him at the instigation of the victorious Greeks. There in those half-savage lands, Polyxena, Polydorus and last of all, my mother, died without even the consolation of knowing Helenus was still alive. Hecuba died, cursing the Greeks as they mocked her.

So the voyage went on. We came to land at Euboea, where they said Agamemnon had sacrificed his own daughter to get up a wind to take the fleet to Troy. Straight away Neoptolemus bore Andromache away to his mountains in the Epirus, for he wanted to have her all to himself. It was later she became Helenus' wife.

I was dragged on deck, injured, fouled and starving. The women screamed when they saw me as I stared round blindly and desperately for my mother and sisters. The women looked after me as well as they could, and told me my mother and sisters had gone on Ulysses' ship.

The other Greek ships lay in the bay on sparkling sea. Above were wooded cliffs. So this was Greece, home of the monsters. I had thought of it as dark, yet it was not unlike our own land. The women, in spite of their own fear and distress, were kind. They washed me down with sea water, which, though painful, was cleansing, but they could not cleanse me of Agamemnon and they knew it. One woman tried to push a small pebble in my womb, sure protection against conception, she said, but it was too painful. I was too torn.

That evening the village women came with a waggon, with food, broth, bread and roasted meat for the soldiers. I ate soup and bread. Like Andromache I had resolved to starve, but still I ate. Agamemnon came among us, and I flinched and trembled from him. Nature is very strong – we eat in order not to die, we cower from those who have hurt us. At the same time, though I lay at his feet, trembling, smelling him, one glance showed the death-mark spreading on his face.

I slept out in the open that night in the bay, surrounded by trees. The women were kind to each other. Many had been raped, others expected it. Even as we slept we were awoken by a man hauling a girl in our midst to her feet and dragging her away. At dawn I myself was pulled up and taken to a chariot drawn by two horses. I was tied upright by ropes, as I have seen men rope themselves in before battle so that they can fight on, though wounded. A soldier positioned himself behind me and there I stood as dawn came, and birds began to sing.

Later, Agamemnon got on to the chariot, picked up the reins and we went off. He was still in his battle armour, I beside him, my gown torn, stained and dirty. So Agamemnon and three more chariots and some twenty-five mounted soldiers set out for Mycenae, a hundred miles away. Travelling fast, in helmets, plumes waving, we went through the countryside, where the farmers and villagers came out to watch us go. The soldiers shouted out who I was as we travelled. I was in pain, half-conscious, yet I knew the soldiers knew, as did all the people we passed, that their chieftain had raped and beaten me. This was the return of a triumphant general who had been away for over a year, and a display for the people. Some laughed at me or jeered and shouted but I was aware that some did not.

We went through the streets of Thebes, then Corinth. Those streets were magnificent and were lined with people but there were many more women than men, and they looked tired and pinched. The children were hollow-eyed, some ragged and barefoot.

In the cities we slowed down for the king to display himself, and me, the emblem of his victory and our defeat. The crowd cheered and called out insults.

One of the soldiers cried, 'See – here is our leader with Cassandra, Troy's princess.'

A man called back, 'Wash her and I'll take her off your hands.' There was a laugh, more jeering until a woman's voice cried out, 'Where's Helen? Where's Paris' whore?' and that cry was taken up with more enthusiasm than the other.

The soldier tried to distract attention by crying out, 'We have the riches of Troy, travelling behind.' There was more cheering, but the cry came again, this time from a man lacking a leg. 'Where's Helen? Bring us the bitch. Never mind the prophetess. Bring us Helen!'

Agamemnon whipped up the chariot, the men followed suit. We galloped out of Corinth at speed. I could see now that this war had cost the Greeks dearly. They were poor. Their men had died. They had suffered for the ambitions of their leaders. There in Greece I saw that defeat is bitter and even victory is cruel.

The soldier behind me said our horses were tired and indeed they were, but Agamemnon's desire to leave the city and its less-than-admiring crowd made him push on, paying no visit to its ruler, not even changing horses.

We rested in a grove beyond the city while fresh horses were brought out to us. They untied me, and I lay on the ground.

Mycenae lay ahead. A messenger was sent before us with a trumpet to tell the palace we were coming. I saw Agamemnon on a hillock with his officers. He glanced at me and grinned as I had once seen an angry ape grin, but the mark on his face was still spreading. Not many days were left to him now.

It was in the grove that they hauled me up, stripped off my torn and filthy dress and put on me a red, embroidered dress. This was done on Agamemnon's instructions. An old soldier, eyes averted, dropped it over my head to cover my bruised and wasted body. Agamemnon had bitten my shoulder and it was festering. This soldier had stared as I took off my dress but turned his head away, ashamed, I suppose, when he saw what the great general had done. I said nothing. He brought me some wine, and I sat down on a rock by the roadside. I was thin, my hair matted and tangled and I knew my face must be bruised. I felt too, my womb was festering like the bite, with Agamemnon's poisonous seed. But I was bewildered by the attempt to make me presentable for the arrival at Mycenae. No one would be surprised by violence towards a captive, or, of course, rape. Agamemnon had no need to attempt to hide his maltreatment of me. The soldier spoke to me, not unkindly, but I ignored him. He could not be innocent of my people's blood. He had killed. He, too, had raped. Now he was home, perhaps he was beginning to be shocked by some of the things he had done. In a little while he would be ploughing his field, pruning his vines, telling his neighbours of his brave exploits. His wife would show off her Trojan bracelets, his daughter's dowry would be golden earrings from Troy, no doubt. His sons would play soldiers with his dented and battered sword. He would buy a widowed neighbour's field. Now I lay down on the grass, in pain from my womb and bruises and the cracked ribs, jolted badly on the journey. I felt quite empty, except for the most intense fear for what was left of my family.

We would reach Mycenae at dusk, I imagined. And what was to happen to me then?

I do not suppose Agamemnon knew, as he searched out a dress from the loot he was bringing back to his palace, that the garment he had found for me was the old ceremonial gown of Troy's oracle. After they had killed the woman they must have stripped her and thrown her clothes and ornaments on to a heap. It must have been fated that he was to give me that dress, invested with a hundred years of power held by the oracle, and given to her by the goddess. I, of course, who from childhood had tried to avoid becoming the oracle, had now been forced to assume her clothing, and her role, here in Greece, just as we were about to enter Agamemnon's stronghold. I knew, in my weariness and pain, that strange and terrible events were about to take place.

THIRTY-SEVEN

Thessaly

AFTER HELEN saw my son Diomed in the yard, I led her, because she was too startled to be able to move of her own volition, through the snow and back to the house. Diomed held her other arm. It was easy to understand her feelings – she had seen what must have looked to her like a ghost, not just Agamemnon returned – and he had been dead now for over twenty years – but Agamemnon in youth, as she must have known him when she was a girl.

A whole story now revealed itself to her – that I had borne Agamemnon's child after his death, hidden both of us in fear all those years, knowing the child of a Trojan princess and the great leader of the Greek alliance could only be seen as a threat to the kingdom. After the war, the alliance had at first been ruled by her sister, then by her nephew, Orestes, who had never been popular. My son, with his astonishing resemblance to Agamemnon, might, if he ever chose to raise an army and challenge Orestes for his throne, have gained the support of the population and become king himself.

Naomi walked behind. I felt her agitation and shared it. This visit was a most unlucky event.

As Diomed grew up, his resemblance to Agamemnon had become more and more marked. Slowly, from his childish face, the lineaments of the dead king emerged. He grew tall – taller than Iphitus or his brothers and sisters. I had known from his birth he might be in danger from the rulers of Mycenae. As this resemblance to his dead father grew it became more and more obvious he must leave Greece before he became a man. My husband of course knew Diomed was not his child. He must have been as convinced as a man can be that Agamemnon was Diomed's father, but he said nothing of any of this. He was a kind man and part of his kindness lay in silence. Agamemnon was dead, but many had seen him, and all who had seen him would remember him. No ruler could risk Agamemnon's old soldiers rallying to his son, however unlikely it was.

The only way to ensure Diomed's safety was to send him away from Greece. So as he approached fourteen years old, I sent a secret message to Helenus, undisturbed lord over his own wild area, and despatched the boy to his uncle. This caused me great suffering. He had little experience of anything but life on his farm. Helenus had put him in the charge of an Egyptian captain, who had taken him to King Rameses in Egypt. Pharaoh (no friend of the Greeks) had kindly found him a position in his army. And there he had prospered. Perhaps he had inherited his father's gift for war.

It had been wrong not to tell Diomed why he was being forced from his home. I believed it must have been Helenus and Andromache who had, gently, I am sure, told him of his origins. What he had thought on hearing the terrible story of his birth and parentage

448

I could not know. Yet he seemed to have sustained the shock and the toughening experience of Pharaoh's court. He seemed still the same open, straightforward individual he had always been.

The horror now was that after all the efforts made to save him, by a terrible mischance, a matter of only a day, he had now encountered the woman who could do both of us more damage than anyone else in the world. She knew who I was, she had known the face of Agamemnon. She could betray both of us to the king, her son-in-law. He would not be happy that his father had another living son, the image of himself, a soldier (as he, Orestes, was not), another Agamemnon to follow the one still praised in ballads and songs, recalled sentimentally by his troops, a god among the Greeks.

Naomi – I could read her mind – thought a dagger in Helen's ribs the best and only answer to our predicament. She was right, but I could not and would not take up the methods of that perverse and blood-spattered family – could not commit yet another murder which would, according to their own tradition, create another series of murders, lengthening that long chain of death and revenge inside the family. They had killed and killed – enemies, friends, each other – over generations. If I despatched Helen with a knife – and it would not have been hard – it would be clear proof that the family taint or curse, rather, had not disappeared. The slayings would continue. I had watched Diomed in childhood, dreading that some day bad blood would appear in him. It had not. So I thought, was I to do the deed which would stir it up?

Some other means to silence Helen had to be found. But I could not imagine what that might be.

It was an uneasy feast we had that day. We shared it with the soldiers who had accompanied Diomed. It was impossible to talk privately, but huge questions hung in the air. Helen's gaze was almost continually on Diomed, as if she saw a wonder, like a fountain springing up suddenly in the middle of the room. Diomed was equally fascinated by her. And I thought of that rapid remark he had made when he first arrived, that he planned to take me to Egypt.

I had been so horrified by the prospect of his meeting Helen, I had not paid sufficient attention to what he had said, or how he had said it. Thinking now, I realised it had not sounded, simply, like a filial desire to have his mother under his care and protection. There had been too much urgency in his tone. Also, he had not raised the topic again, as he might have done, while we ate. It was as if because Helen was present, he was not prepared to say any more. She, however, spoke of her own departure – her waggons were loaded, she might have left hours ago if we had not taken fright at the arrival of unknown people and she hoped there would be no more snow. As she talked though, her eyes rarely left Diomed's face.

Meanwhile Diomed spoke to her in the courteous manner of one meeting a previously unknown relative, but without making it too obvious to his men there was any relationship. That grim and shameful history would have done him no good in the eyes of his soldiers. Although he was apparently open and candid, I saw his attitude to this situation was extremely cautious.

The men, of course, were intensely interested when

they found themselves feasting with the legendary Helen. She bore their scrutiny of her blemished beauty with calm. She must have been perpetually subjected to that look which always said, 'One can see how lovely she must have been – once upon a time.'

I went out to fetch more bread – the soldiers were hungry. Naomi caught me by the arm. She said, 'I'll kill her. If I don't, she'll destroy us.'

'No,' I told her. 'The killing's stopped.'

'You dream,' she said. 'This is one death, well deserved, to save our lives. This has nothing to do with the past.' She seemed to cast her eyes sideways, as if the past, figures locked in combat, a burning city, lay there in the corner of the room. In a sense now, it did. She said, 'That's over. Come into the present.'

'It's not over. We see that now,' I told her.

'Never mind. Never mind,' she replied urgently. 'This is not a poem or a ballad. This is real life. She can return to her husband or to Orestes, to any one of a number of kings and leaders – she will tell them what she has seen. You – Diomed. From that moment on, our lives aren't worth a pin. If she does that,' Naomi continued, 'we'll become part of some hideous sequel to what went before. Do you want that?'

She touched me on the raw. 'No killing,' I said obstinately.

She gave me a furious, scornful look. 'Then I'll go to my man across the hills, now,' she said. 'And take my boy. I won't have him die, for you. I may not return.' And she was running for her child, asleep in her room, in an instant. I returned to the table.

'My men can escort you some of the way,' Diomed was suggesting politely to Helen.

What had Helen said while I was gone? 'You can't be leaving now? It'll be dark soon,' I said in alarm. I did not trust her. I felt safe while she was under my roof. Once she was gone, I would fear her.

But now she was determined to leave. 'It may snow again, as you have said. We have just enough light to get us south to Pinios. There we will spend the night and make a good start in the morning.'

There was no stopping her. In the courtyard I pleaded, 'Say nothing of all this, Helen. Let the past remain the past. No one plans any harm to anyone. You and I – we have seen enough ambition, killing, soreness of heart. Let matters rest. I promise you we will do the same.'

She was getting into her litter, her men all round her. She smiled that lovely smile. 'We have all suffered,' she said. 'The gods cannot require any more of us. I have been involved in enough destruction. Do you think I want more? I have never been a vicious woman, Cassandra, nor an ambitious one. My sister and I were two sides of that coin – she, all rage and desire, I only requiring love, and peace. You know that well, don't you?'

I nodded. It was true, Helen had no lust for rule, power, cities or gold. She took the products gladly, but she never worked, schemed or fought for them, or asked others to do so. She spoke the truth. She only desired love, peace, comfort, ease of mind. Of course, we had all paid a high price for all these innocent desires of hers.

She put her hand in mine, the good one. 'I wish you only well. You, too, need peace. You have it now, with the respect of your neighbours and your fine children. You can be assured of my silence. What good would it do me to harm you?'

Those great blue eyes fixed me. Her charm and sincerity flowed over me. I said, 'Thank you, sister. I'm glad our battles are over.'

Diomed and I saw her waggons and men depart. At the bend in the road, she turned to wave.

Inside the house, no longer playing the part of the slave, Naomi, her child held in one hand, a big bundle in the other, rounded on us. 'You should have killed her,' she cried. 'Now what will she do? It isn't as if you don't know her of old.'

'She'll be silent,' I told Naomi. 'She said she wanted no more deaths. She even asked me what she would gain now by betrayal.'

Naomi turned on Diomed, and shouted at him, 'Do you trust her?' She showed no respect for this man, whom she had mopped, fed with a spoon, scolded and watched like a hawk as he grew, knowing his parentage and fearing some evil would come out in him.

We argued fiercely. It was not too late, Naomi said, for the Egyptian soldiers to go after Helen and kill her. Her attendants were callow men – Diomed's men were veterans. Diomed was reasonable: there were reasons why that course was not only undesirable – repugnant to him, he said – but also unnecessary. I argued, too, for allowing Helen to live, but seeing Diomed after so many years made me remember his birth on the farm, assisted only by Iphitus' mother and sister. 'Look! My son's son!' the old lady had cried, holding up the yelling, bloody infant, her suspicions of the peculiar, alien bride subdued, though not for long. I remembered the joy of his birth, mercifully untainted by thought of his father. But now, the past crowded in on me; while under the hanging depicting goddesses and seasons, Diomed, Naomi and I were locked in argument, I was, in memory, returning to Mycenae, long ago.

THIRTY-EIGHT

Mycenae

I stood surrounded by guards in the courtyard outside the great hall at Mycenae, high above the sea. Gazing in awe at the vast palace Agamemnon had had built for himself, I began to feel the force of the gown I was wearing, that red gown with the old thready embroidery of animals, snakes, birds, in green and blue, so old the colours had faded and the patterns were almost lost. Yet the garment had taken magic into its fabric, I knew. I also knew it had been torn from the oracle of the hill, that woman I had feared so much all my life, who had been struck down with her arms uplifted at the gates of Troy, delivering a fearful curse on her killers. The gown was imparting its magic to me. I am sure that some power far beyond Agamemnon had prompted him to select the robe and give it to me. We had not gone far along the road to Mycenae when I began to feel the atmosphere it carried. What prophecies and what sacrifices had not entered into its fibres, what secrets had it not heard? Every thread knew the bellowing of beasts for sacrifice, wild music, fire, all the practices of the goddess.

A chill came in from the sea. I had forgotten. The year was ending. At home we would have been harvesting, picking our fruit, pressing our wine. But I was in this faraway and barren land, the tip of the world, wearing the oracle's gown, power mounting in me. We ascended the steep hill, passed through the mighty gates of the fortress and were there at the palace of Mycenae. I stood alone, guarded in the courtyard.

I watched the queen, Clytemnestra, leading her daughter by the hand, come out to greet her lord. He was tall, dusty, in battered armour, scarred and washed only by the sea at Aulis. She was dressed in a gown blue as the sky and in her hair was a fillet of flowers. At the last moment, she dropped her daughter's hand and ran towards her lord, like a girl, arms outstretched. Her daughter, Electra, stood for a moment, then ran after her. As Clytemnestra ran, face alight with joy, the blue gown fluttering round her shapely limbs, I saw deception. This was not a bride rushing to her husband, as she wanted him to think. She was a sheet of fire, driven by wind towards a hayfield; she was an arrow tipped with poison speeding towards a great lion; she was the dagger of gold coming down on the white oxen. She was the priestess, Agamemnon the sacrifice.

Clytemnestra embraced her warrior, speaking to him gently in a voice too low for anyone to hear. The girl, Electra, had halted in her run towards her father and stood between the group of Clytemnestra's women and the reunited couple. The expression on her face chilled me. It was terrible to see behind the sweetness and passivity of that child-woman's face such cunning and bad intention. The girl hated her mother, that was clear. Time froze. There were the couple embracing, the girl looking on, the women, soldiers, all watching the reunion of Agamemnon and his queen. It was as if that moment would last forever.

For me the scene was beginning to lose form and colour, dissolving into grey mist, streaked with red. I felt behind the palace walls a man watching. I felt his fear, his desire for murder. He was like a huge, grey toad, waiting. But then the mists cleared from my eyes. The trance into which I was sinking suspended itself for a little while.

There was a disturbance. A column of Greek soldiers, a line of chained captives, two chariots, then waggons, piled high, were coming through the gates. A contingent of Greeks must have landed at a port lower down the coast from Aulis and had evidently arrived at Mycenae from the other direction. In the long line of chained slaves between a tall boy and a collapsing woman I saw Naomi, carrying a baby. She saw me, but gave no sign. It seemed fate had brought us both to the centre of this wasps' nest and she was showing every caution. Then she turned her head towards the gates. Clattering in came Prince Aeneas, son of my father's oldest adviser, Aeneas the Trojan, still in his armour and driving a chariot, while the rest of his countrymen and women came in chains.

My astonishment was great. Naomi, having indicated Aeneas' arrival, now cast a half-look of great significance. It told me Aeneas was a friend of the Greeks, must have been a friend even before the city fell. This explained the ease with which he had seized his child from his wife's arms then managed to escape with him and his elderly father from a burning city filled with victorious Greeks, a city from which no other Trojan warrior had escaped alive. But I wondered what had he offered in exchange for safety for himself and his family? Years later, of course, Naomi told me she had recognised Aeneas as the visitor to Tenedos the night before the successful Greek assault on the city. That was when Aeneas had given away the only secret the Greeks could have wanted, the secret of the tunnel and the position of the tunnel's mouth.

However, I was still barely on this side of consciousness. Aeneas in his chariot, the united couple on the flagstones before the palace, the trailing girl, Electra – all seemed to me like little wooden puppets, mounted stiffly on a little stage in front of crudely painted scenery. Even the relief of seeing Naomi alive and the shock of the terrible perfidy of Aeneas were soon lost to me. The last event I recall was witnessing Queen Clytemnestra taking her husband's hand and starting to lead him with great dignity into the palace, smiling up at him as they went.

I screamed, heard my own scream, had a vision of the queen behind the thick walls of the palace gently bathing her husband in warm rose-petalled water, already prepared, and saw her gracefully hand him wine. Then, as he stepped from the water, erect, lusting for her after her ministrations, I saw her advance towards him, with a cloak of fine scarlet she had woven for him with her own hands, throw the cloak over him, covering his head, saw her raise her hand, with a hidden dagger in it, as he, at first laughing, then struggling, tried to push the enveloping cloak from his head and arms. I saw her plunge the knife into his heart. I watched her strike and strike again, saw Agamemnon wildly, then more weakly attempt to escape. I saw her lover, the grey toad, rush in, knife raised, to add his blows to hers. They stabbed him a hundred times, before he fell, and after, as he lay writhing and struggling inside his scarlet caul. They went on striking into him, on and on until they were at last satisfied he was dead.

I must have told all this, arms raised, as the captives screamed at my words and the soldiers stood appalled and astonished. Towards the end, Aeneas, they said later, jumped from his chariot, ran to me and struck me to the ground. Then he wheeled his chariot and was off, appearing to have other business in other places to conduct, as men like that always will.

When I next saw the sky, the air around me rent by cries and screams, I was lying on the paving stones before the palace. Turning my head, I dimly saw a tall, black-bearded man, many soldiers at his back, carrying the great body of Agamemnon from the palace. This he threw to the ground. I saw Agamemnon's big hand, my father's heavy gold ring on his finger, red with blood, only yards from me. Then I saw a man's foot in a sandal, a braced, muscular leg beside me, heard the clash of swords. Agamemnon's men were fighting the men of the palace, to avenge their leader and kill the murderess wife and her usurping lover. But I could not rise, through weakness. I would die here, I supposed – die trampled, probably – but I had long expected death at Mycenae and I felt nothing.

Then I was hoisted up, across an armoured back, by someone strong and skilful enough to get through fighting men without damage, and carried safely back through the battle taking place in front of the palace at Mycenae. I first found myself being heaved across the courtyard at a run. I saw hand-to-hand fighting, the corpse of Agamemnon, with his poor daughter crouched over it, as men fought round her. The terrified captives, still chained, were trying to scuttle off to shelter in a corner of a wall. I felt the plumes of a helmet in my face.

Aeneas grunted, 'Be still, lady. Do nothing or you are a dead woman.' He had left his chariot on the road to Mycenae and it was down the road to the chariot that he carried me. He dumped me on the floor, shouted to me to stay there, and be quiet, then whipped up his horses. We began to move at a fast, rocking pace. 'Some will call me traitor,' he shouted to himself more than me. 'But I – I – shall live on with my son, to celebrate the name of Troy.'

From the floor of the chariot, I muttered weakly, 'You disguise treachery with a pious statement.' He heard me.

'Troy would have fallen, then or later. The Greeks would never have given up their ambitions,' he said. He was standing straight, muscles straining, whipping his horses like a madman. I had seen him like that in battle. Even in treachery, he looked the hero.

'Boughs that don't bend break in the wind,' he said.

'If they bend too often, they grow crooked.'

'They grow all the same, and bear fruit. Remember that, Cassandra.'

I hated his justifications. Yet whether his advice about bowing to the wind influenced me or not, I ended up – perhaps to my shame – accepting things as they were, and living on.

We were twisting and swinging round bends, the sky above me was full of wheeling clouds.

'Where are you taking me?'

'To some friends at Pylos. I have a ship in port

there. I'm leaving Greece – and poor Troy – far behind me. I've done with all this. I'll give you to people who will help you, find you a husband. I'll pay them. I don't want you to die, like the rest.'

We said nothing more. We careered on. I thought of Agamemnon dead at the hands of his own wife. Later I asked him where Helen was, was she alive, but he knew nothing. No one knew. It was as if she had disappeared. And I thought of Aeneas above me, driving the rocking chariot, the man who had betrayed his country, caused the deaths of his king and queen and hundreds of his own countrymen, even his dearest friends, yet had for no reason I could guess, decided not to betray me, the least important member of my family.

THIRTY-NINE

Thessaly

ELEN HAD gone, Naomi had taken away her child. Diomed and I were alone, with much to speak of. But we had had almost no time together before we were interrupted. During that period we spoke, as was only right, of his father, the man who had reared him, who had died while he was away. He had been placed in a circular tomb buried half beneath the ground, according to the customs of this country. This tomb was on our hillside among the olives. Diomed planned to go there at dawn to offer prayers for his father, or rather, the man who had been to him all that a father should have been. He confessed, 'When I found myself with Helenus and they told me who I was, at first I wept for you. Then I wept because the man I had always thought of as my father was not. I envied my brothers and sisters. Helenus tried to console me by saying I should rejoice at my noble birth, but that did not seem enough. Have you told them – Iris, Penelope, Phaon and Dryas – of this?'

'I dared not,' I said. 'I never spoke of it, even to your father, though he knew. I was afraid for all of you. And it was not hard to be silent about those days. There was much I preferred to forget, or push from my mind. Of course it was my duty to speak, to tell my children of their grandparents, of Priam and Hecuba, and of my brothers and sisters, but the danger was too great.'

Then there was disturbance outside. The messenger had reached my son-in-law, Telemon, and told him that strangers were arriving at the farm. Telemon had promptly collected my son Dryas, Dryas' brother-in-law and his tough old father. So a group of four, sturdy local men had all arrived on a waggon ready for a fight if necessary. Discovering that instead of trouble, Diomed was with me, there was great joy and excitement. Dryas embraced his brother, examined his weapons, embraced him again and wept. Soon they were talking excitedly. Meanwhile Telemon sent for my daughter Iris, and a further message went to her sister Penelope married to the harbour-master at Pinios. I wrote the message, knowing few could read. It urged her to be discreet about her departure since Helen and her retinue might be arriving just as she was leaving. Pinios is not a small place, but the hasty departure of the harbour-master's wife to her mother's home, combined with the coming of the Queen of Sparta from the opposite direction, might cause gossip and speculation. People are often ingenious enough to take unrelated events and on scanty evidence construct a story too close to the truth.

So Dryas was here, Penelope and Iris on their way and only Phaon, away on his ship, carrying wool to Thrace would not be here to greet the brother he had not seen for so long.

Happy as I was about this reunion, I still had doubts and fears. Dryas, Iris and Penelope were meeting their brother again after seven years, an occasion for joy, but the collision of Helen and Diomed seemed to me sinister and ill-fated. And I had spent so long keeping my secrets, and then, lately, only telling my story by means of those blackbird tracks on that thick yellow-brown papyrus, that I dreaded revealing my own past. But the time had come when I must do it and I felt the pain in anticipation – the pain of a splinted limb, when the splint comes off. In exile, from myself as much as my country, I had learned the frozen comforts of silence and forgetting.

Nevertheless it was a wonderful moment when Iris came in with her little daughter and early next day Penelope and her husband, both wide-eyed. Penelope exclaimed, 'We left at night and even as we left the town, a troop of men, a richly-loaded waggon, a litter containing a wealthy woman it seemed, passed us as they entered the town. We could not guess what she was doing on the road south. Did she come from here? And where is Diomed?'

'At his father's grave, with Dryas.'

'You'd best give your mother and sister a hand,' Penelope's husband told her. And so Penelope turned to, for by now there were thirteen of us in the house, Diomed, Dryas and his brother-in-law, Telemon, Iris, Telemon's father, Penelope and her husband, Diomed's four soldiers and, of course, myself. We slept on the floor, were eating barley and drinking wine which could hardly be spared. Yet another animal had to be killed. Everyone was enjoying themselves. My daughters made bread, a cauldron of lentil stew with herbs. We set up a spit in the yard to roast half a sheep, leaving Dryas to attend it in the cold wind which had arisen. Penelope's husband and Telemon's friends settled down to talk with the Egyptian soldiers and Telemon and his father-in-law took a tour of the farm they hoped one day would be theirs.

As we prepared the food, I told Iris and Penelope, 'The farm belongs to you and your brothers but Telemon had better farm it. I will state this in front of everybody when he returns, so that there will be no quarrelling later.'

'Will you live with us?' Iris asked.

'I shall be gone,' I told her.

'Gone where?' Penelope asked.

'I don't know. It is something I feel. Look,' I told her, 'there are bad times coming. You must be very cautious, all of you.'

'Mother!' came Iris' impatient cry. My visions, which of course had not completely ended with the fall of Troy and its terrible sequel, had afflicted their childhood. They took these periods of time when I was locked in visions for granted at first, as children will, then, discovering it was unusual, they came to dislike the times when I was not myself, not really with them, not about my proper duties. They certainly never believed what I told them. I spoke on, firmly, telling Iris, 'There will be an invasion. Make no mistake. Telemon, your husband, will conspire with the invaders. Penelope – tell your husband that resistance will be useless.'

Iris, infuriated, left the room. Penelope, a quiet young woman, rested her hands on the dough and stared at me, kindly and patiently.

'Fetch Iris,' I said. 'We must go on with the work. I have a great deal to tell you, and it must be said before Diomed returns. It is a most shocking story and best if we have something to do with our hands while you listen. It is also a dangerous secret you may not even tell your husbands.'

'Mother – are you sure? You have been living alone for some time,' Penelope said. She thought I had become mad.

I went out to Iris myself. She was standing in the yard, watching Dryas turn the spit. I asked both of them to come into the house with me. Inside I said again, 'Before Diomed returns you must know this – there is danger coming to all of us. Dryas, you will be a busy man, making swords, not plough-shares and billhooks; Penelope, your husband would do well not to resist, to allow the harbour to be used by the enemy.'

'Mother!' she protested.

'Mother,' Dryas said patiently. 'Mother – please –' But I swept on.

'There is much I have to say, some of it is painful to speak of, and at least for a time, no one must know what I tell you. You may not believe me, but you will find out what I say is true in the end. As I speak, I beg you, do not interrupt me. As I say, the telling will be painful, more so if you question me.'

And so I told them of my birth and family, of the war between Greece and Troy, of the fate of my family, which was of course, in part, theirs. I was forced to tell them how, as a captive, I had been raped by Agamemnon, and how after my rescue, I had borne his child, their brother. I said that it had been for his own protection that he had been sent to Egypt. As I continued, I went on with the preparation of the meal, though my eyes were full of tears. I did not look at them, though I knew they were standing silently, staring at me. Then I looked up. Dryas, knife in hand, was frowning, trying to work out if he believed me or not, Iris looked blank. I believe she was comparing what I said with the stories they told and songs they sang about the war. She was adding up the evidence. Penelope believed me. She was weeping into the bread. 'Don't weep into the bread,' I told her. 'When you see your brother I hope you will all treat him with respect. The circumstances of his birth are ignoble, but you must not shame him. He is the same brother he was, remember that.'

'This is the most horrible tale,' Iris said. 'If you invented it, Mother, you are mad and wicked.'

'I may seem to you to be of the blood of the enemy,' I told her, 'and nothing better than a slave, a raped captive. Remember, the ballads you hear were composed by the victors. Remember, those slaves you see drawing water, being beaten by their masters, were once free, and brave. Remember, I am telling you of your own kin. In that, I do my duty to you and to them. You may feel obliged to reject what I say as untrue, but remember you have a child, and that child is the grandchild of the King and Queen of Troy.'

If Iris felt the shame of her descent from disgraced enemies, Dryas had different thoughts: 'As a result of all this shame, nevertheless Diomed is a captain in Pharaoh's army and I am the village blacksmith.'

'Go with your wife to Egypt, then,' I told him. 'Diomed will help you.'

Iris was beginning to put things together. 'Where's Naomi? Why has she gone? Who was the woman – the woman on the road with soldiers?'

The light failed in front of my eyes. I muttered, I think, 'I cannot say her name,' and fell.

They put me to bed. Diomed told me later that

when he came in, his brother and his sisters embraced him though they had had no chance to speak privately to each other at that time, the house being so full of people. I lay in bed, ice-cold, with a faint pulse and breathing so shallowly they feared, mistakenly, for my life.

That afternoon twenty soldiers came, snatched me up, seized Diomed and took us away. They were armed and ready. Resistance was useless. Before long I and my oldest son were standing before King Orestes at Mycenae. I should have known – I should not have believed her – Helen had betrayed us.

We had a long journey in a waggon guarded by soldiers. They had been told only that the Egyptian general was a spy, and his mother one of his informants. At first these men treated us with the same brutality and indifference they would have shown to any captive. We spent the first day tied hand and foot, lying on the floor of the jolting waggon. But at night, as Diomed slept on the ground and I lay awake, I heard one of the men, who was about forty years old, talking to some of the others round the fire, at a distance. I heard Agamemnon's name more than once. I believe the man, who must have fought in Troy, had spotted Diomed's resemblance to his former general.

The next day they were careful, even wary, of Diomed. They had concluded there might be more to this than the arrest of an enemy spy. Diomed's clothing was Egyptian, but his appearance was not. My arrest, since I looked an ordinary farmer's wife, made the whole situation even more puzzling. They untied our feet and we were able to sit, leaning against the sides of the waggon as it travelled. Meanwhile the soldiers with us in the waggon tried to find out more about us. We both maintained that Diomed was indeed a general in Egypt, only visiting his old home after many years away. Was their king mad, we wanted to know, to be sending bands of soldiers to remote farms far from his own realm, in order to arrest an innocent man, and, even more foolishly, his mother? Pharaoh, Diomed told them grimly, would not be pleased to have a captain of his snatched and carried off, tied up in a waggon, on the command of an arbitrary, petty princeling. The soldiers became increasingly uneasy. Jolting in the waggon, there was much we could not say in front of Orestes' men. Diomed muttered merely, 'We've had no chance to talk.'

I told him, 'There's been so much to say, no time to say it. I don't fear Orestes. The fear comes from another direction.'

'Do you know of the Sea People?' he asked me.

The soldiers' captain's suspicions aroused, he interrupted angrily, 'Sea People? What do you know of them?'

'I am one of Pharaoh's captains,' Diomed replied calmly. 'How could I not know of them?'

'Who are they? What is the sea they come from?' I asked.

'An army, tens of thousands strong,' he told me. 'Egypt has already fought a battle with them. They sailed into the delta of the Nile and attacked in force. They were barely driven off. When I left Memphis ten days ago, a report had been received suggesting they were about to attack Hattusas.'

'Hattusas? Impossible! No one would dare attack that city,' I exclaimed.

'Well, the kingdom is weaker now,' Diomed told me, and then stopped speaking. A farmer's wife seeming to have too much knowledge of other lands and nations would revive our guards' suspicion that both of us were spies.

'What people are they, these Sea People?' I asked more cautiously.

'They're of many races – the Philistines, the Gasga people, old enemies of the Hittite king, Lukka pirates, Lycians, Lydians, some Trojans – '

'Trojans,' I said, astonished.

'The Greek victory in Troy meant heavy Greek occupation of the coastal areas and inland regions,' Diomed told me neutrally. 'But it destroyed the system of alliances with King Suppiluliumas – of whom you may not have heard,' he added delicately. 'Forgive me, Mother, if my explanations are confusing. You have led a simple life and may not know of great empires and lands far off. However,' he continued, 'our country,' by which he meant, of course, Greece, 'would not yield to the bullying of the Hittites, would not pay tribute to Suppiluliumas, their king, but this breaking down of the old order led to instability.'

'Treachery and disobedience,' interrupted one of the soldiers, who no doubt served in the area and had bitter memories, perhaps of a comrade knifed while making love to a girl, or hunger caused by the population hiding food from the army.

'Indeed, indeed,' said Diomed. 'But let us admit the kings of Greece could not control the area completely. Sometimes, in fact, they quarrelled among themselves

470

– as we know.' He turned to the older soldier who had evidently served abroad. 'You were at Miletus?'

'I was,' said the man, unhappy at the thought.

'Achilles,' explained Diomed, 'attacked King Orestes claiming that he himself had conquered the city of Miletus many years before and that Orestes should not be ruling it, taking taxes and so forth.'

'Thus Greek fought Greek for this city you name?'

Diomed nodded. I did not ask who had won. The soldier's face told the story. Achilles had taken back the city he had always considered his. It seemed the Greeks had taken over the mainland, refused to agree with Suppiluliumas, fought among themselves and lost control. A vacuum had been created. The disaffected of the area then linked up with the Hittites' traditional enemies from the Black Sea and beyond and with others, drawn, it seemed, from the east beyond the mountains. These, whom they called the Sea People, had become powerful.

'He is dead now,' Diomed told me.

'Even in our remote area,' I said, 'we heard that sad news, and wept.' I had, indeed, wept for Achilles.

The soldiers exclaimed woefully, they spoke in praise of the dead man. I again felt great grief for that wild, angry, kindly man.

'But these Sea People,' I asked, 'who are their leaders? To whom do they owe allegiance? Where is their capital?'

'They have many leaders, offer no one allegiance, have no capital,' he told me. 'And they might by now have taken Hattusas.'

I bowed my head, to hide my shocked expression from the soldiers. If I were who I said I was, this information would not have had any great significance for me. I sat silently looking at the floorboards. 'My fear was from another direction,' I had said earlier to Diomed and he immediately asked me what I knew of the Sea People. The enemy attackers I had seen in dreams had a name now.

Diomed and the soldiers were talking together.

'The Sea People have ships then?' asked the old soldier, the one who knew Agamemnon's face.

'Many ships,' Diomed told him. 'And a big land army.'

'You're saying they might come here. No one attacks Mycenae. It's too powerful. Too well-armed, the army too strong.'

'If they dared to attack Egypt, why would they not come here?'

'They would hear of us and fear us.'

'Do you know the size of Pharaoh's army, the number of his ships?'

The soldier said, 'Well. The size of an army isn't everything. If they're attacking the capital of the Great King now, they won't be here for a year or two.'

'I expect you're right,' said Diomed, but only to keep the peace with our captors. He did not believe what the soldier said.

I again saw that fleet of ships sailing through mist which I had seen in a vision. I saw the dark hordes of raiders drawn from many nations engulfing the world we knew. But they could not, I thought, harm Troy. It was already destroyed.

For the second time, and again a captive, I was brought up the steep hill to Mycenae. There were

472

indications that if Orestes' soldiers did not believe the Sea People would dare to assault Mycenae, the king himself was not so confident. Anyone who had seen a city preparing for war would recognise that Orestes expected an attack. Gangs of men were putting an extra layer of stone all round the city's thick walls. Once we were through the gates and inside I saw a heap of copper ingots outside the smithy. The smith was still at work, though it was dusk. Weapons were being made. Baskets of wheat were being carried into the storehouse. Diomed looked expressionlessly at the soldier who had told him Mycenae expected no attack.

The old soldier shrugged. 'They must have had some fresh news.'

Diomed told me, as we were pushed out of the waggon, 'This was why I came to visit you – to urge you to return to Egypt with me.'

I nodded but could not speak. We were crossing the square where Agamemnon's body had been thrown. It was as if he still lay there, with his arms spread, huge, bloody, the red cloak still entangling his legs, trailing over the stones of the courtyard.

Then we were marched in to see Orestes. He sat beside his wife, Helen's daughter. But I had seen the flash of a blue gown disappearing through an entrance even as we were thrust unceremoniously into that room. I saw also costly hangings, gold vases displayed on an ebony table, along with a well-shaped ewer and cups which had come from my parents' store.

Orestes, unhappily for him, perhaps, resembled his dead mother, not his father. He was slender, not tall, and had a dark, narrow face, small-boned, even feminine, and fringed with a black beard. His black hair hung, uncombed, beside his face. He had been king in Argos now for more than ten years. Some of the dignity of kingship sat on him, but beneath it he seemed uncertain.

His wife, Hermione, unhappily for her, perhaps, did not resemble her mother, Helen. She, too, looked like Clytemnestra, though she was less beautiful. Like brother and sister, these cousins sat in stately robes, each assuming the regal position, their arms laid along the arms of their curved wooden chairs, backs straight, feet planted side by side. Yet something in their manner did not speak of perfect ease.

The only other person in the room was a court official, a young man also in a robe.

No one in the room could have recognised me – except perhaps Orestes, but when we had met, so long ago, he was mad and as I looked at him I observed he did not know me. On the other hand, there might be some soldier or official of Agamemnon's nearby who would see in the woman I now was the young princess of Troy.

And I had seen Orestes blink as Diomed was pushed in. He had not seen his father since he was eleven or twelve years old and the Agamemnon he would have seen then was a warrior, almost forty years old. Nevertheless, from Diomed's appearance he must have concluded that Helen's story might have been true. There was a possibility this unknown man was Agamemnon's son – and if he was, then the rest was true. I was Cassandra.

'Are you indeed Cassandra? Are you Diomed, her son by my father?' he said, in the flattened voice of royalty. It was a deep voice, belying his unimposing appearance, and it echoed round the pillars of the room.

Diomed replied for both of us, as was only suitable, for no Greek farmer's wife would respond to a king. He said, 'There has been a mistake, Lord. I am the son of a farmer from Thessaly, Iphitus of Tolos. I have been fortunate enough to have been distinguished by the Pharaoh of Egypt. This is my mother, Iphianissa of Tolos. I returned only days ago from Egypt to visit her and to see the tomb of my father, who died two years ago, while I was absent in Egypt. That is all. Before we had a chance to greet each other, even as I returned from my father's tomb, your soldiers seized us from our home and roughly brought us here. Now we have false names put upon us by you. This is unfair. The King of Egypt will be much annoyed if you hold one of his captains in this illegal manner.'

This speech made Orestes unhappy. His eyes flickered towards his wife's.

'We have it on good authority this woman is Cassandra of Troy, and you her son,' she said.

'That is absurd – let the accuser come here and speak and say what evidence he has for believing what he says,' Diomed answered boldly. This was risky: if Helen appeared, and I knew she was in the palace by the sight of that vanishing gown, and if she then made a direct statement she knew me to be Cassandra of Troy, we were lost. I could only hope that, though she dared to betray us, she would not dare to face us. I knew her. She might act, but would not wish to see the results of those actions. She would not have the courage to confront us and say what she knew. She must have agreed this with her relatives beforehand, or she would have been seated in the room when we came in.

'There are those who will recognise your mother,'

Orestes told Diomed. 'They will also say if you resemble my father.'

'There are those who may say they recognise a woman briefly seen twenty years ago in this woman here. But all know Cassandra is dead. There may be those who say your father could have been mine. Any man can be any man's father, as you know,' Diomed replied firmly. He went on, 'Lord, this is an injustice, and can never be other than an injustice. And as a soldier, I know you have more important enemies to think about than a farmer-woman and her son. You are thinking of the past – I speak respectfully – when the future is demanding your urgent attention. You are reinforcing your walls, equipping your army, supplying your city. As we travelled I saw watchmen at the coast, bonfires ready to be lit in warning if an enemy attacks you by sea. Let us go, my Lord, to attend to our business while you attend to yours. We are not who you think we are.'

All this time I had kept my eyes to the ground and twisted the folds of my woollen gown in workworn hands. I felt Hermione's gaze on me, but did not meet it. Diomed's last statement, cleverly drawing the king's attention to his fears of invasion, had, I thought, made the king hesitate. Nevertheless they produced a grey-haired man who had been one of Agamemnon's sergeants aboard the ship which had brought the Trojan captives to Aulis so long ago. We went through an embarrassing performance. He was instructed to come close to me and scan my face, to see if I was the woman he remembered. I slackened my jaw and screwed up my eyes, staring at him as stupidly as possible, like a woman stunned by everything happening to her. He said, and I had known he would, that

476

I was Cassandra. I burst out, in the accents of Thessaly, 'You call me Princess of Troy, you fool. How can I be? I have never left Tolos. You must be mad. Cassandra is dead. Everybody knows that. It's in the ballad, sir,' I appealed to Orestes, falling to my knees, 'do not believe him. I'm no Trojan, nor my son.'

'Lord, I beg you,' said Diomed, 'do not allow my mother to be humiliated in this way. She is a simple woman, a widow, a farmer's wife, a good mother to five children. She has been taken brutally from her home on a suspicion, a vicious rumour. This reflects badly on that reputation for wisdom and justice which has reached all parts of Greece – and further, to the coast of Pharaoh himself. If you cannot produce a better witness than this man, who saw Cassandra of Troy briefly, for a week perhaps, on a ship, so long ago, please accept that your informant was mistaken, a mischief-maker, perhaps even mad.'

Again it was a clever speech, involving Orestes' reputation, of which he was naturally jealous, the impression all this would make on Rameses of Egypt, if reported, and Orestes' own suspicions and dislike of Helen.

'Well,' he said wearily, 'let us keep you a day or so, to look into this matter further.'

Obviously he and his wife would go back to Helen, perhaps insist she confront us. Diomed protested, but it was no use. The soldiers took us through the doorway where I had seen Helen's gown flash, to a windowless stone chamber, which, though small, was nevertheless furnished. Food and wine were brought to us. Then we heard the crossbar of the door imprisoning us thud down.

We spoke into darkness in low tones, fearing that

we would be overheard by the guard outside, even though the door was thick. 'He'll re-question Helen, then let us go,' Diomed asserted. 'Let us hope she doesn't agree to confront us.'

'I don't think she'll dare. She can't bear anything which is not pleasant. And I think she fears me a little.'

Diomed sighed, 'Naomi was right to suggest murder.'

'I know it,' I said. 'Helen needs to trick her way back into Orestes' favour. Plainly, she daren't return to Sparta.'

'We hear songs and sagas of the nobility of that war,' he said disgustedly. 'Now this shameful affair, an ignoble sequel.'

'The songs and sagas are for Greeks,' I told him. 'In life, war creates war, evil deeds give rise to others, lies and murders create more lies and murders, and there is no nobility about it.'

'My soldiers will have sent messages to Egypt.'

'Pharaoh could come too late.'

'Let us talk,' he said. 'We have much to say and if we are to die we should say it now.'

He woke before I did that night. His soldier's instincts alerted him to the sounds of fighting. We sat in the darkness, hearing far-off shouts, the clash of metal.

'They're defending the Lion Gate,' Diomed told me. 'I doubt if it's a neighbour. The soldier was right – few of those who know of Mycenae would dare to attack her. Only the Sea People.'

'Mycenae is doomed. I have known it for a long time.'

'The king is no general,' he said. 'You can see it in his face.'

'Small help for us,' I said. 'We may avoid being killed by Orestes only to be killed by those who triumph over him. Questions are not asked in situations like this.'

'We must try to get this door open.'

We battered at it with a stool. It was no use. The door was too thick, the bar across it heavy. It barely trembled under the blows. All the while the battle came closer. 'They're through the gates, the Greeks are being pushed back to the palace,' Diomed told me.

I reminded him, 'I have heard these sounds before.' The noise of swords and shields and the shouting came closer. Then there were sounds of crashing vessels, the thud of things being thrown about, the sounds of looting.

We stopped trying to break the door open when we heard heavy feet outside, the sound of swords hitting shields. To spare Diomed having to explain to me what I well knew, I said, 'The Greeks are overwhelmed. Now the killing and looting begin.' As if to confirm this, in the distance a woman screamed. Diomed took up a position in the doorway as if to fight for his life.

'You are unarmed,' I said. 'Better to talk, if possible, than fight.'

He nodded. We stood in the middle of the room and waited for the door to open. I thought how terrible it was to have struggled for my own life and Diomed's for so long just in order for both of us to die in this awful place.

Then the crossbar on the door was flung back and

a man in armour filled the entrance. He stared into the darkness, looking for enemies. From the sounds, there were others behind him.

'No treasure here,' said Diomed. 'Only two captives, who will be ransomed by Pharaoh if you spare us.'

It was then that I heard the sound of my native tongue again, after so many years. The man in the doorway, sword in one hand, a torch in the other, could evidently speak little Greek, those behind him less. As he peered at us, wondering who we were, trying to understand Diomed's speech, a voice from behind him said, 'Who's there? Are they armed? What's happening?'

The man in front, sword poised, came in further. 'Captives, I think. They're unarmed, a man and a woman.'

Both men spoke the language of the country people of Troy. The man in the doorway was moving towards Diomed, sword raised, when I said, my voice cracking with fear, my tongue rusty after so many years of disuse, 'Put down your sword. We are Trojans.'

He stopped. 'Who are you?' he asked. The men behind were crowding him, saying, 'Has the woman any rings?'

'Who are you?' I asked.

'Towilas, son of Tacho of Cassawa. And you?'

The men behind had fallen silent, half-hearing. He shouted, 'Trojan slaves.' They had come across others, I am sure, as they fought up from the coast.

I was overcome with joy. Tears filled my eyes. I could hardly speak. 'Is Adosha, your mother, still living?'

'She is,' he said in astonishment.

Adosha must have told him no doubt many times in winter how she had been put in charge of mad twins by the Queen of Troy and had reared them and endured war and siege. She must have told him of the deaths of Hector, his father, and all from the Trojan royal house. But had she told him Hector was his true father? Weeping, I saw Hector's son and my own son, Agamemnon's, face each other in that little room. I asked, 'Have you driven the Greeks from Troy?'

Diomed asked, 'What are you saying? What's happening?'

Adosha's son laughed, 'They all ask, have you driven the Greeks from Troy? We have. But who are you? What is your name?'

'I am,' I said, for the first time in twenty years, 'Cassandra, the daughter of Priam and Hecuba of Troy.'

FORTY

Returning to Troy

W<small>E SET</small> sail for Troy only a week later. We returned to Thessaly under safe conduct from Towilas to collect a few things from the farm, for there was no knowing what conditions might prevail in Troy when we arrived. The city had been sacked again, the land again wasted.

Naomi persuaded her lover to leave his employer, telling him if he went to Troy he would get land, fertile, well-watered by rivers, of his own. This I believe to be true – Towilas will see to it. So Diomed, I, Naomi and her lover commandeered a waggon and two white mules. Piled high, we went to Pinios. I parted again from Diomed. He urged me to go to Egypt with him, but I told him I must see Troy first. I yearned to see my native land again, and desired also to finish my own account. I had rescued the papyrus from the farm, with domestic items – two ewes, a ram, a crate of chickens and storage jars of grain, oil and fruit – and I knew I must tell my tale, or the other voices, of Greeks, warriors and ambitious kings would overwhelm me. Perhaps even now they will, whatever I do, but I must make the attempt.

So Diomed returned to Egypt and I to Troy. I will try to live in Troy again. It is a midden compared with the old city, for it is built on two sets of burned ruins – the Trojan city and the one the Greeks rebuilt later. Towilas may, if he survives, declare himself king of the new Troy. He has every right, by blood and by conquest. Adosha will certainly declare herself queen (until her son marries, and then I pity his bride) so she will be queen and rule over me. Fate brings many things on us.

I know the fates of the mighty. I shall be happy in my obscurity. I have reclaimed that little piece of land I was given at my betrothal to the Phoenician. I shall cultivate my land, and write my story of Troy and then, when I have finished, perhaps I shall go to Egypt or to Phoenicia, to see if Arvad still lives or go wherever I please, for my story will be told, I will be free at last.

AUTHOR'S NOTE

THIS BOOK IS a work of fiction, but readers might be curious about how much of it is factually true, how much based on the old legends of Troy and how much my own invention. Much could be said, enough for another book, but here is some of the basic information.

There was probably a war in Troy between the Trojans and the Greeks, some three thousand years ago. The most popular date for this is 1250 BC. The site of Troy was probably near Cannakale on the

Aegean coast of Turkey just north of the Dardanelles. In ancient times people may have known of the site, but over the years it began to be assumed that the story was entirely legend and the city also. It took a German businessman and amateur archaeologist, Heinrich Schliemann, to decide that, as far as he was concerned, Troy had really existed – and he would find it. He went to the site in 1870 and started digging, finding the buried city now generally accepted as having been Troy. After that, he then went on to discover Mycenae – one of the most wonderful and fascinating stories of archaeology. In a way it still goes on. For Schliemann donated much of what he called the Treasures of Priam to a Berlin museum. In 1944, in the confusion of war, all the Trojan items disappeared, looted, it was supposed, by allied troops or removed by fleeing Germans. It was thought the Treasures of Priam would never be seen again, until, in 1992, the Russians confessed that these objects, along with many others, had been removed from Berlin during the Russian advance into the city and were now under lock and key in St Petersburg. But so far no one has seen them.

At the time of Troy there was indeed a great Hittite empire, as described in the book. Based in Anatolia, it stretched to the east, up to and over the borders of what are now the CIS, Iran and Iraq, and ran south down into what is now Syria. I have seen Troy as one of an important chain of coastal cities, ruled independently but allied, for reasons of mutual gain, with the Hittite kings. Ethiopia also existed as a kingdom, ruled by queens called Candace. One of the principal cities was Saba, which was probably where the Queen of Sheba came from to visit Solomon. Also –

though it is fanciful, it is not impossible that Naomi, Cassandra's servant, was indeed an Israelite following Moses through the wilderness after the flight from Egypt.

The Sea People, too, existed, though little is known about them. They were not one people or particularly connected with the sea. They left behind no records, did not settle, created no cities. Nevertheless, around the time of the Trojan War they certainly more or less destroyed the Hittite kingdom and made several attacks on powerful Egypt and were barely defeated. When they turned their attentions to Greece, they wiped out Mycenaean civilisation all over the Peloponnese, killing or scattering the population. By the time Homer came to write about the Greeks (a loose term but convenient) his countrymen were not even of the same race as the warriors of the Trojan Wars.

The Amazons, led by Penthesilea, were certainly part of the Homeric tale, but little else is known about them.

About the Trojans nothing is known, not their race, language or religion.

People might find it curious that throughout my book there is no mention of the pantheon of Greek gods and goddesses we read of in Homer. But the Mycenaean Greeks probably did not worship them. Excavations in Mycenae contain many religious objects, figurines of women and animals being common, but there is nothing, apart from some rudimentary pottery figures, which might suggest the beginnings of the Greek religion, with which we are familiar, to suggest the Greeks at the time of Troy worshipped the Greek gods as we understand them. I have also made suppositions about the religion of

Troy. The worship of the tri-partite goddess – girl, woman and crone – was very common in Europe and the Middle East at the time, the goddess being known by various names (and, incidentally, the name Hecate is a variation on the name Hecuba). Evidence either way is inconclusive but both the Trojans and the Greeks may have practised a religion like this.

The chief source of my story is Homer's *Iliad*, though the tale told there is short, beginning when the war had been going on for ten years and ending with the death of Hector. Homer composed his poem (probably drawing on ballads and songs sung and recited during the pre-literate days) in about 700 BC according to the conventional dating, so there is a gap of five hundred years between *The Iliad* and the Trojan War itself. The rest of the story comes from the Greek dramatists, calling on the old legends. They wrote of the war and its sequel, two hundred years after Homer.

Other parts of the book are taken from Virgil, writing in Latin at the time of the Emperor Augustus – over a thousand years after the Trojan War.

I have told the bones of the story, but altering and changing it as I went along. The major change in the story is, of course, that Cassandra is alive twenty years after the war. In the original tale, although her brother Helenus and Hector's widow did survive, Cassandra was killed in Mycenae soon after being brought as a captive from Troy.

The geography of the area I describe is probably much the same, though rivers may have changed course – the chief difference is that most places would have been more heavily wooded than they are today and other areas less denuded of grass. A combination of the human need for firewood and grazing for sheep and goats has altered the landscape.

Finally, I regret any disappointment to readers because the Trojan horse is missing. It's a wonderful story, but it proved quite impossible to include in the book.

Hilary Bailey
The Cry from Street to Street £4.99

In 1880, young Mary Kelly flees the horrors of Whitechapel slum life
to survive triumphantly as a brothel keeper in Canada. Eight years
later, she returns to East London to rescue her two sisters, but she
arrives just as Jack the Ripper begins his dreadful career . . .

Plunging ever deeper into the darkest side of Victorian London, Mary
begins to lose all her defences against the life from which she came –
until eventually she herself faces the murderer . . .

'The strengths of the novel lie in the meticulous charting of Mary's
journey on foot . . . strong on local colour and description'
MAIL ON SUNDAY

'This is a work of which local colour comes as dense and enveloping
as an old London particular . . . [an] atmosphere of murk mixed in with
an East End jauntiness . . . [an] engrossing novel' SUNDAY TIMES

'Hilary Bailey has a magic power of evocation' THE TIMES

All Pan Books are available at your local bookshop or newsagent, or can be ordered direct from the publisher. Indicate the number of copies required and fill in the form below.

Send to: Pan C. S. Dept
             Macmillan Distribution Ltd
             Houndmills Basingstoke RG21 2XS

or phone: 0256 29242, quoting title, author and Credit Card number.

Please enclose a remittance* to the value of the cover price plus £1.00 for the first book plus 50p per copy for each additional book ordered.

*Payment may be made in sterling by UK personal cheque, postal order, sterling draft or international money order, made payable to Pan Books Ltd.

Alternatively by Barclaycard/Access/Amex/Diners

Card No.

Expiry Date

_____

Signature

Applicable only in the UK and BFPO addresses.

While every effort is made to keep prices low, it is sometimes necessary to increase prices at short notice. Pan Books reserve the right to show on covers and charge new retail prices which may differ from those advertised in the text or elsewhere.

NAME AND ADDRESS IN BLOCK LETTERS PLEASE

. . . .

Name _____

Address _____

_____

_____

_____

6/92